I0627321

A Poem Penned in Poison

TALES OF
WONDER AND WOE
BOOK 3

R. DUGAN

Copyright © 2025 by R. Dugan

All rights reserved.

The story, all names, characters, and incidents portrayed in this production are fictitious. No identification with actual persons (living or deceased), places, buildings, and products is intended or should be inferred.

No part of this publication may be reproduced, distributed, or transmitted in any form or by any means, including photocopying, recording, or other electronic or mechanical methods, without the prior written permission of the publisher, except as permitted by U.S. copyright law. For permission requests, contact:

Renee Dugan
reneeduganwriting.com
renee.s.dugan@gmail.com
PO Box 1265
Martinsville, IN 46151

Book Cover by: The Odd Seed

Map by: Jess Khoury

ISBN: 9781958927205

First Edition: October 2025

DEDICATION

For all those who make the hard choices for the right reasons, who stand their ground when it's unpopular, who take the fall so truth can rise up.
Keep fighting the good fight.

And for my nephew, who taught me the imperishable, world-wrecking love one holds for their siblings' children.
If I can help lead you into adulthood as the man you're meant to be, it will be one of my favorite parts of my own legacy.

HADRASS-DRUI
Valorkeep
Amalgard
Fortress Ferregrand
VENSAIR MOUNTAINS
Umbrah
Rastra
Sunivale
To Mithra-Sha
Hyraith
Aldran
Thrasmund
Reccard

CHAPTER 1
WISH-AWAY DAYS

*O*NE DROP OF POISON *is all it takes.*

The most famous lesson from the professors at Harrow Hall—haven for healing and poison studies in the land of Mithra-Sha—coursed through my blood with every churn of my heart. It was as much a part of me as my mother's smile and sensibility, my father's laughter and easygoing ambition, my four brothers' teasing nicknames and our matching smiles and the same streak of mischief in our eyes when the light caught them just right.

That lesson had shaped my life from the first day I'd set foot inside those ancient stone walls, a new initiate of nearly ten years old in hand-me-down clothes and uneven braids...one among many in a crowd, determined I would never find myself lost in it. I'd hung on that thrumming edict declared over a vaulted chapel full of youthful bodies, half quivering with fright, half with excitement. And mine with a bit of both.

One drop can destroy everything.

And waking yet again in a cold sweat, tears staining my cheeks, palms slicked with sweat that soaked in a little too much like blood...I had never believed it more.

Breaths shuddering in my lungs, I shoved myself upright and squirmed to escape the confines of silk sheets and a down duvet. Pain creaked in my joints from the tension that had squeezed like a torniquet while I slept, and my heart thundered as if I'd been running.

As if I could ever really *stop*.

I bent my knees and rested my elbows on them, shoving my hair from my brow; my flickering gaze caught glimmers of dusky brown curls limned in moonlight, and a pang shot through my middle.

Mama's hair. Though I'd celebrated more than twice the birthdays without her than those few special ones we'd shared, on nights like tonight the craving for one of her quieting embraces was so keen, it hurt like a stomachache.

Pressing my eyes shut, I fisted the hair at my temples and bent my brow between my elbows, rocking slightly.

Count to three, Miss Weathers. Another lesson from Harrow Hall. *Then work with what's before you.*

"One,"

A whisper to the creeping midnight shadows.

"Two."

A deep breath in, an exhale blown over rounded lips.

"*Three.*"

I peeked my eyes open again, taking in the spacious span of the spare room in my father's fancy house that was always kept just for me: gauzy white curtains neatly shielding the glass balcony doors and the washroom's handcarved wooden doorway, inside of which the fluffiest towels in the country of Mithra-Sha could be found. The bureau full of clothes my father gathered during his ventures as the country's most prolific and well-loved peddler. Potted plants in macrame hangers strung from every exposed wooden beam, ferns and hanging moss and herbs his housecleaners graciously watered in my father's frequent absences so that they were always green when I stayed with him.

The square of a window fitted into the ceiling, shedding moonlight onto the writing table where I'd hung my satchel and a few carry-along belongings when I'd arrived. The comforting scent of cotton and freesia—a signature scent I'd spent years concocting with fragrance oils, just for myself—drifted from its seams.

One. Two. Three.

I freed another long breath and carefully unbent my legs, disentangling my fingers from my hair and smoothing down my quivering abdomen, my tremoring thighs, my stiff calves.

The nightmares were back. And didn't that just figure? Not even two days I'd been visiting the city of Vallanmyre, and already Mithra-Sha's bustling capital city had wound its fingers around my head and heart, stitching sinister reminders all over my dreams.

Reminders of why I alone among my family no longer called Vallanmyre my home. The reason I was the only member of the ruling Sha's inner circle of advisors who lived an airship's ride away from this city...and why I never told any of the patients I treated in my new home city of Dalfi that I was an advisor to Sha Arias Lothar at all.

Arias had plenty of trouble on his plate without adding mine to the roster. Nerves sizzling, I cast off the bedsheets and slid from their smothering grip.

My bare feet made little sound on the polished wooden floors of my father's attic room, and even less on the braided rugs that sheathed the steps down to the lower levels. I picked my way past the second floor, where spare rooms were kept for each of my brothers, their names engraved on their doors: Patryk, Felyx, Conor, and Behn. None of them were here tonight...Patryk and Conor at home with their wives, Felyx likely moonlighting as a gondolier for the romantically inclined along the water channels he helped clean and maintain during the day. And Behn...he was off on a musical journey of sorts, playing his newly-acquired six-string instrument in the cities and villages beyond Vallanmyre.

It was only Papa and me. And tonight, it felt like it was *only* me, a lonely shadow in silk pajamas floating into the kitchen. Lighting the stove, pouring milk into a saucer, mixing in drinking chocolate and honey and crushed vanilla and a bit of powdered bone broth. And then, kneeling on the granite countertop, I retrieved a special sachet Papa stashed on the very top shelf...a spice blend from Hadrass-Drui, the Land of Spice and Secrets.

Notes of cinnamon, clove, nutmeg, saffron, and a dash of chicory filled my nostrils at the first whiff, and a moan of delight bubbled in my throat. I didn't dare ask how much Papa had paid for this sachet in the Hadrassi district of Vallanmyre's flourishing marketplaces, but it must be expensive for him to have hidden it where only his children and none of his many guests would ever find it. So I was sparing with how much I sprinkled into my hot cocoa, though my mouth watered for more.

Choosing a mug was a feat...not for the head, but for the heart. The cupboard was the only part of the house that did not reflect the wealth my father had built after he'd become the sole custodian of his five children, when I'd been scarcely nine and Patryk, the oldest, freshly sixteen. Every mug was handspun, chipped, and faded with age and use...each one crafted by the loving labor of my mother's hands.

A mug for each of us with our names etched into it. Mugs studded with false pearls and painted in whirling purple-blue tones reminiscent of the merfolk in my favorite childhood bedtime stories. Mugs laced with flowers and bumblebees and clouds. Sturdy mugs sculpted with tiny swords and shields.

I chose a meadow green one, its shade as familiar and comforting as the plants that adorned my room. Then, cocoa in hand at last, I made my way into the sitting room, lined half with bookshelves and a fireplace, and half with floor-to-ceiling windows.

The view of Vallanmyre was breathtaking across one of the city's numerous canals. Arched, two-toned cathedrals honoring two-faced, fickle Luck, homes of varying levels and luxury, sprawling markets, domes, and spires all glowed with late-night lanternlight and glistening globes. Those multihued lights encased in glass posts were warmed slowly by the sun throughout the day, and at night they paved Vallanmyre's avenues in dapples of prismatic color, their reflections winking secretively across the black, churning canal waters.

"I've got a secret, too," I murmured, lowering myself onto one of the lounging chairs before the windows and tugging my mother's old, knitted blanket across my lap.

It was just my imagination—scents did not survive two dozen years past the person to whom they'd belonged, even for a sharp nose like mine—but I liked to think there was a trace of my mother's gardenia perfume still hidden in some fold of the thing.

Settling back, I stared across the city that had been my home for so many years...and let the sweat of a warm mug replace the sweat of nightmares.

I only had to linger until week's end. For the past two years since his father's abrupt abdication and his own ascension as Sha, Arias Lothar had insisted the five—and now six—members of his inner circle convene every few months from our various tasks to update and report to one another.

From Audra Grissom and Reiko Nayori, a report on the status of Storycraft, the power which created tangible things from storytelling. For years, Storycraft had been broken, the endings of all the stories vanished completely. Now that it had returned, by the work of Audra's own hand, Mithra-Sha was beginning to truly flourish again—from farmlands to cities to commerce and more.

From Arias's sister, Shadress Mahalia Lothar, a report of the high-ranking leaders of the country...the influential, the powerful, the people like my father and those even more wealthy and persuasive than him. The exact sort the Sha's softspoken, keen-minded sister could coerce—or eavesdrop—into reporting on dissatisfaction and schemes among city leaders and trade magnates across the country.

From Wyat Jaymes, Mahalia's bodyguard and a true soldier's soldier, a report of how our borders fared. Though he was young, and in some ways untested, he took his duties as seriously as any seasoned military man. I'd been impressed more than once when he'd caught wind of unrest from Amere-Del to the south or Hadrass-Drui stirring on the far side of the Vensair Mountains to the east, well before any official reports were made.

From Jaik Grissom, Arias's best friend and his own bodyguard, a report of how the army itself was performing from its generals and emissaries...and how the ongoing efforts proceeded with rounding up the manifestations of Misspoken stories born of broken amplifiers across the country, and destroying them. A task cut evenly between the military and the Storycrafters...sword and story, working in tandem.

I didn't envy him *that* task, but Jaik had leaped on it without hesitation as soon as he'd become Arias's right hand and head of the military forces in Vallanmyre. And now he had Audra's help, husband and wife forging a near-ly-unbeatable force.

And from myself...

Reports on the wellbeing of Mithra-Sha. How it was truly healing...how its lingering pain pushed through, and where, like emergent diseases and broken bones through tender flesh. What new plagues were in outbreak? What herbs and brews were being abused? What wounds of the mind, the body, the soul still begged healing after all the lack the country had suffered during the years without Storycraft?

These weeks in Vallanmyre were always the heaviest of the year. Because a report was not a guarantee of a cure...and some of the things I told the others about couldn't be managed with a tonic or a torniquet.

Despite how Mithra-Sha had clawed its way back to a semblance of pros-perity over the past two years, hurts still festered below the surface. Unrest, doubt, even dissidence against the Lothar name, after the paranoia and resulting injustices of Arias's father had been revealed.

The death he had caused out of sheer fright. The way Storycraft had lashed back at him, tearing away the endings and all the power of stories for years. What that had done to the country we all loved...and to people we loved, too.

And that left me wishing away the days in the city, even the ones that meant I would see Audra—my closest friend since Harrow Hall—and the others. Wish-ing I could return to my quiet home in Dalfi, striped in shadows from passing airships, to the perpetual scent of potpourri dishes and herb pots cultivated on the rooftop, and the furniture and foodstuff arranged just so.

To the wounds and struggles and people I *could* help.

The tread of heavy feet crunched into my straying thoughts like boots through winter foliage; a familiar scent of sandalwood and pipe smoke wafted over me—a perpetual reminder of a bad habit unbroken despite my warnings over the years—and then my father lowered himself into the lounging chair beside mine.

Something unknotted itself in my father's presence; just watching him toss another hand-stitched blanket over his broad girth, settle in, scratch absently at the stubble he always let grow out during furloughs in Vallanmyre before he was off traveling and peddling again.

Finally settled, he flicked me a glance, brows raised nearly to the far-thest-reaching curls of his graying chestnut hair. "What are you doing up so late, bug?"

A flicker of a smile stitched up one side of my mouth; though it had been a lifetime since I'd been the little girl crawling through the garden of my childhood home, rolling in the dirt and asking my mother the name of every plant I encoun-tered, I hadn't convinced my family to shed that nickname. And, if I was being honest, there was something comforting about it these days; the notion that some piece of that innocent girl could still live in a woman with blood on her hands.

My smile slipping away, I glanced down at my frothy cocoa. "Just...couldn't sleep. What about you, Papa?"

"Ah, the same." He spanned an arm along the back of my chair, reclining in his. "Always get this way before another peddling venture. Though this should be nice...Behn and I will happen to be near Tavris about the same time, so we made plans for a meal and shared board for the stay there. It'll be good to see him...claims he has some exciting news to share."

"Whatever it is, I'm sure it will be wonderful...just like him." My heart pinched at the thought of my youngest brother—my childhood playmate and the closest friend I'd had until Harrow Hall. Though we'd written plenty of letters since I'd relocated to Dalfi, we hadn't seen one another.

My father, Patryk, Felyx, and Conor were all married either to wonderful women, or to their work. They tended to think my sudden uprooting of my life and fresh start in an airship port city had been nothing more than a business decision. But Behn—a poet, a musician, the freest spirit of us all—would know better. He'd always been able to look into my eyes and know if I was lying.

Avoiding him had been a necessity for so many years. But that didn't mean my chest didn't ache at the mention of his name.

"Tell him I love him."

I ducked my gaze back to my drink, avoiding the glance Papa leveled my way from the side. "Something bothering you, Naomi?"

I bit my lips together; it was rare for him to pursue personal matters, especially with me. Despite his doting nature, he struggled a bit with the intricacies of parenting a daughter.

For just a flash—a traitorous, dangerous heartbeat—I wanted to tell him; I wanted *someone* to know the truth about me.

How leaving Vallanmyre had not been my desire. How abandoning my family and friends had been the furthest wish from my heart. How I'd had the exact life I'd dreamed of here in the capital, close to all my friends, enamored with a quick-paced life of danger and challenge...until one terrible day that had changed everything.

One drop is all it takes.

Swallowing, I spared my father a quick smile. "Nothing out of the usual. I'm just adjusting to sleeping in a different house again."

"Fuss-bug," he teased, tugging on a lock of my hair. "Oh, that reminds me! Word must have spread from the Shastah that you're visiting again. There was a note here for you this afternoon."

Frowning, I pushed myself up straight in the lounging chair. "A note?"

He nodded, then shuffled off to root through a stack of letters on the cherrywood table beside the fireplace. I watched his every movement like I would an ailing patient's, each thud of my heart churning new thoughts to the surface.

The only people I regularly met with during my visits to this city—my brothers, Arias, and his inner circle—wouldn't leave me a note, they would speak with me face-to-face. And anyone enough of a stranger to send a *note* shouldn't know where I was staying at all.

My scalp prickled, the fine hairs on my arms and nape standing at attention when my father returned carrying an innocuous envelope, marbled cream linen with my name etched across it.

Innocuous...but the stock was heavy when my father laid it in my hand. Too fine for common households. And the ink was pure and rich, deep ebony...not the watered-down stuff often sold in the markets that bled and faded gray within the hour.

"Who...who did you say left this?" I rasped.

"I didn't." Papa eased back into his seat. "It was just there on the stoop when I came home this evening."

Scalp prickling, tension winding down my arms and seizing my wrists like thorny vines, I flipped the envelope over and brushed my thumb against the plain wax seal; then I broke it and wiggled the contents loose.

A single sheet of paper, the same texture and color as the envelope; a pair of lines, written in shining sable ink.

But, like one drop of poison, they destroyed *everything*.

I know what you did.
Meet with me at Harrow Hall tomorrow at sunrise to discuss your future.

CHAPTER 2
TURN AND RUN

I COULDN'T EXPLAIN TO my father why I'd gone, as he described, *bone white*.

I couldn't force myself to show him the letter. To bring him any nearer to a horrible truth hinted in ink; the part of my past that made me a stranger to him, to everyone I loved...finally catching up with me.

The next clear-headed moment, I was back in my room; I was ripping my satchel from the back of the chair at the desk and throwing it onto the bed, hurling clothes into it, my perfume bottle, then grabbing my cloak, pulling out my boots from the closet.

And the thing that stopped me, leaning against the bedpost and tugging them on, was how I had lived this night before.

A mad dash in the dark. Half of my things forgotten until my father had brought them to me months later. No proper farewells. No last looks back. Fleeing from Vallanmyre to Dalfi. Starting over.

Always running, running, running.

And here I was, about to do it again.

My legs gave way, and I dropped onto the edge of the bed, cupping my mouth with both hands—choking back a scream.

I know what you did.

This couldn't be happening—not after all these years. Not when I'd given up *everything* to ensure it never would.

Every inch of me ached to escape the capital like I had the last time. To slip away before the threat in those five luckless words could land against the back of my neck like a dagger.

But...

I knew where that road led: more running. Never feeling like there was a home to come back to. Broken friendships, severed ties, relationships that only existed in the written word, an empty house, *loneliness*.

If I ran now, I could *never* come back to Vallanmyre. I would never have the strength to face the risk of being caught by whoever had sent that note.

This was the breaking point. This was my only chance to choose whether I would stay and risk it, or run forever.

My hands smoothed up my cheeks, the heels of my palms grinding against my eyes. Damp heat kissed my skin.

I don't know how to stop running.

But maybe, this time, I had to try.

Running wouldn't change what this stranger knew. And *I* had to know *how* they knew...and exactly how much.

With shaking fingers and tearstained cheeks, I unpacked my satchel again. Legs aching at every joint, I pushed myself back onto the bed and lay with my head buried in my pillow. The memories of an awful dream—and a truth just as horrific—pounded the insides of my skull.

This time, I stayed. I didn't run.

But I didn't sleep, either. Not when the same nightmare was waiting for me if I closed my eyes.

CHAPTER 3
IN HARROWED HALLS

A THICK, SODDEN CLOUDBANK wept rain in deathbed tears when I scurried through Vallanmyre's streets just before dawn, no better rested and ridiculously more anxious than last night.

Because this unexpected jaunt across the city, stealing like a thief through the night's last shadows with the thick, heavy cardstock crushed in my fist and jammed into my pocket, was not a dream. No matter how badly I wished it was, like the kind of horrible diagnosis every patient wished they could blink awake from.

The city certainly *felt* like something from a dream. Caught somewhere between rousing and resting, its usual predawn bustle dampened by the deluge, Vallanmyre struggled in lurches and lulls of shop lights flickering alive and open vendor stalls still covered, waiting for the storm to pass. Distant lightning flickered to the west and thunder grumbled in low peals, as if even the storm shied from the coming day.

I wished *I* could shirk necessity; I wished I was anywhere else and doing anything but heeding summons from a hidden face to the place of my adolescent training, like a lapdog tugged on a leash.

Dodging puddles in the cobblestones and stepping up onto the curb, I squinted from beneath the folds of my cloak's soft jade hood. It was the attire of a first-classed healer, a system we'd borrowed from the Storycrafters in Fablehaven Academy—though *our* cloaks didn't shift color like theirs.

Initiates at Harrow Hall wore ivory-white, a color of fresh minds waiting to be stained, scoured, and sullied. To take on the marks of the brutal learning that would make them competent.

We wore brown cloaks the longest, through our middle years at the Hall. The color of soil and growing things, of roots digging deep into the earth, of fertile minds nourished and ready to receive things that would be watered, then sprout and define the shape of our lives.

We wore green when we earned top marks, when we graduated. Only a handful stayed for ten full years of training to earn this color; though brown-cloaks could serve in infirmaries, they would never practice healing on their own. They always answered to a green-cloak in charge; to try otherwise meant disbarment from healing altogether.

I'd once fancied that my cloak was greener than most...a nod to how my professors had praised my talents and lauded my studies. How my ambition surpassed many of my peers, even in ways that made the rest of them uncomfortable. The professors, too.

But now I knew precisely how green looked when it was stained red—dangerously close to brown.

I shook that thought away, unleashing a cloud of freesia-scented shampoo from my curls that stoked my courage just a bit as I rounded a hook in the avenue—and my strides ground to a halt.

There it was, up close for the first time in too many years: Harrow Hall, a sprawling complex of interlocked stone, higher and mightier than most of the apartments and trade buildings that framed the street, its numerous levels all twined in ivy or shaded by soaring trees that likely outlived Vallanmyre itself. It reposed behind its wrought-iron fence, every post topped in a rose-and-thorn finial...beautiful and threatening in the same breath.

I'd spent the better part of adolescence inside those cavernous stone halls and darkened apothecary rooms, tending the herb beds and gently teasing life into the poisonous plants, and somehow it still had the indecency to knock me breathless just by looking at it. I'd always argued with Audra that Harrow Hall was far more beautiful than the spire of Fablehaven Academy beyond it, full of gabled roofs and balconies, stuffed to the brim with books.

Tangibility. That was what Harrow Hall was made of. There was an ancientness to it, almost a breathing sort of sentience in the thick-cut, uneven stones and jutting pinnacles and facades...as if all the blood spilled in its halls had seeped into the seams, mortaring the stone, imbuing it with life.

Harrow Hall *whispered* at my approach. Songs of life and death curled up from the grass on either side of the pavestone walkway, up to the sable fence that ensconced the grounds and gardens. Those gardens brimmed to the overflow with life-giving herbs—and in darkened corners barred to the newest initiates, death-dealing ones as well.

My heart stuttered when I crossed the street to the swooping gates; Arias's grandfather had ordered them sealed to public entrance years ago, after a pack of rowdy soldiers-in-training had provoked one another to steal from the garden only to find themselves victims of toxicity. But today, the silver rose lock was unhinged, the gate just barely pushed open.

Occupied. Anticipating.

I pressed a kiss to my trembling fingertips and grazed them over the black gate, breathing out the old initiate's prayer I'd learned from the graduating class my first year:

Three things I pray in my craft this day:
Compassion for the ill
Skill to heal and not to kill
Confidence to make the choices no one will.

Hinges groaned and iron creaked inward, brushing aside fronds that yellowed in the face of autumn's rapid approach. Puffs of scent touched my nostrils like the perfumes of old friends passing by...tomato and marigold and lavender. Dry vines curled at the edges of the immaculate path to Harrow Hall's receiving door, winding beneath wisteria and willow trees to the wide front steps where Audra and I had sat for more afternoons than I could count, backs propped to the opposite railings, the soles of our boots pressed together while we scribbled feverishly over our examination papers.

Nostalgia thickened in the base of my throat as I mounted the steps, my feet instinctively skipping the middle one with a hop and a pirouette—a game of ours that was imprinted in the motion of my muscles. Then I was up to the door, fingers pressed to the weathered gray wood whorled with embered slashes.

It, too, gave way beneath the brush of my hand.

Heart clamoring, I ducked into Harrow Hall's soaring entry nave.

Even the pad of my jewel-studded flats echoed in the soaring vault of the ceiling; the broad stone columns, topped with second-level mezzanines and hand-carved balustrades, captured the swish of shedding my cloak and hissed it back like a threat.

The hair on my neck rose; I had never seen Harrow Hall so empty, so tomb-like. True, they were between sessions now, with the end of summer looming. Many initiates came from farming families and had to return to Vallanmyre's outlying lands or the smaller towns and villages to assist with the crops. But Headmaster Glover always had one of the professors watching the door.

I couldn't bring myself to call out as I eased deeper into the nave. Serving closely with soldiers and Storycrafters and growing up with four older brothers had ingrained a sense of danger so deep in my bones, it was almost a disease.

Never be the first to give away your position.

Funny how the principles of mortal combat were so like the standards of *hide-seek-find.*

Shadows enfolded me ahead and behind; halfway down the nave, my sensitive nose caught the brush of a smoky aroma.

One of the receiving rooms was lit from within, shedding a dusky red-gold glow across the smooth, wide-cut stones.

My steps churned to a halt. For half a moment, my weight balanced on my back foot—ready to run.

Whoever lurked in that chamber, if they were the one who had sent the letter, then they held all the power in the world to change my fate forever. One flip of Luck's two-faced coin was all it would take...I might never go home again.

One last chance to flee.

It demanded all my courage to shove my heavy feet closer to the doorway; to enter the chamber with my head high.

This room was one of many where initiates gathered for studies around steaming mugs of coffee and cocoa—or where patients waited to be called for free care in exchange for the experience untested healers gained from their cases. Each and every chamber lining the nave was sculpted precisely the same: a hearth, a stone bench stuffed with sitting pillows ringing both halves of the circular room, a set of chairs and a low table at the center.

A single figure perched in one of those stuffed armchairs, her posture betraying her name even before the slant of firelight revealed her face.

Dark hair, russet skin, high cheekbones—eyes like black fire. She'd thinned some since I'd last seen her; after her husband's abdication, we'd rarely crossed paths, because that was what Arias had requested.

And I had always held more love for Arias Lothar than I had for his mother.

CHAPTER 4
DOCILE, DEVOTED, DECEIVED

SHADRE CALTEN LOTHAR WAS a woman of presence.

As an initiate, I'd been smitten by it; as one of the many high-marked healers serving in the royal family's Shastah for years after graduation, I'd respected it. And though she was now a ruler in name only, her retained title a formality until Arias found a wife to take it...still, my spine locked and my shoulders drew back when our eyes met.

"Where is Headmaster Glover?" I asked.

"Absent," the Shadre replied tersely, "along with the rest of the professors. I thought you might prefer to have this discussion in private...and somewhere familiar to you."

A wince worked its way across my shoulders before I could stiffen them against it. The Shadre settled back in her seat, crossing one knee over the other, studying me up and down.

"It's been some years, hasn't it?" This question was inflectionless—more a statement of fact. "My son has kept you busy."

I slipped a bit deeper into the room, letting the fire warm my right side—begging Luck that that would be enough to chase away the shivers that crawled up my legs. "He has."

"And how is Arias faring these days?" No more inflection to this question than the last, but pain darted through her eyes.

Well, that answered one of the countless questions lurking in my head: Arias had made no strides to reconcile with his parents. Which was just as well...I'd lost every bit of respect and affection for Arias's father when I'd learned he'd committed murder to maintain power and possession over the most powerful Storycrafter of our time.

Besides the fact it was Jaik he'd murdered. And Audra he'd been so desperate to possess.

I would never stop being grateful for the complicated mess of Storycraft that had brought them both back to us, through sundered tales and desperate love. But it had gashed apart Arias's relationship with his parents so brutally, I wasn't certain even the creator of the Wellspoken World could mend it.

I couldn't be certain Arias *wanted* it mended.

Which had left his father in seclusion for the last two years and his mother hovering at the fringes of her children's lives, seeking a way in. Mahalia still spoke to her, if infrequently, but Arias had settled for formalities...and requested we all do the same.

I almost wished this meeting could be about that. Not...

My fist strangled the note in my pocket.

I know what you did.

Even with her husband no longer Sha, this woman had every bit of power to destroy me with the truth.

One drop is all it takes.

"You don't seem surprised to see me here, Miss Weathers." The Shadre's gaze drifted to the hand shoved in my pocket. "Was my note really so revealing?"

The question felt oddly like a test.

"The ink was clearly good quality—thick, dark—and the note was excellent stock. Too costly for most people to afford, and certainly too fine to be wasted on sending letters without some authority behind them." I skimmed my free hand along the back of the nearest seat, slowly circling it. "I could only think of a handful of people who wield that authority, who might also find out where I was staying, and when, while I visited the city...and who would send a note, rather than speaking to me personally. Your name was obviously on that list, Shadre."

In truth, there were several other *someones* with the clout to send threatening letters scripted in fine ink on fashionable cardstock...and with the desire to see me tried for what I'd done. But if *they* knew enough to send that letter, they wouldn't have sent it at all. I would already be in chains, on my way to stand trial.

The thought weakened all the strength in my knees; I slipped around the edge of the chair and sank down on its edge before I could make a fool of myself and drop to the floor.

Shadre Calten regarded me with a faint twist to her lips, the slightest downward slope of her brows. "You're an observant woman, Healer Weathers."

I shrugged. "My father is a peddler. He taught me to notice the quality of things. It's how you keep from being swindled."

"Or how you learn to swindle others, hm?"

My pulse jolted; lacing my fingers together in my lap, I reclined against the seatback. "I haven't swindled anyone."

"My son might disagree. Or does he know *everything* about the woman who sits with his inner circle, speaking of healing with a forked tongue as two-sided as Luck's fickle coin?"

Shock—and rage—struck like a blow to my sternum. "I haven't been *lying* to Arias, if that's what you're—"

"Lies can be spoken, or truth can be omitted," the Shadre cut across me coldly. "Whichever it is, Arias doesn't know, does he? He hasn't the first notion what docile, devoted Naomi Weathers is capable of."

Heat streaked across my palms, a flash like sweat—like blood—pouring across the creases. Cold, corroded chills lanced through my insides, lacing me deeper into the seatback. But there was no escaping the Shadre's hawkish stare, the cool triumph rearranging the sharp angles of her face as she watched the blood drain from mine.

Her note had not been a bluff, a misdirection to a false diagnosis.

She *knew*.

"Wh—" *Who told you? When did you learn this? What now?* All the questions built in the back of my throat, thickening like contamination beneath the skin. But only one escaped, after endless, breathless seconds: "Why call me here instead of sending soldiers to arrest me?"

My cheeks warmed at the humiliation of the thought—because Jaik would've likely been responsible for such an arrest. And I couldn't even begin to fathom how either of us would've looked the other in the eye while he clapped me in irons.

I'd been spared that for a reason. And with every heartbeat that thudded past, my desperation to know it grew.

Slowly, Shadre Calten eased back as well, smoothing her palms over her cobalt gown. A stray aroma of mint and melon floated my way, tickling my nostrils. "Your crime was perpetrated many years ago, Miss Weathers. As it happens, the talents that equipped you to commit it may prove useful in solving a more emergent problem."

A dull, delicate hum overtook my hearing; surprise prodded me up from the seat. "I'm sorry, Shadre...are you *extorting* me?"

A slow, upward slide of one sculpted brow. "I am preparing to offer you an ultimatum which may spare you the stocks, a vicious public trial, and a lifetime in Vallanmyre's most well-guarded prison. Or worse." That brow twitched downward, slanted inward with the other—goading me to the inevitable conclusion of what *worse* would be. "Unless you would prefer this conversation to end with a simple arrest?"

My mouth dried out like a cloth bandage on a clothesline. Heat choked my throat and swarmed the backs of my eyes. "To what *emergent problem* are you referring?"

Triumph flickered in the otherwise empty smile that slashed across her face; she folded her hands in her lap, posture mirroring mine. "Tell me what you know of Hadrass-Drui."

Like an initiate in one of this complex's many lecture halls, my mind tilled through various lessons, dusting off notions and knowledge I hadn't had much reason to touch in the past decade-and-a-half...

Except for once. A piece of the choice that had changed everything.

"The Land of Spice and Secrets." I tapped my fingers against my opposite knuckles, a familiar rhythm I'd learned for recollection. "Ruled by Drui Athicus Moraven and Druaeva Estrella...your parents."

A slow blink. "Go on."

I rummaged a bit further, through things I knew from Arias and Mahalia's stories of their mother's homeland. "Your sister Serai is next to inherit. And your younger brother, Caspian, serves as spokesperson for the Moraven family across Hadrass-Drui. It's the second-largest country in the Wellspoken World, famous for its exports of spices, cloth, and dye, and—"

"For its assassins."

I quieted.

For a long moment, the Shadre and I gazed at one another, the crackle and pop of the hearth the only sound subverting the silence.

"Shadre, what is this about?" I dared to ask.

Her gaze strayed slowly to the hearth. Still interlaced, just like mine, her fingers tightened until her knuckles popped pale against her tawny skin.

"Hadrass-Drui is a complicated place." Musings—memories of her childhood home—guttered in time with the fire's reflection dancing against her eyes. "Secretive, secluded...and currently facing a threat unlike any it has suffered before."

"What sort of threat?"

Her focus pierced back to me. "An assassin targeting its most elite."

The breath fled my lungs in a rush. "Flipping *Luck*. Does Arias know?"

"He hasn't, but he does now." The Shadre's throat clenched, and a slow blink produced a silver sheen across her eyes; with the next, it was gone. "My sister's son, Phineaus...he was the latest mark."

Disbelief bolted me flush to the seatback again.

Phineaus. Arias and Mahalia had often mentioned their cousin with his thick, sandy-brown hair and goldenrod eyes. How he'd taught them to play—and cheat—at cards. He'd bought Arias his first dagger and showed him how to use it. He'd given Mahalia her first taste of strong spirits. He'd inspired the desire for the Sha's title in Arias with his own ambitions for change, though Phineaus was third in the noble line behind his parents and uncle.

Arias and Mahalia had only ever spoken of him fondly, even wistfully, though they hadn't seen one another in years. And now... "Is he—?"

"He survived." The Shadre's curt retort freed a *whoosh* of breath from behind the lump in my throat. "But barely, and not unscathed. He is the first we know to have lived after this assassin's strike."

"Which assassin? And how did they get so close to the Drui's own *family*?"

"That," the Shadre said, "is precisely the mystery my family is desperate to solve, before this person strikes again...before they strike *Phin* again." A faint twist of her mouth was the only sign of just how deeply that notion disturbed her. "They are so desperate, in fact, that they enlisted the help of their estranged daughter and sister, by all accounts little more than a Mithran bedwarmer in the eyes of Hadrass-Drui." A cold smile fractured across her face, so utterly devoid of mirth it chilled me to the core. "So desperate that they are seeking aid from *this* country to help find this elusive assassin before Phin is attacked again."

All the air fled my lungs the gust of a half-squeaked word: "*What?*"

"Hadrassi forces have failed to find him yet, and now time runs short. So you, Healer Weathers, are going to Hadrass-Drui as my personal dispatch. You will assist the Hadrassi sentinels and my father's advisors in bringing this killer to his knees."

My mind stumbled and stuttered, clawing for another test in her words. A jest. A mistake. "Shadre, that's...that is absolutely *impossible.*"

"Is it." Her frosty tone did not imply a question—more of a dare that I defy.

Shifting to the edge of the seat, I spread my hands in a showy flash indicating my whole person. "What in flipping Luck makes you think that *I'm* some sort of match for an assassin?"

"Oh, I can't fathom, Miss Weathers. What *would* make me believe you could think like such a murderer?"

I stilled. Swallowed. Stared at her.

"From what I learned from the report of a certain Initiate Raynes some years ago," she went on, missing—or ignoring—the flinch that gripped me at that name, "you are adept indeed at playing an innocent part while masking your true nature. And you can keep a secret of the most sinister sort for quite some time."

Initiate Raynes. The ashen taste of shock and regret and fury coated my tongue; the memory of a wide-eyed, pallid face surged in their wake, a girl's tearstained gaze between curtains of dark braids dragging after me across a stifling room, my bloodsoaked hands plunging into frigid water—

You will forget everything you saw here, Raynes. You will never breathe a word of it, or write a word of it, or even allude about this moment to anyone. Or I will make absolutely certain you never so much as thread a suture needle or lay eyes on the inside of an infirmary ever again.

I blinked away the memory, then knuckled a streak of heat from my cheek; my vision cleared to the sight of Shadre Calten, the faintest sideways bend of her head as she assessed me.

So. Raynes *had* told, after all. And this entire time, someone had been waiting to wield that knowledge against me.

"You are also the only one I know who possesses these secretive qualities," the Shadre went on, "as well as having scored the highest marks of Harrow Hall's graduates in recent account—for both healing and poison studies. You never shied away from those darker designs, unlike most of your peers." A vicious divot grooved between her brows. "One need not wonder how you achieved so high in the subject, now, do we?"

Copper washed between my teeth as they ground through the tip of my tongue.

"All of this considered, Miss Weathers, you possess every single talent required to accomplish this task," the Shadre finished. "And unlike your peers, you are in no position to refuse...not if you wish to remain a free woman."

I swallowed the taste of blood from between my teeth; better there than lurking in my hands. "And how do I know that if I do this, you won't have soldiers waiting to arrest me when I come home?"

"You don't. But you can rest *assured* that if you do not do it, they will be waiting to arrest you the moment you set foot from this room."

My breath hitched. Behind it, a sob started building.

"An *assassin*, Shadre," I croaked.

"Not merely an assassin, I'm no fool. I wouldn't pit you against blades or rifles," she scoffed. "This assassin is himself a poisoner."

On heartbeat thumped by. Two. Then three.

"That's why they're searching for help outside their borders." The whisper floated from my lips. "They don't know who the killer is, or who his connections may be. So they don't trust any poisoner or healer of their own to find him."

"Anyone could *be* him." The slightest tilt of her chin. "A murderer masked in shadows. Someone near enough to have struck the ruling family of Hadrass-Drui." The faintest quiver tilted her words. "Tell me you are no match for *that*."

I couldn't.

She was right...I *had* received the top marks among my class in poison studies. I'd taken that very first lesson, absorbed that first drop, and let it spread through my veins until it had consumed me with curiosity. I'd shouldered Audra's teasing about my interest in the wicked romanticism of poison...the bane of the wealthy and elite, of tragic lovers, of shadows and the night. I'd learned to shrug off the sideways glances from my classmates and the strange looks whenever I broached the subject in public.

And then...in a moment of desperation, I'd let one drop fall. And it *had* nearly destroyed everything; it was *still* destroying me, at this moment, in this place where I'd first learned of it.

"The choice is yours, Miss Weathers," Shadre Calten added when I didn't speak. "To Hadrass-Drui, or to the stocks. What will it be?"

CHAPTER 5
RECLAIMING THE CRAFT

"Y OU WANT TO GO *where*, precisely?"

Grimacing, I leaned my folded arms against the drinking counter at *The Bean and Brew* and inhaled the steam from a signature mug of pumpkin hot cocoa. A coffee and teahouse by day and a tavern by night, this place had become a favorite haunt of Arias's inner circle when we needed an escape from the suffocating blend of duty and memory that stifled the Shastah most days.

It was different for each of us, but today, the ache in my chest had nothing to do with notions of lost friends or the cruel former Sha. It was all the cruelty of his wife.

I wished the spicy steam of *my* drink would clear my head like it usually did. But every waft of cinnamon and nutmeg reminded me of a Hadrassi spice sachet, and why we were here...and what I'd just asked Arias, seated next to me, dark curls deeply ruffled and plastered against his russet brow, frowning as he waited for me to correct myself from what was surely a mistake.

Surely is.

"Hadrass-Drui." Slowly, I peeled my head back to meet Arias's wide-eyed stare. "I have business there."

"You can't be serious." His broad palms swallowed a steaming mug of dark coffee half-whole. "What business could you possibly have in the Land of Spice and Secrets? You've never even set foot over the border!"

Why don't you ask your mother?

I swallowed the snappish retort; Arias needed sass less today than he ever had. Holding his gaze had never been difficult before; we'd even had staring contests over the years to pass time, or to settle disputes over unpleasant tasks. But ever since he'd become Sha...

Looking into Arias Lothar's eyes was like staring into graves before they drizzled dirt over the corpse.

But I forced myself to do it now, while he faced me; to search past the shock and uncertainty, to find the strain, the struggle, the fear lurking behind it. The exhaustion swimming in his eyes, dulled by worse than the low-toned lighting.

"Arias," I murmured, pressing the pads of my fingers to my mug until they warmed through, "I think you know why."

A harsh swallow bobbed his throat. His gaze dropped to his mug.

"Someone tried to take Phineaus from us." The break in his cousin's name shattered a corner of my heart, too.

I squeezed his wrist. "We can't let that happen, Raz. We can't let murder shake the Hadrassi ruling family...not with how it would shake Mithra-Sha, too."

A sharp heft and dip of his broad shoulders; then he cast his gaze my way again. "Where did you hear?"

"As a matter of fact, your mother told me. I know," I flashed a palm before he could retort, "we try to avoid contact with your parents. But I couldn't precisely ignore it this time."

The truth—as much of it as I could give him.

"Then you know he was nearly murdered." Arias's gaze hardened like flint, a needling tip driving deep beneath my breastbone. "And you're asking to visit the very place where it happened...*why*?"

"Because no one knows yet who did this, or exactly how." I laced my fingers tightly around my mug, willing the warmth from it to flare into true courage somewhere beneath my skin. "That means the danger could be more than just Hadrassi, it could extend to other members of the Drui's family. To his estranged daughter...to Mithra-Sha's new ruler."

The way Arias streaked a hand back through his thick, dark curls, his remote stare flashing to the bulletin board behind the drinking counter and taking in the *Wanted* posters hung there, suggested he'd already considered that possibility.

Another weight to add to the impossible spread of them dumped across his shoulders.

"Arias, we've been friends since I was fifteen," I reminded him gently. "Your troubles have always been my troubles. I have *always* done whatever I could to help keep your family and this country safe." And if his mother kept her word, he would never know just *how much* I had done to ensure that. "Right now, your cousin is in danger, your mother's whole family might be in danger...which means *you* might be in danger. And Mahalia."

I hated the way his shoulders tucked in at the notion; but healers learned early and often which threads to tease to convince a person to commit risk for the hope of reward.

"Hadrass-Drui is being plagued by a poisoner," I added. "And you know that's one of my areas of expertise. All I need to do is travel to Hadrass-Drui and put my talents to use. I can be home in a few weeks...a few months at worst."

Skepticism deepened his grunt as he sipped his drink.

"I know you're concerned with the risks." I laid a hand on the crook of his elbow, drawing his attention back to me. "But consider the risks if I *don't*. This threat needs to be mitigated, and your mother asked me personally because she believes in my talents."

A quieter scoff. He said nothing.

Swallowing, I added, "It's not in me as a healer to see a hurt and not try to heal it. No matter who is hurting."

Which had only been a lie once. But once was all it had taken to land me in my current predicament.

Arias took in a shuddering breath; then he laid his hand over mine, squeezing it in the bend of his arm. "I want you to know I don't like this one bit, Naomi. Not one." His voice dipped slightly. "But I am *not* my father...I swore I'd never dictate where anyone on my council could go."

A last tightening of his fingers; then he freed my hand and slid his arm from beneath it.

"If this is how you see fit to use my trust and your talents, then I trust *you*," he said. "But I'd like reports. I want to know when you arrive and when you depart for home. And...how Phin is faring. I want to hear that, too."

I blew out a breath, despising the easy victory almost as much as I was relieved for it. Winning was hollow when it was his father's betrayal that had secured it...when I had known where to push to slip free.

If only escaping his mother were so simple.

Plastering on my widest smile—the one I'd flashed at countless patients when a poor prognosis landed in my lap—I shoved my shoulder against Arias's. "I'll be back before you even have time to miss me."

Lightly, he spun his coffee mug. "I never have time to miss anyone these days."

And that was the state I was leaving him in. Leaving all of them. Not for some noble reason, even if I could braid that lie easily enough into the truth...but because of the blood on my hands that hadn't washed away after all these years.

Tilting sideways on my stool, I rested my head on Arias's shoulder. "I'm so sorry this is happening."

A shudder of an inhale; then he pressed a chaste kiss to the top of my head. "That makes a pair of us, Noni."

"If it's any comfort, I'll do whatever I can to make sure it ends *now*."

"The only comfort I need—" His tone steeled, a flawless, almost frightening match for the rigid cut of his jawline, far too reminiscent of his mother's, "—is to know my cousin is safe and this *poisoner* can never hurt anyone again."

A quiver squirmed through my insides. "I'll make certain he never does."

CHAPTER 6
FAREWELL GIFTS

THREE DAYS AFTER MY meeting with Calten Lothar, the hum of an airship finally quieted my racing heart.

These Storycrafted ships, maintained by the most talented craftmasters and repairmen in Mithra-Sha, were the swiftest method of travel in the Wellspoken World. My father often raved about how the landscape of the peddling trade had changed unalterably for the better when airships came along from some Storycrafter's imagination. And I had lived in their tethered shadows for years in Dalfi, treating the inevitable wounds that came with working these great, clunking ships that rode the back of the wind rather than the waves.

But sitting in the small, stifling quarters granted by the airship's captain, hugging my travel satchel to my chest and breathing in the comforting aroma of earthy herbs from its fibers, I could only think of how I'd once fled Vallanmyre on an airship just like this one, with barely a goodbye to the people I loved most. And now, just like back then, my chest loosened and my lungs expanded more fully with every mile we chugged through the wind currents, further and further from Vallanmyre.

Even a journey to face an assassin was a Luck-loved escape from what the Shadre knew.

Tucking my face into my satchel, I breathed out—long and slow.

One. Two. Three.

Then I swiftly unbuckled the straps and laid out my belongings. Whether it was an unfamiliar infirmary or a strange city—or, in this case, a new country altogether—this ritual always took the edge off my nerves like a painkilling herb.

First, my favorite books, the ones I'd loved the binding right off of: pocket-sized volumes about herbs and triage and poisons. I grazed a hand over the cover of that one, wishing I could absorb every speck of knowledge I'd need for this mission by touch alone.

If only.

Beneath that, my sachets and tincture bottles, banded inside a leather pouch with flowers etched deep into the top flap; along the base ran the initiate's prayer I'd learned in Harrow Hall. I unlatched the pouch and explored its contents by the familiarity of various scents: cures for illnesses, inductions for vomiting, coagulating agents...things I'd been given as part of my graduation from Harrow Hall and never needed to touch, but never dared travel anywhere without.

Poison wasn't particularly prolific in Mithra-Sha—though moreso now than before we'd had a Hadrassi Shadre and stronger trade with our neighbors beyond the Vensair Mountains to the east. Still, every student at Harrow Hall knew how abundant poisons were even in the borderlands of our country, along the tiny skirt of the mountains where the Alusia River flowed into the small country of Navar-Bane.

We were all trained, just in case we ever treated a patient—or became a victim ourselves—of such things.

Grimacing, I tucked the pouch aside with a prayer to Luck I'd have no more need to open them in Hadrass-Drui than I ever had in Mithra-Sha.

Next, my clothes; I'd only brought a few changes, since it was likely I'd need Hadrassi attire to blend in and play my part. And I couldn't deny the spark of excitement that flared at the thought of buffing out my wardrobe with highly-coveted jagged skirts and peplum tops—the sort Mahalia often wore.

Grinning, I rifled through the mound of muslin, linen, and lace, folding them in neat stacks: tunics, skirts, handkerchiefs for tying back my hair while I worked. Then it was on to the assortment of effects I hadn't planned to bring with me...the gifts my friends had insisted I bring when, this time, I'd risked a real goodbye.

Emotion balled thick in my throat as I laid them out side by side. First, a dagger Jaik and Wyat had chosen specifically for me, the perfect weight and balance for the handful of lessons they and Arias had given me in defending myself from handsy patients and wicked soldiers over the years.

"Just in case," Jaik had warned, his smile lively but concern etching his eyes. "You never know with Hadrass-Drui."

From Mahalia, a perfectly-rendered map of the Hadrassi capital, Amalgard, sketched by her own hand. She'd darkened the path from the port through the lower town, to her grandfather's fortress—an easy guide for me to follow once we landed.

From Reiko, a blank journal with flowers etched in a deep oval recess, ivy twining the edges. She'd pressed it into my hands but not let go herself, her gaze boring into mine. "I got this from Gareth, down in the lower town...he's the best bookbinder I know, so it should hold up to whatever you get yourself into."

From Audra, a Storycrafted quill and ink—the plume ridiculously and wonderfully overpuffed, and the inkpot appearing empty at first. But she'd explained she'd crafted it herself, an ink that didn't show on paper unless it was held up to light at very specific times.

"I thought you might want to keep whatever you write in your new journal secret." She'd smiled when she'd said it, but concern had haunted her earnest gaze.

Arias's gift I already wore, tucked onto a string around my neck and slipped beneath the collar of my tunic: a decadent brass key, its shaft woven with thorny vines, its bow honed into the shape of a jewel-studded rose. It was a family heirloom—a Hadrassi vault key. It had been his mother's, a token of her heritage...and it just might save me some trouble during my search.

Surveying the gifts from my friends spread out on the drab olive bedspread, something prodded low in my gut...a sharp mingling of sorrow and shame.

These didn't feel like the sort of gifts you would give to someone you expected to see again in a few months. Not deathbed gifts, but...like all of them were holding onto the memory of how I'd left Vallanmyre with no warning and hardly any explanation all those years ago. As if they expected the same thing to happen again now.

I stroked my fingertips over the gifts, one after the other. "I will come back."

I blamed the thick, churning silence for how the words sounded.

A bit like a prayer.

A bit like a lie.

CHAPTER 7
CITY OF SKULLS AND SHADOWS

M Y FIRST GLIMPSE OF Hadrass-Drui's capital stole my breath away.

I'd spent most of the voyage belowdecks, paging through my book of poisons, preparing as best I could to pit wits against a trained assassin—someone powerful enough to have almost killed the Drui's own grandson.

I couldn't afford a single misstep.

I was buried deep in those notions—and deeper still in my notes, sipping a miserably thin and savory cup of tea, the only drink besides water the airship stocked—when the bell clanged outside my small chamber to signal our arrival.

Three bells for three minutes. We were *close*.

My heart bounded into my throat, and I snapped my journal shut. Winding the twine around it with a few deft swivels, I launched to my feet and ducked from the room, pulling my knit cardigan up my shoulder as I went. Pivoting my hand along the rosined banister, I hauled myself up to the topdeck with the flurry of soldiers gathering at the railings.

For some of them—just like me—this was their first time in the heart of Hadrass-Drui.

And...there went my breath.

Amalgard loomed in blackened spires and skull-shaped finials, in soaring obsidian cathedrals with candlelit steps and rook towers standing stalwart like fists raised against the sunset sliding from the east. But there were also collisions of color to contrast the dark stone and marble from which their architecture was hewn; riots of rich magenta trees, lurid emerald shrubs, sizzling pink pomegranate lights, and brassy yellow street lamps against the bruise-blue dark, all spurting like blood from severed arteries.

Most striking of all as we sailed lower and lower was the menagerie of painted glass mosaics sparkling in countless windows and rooftops. They flared the same hues as much of the plant life and lanterns, gleaming like chipped teeth knocked loose from a fighter's jaw.

My own jaw tensed as I soaked in the mishmash of deep shadows and brilliant shades of glass and plant life, fingers curling over the sleek railing. I had never seen flowers in so many colors; who knew how many of them were poisonous?

Suddenly, my preparatory work belowdecks with my nose buried in my books seemed worthless. To think that my answer lay pressed like petals between pages and not growing out there in brilliant bunches snaking between sinister towers...

Just what, *exactly*, had I gotten myself into?

CHAPTER 8
BLADE IN THE DARK

AMALGARD HAD NO AIRSHIP ports, which demanded we make our landing in the spacious harbor from which the low clouds rolled in like an ominous portent. From the water, we would make our way to the docks, and then...Fortress Ferregrand.

The home of Drui Moraven was a sprawling, steepled complex winking with fuchsia and gold stained-glass windows, its uppermost towers wrapped in the drizzly mist from the harbor on whose edge it perched. Thunderous waterfalls roared from beneath it—so much like the Shastah that perched on a plateau above Vallanmyre, it drilled a pang of melancholy recognition through my heart.

But *unlike* the Shastah, the Fortress was separated from land by a broad moat on one side and the sea on the other, accessible only by a retractable bridge; and that was currently upraised, shielded on both sides by pike-walled guardhouses.

Defensible to the uttermost.

"Drui Moraven knows how to guard his flanks." I gnawed the tip of my thumbnail, studying the pinnacles of soaring stone as we scraped by them, descending toward the choppy waters. "Every bit as suspicious as Arias and Mahalia always said."

Which meant that whoever had attacked Phineaus was a trusted visitor...or someone incredibly skilled, to slip past the Fortress's obvious defenses.

The lurch in my stomach had nothing to do with how the airship skimmed the whitecap, jolted, and settled with a body-wracking *splash* in the waves. And the buzzing in my head couldn't be blamed on soldiers barking orders to *drop anchor* and *prepare to row to shore*.

Perhaps I shouldn't have let the terror of a trial and sentencing goad me into this. Because death at the hands of a poisoner was suddenly feeling quite a bit more likely.

Scrambling belowdecks, I repacked my satchel faster than I ever had, belted on the dagger from Jaik and Wyat, and shook hands with the airship captain on my way back up the steps. I was ready at the shipside, bouncing from my heels to the balls of my feet and back again, by the time the soldiers lowered the gangplank.

Five of us descended to the harbor wharfs; the escort of four heavily-armed soldiers was a comfort and also precisely how I imagined being walked to the stocks would've felt. Both thoughts had me flexing my fingers around the satchel strap lashed across my chest as we slipped along the empty, silent docks and sank into the shadows of Amalgard's lower town.

The buildings staggered like crooked teeth, all mashed tightly together; the seams between were barely wide enough to slip an arm into, but that was almost a relief. There were fewer places for crafty figures to lurk as we hurried along cracked cobblestones and up toward the more refined architecture of the Hadrassi capital.

Armed with the map Mahalia had sketched, at least we didn't have to wonder where to go; the path to Fortress Ferregrand was laid out for us like the Spine, the great road that traveled the heart of Mithra-Sha. All that was left to do was walk it...and to try not to feel like I was being escorted to my own destruction.

Fog rolled in on our heels, muffling even the resonance of our footfalls as we hurried through the streets. The soldiers were all quiet, heads on a constant revolution, scouting the branching sideways; it shouldn't have felt so eerie in the emptiness of the middle of the night, but something about the mist and the shadows seemed malevolently watchful.

I checked my stride to match the senior soldier in the small regimen. "Captain Savar, isn't it?"

He dipped his head, keen gaze still hunting the darkness. "You've certainly chosen an interesting challenge coming here, Healer Weathers."

"Don't I know it." I chafed my thumb over my satchel's woven strap. "Have you ever visited Hadrass-Drui before?"

"Once." A glint of memory ticked at the corner of his mouth. "I was a member of the retinue who escorted Shadre Calten—Druella Calten, as she was at the time—from Hadrass-Drui to Mithra-Sha for her wedding."

"That must have been quite the escort." I couldn't help smiling at the thought of the Mithran army clashing with a younger, high-headed, steely-eyed Calten.

"It was not a chatter-filled trip." Captain Savar snorted. "I was the most inexperienced aboard the airship...absolutely smitten with the Druella, as most young men tended to be." A trickle of the shadows that clustered the edges of the street perforated his gaze, slinking slowly from storefront to storefront as we passed through a deserted plaza. "I also remember this place...how *haunted* it felt. Desolate, even in the daylight."

I swallowed a prickle of fear that needled in the base of my throat. "How do you mean?"

"Hadrass-Drui is a Luck-cursed land, Miss Weathers." The gauzy fog deadened Captain Savar's voice. "A home for liars and killers and thieves. If it were my say, we wouldn't leave a Mithran here to face its harms alone."

I hated the shiver that crawled down my arms at that remark...almost as much as I hated how they echoed a softer shade of a far more sinister threat. A threat that had started me down the road to this land, Luck-cursed or not, a very long time ago; a threat that made me wonder if Captain Savar might've preferred me in chains, if he'd known what I'd come to Hadrass-Drui to escape.

I rested a hand on the Captain's arm, hoping to quell his suspicions and my nerves at the same time. "I won't be alone, I'll be with the Shadre's family."

Savar's sharp eyes fell on me. "That concerns me all the more. The Moravens are—"

But I would never learn what the Moravens were—not from him.

Because all it took was that one moment—that single distraction, his gaze turning away from the street, falling on me—and then...

Chaos.

A burst of running footfalls; a bellow of curses. A lean body swooping down like some dark vulture from the rooftops that girdled the plaza. I barely had time to shout, "*Look out!*"

Then blades flashed like needles winnowing into rendered flesh.

Before horror had even finished dousing my body in an icy, breathless chill, before I could muster a scream past that, two of the soldiers were dead, cleaved open from sternum to waist.

Captain Savar whipped his rifle up to his shoulder. "*Run, Miss Weath—!*"

My name didn't make it past his throat before the column of it fell open in two neat strips, slashed wide open from ear to ear.

And then I was screaming.

And then I was *running*.

Rifleshots popped—the last soldier making a valiant stand that went dead silent far, far too quickly. A sob tore from my lips; I clutched my satchel strap tight to my front and forced my feet to pound the pavement harder, quicker, gobbling one span of darkened street beyond the plaza, and then another. And another.

The fog faded as the avenue climbed—and when I rose above it, the thrum of pursuing footfalls hammered against my ears. No longer silent, no longer stalking...the person who'd murdered those soldiers was chasing me down like prey.

"*No, no, no!*" I pleaded to Luck itself—then bore down my breath and stretched every stride for all it was worth.

Huffing breaths behind me. A shriek of blade whipping along stone—not a throw, not a blow, just a taunt. A promise of the painful death that was about to bury itself in my flesh.

Twisting down a side alley, I palmed the narrow walls on both sides, gripping the stone until it tore my fingertips, thrusting myself further and faster. My throbbing feet flew over disused fruit crates and tumbled stacks of brick and stone until I reached the opposite mouth, bursting free into a wide span of open cobblestone verged by greenery.

And there it was, a jutting, brilliant beacon ahead, just beyond the coniferous trees—Fortress Ferregrand, rife with towers and parapets and archways of silver-gray stone, its mosaics agleam, firelight bleeding down its pillars and columns in tawny sprays. The roar of waterfalls at the edge of the moat filled my ears like a chant of salvation as I fled toward them.

The guardhouse on this half of the bridge couldn't be more than a half-mile ahead, just beyond the stony footpath and encroaching evergreens. If I could make it that far, flash the key around my neck, then—

Pain erupted across my front—searing, slicing, ripping me backward on my heels. My satchel strap tightened like a torniquet across my throat and down my front, smothering the shriek that punched upward from my throat as rough hands seized the leather bag. I pirouetted in place, rearing up my arms and pivoting out of the satchel strap; it whipped over my head and I stumbled backward—my gaze lunging to follow the impact as the bag thudded aside on the cobblestones, then hurtling back to my pursuer as I scrambled out of his reach.

I couldn't see his face beneath his hood. I didn't *care* to; his front was soaked in soldiers' blood. It dripped from the side of his fist—the fist that strangled his gore-strung blade, thick globules plopping on the cobblestones with every step he advanced.

Stalking again. He knew I wouldn't dare turn my back on him like this; but the way he balanced the knife was a warning that, when I crossed some invisible threshold, took one too many breaths, stepped over some unseen line, that blade would gorge itself on *my* blood next.

My ears roared with the memory of what sounds flesh and muscle and bone made when they sundered. Scalpel, bonesaw, blade, it didn't matter...it was a song every healer knew.

And it was about to play for *me.*

My back collided with cold brick; I fumbled my own dagger from its sheath, its weight cumbersome in my grasp pitted against the featherlight hold the man held on his. My mind staggered over the lessons that were intended to serve me in moments like this—

There were no moments like this. Not for me.

I hadn't been on Hadrassi shores for a half-hour, and already I was staring down death. And I didn't have the ignorance that served other people in these situations, to ignore what it would sound like, smell like, taste like—*feel* like—

It was as if Shadre Calten had sent me here for a different justice altogether.

Count to three. Another lesson from Harrow Hall wailed in my mind as the man palmed the blade from hand to hand. *Count to calm. Then deal with what lies before you.*

One. I fisted my hand tight around the dagger.

Two. The man coiled to strike—as silent and lethal as a seizing, failing heart.

Three.

CHAPTER 9
THE SUBTLE SAVIOR

I BARELY SAW IT happen.

One moment, we were alone in the street, and then...we weren't.

The same instant the man tossed his blade, caught it by the tip this time, and arched forward to fling it—a second figure slipped from a hidden seam between two shops behind him. And, casual as a handshake, smooth as an embrace, he flashed an arm around my assailant's neck.

Arterial blood sprayed, a fount opened for the fifth time that night. I slammed my fist to my mouth, stifling another scream that belted across my tongue just for the sake of it as the murderer folded down on the cobblestones, his knife clattering uselessly from his hand and skidding across the street to rest at my feet.

And a stranger hovered unbothered above him, cleaning blood from his own blade against the hem of his coat.

I couldn't wrench my gaze from him; like one wound stifled and another beginning to bleed, he was the newest danger. He loomed taller than me by a head, leonine, swathed in Hadrassi core shades—black trousers and a burgundy shirt fletched in flickers of silver thread, and a deep cobalt cloak that pinned at his left shoulder. Black hair streaked back from his pale brow, and he wore a mask...sleek black metal fitted above a cowl drawn up to rest over his mouth and nose. Set deep in those angled eyeholes, his stare reminded me of Arias's—grave-dark, fathomless.

Fixed on me.

With a guttural chuff, his blade retracted...disappeared into the cuff of his shirtsleeve with a whir of unseen mechanisms that grated against my nerves. Spreading his stance, he tugged down his cowl to reveal high cheekbones and a bearded jaw. Then he showed his empty palms and dipped his chin a bit, peering at me from beneath his lashes. "Are you hurt?"

"I don't...I don't think so." But was I about to be? If one murderer could slip through the alley cracks of Amalgard and cut down four soldiers like shears through stanch cloth, couldn't another?

Couldn't *he*?

I angled my blade outward, its lethal tip level with his liver; not wise to provoke him with a threat, but I had no interest in goading him with a show of weakness, either.

"I can see you don't trust me." His gaze slid down to the dagger, then back to catch mine. "That's good. You shouldn't." His lips snagged downward when my breath hitched. "But it would stand to reason that if I preferred you dead, I'd have had no reason to intervene just now."

I forced that held breath out in a rush of, "Unless you wanted the pleasure of the kill for yourself."

One dark brow lifted, driving furrows deep into his forehead. "The *pleasure*—?" A humorless smile slashed up the corner of his mouth, and he half-pivoted away from me, then angled back again. "Sullied *souls*, you're mistrustful, aren't you?"

"Tell me I'm wrong. You didn't so much as blink before you killed *him*." I stuck my chin at the man lying between us, his blood veining the cobblestone cracks.

"*Him*, I had business with." The man stepped lithely over the corpse, circling off to my right with a long-limbed grace more often possessed by wildcats; I couldn't even bring myself to blink, watching how every leisurely step stirred the fog that had closed in around us again. "You and I, we don't have any business. Do we?"

He tucked to a knee, lifting my satchel and bearing it out before him as he approached. My breaths quickened, every muscle winding so tightly it bored pain into my joints. The wind seethed through the crooked streets behind him, chasing a smell of fennel and pine from the folds of his cloak; it tickled my nostrils, not in an unpleasant way...in fact, it cleared my head some, like smelling salts.

Awareness prickled along every nerve when the man halted before me, satchel offered out. "You dropped this."

Keeping my knife aimed between us, I snagged the strap and tugged; he didn't release it.

"You're bleeding," he added.

The moment he said it, I became aware of it: a warm trickle sliding down the column of my throat from the abrasion the strap had made.

"I'll live." I didn't dare take my eyes off his.

"Yes, I believe you will." A faint tilt of his head. "And you're welcome for that."

"*Thank you.*" The words emerged taut with annoyance. He *still* wouldn't release my flipping satchel strap.

"You're awfully rotting feisty, for a woman who almost had a blade thrown through her eye." His attention dragged up the length of me, and every hair on my body rose under the caress of that careful gaze. "Perhaps you're in shock."

"I know what shock is," I snapped. "I know how to manage it. I don't need your *opinion*, I'd just like my things."

All at once, he released the satchel strap—then, just as swiftly, his other hand snapped out and caught my opposite wrist. With a painless but irresistible swivel, he spun my hand and pried the knife from my fingers, holding it away from me behind his back.

"*Hey!*" I barked—then froze.

Not because he'd disarmed me. Not because he could likely murder me eleven different ways from Luck. But because he still held my disarmed hand—and lifted it in his gloved grip to press a kiss to my knuckles.

"No need to fret, troublemaker," he said. "I'll return this as soon as I'm convinced you're not going to stick it in my liver."

"Forgive me if that hardly makes me feel any *safer.*"

"Would you feel safe if I escorted you to the guardhouse?"

I stilled. He canted his head.

"Wasn't that the direction you were running when he caught up to you?" A flick of his deep attention toward the corpse behind him. "Or was it just coincidence you happened to be moving toward Amalgard's most well-armed outpost with an assassin on your heels?"

My breath squeaked out. "An *assassin.*"

A murderer, I'd known—and that he'd brought down talented Mithran soldiers without breaking a sweat had certainly hinted that way. But hearing it confirmed by a Hadrassi made my stomach churn right on the verge of vomiting.

"Haven't you heard?" The man freed my knuckles and tossed my knife to his other hand, offering me the hilt. "Anyone and everyone in this country might be."

There was a dare in those words to ask the question sizzling on the tip of my tongue: *Are you?*

I accepted the knife instead, stabbing it into my sheath...and the moment it snickered into place, an awful, aching realization pulsed through me.

Those Mithran soldiers were *dead*.

It could've been Jaik. It could've been Wyat.

It had almost been *me*.

Cold sweat beaded across my brow; sucking in a harsh breath, I braced my fingertips back against the wall and shoved up from it, swaying forward. "Those men—the ones escorting me—I have to go back. I can't just leave them—"

"Ah-ah-ah." A light backstep dodged this sinister savior straight into my path, hands outstretched again. "Believe me, troublemaker, you'll be far worse off if you're caught by the city's sentinels, surrounded by dead men with a puny pigsticker in your sheath."

I flinched back from the tips of his gloved fingers, tightening my satchel strap against myself. His fingers curled into slow fists, then dropped to his sides.

"I'll show them *him*, then." I nudged my chin at the corpse. "That will corroborate what happened."

"Yes, it would, if he would still be here by the time they come. But he won't be."

A chill scraped down my spine. "How do you know?"

Something pained flashed through his eyes. "Because I lived in this city long enough to know how it makes things disappear." He offered me his bent elbow, body angled toward the rocky footpath and the treeline I'd thought would be my salvation. "Just as the sentinels know how to make bodies vanish. Come market time at sunrise, there won't be a trace of blood left in the sidewalk cracks, and your friends might as well have never lived. So, unless you'd like to risk your soul on whether you'll join them..."

I eyed the offered elbow, licking drops of sweat from my upper lip.

This was absurd. I shouldn't even be considering it, but...

"I make it a point not to accept a man's help without knowing his name." I darted my eyes back to his face, gauging his reaction. "That's gotten me into heaps of trouble before."

"You, in trouble? Surely not." His sharp smile softened at the nearest edge. "I make it a point not to share names with people I have no intention of ever seeing again. But for the intents and purposes of getting you to move your feet so I can finally be on my way home, you may call me Kai."

Kai. A simple name, short, clipped...it rolled off his tongue like a story. Like there was more weight behind it than I would ever fathom.

Fog stirred as I stepped forward, my feet latching like lead to the cobble-stones. Distantly, a dog howled; voices clamored, slurred by the mist.

I slid my hand into the crook of his elbow. "Kai it is, then."

We left the assassin's corpse in the street, moving at a market browser's pace to the edge of cobblestone and untended rock, the trees wrapping us in a piney, herbaceous embrace. Kai cleared his throat. "And? What should I call *you*?"

"You seem partial to *troublemaker*, and I'm not feeling inclined to correct you." I skimmed a glance over my shoulder, shuddering at the bloodied pool spidering out beneath the corpse behind us—still visible even with the undergrowth tucking in at our backs. "Not after tonight."

"But I take it this is not your first brush with trouble." He batted aside a low-hanging cluster of pine. "You're taking it remarkably well."

"That's the thing about shock, I suppose." My teeth chattered slightly. "It keeps you strong until you no longer need to be."

"My experience may be lesser than yours, but I've never seen shock empower someone to face an assassin with blade in hand knowing they stood no chance against him." His face tilted down just when mine lifted, our gazes locking. "That was courage, troublemaker."

"Or foolishness." Which was what *this* was, too.

He didn't correct me, and we didn't speak again as we hurried through the darkness, hand in arm—until Kai slowed, and finally stopped, angling a nod to the glow of firelight fanning between the trees. "You were close...closer than most would make it with an assassin on their heels. You hardly needed an escort at all."

"I wish that could make me less grateful for it." I stepped away from him, nearer to the fire's beckoning golden warmth, to the promise of safety within lofty stone walls...but something had me pausing. Glancing back.

Kai lingered, posture immaculate, head tilted...still measuring me as if he'd keep doing it until I crossed the threshold to the guardhouse. Until my safety was assured.

And I had no reason to trust that more than anything else in this city that had already tried to steal my life...except that he'd distracted me from my fear twice now. And he'd brought me this short distance, and he lingered, waiting for me to carry on.

I snugged my satchel tighter to my hip and stuck out my hand. "That concludes our business, I suppose."

"So it does." But something twinkled like a secret in his eyes when he stepped forward and took my hand—and rather than shaking it, he flipped it, pressing another kiss to my knuckles. "But something tells me this won't be the end of the trouble you'll find in this city. I'll be here and there...if you need me, you can always call out."

I snorted. "That isn't going to happen."

"I suppose we'll see, won't we?" A wicked grin flashed beneath the curve of his mask; then he spun me by the hand like a dance in the Shastah, shoving me toward the treeline. "I'll be watching, troublemaker. Now, do us both a favor? *Run.*"

Maybe it was the shift in his tone, how it dropped, turned gravelly...something that all at once made me feel like I was about to be chased again. But I gripped my dagger hilt in one hand, the satchel strap in the other, and for the second time that night I fled like my life was in the balance. I crashed through the undergrowth and to the guardhouse gate, slamming both palms against it with all my might.

"I need help!" I screamed, rattling the iron with all the strength in my bones. "Help, *please*—I'm from Mithra-Sha, I was just attacked by an assassin, my escort is dead...*let me in!*"

There was a flurry of banging doors, of creaking winches and chains, a fluster of grabbing hands and snarled demands and me flashing the key around my neck and my papers from my satchel over and over again.

All of it became a riotous hum in my head as the warmth of six-foot-thick stone walls closed around me, as the Hadrassi sentinels hustled me to safety...and when I was there, I finally, *finally* broke.

A hailstorm of tears. Chest-wracking sobs. I saw those soldiers' faces, heard Captain Savar's command to flee. Felt Kai's fingers locked around mine, his lips brushing my knuckles, his arm slipping from my grasp.

I saw the assassin with his arm raised to strike, knife braced to throw—and Kai separating, shadow from shadow, coming to my rescue.

And I *knew*, deep in the pits of my chest, that he was right: this city would swallow every evidence of my near-death whole, as if it had never happened. But Hadrass-Drui had marked my arrival, stained it in blood and death.

As if that was everything I could expect for as long as I was here. Until I escaped...or this country was the end of me.

CHAPTER 10
FORTRESS FERREGRAND

I DIDN'T REMEMBER FALLING asleep in the guardhouse—though at some point the exhaustion from the running, the crying, the panic and terror must've all caught up to me. Because one moment I was leaning against the wall of a small, windowless room, wrapped in a stale blanket and breathing deeply to ease the shudders in my arms and legs; a pair of sentinels watched me unblinking from the corner, while another ran the bridge down and hurried to speak with the Drui, or so they told me.

The next thing I knew, I was dragging my itchy, exhausted eyelids open to mosaic light.

For a moment, I lay completely still, equal parts fascinated and frantic at the abrupt shift in my surroundings. Was this what it felt like for patients when they succumbed to ether?

I let my gaze rove the room, adjusting, drinking it in, bringing patterns to life and light. And by the time I'd seen most of it, I was in love.

The prismatic mosaic on the far wall cast everything in a rouge of pink and emerald. A curved sofa hugged close to a hearth and around a table on one side of the room; the other held the bed, a brass washstand, and a gilt-framed mirror. The sloped roof was patched with another mosaic, this one in chinks of gold and green that matched the paint on the walls and the detail in the wainscotting.

And everywhere, there were fabric plants: bunched into corners, strung over the hearth and mirror frame and curling around the four posts of the bed. The canopy itself was an imitation of an ivy curtain, the spread a deep jade; it was like climbing out of a meadow when I sat up, shoving the thick duvet aside.

This must be Fortress Ferregrand. It was a marvel I'd slept the whole way here...I couldn't imagine letting any stranger touch me, much less *carry* me, after everything—

A bolt of fizzling memory brushed through my knuckles.

Slowly, I curled my hand into a fist, then swung heavy legs from beneath the bedspread and padded to the mosaic wall. Brushing my fingertips over the sofa's low back and the washbasin's silky-smooth sculpting, I breathed in the scents that puffed from them: cleaning solutions and fabric wash and just a hint of the spice that hung over Hadrass-Drui in a perpetual haze.

Then I came to the window and lost my breath altogether.

Amalgard was *magnificent* from this angle—a view from the fortress fore-front, looking across the thundering moat and the lower town, out toward the markets and spires and cathedrals with candle wax slicking their steps. I edged close enough to the glass that my breath steamed it, my fingers streaking over the thick, smooth cast, skimming the whorls of indelible iron between every pane.

Beautiful, but functional. Which was how everything in this fortress had looked from the airship last night.

An involuntary shiver dragged its icy fingernails down my spine, blood-stained memories nudging at the corners of the relief that wrapped around me like a cozy blanket.

I was safe for now...but I'd have to go into the city again sometime. And I didn't suspect the idle promises of a shadow-spun stranger were going to really count for keeping me safe from the next assassin or mugger or ill-intentioned bastard I crossed paths with.

I'd need a sentinel guard for this.

It was as if the resolve that bolted through me at that thought summoned a knock at my door; I spun from the window just as the heavy wooden slab in the recessed frame swung inward, and a willowy figure glided into the room.

She hardly looked real: a handful of years younger than me, judging by the roundness of her face, her lean frame wrapped in a gauzy lavender-pink dress with a rosebunched bodice and tulled sleeves that draped around her upper arms. Her hair was such an ash-blonde, it gleamed almost silver in the daylight; I couldn't help staring, and our gazes locked for half a heartbeat when the door clattered closed. Then her bright blue eyes averted, and she wrapped one arm around her middle, the other hand crawling up to twist a tress around her finger. "It's...rather eyecatching, isn't it?"

I stifled a curse. What was I *doing*? I'd learned my first year in Harrow Hall not to stare at whatever came through an infirmary door, whether it was weeping pustules or disease-bulged eyeballs or limbs half-severed by farming implements or whipping airship rudders; unusual hair should be absolutely no different.

"I'm so sorry." I edged around the sofa, snatching my cardigan where someone had draped it over the back and slipping my arms into the familiar, scratchy-soft comfort of its sleeves. "I didn't mean to make you uncomfortable. I once dyed my hair an absolutely unbelievable shade of berry-pink. My brothers didn't let me forget it for years after. I think my youngest, Behn, almost forgot my name wasn't actually *Franny Fuchsia.*"

Her gaze darted back to me, the lightest smile stitching up the corners of her lips. "You have brothers?"

"Four, all older." I settled on the sofa's low back and rested one leg off the floor.

"I have an older brother and a much younger sister." She blinked, then shook her head. "Of course, where in the grave are my manners?" Several swift, smooth strides put her in reach to offer her hand. "Luminae Moraven."

I slid off the sofa back, shock crackling through me the same precise temperature as the cold stone against my feet. "Druella Luminae?"

"Unless there is another Luminae Moraven they've been hiding from me all these years." A tentative smile backed the joke.

Grinning, I took her hand and squeezed it. "If they have, I can't imagine her style is as stunning as yours. Your hair is just *beautiful,* and the way that dress complements it..." I clicked my tongue. "Perfection."

"Oh...thank you." She withdrew a bit, freeing her hand and tying another cord of hair around her knuckle. "My mother says the lavenders and pinks wash my skin tone out."

I snorted. "Not that I'm one to insult a ruler's taste, but in this case, I think your mother should have a healer see to her eyes." The cardigan slid down to hang in the crooks of my elbows when I rubbed a rush of chills from my upper arms. "I'm sorry, *that* was rude, I just...my arrival to the city has made everything a little more difficult to manage gracefully."

"Yes, I heard." Sympathy softened the Druella's wide eyes. "I wish I could assure you that was an *uncommon* welcome, but—"

"I've already been well-informed of the perils I've gotten myself into by coming here." A flash of night-sky eyes and a tilted head cut through my mind; I batted the memory off like a pair of bandage shears wielded by a haphazard first-year initiate. "So! I'll wager a teensy guess that the fourth in line to the Hadrassi ruling seat didn't come to the guestroom just to see if I was awake."

A flush colored Luminae's cheekbones. "No, I did—I mean, my mother sent me to see if you were awake, *and*—"

"They want to meet with me." That made sense—in fact, given the angle of the sunlight slanting through my window, it was a wonder the Moravens had let me sleep this long.

Sympathy for a woman who was almost murdered was one mark I could give in favor of the Moraven family. *Transporting her unconscious to a room, dressing her, and leaving her unguarded* was a questionable second.

"Very badly, yes." Luminae smiled sheepishly. "Is now a good time?"

"I have the very keen sense that *good* and *bad* times aren't precisely taken into account in situations like these." I scooted past her toward the round closet door etched into the wall across from the bed. "Just give me a moment to make myself presentable."

The guest closet was everything I'd dreamed it would be: deep and broad and well-stocked with dresses of various sizes and cuts, most in dark Hadrassi shades. I chose something green by the dim light spilling around my shoulders, some of my tension easing with the color of plant life and growing things slipping against my skin.

Tugging the sleeves off the shoulder and adjusting the cuffs that layered it at the elbows and wrists, I slapped on a leather bracer over my belly that I could easily tuck my sheathed dagger behind. Then it was back into the cushy comfort of my well-fitting flats, tying my hair back in a braid, dabbing on a bit of perfume from the mercifully-unbroken teardrop bottle in my satchel, and finally adjusting the layers of the ruffled, serrated skirt.

"Done!" I announced to Luminae, who'd drifted to the window and peered across the city while I readied myself. "What do you think?"

She assessed me with the smallest half-smile, and it struck me that there was no feeling behind it whatsoever. It was a trained little grin, something required by station; that made it all the more obvious when warmth perforated those cool blue eyes. "You look perfectly Hadrassi."

"Thank you." *I think.*

We slipped out into the hall, a smoky scent of fire and cold stone rubbing my nose when we emerged. The corridor was lined with torches—likely the culprit of the firelight glow that'd beckoned me like a moth toward the Fortress last night—and across from my door, archways led to an inner mezzanine. Tree limbs, already yellowing into autumn tones, brushed against the balustrades and even the balcony floor. These guest quarters had to be on the second or third level.

Poking my head out beneath the nearest arch, I counted up the rows of windows above, all the way to eight.

Fascinating choice to arrange the guests on the lower levels, given what my brother Conor had told me once of Mithran architecture: our ancestors would usually place guard rooms and serving quarters on the bottom floors, then the family in the middle, and the guests at the very top. It made visitors feel safe in the event of an attack.

It seemed Fortress Ferregrand had been built with as many layers of defense between its presiding family and danger as possible, guests be lucked out.

Luminae scuffed a foot on the corridor floor behind me...the quietest and most polite sign of impatience I'd ever heard. I ducked back into the hall. "I'm sorry. I just love growing things."

Luminae smiled fretfully. "I wish I didn't have to rush you, but—"

"Duty calls." I nudged her with my shoulder, and she turned us in the right direction.

"So," Luminae ventured as we walked, "my mother tells me you're our guest from Mithra-Sha." When I nodded, a spark lit in the depths of her eyes. "I've heard the tales in your land are just *magnificent*. I'd love to hear about that...storytelling shaping the country itself."

"You're keen on stories?"

She hooked a strand of hair behind the shell of her ear; that exposed a cuff on it in the shape of a mythical dragon, coiled along the arch and with its tailtip pierced into the lobe. Several fine, long silver chains dangled from its back, nearly brushing the top of her shoulder.

"I love history," Luminae admitted. "I'm an apprenticed scholar at Valorkeep—that's where we house our annals, records, and the first editions of every fable, storybook, and poetry collection in Hadrass-Drui." A wistful sigh floated from her nostrils. "It's the most beautiful place you can imagine. Towers full of tomes. Halls dedicated to nothing but chronicles and ancient artifacts..."

I couldn't help the smile that curled across my lips. "Well, I'm not much of a storyteller myself, but two of my closest friends are. I'll share what I can about Mithran history sometime."

"I'd so enjoy that." Luminae knotted her fingers, thumbs twiddling, gaze fixed down the hall. "I miss the smell of old books."

The way she whispered it was like a secret confession. "Can I ask why you're here, then...not at Valorkeep?"

Her slim shoulders stiffened; her harsh swallow was audible. "When I heard about Phin, I...I came straight home."

Well, of course *she did*. Her brother nearly murdered, a threat for which they had no defined motive yet? If nothing else, Luminae ought to be here for her own safety...as should all the Moravens.

I quickened my pace, and to my relief, Luminae did the same, guiding our course through serpentine stone halls past mosaic after mosaic and the ensconced torches that set them dancing like liquid fire. We climbed through winding turret stairwells and crossed countless halls of diamond-patterned floors, each one dipped in its own distinct shade owed to the painted glass set into the roof. I could tell which sides of the fortress we traversed by the strength of the colors—brighter in the east where the morning sun fell through them, duller in the west by its indirect glow.

I'd never been fighting fit like many of my friends, but I'd always ensured I was strong enough to stand on my feet and perform delicate surgeries for hours at a time without needing rest. Even so, I was a sweating mess and my calves screamed profanities by the time we ascended what I hoped to fickle *Luck* was the *absolute last* staircase, reaching a corridor more heavily guarded than the rest.

Luminae passed through the sentinels like a sweet summer wind, ignoring their creaking armor and shifting steel when they watched her passage with bladed intensity. Clearly she was used to this level of attention...a girl grown up in a fortress full of doubt and suspicion.

I smoothed my hands on the ridiculously-soft velvet of my Hadrassi dress. *It's time to impress them, Franny Fuchsia.*

Ugh. *Behn.*

But at least I had my brother's good humor to bolster me as I followed Luminae between the two rows of sentinels seething with quiet, almost malevolent focus, all the way to the soaring double-doors at the end of the hall.

CHAPTER II
PET POISON STUDY

T HE ROOM BEYOND THE thick doors prided itself on starlight. The stained glass of the turret's vaulted ceiling was pleated in shades of dusk—deep blue, bruise-purple, pink-gray. Even though it was midmorning, it gave the room an air of twilight that was both eerie and oddly soothing.

A black-and-white tiled floor staggered away from the tips of my flats, intersected with blackwood pews that all faced the same way: toward a dais housing a long table with eight seats. Two were high-backed, all ornately cushioned and hewn from the same wood as the pews. And the people seated at that table, I had to assume, were the Moraven family.

Athicus and Estrella, the Drui and Druaeva, flung a one-fingered salute to age just by breathing in those seats. Both had to be nearly a hundred, but their gazes were wicked sharp, fixed on us the moment Luminae stepped through the door.

On their right, Druella Serai was unmistakable. Not because she held herself stiff and sharp like a blade in a sheath—though she did—and not because of her position at her father's right hand—though that was also a dead giveaway. But the inky shade of her hair and the furrowed pluck of her brow and the way she watched me without blinking, like a panther eyeing its prey from a shadowy branch...

Oh, that was Calten's older sister down to the last little narrowing of her gaze.

Her husband, Varros, was grayer than I'd expected, barely a trace of sandy-brown hair left. He seemed wearier, too, across his lined eyes and down-turned mouth, in a way that made me think of farmers and airship captains who'd come through my doors in Dalfi—people worn beyond their age from strain and struggle.

Perhaps the life of a Druavas-by-marriage didn't agree with him as much as the notion of marrying Serai had...especially after the fate his oldest son had nearly suffered.

Arias's haggard face dashed to my mind; I blinked it swiftly away, just in time to breathe out a whispered protest when Luminae abandoned my side. Gliding between the pews, she mounted the dais and settled primly on her father's left—leaving one open seat between them that must've belonged to Phineaus. So the other seat was likely for her much-younger sister.

How nice for them, having a table to share. Meanwhile I was shouting distance away down the row of pews and feeling like I'd been tossed into a trial after all.

My only reprieve came from the door rattling open behind me, drawing every eye in the room—including mine—to another figure who swaggered in to join us. And all at once, the edge of my nerves blunted just a bit.

This man's blood-relation to Arias was *unmistakable*. The same tawny skin, the same tousled, dark curls—though his were grazed with threads of silver—even the same angle of growth on his bearded jaw. He breezed by me in a cloud of cypress and mint, dressed in a long, dark robe undone over his bare chest and low-waisted trousers.

Druavas Caspian. The uncle Arias had always spoken of with the greatest fondness out of all his mysterious and often unwelcoming Hadrassi relatives.

"How nice of you to join us, Caspian." Drui Moraven's voice was as paper-dry and onionskin-thin as his wrinkled complexion—as if his son's choice of attire and lack of punctuality sucked the last freckles of life right out of him.

"Apologies for being late," Caspian called to the Drui as he crossed the room. "I would've been on time, except I didn't want to be here, so..."

Spinning the seat next to the Druaeva on one foot so it faced backward, he dumped himself into it, hugging his mother around the shoulders and glancing my way. My heart jolted when he offered me a smile and a nod, the closest thing to encouragement from any of them.

Swiping the sweat from my palms, I approached down the path between the pews; the luck-charm coins on the anklet chain I never took off whispered sweetly with every step like a friend nudging me along, ensuring me I was doing just fine. "It's an honor to make your acquaintance...all of you. My name is Naomi Weathers, I'm—"

"We know what you are," Serai cut across me curtly. Not who, but *what*. "You're my sister's pet poison study."

My heels clapped against the sleek tiles, indignation tightening around my throat. "*Pardon* me?"

"What my devastatingly ill-mannered *older* sister is trying very hard to say," Caspian interceded before the heat flushing up my neck could manifest itself in a malignant tirade that would be the envy of that dragon cuffed on Luminae's ear, "is that we're intrigued by the aid Callie's sent us."

"She couldn't bear to spare us a *contingent* of Mithrans...she sends a single healer." Druaeva Estrella searched me up and down with a piercing look *entirely* too much like her middle child's. "Not even a poisoner."

"Mithra-Sha doesn't have poisoners like yours." Oh, did that sound superior as all Luck. I softened it with a smile. "But I don't have to *be* a poisoner, just to know how they do their work...their studies."

"Do you have any idea why she only sent you? Someone so young and...fresh in experience?" Varros demanded.

Likely because she doesn't have a life-ending threat to hang over any other healer's head that would make risking this absolutely murderous country worth their while?

"I'm all you need." I stitched that sweet smile into place, spreading my arms in a shrug. "I have the top marks of any graduate from Harrow Hall in decades, for both healing *and* poison studies. And..."

I know what it's like to take life. To think that way. To poison someone. To let one drop destroy something that can never be repaired.

"And?" The Drui prompted when I lost my voice.

My eyes leaped to Luminae. She fiddled with the bodice of her dress, not even glancing my way—like her mind was miles away.

Luck, I wished *I* was miles away from this family's cumulative stare bolting me to the floor.

"I know how to think like an assassin." I dragged my focus back to the Drui. "Like a poisoner. And I have a vested interest in the safety and security of your grandson and granddaughter in Mithra-Sha...as a member of Sha Arias's trusted inner circle, I'm the most qualified in the most ways, even if I lack for age and experience in others."

And you have enough age to make up for both of us.

Conferring glances bounced between the Drui and Druaeva, and Serai and Varros, for several heart-stopping moments. And I realized just then that I hadn't the faintest notion in all of Luck whether they were really going to accept my help, or not...or what that would mean for me, if I didn't fulfill Shadre Calten's demands.

Would she consider it enough that I'd tried—that I'd almost been gutted already for trying? Would she let me return to Mithra-Sha with a secret kept between us? Or would I have to come back as her personal lackey, spy in Arias's fold, servant to her every whim...knowing the instant she was ever displeased with me could see me thrown in the stocks?

Pet poison study, indeed.

A resonate *clap* startled me out of that dark spiral of thought; Caspian leaned on the table, arms outstretched, hands clasped—grinning. "Well, I like her. So when do we get started?"

"Serai?" Athicus prompted.

The Druella reclined, waving a hand studded with obsidian jewels on every finger. "Fine. Use her, let her search, let her stumble around and fall into danger for all I care. Just know, Father, that I'll continue my *own* search in the meanwhile."

"You do what you must to feel your family is secure." Estrella's glittering gaze hadn't moved an inch from me. "I for one am glad to have some aid whose intentions we can trust. From what Calten suggested, you are very highly persuaded to see this through and have this poisoner brought to justice, aren't you?"

Funny how mothers and daughters could wear the exact same knowing look. Papa had always said I'd inherited that from *my* mother, but she hadn't lived long enough for me to remember what secrets looked like when they lurked behind her eyes.

With the Moraven women, it was like stars winking in the blackest night.

Well, just flipping wonderful. Estrella knew what I'd done, even if the rest were ignorant. Which meant she'd likely be watching me more closely than anyone...and reporting to Calten.

Luck, can't I catch a respite? Just once?

But Luck had abandoned me, apparently; I had to make my own. So I built it out of a bow and a bent head—out of respect I'd learned in a position I'd earned by the same talents these people scorned. "I'll get started searching right away."

Caspian was the first to rise, screeching his chair backward and setting his elderly father wincing. Luminae leaped up after him like her cushion was on fire, scurrying around the table to fall in on one side of me; Caspian took the other, slinging an arm around my shoulders with startling familiarity. "Let's have fun, shall we?"

Luminae eyed him reproachfully around my side. "Nothing about what's happened is *fun*, Uncle Cass."

Caspian blew out a breath, and as we stepped through the iron doors again, he stooped a bit, his arm weighing heavier around my neck. "No, it's not, not really." He hiked a thumb over his back. "But they're frowny and fretting enough for all of us and then some. Someone has to balance out all that morbid apprehension."

He steered us to the end of the hall, down the winding staircase—then the opposite way we'd come down the next corridor.

"Where are we going?" I demanded.

"To visit Phin." Caspian slipped his arm from around my neck at last. "He's absolutely livid he wasn't invited to your introduction."

"Tell him to visit a festival. Or better yet, a public trial." I banded my arms around my waist, hugging warmth back into my chilly core. "I'm certain he'd find entertainment of the same sort."

Caspian and Luminae swapped a glance around me that felt like the last bolt driven into a coffin. Then Caspian sighed, scratching under his hair. "You have to understand our family...even if they *want* help, they don't ever want to ask for it."

"My mother writing to Aunt Callie was pure desperation," Luminae added softly. "Because of Phin. If it was *anyone* else, her pride wouldn't have allowed it."

Something pinched in my throat as I watched her from the corners of my eyes, her long, slender fingers fussing with the tulle fringe of her sleeve. *Even if it was you?*

"But desperation can only change so much of a person," Caspian added. "They want you here. They want the help. That doesn't mean they aren't skeptical of it or expecting some sort of double-cross. Or a failure."

None of which I could prove away with diplomacy or sweet words or smiles. This was a country of quick pace and swift action—I'd already experienced that in the worst way. Which meant the *only* way I was going to shake off the displeasure and wariness from this ruling family was by swift action of my own.

I reeled my shoulders back and held my head high. "Well, I suppose I'm just going to have to prove them wrong."

CHAPTER 12
POEM PIECES

As we started downward through the Fortress by a sharp curve into a descending stairwell, I braced my hand to the cool stone wall. "Tell me everything you know about this assassin."

"We suspect he's responsible for at least twenty deaths since all of this started." Caspian's tone dipped gravely at that heart-stopping number. "And likely more before he settled on a pattern."

"That pattern being—?"

"He only targets high-ranking Hadrassi elites." His grimness fractured into something almost like grief. "City leaders. Town organizers. People in charge of important trades and routes. Folks who help keep this country stable."

That sounded a bit like reports we'd heard of power trading hands in Amere-Del just before Arias had become Sha. "Is he some sort of revolutionary?"

Caspian's bark of laughter rang almost painfully loud in the narrow turret. "Ah, no. No, most assassins don't kill for a noble cause. It could be a flex of power, a show of strength or displeasure..."

"It could be *anything*." Luminae's voice floated back to us as she stepped between another handful of guards and through a doorway at the base of the turret. "And that's what's so frightening about him."

We emerged into a windowless corridor, thick and muffled and lined with guards; tapestries and heraldry hung along the walls, decadent in every color. But even the bright shades couldn't ease the suffocating feeling of being buried alive in a place so stifled that not even an echo traveled ahead of us.

"Family corridor," Caspian explained as he brushed ahead, taking the lead.

"What else can you tell me about the assassin?" I lengthened my strides to keep up with him.

"We know he's a poisoner, obviously. Every death has been the same pattern: the body found in a locked room, no signs of struggle or of suffering. Just a corpse and a note."

"A *note*?" Well, wasn't that the pinnacle of dramatic? "What sort of idiot assassin leaves a *note*?"

"One who wants us to know every death he's responsible for."

A fair point. "Well, what do the notes say?"

"They're pieces of a poem," Luminae piped up. "If you line them all up, they're the start of something."

"But not the end," Caspian said. "And no hint of where it *will* end, either."

"But that's how the assassin earned his name," Luminae added. "Most established ones have them. They call him *the Poet Poisoner.*"

Oh, please. No wonder he had a thrill for the theatrical. Pinching at the headache blooming across the bridge of my nose, I sighed, "What have you ruled out?"

"Just about everything." Caspian's steps slowed. "Poison in the food, poison in the drink, poison in the air..."

I dropped my hand, eyes popping open as a thought rammed itself into my head. "You said the assassin leaves a note at every deathbed. You've checked the paper? The envelope?"

"Dusted high and low. No particles of poison on either."

Dramatic...and crafty. "What line did he leave for Phineaus?"

Caspian halted with his hand on the doorknob, eyes cutting to Luminae again.

"That's the interesting thing," he admitted. "No poetry this time. Just his name on a note. And then, an hour later..."

"My mother found him." Luminae's voice quavered. "Choking on blood, more dead than alive."

And that was the last image of Phineaus Moraven they offered me before the door to his chambers swung wide.

CHAPTER 13
PLAY THE PART

T HE FIRST THING I noticed about Phineaus was that he was, definitively, very much alive.

And, more to my relief, he didn't *look* like a man who'd almost choked to death on his own blood, either. In fact, he looked more alive than my brothers after a hard day's work: hunched over ledgers scattered across his lap in a stately, functional bed, pushed against the wall of a stately, functional room. It looked as if the desk in the corner saw more use than anywhere else, and the walls were absolutely stuffed with bookshelves on one side and weapons racked on the other.

His head flashed up when we entered, goldenrod eyes locking with mine. Shock parted his lips; he tossed a stray thatch of russet hair from his eyes, setting aside his fountain pen and yanking his blanket halfway up his bare chest. "Uh, *Uncle*? Bit of warning next time?"

"Oh, she's not here to ogle your chest, get over yourself, will you?" Caspian kicked the door shut with a jarring *slam* that did indeed rip my focus away from the Druavas's not-unfortunate physique. Luminae breezed past me to settle into the chair behind the desk, curling her feet beneath her body; Caspian reclined against the door with arms folded.

"I just—wanted to have a better first impression." Phineaus's gaze averted from mine.

Oh, flipping Luck. As if he was the first shirtless man I'd ever laid eyes on. As if I cared about *that*.

"Naomi Weathers." I approached the bedside and offered yet another hand-shake. "Druavas Phineaus, I presume."

"Ooh, she's keen." He grasped my hand tightly, eyes glinting with merriment. "It's Phin, please. Only my mother calls me Phineaus...and usually when I'm in trouble."

"It sounds as if you *are* in a bit of trouble," I pointed out.

"Well, if it's the kind that gets me rescued by a beauty like you—"

"Phin? Ew," Luminae scolded.

"I knew we should've waited for a formal setting to introduce them," Caspian groaned, knocking his head back against the door.

"Well, you can blame my mother for that." Phin released my hand with a last squeeze; I was oddly relieved he hadn't kissed my knuckles.

"No, you can blame *yourself* for it," Caspian shot back.

"The rot-brained idiot snuck out last night to stroll the gardens and explore the library," Luminae snorted.

Coughing shortly into the side of his fist, Phin cast me a sheepish grin. "I don't like being confined to bed."

"And you never have, which is why you had festering lung *twice* before you turned ten." Though disapproval soaked Caspian's tone, there was nothing but affection in the way he crossed the room just to muss his nephew's shaggy hair.

Phin swatted him gently off. "Besides, I'm healthy enough to think, and the more I think, the more I want to move. I should at least be taking notes, searching my rooms, trying to come up with patterns—"

My brows arched. "You're helping them solve your own attempted murder?"

"Yeah, well." Phin shrugged one muscular shoulder. "They say if you want a task done properly..."

"Leave it to the professionals who are *trained to do it*." Caspian popped him on the back of the head.

"The professionals have tried, and where has that gotten me?" Phin huffed, rubbing his skull. "Bedrest and a constant guard if I so much as leave for the washroom. Can you blame me for giving them the slip yesterday?"

Blame? Not at all. But I carefully tucked away the knowledge that, while his family was Luck-bent on keeping him safe at all costs, Phin seemed to possess a streak of reckless independence that disregarded their wishes.

"Tell me what you've learned." I settled myself at Phin's feet.

His eyes brightened from goldenrod to rich amber; he shoved himself up fully among the pillows, then winced, wrapping a hand around his ribs—guarding just above the organs on the right side. My mind delved at once through possible poisons that affected that half and those organs in particular—none of it good.

"The Poet Poisoner is a newer presence among the named assassins." Caspian settled himself into the nook where the thick stone walls cornered, arms folded, expression oddly remote. "Relatively speaking. It's only within the last year or so that his work became identifiable. Then he was given the name, which seems to have only emboldened him."

"And nothing in the past year has given you any sort of hint as to who he might be? What his precise aim is?"

Phin and Caspian were both silent for a long moment.

"Besides targeting the elite, no," Caspian sighed at last. "And even that has been staggered. Variegated to the extent we can't predict precisely where he'll strike next. Or if we do, then he changes targets at the last instant."

"What we do know is the Poet Poisoner has kept a strict code of his own, a pattern, with a calling card and everything...like most Hadrassi assassins are trained for." Phin skimmed his thumb along his lower lip. "Every crime he's committed could be traced back to him, if we could just catch the rotting bastard."

"Language," Luminae piped up from the corner.

He stuck his tongue out the side of his mouth in her direction, then was serious again when he added, "Every attack of his fits the code...except mine."

Caspian nodded curtly, reclining against the wall and dashing a hand back through his hair. "It's the first time since we began tracking his movements that he's broken his patterns."

"Are you certain it even was the same assassin, then?" I demanded.

Caspian shrugged. "The target fits. As does the lack of tracery, the way he finds his way in and out without being seen, the method of murder with the note left behind, and the penchant for poison as opposed to weaponry. But the act *itself*..."

"It was vicious, it was bloody, it wasn't *like him*," Phin finished grimly. "Not the same poison, not the same symptoms."

"Someone copying his patterns?" I guessed.

Caspian shot me a lopsided smile void of mirth. "To have the exact talent he possesses for evading notice? To use poisons the way he does, as his signature style?"

"It was him." Phin's conviction was as adamant as the set of his jaw. "Or someone associated with him."

Quiet tumbled over the room like a thick sheet cast across a corpse. For a long moment, none of us spoke.

"You're suggesting he has a *partner*?" The words strangled me, barely dodging the lump that lodged in my throat.

Flipping *Luck*. Facing one poisoner assassin was its own matter. But *two*...

"It's quite possible." Caspian tapped this thumbs against his elbows. "Most assassins enleague themselves with a guild or group of some sort, for the trading of secrets and information, or to meet common goals."

"That's why we can't just hunt him down and be done with it anymore." Phin shoved a fist into the pillows, propping himself up higher again. "We need an infiltration. A way to find out who he's partnered with, who his guild might be...if he's starting one of his own, even."

"And what their intentions are." A dangerous light gleamed in Caspian's eyes—the greatest likeness to Shadre Calten I'd seen in him yet.

"Do you think you can manage that?" Phin's tone gentled slightly, concern deepening the pained, sleepless lines that traced the corners of his eyes when they searched mine. "Not everyone can play that kind of part."

A retort tickled the tip of my tongue...and perished there.

Play a part? I'd been doing that for years, hadn't I? Ever since I'd fled Vallan-myre...my friends and family, they all saw me one way. But beneath the surface, I was entirely another. Sometimes an absolute stranger wearing the familiar scent of cotton and freesia, wearing the clothes I loved, making music with every step she took. A stranger even to myself, playing the part of the benevolent healer when malice marked her hands.

I fisted those hands in the pockets of my cardigan, leaning back against the footboard. "I can manage."

I had to. Not only for my own sake, for my freedom, but...

This family, suspicious and uneasy though they were, had encircled Phin like a bandage all their own. Their fear for him was stamped beneath Caspian's shad-ow-ringed stare, etched in the bend of Luminae's stooped shoulders, branded in the tears that had dashed across Druella Serai and her husband's eyes. Even Drui Athicus and his wife had worn that concern like a death shroud in the meeting hall.

They didn't deserve the fear and anguish this poisoner had inflicted on them.

As a girl studying in Harrow Hall, I'd known what it was to be hounded, stalked, taunted and harassed by a lustful soldier-in-training who'd thought he had some sort of right to me. That vicious boy had grown into a man with the same nefarious designs, the same lack of self-control...and then with a sword to wield behind it.

Thanks to Jaik's quick hands and deft aim in the Shastah years ago, I no longer had to fear *my* harasser; but the Moravens lived every day now beneath the shadow of knowledge that Phin was the single mark unscoured in their enemy's ledger. That he could strike again at any moment...that he could return in the next breath to finish what he'd started.

No one deserved to live with that terror. And I'd sworn an oath to help where I could, to heal whatever I was able, be it with friend or foe...a vow I'd only broken once.

I wasn't about to break it again.

Swooping in a deep breath, I laced a smile over my lips and met first Phin, then Caspian, then Luminae's eyes. "That's why I'm here. Shall we get started?"

CHAPTER 14
CANDLES IN THE STACK

S TARTING, I QUICKLY LEARNED, was the easy part. Caspian was hasty to help; by the evening of my first day in Fortress Ferregrand, the desk beneath the mosaic windows in my room was stacked with piles of notes and ledgers.

"Reports," the Druavas explained with a bit of a rueful smirk, peering at me from around the latest tower of papers he placed on the last available wedge of open space. "With a sprinkling of speculation for good sport. From sentinels, from family and friends, from soul-senders..."

I paused, hand hovering over the first stack. "Soul...what?"

"So, Callie hasn't carried *every* bit of her native culture over to Mithra-Sha." There was no judgement in his tone—perhaps even a hint of teasing as he perched himself on the edge of the desk. "Soul-senders are the folks who examine a corpse, determine the cause of death, then perform last rites."

I sank into the chair, folding my arms on the stacks and inclining toward him. "What do you suppose happens to souls when they go?"

Caspian shrugged. "Hadrassi tradition holds that every soul becomes a watcher from above." He jerked his chin at the colored glass behind me. "A star for every soul. It's why we light candles on cathedral steps for them...a memorial, but also an invocation of sorts. A hope that the souls of our beloved dead...or the dead we've wronged...will take pity on those of us left to deal with this disgusting world." A smile flicked up the corner of his mouth. "What about in Mithra-Sha?"

I shrugged. "It's much less of a given. Some people think souls linger on, that they stay with us...haunt us. Some think they just snuff out. I've spoken to a few patients who were absolutely certain souls entered new bodies after death...a sort of never-ending cycle."

Caspian bent toward me, wagging his brows. "And what does the healer my sister sent us believe?"

"Honest to Luck, I've stopped wondering," I admitted. "I decided a long time ago that my duty is to the body the soul resides in. If I can't save that, then, well...I can't do much for the soul itself."

"Fair," he chuckled. "Well, you'll find a decent amount about all sorts of souls in these records, I reckon."

I ticked my fingers over the dishearteningly slim spines, which suggested very little information had been gathered. "Too many candles in this stack."

"Too many by far." Caspian was somber all at once, looking over the array of notes—so many dead, and so little guidance or closure pertaining to each.

But at least we hadn't added a ledger for Phin.

"You go and do whatever it is Hadrassi nobility do." I slid the first stack toward myself. "I've got to start reading."

"Well, as the Mithrans would say...good luck, and all that." Caspian slid down from the desk, then hesitated, knocking his fist on it. "And, really...thank you, for undertaking all of this. I know it's not what's usually expected of Mithran healers, and I don't know *how* my sister convinced you of this, but—"

"I like to heal wherever I can." A quick truth to mask the more difficult honesty of what sort of his person his sister really was.

And who *I* was.

"Right. Well, how better to outwit poisoning than with healing?" Caspian cast me a wink, and then he sauntered off through the doors—leaving me alone with my own personal country of books to rule over.

Blowing a stray curl from my forehead, I pushed up from the desk, leaning my hands flat on top of it.

"All right," I muttered. "Let's find a poisoner."

CHAPTER 15
A SYMPHONY OF ACHING HEARTS

MY FIRST WEEK IN Hadrass-Drui ground by with slow days and even slower progress—so sluggish it might as well have been going backward.

There was an uncanny similarity to every soul-sender report I peeled through...not as if they'd been written by the same person, but a testament to the almost surgical precision this Poet Poisoner displayed. There were so *few* deviations between the locations where the bodies were found, the manner of death, the information left behind, that it started to feel like I was retracing my steps.

He was *talented*, this assassin. The few repeating poisoners I'd read case studies of in Harrow Hall hadn't been this methodical in the execution of their methods.

And as for the poison itself...nothing. No trace was left in the bodies by the time the soul-senders tested the organs; no particles were found on clothes or belongings. No one who handled the bodies presented with any matching symptoms—or worse, with similar fates.

They'd even kept the notes left by the Poet Poisoner...each one the next line in some macabre litany of life and death. It took me a full day just to assemble the notes on their heavy, filigreed cardstock to form a pattern of rhyme that made sense:

> *In shadows deep, a poem unfolds,*
> *Of vengeance sought in secrets cold.*
> *A family wronged by treachery's crave*
> *Their souls cry out beyond the grave.*
>
> *A poison brewed with deadly art*
> *Lands like a blade into the heart*

Silent whispers, soft as dreams
A kinder end for gutted screams.

The venom drips from vial to blade,
A deadly dance where debts are paid.
Each drop a promise, justice blind
For those who fell...those left behind.

A taste of bitterness, cruel lack
Falls like a dagger to the back
A plot of pain turned on its head,
As the tale nears its end.

Now raise a toast to beloved dead
Their memory brings us to the end.
For in that end, the poison's art:
A symphony of aching hearts.

And that, sadly, was the best I had to go on. Not a terrible poem, but it was too broad to lead me anywhere specific...which was likely exactly what the Poet Poisoner wanted.

Frustration had me pacing a now-familiar track through the room at the end of the week, rubbing my tired, itching eyes, wishing to Luck I could've found *something*—even if it was awful and an affront to my success here—just so I could feel like I'd made progress.

Even better, wouldn't it be lovely if progress was being made without me? That Serai had uncovered something, or Phin had remembered some infinitesimal detail that set everything right?

Or...well, I supposed it was too much to hope that the Poet Poisoner was the murderer who'd attacked me in the street. That Kai had solved this entire problem for me with one deft slice of a blade.

A streak of heat shot through my knuckles and puddled straight in my core. *Flipping Luck. Stop* thinking *about him.*

That face had showed itself now and again in my dreams this week—the best of the worst that had happened to me since arriving in Hadrass-Drui. He was like a piece out of a story...or like a shard of glass embedded under my skin.

Maybe because he'd saved me. Or maybe because, even after that, he'd treated me more like a person than a nuisance—which was better than I could say for the elder Moravens, who looked at me like something that had crawled out of the moat anytime they caught me outside my room.

Which I halted in the middle of now, shoving my hair back and trapping it behind my head with both hands.

"All right," I muttered to the silence, "this is ridiculous."

I pivoted back to frown at the desk and its absolute disarray. I needed a break—a rest for my aching head. Fresh perspective.

What I needed was some flipping hot cocoa.

CHAPTER 16
THE CHARM OF FORGETTING

T HE FORTRESS KITCHENS WERE exactly what I'd expected: at the base of the complex, hugged by the rock where it perched, chilly and dim by the time I slipped down the many, many flights of stairs to reach it. I paused for a moment to admire the dining rooms themselves—connected by archways, each one sporting mosaic windows looking out over the sea—and then it was through the hall and down another winding staircase to reach the kitchens themselves.

Most of what awaited me there, I expected: deep ivy-green cabinets recessed in the walls, trimmed in black, stuffed with all kinds of fancy dishes. Herbs in sachets and bundles hung on one wall. Glossy tiles, decadent darkwood accents, and vaulted crossbeams angled down to meet protruding posts, delineating the kitchen into sections: preparation, cooking, plating.

What I *didn't* expect was that I wasn't the only one sneaking for a midnight treat.

When I slipped inside the preparation chamber, I almost let out a yelp of shock; because there was a tall, willowy figure painted in light orange from the candles dished on the counter, sitting on the marble edge and helping herself to a jar of custard—spoonless.

Both Luminae and I froze; she stared, finger stuck in her mouth, and I banded my cardigan tighter and raised my brows, hoping my racing heart would calm if I settled on imperiousness over screaming like I'd almost stepped on a spider. "Fancy seeing you here."

She popped her finger from her mouth. "I couldn't sleep."

"I hear a string of murders, including almost your own brother's, will do that to people." I examined the stove and found, with a thrill of cozy delight, that it was just like the one in my home in Dalfi; the cooks even hung the pots in the same place, against the wall behind it "Why so many candles?"

"For the souls of the *countless* cakes and pastries consumed inside these walls." A smile lived in her tone, so I could picture it even without glancing her way. "Both Phin and our little sister Coraline are smitten with sweets."

"But not you, Miss Eating-Custard-In-The-Dark?"

"I don't have space to be as smitten with anything as I am with history."

I snorted. "Do you happen to keep melting chocolate on hand?"

"Only cinnamon infused, I'm afraid."

"I'm not." I stuck out a hand without looking, wiggling my fingers. "Hand it over, if you please."

The brick of melting chocolate struck my palm a moment later, unleashing a powerful burst of musky spice; groaning, I broke off several handfuls, popping one into my mouth while I retrieved cream from the ice chest. I'd endured more than my fair share of teasing from my brothers about my tolerance for bitter chocolate as a child; but I found it rather empowering, being able to enjoy the desserts that sent them gagging to the trash bin.

Luminae hopped back up on the counter's edge, heels striking a rhythm, watching as I measured out the chocolate and maple syrup, then added a bit of fresh vanilla for fun—because why not? "May I try some?"

"You absolutely may." I shot her a grin. "Sharing hot cocoa is one of life's greatest pleasures."

We didn't say much as I worked, but I could feel Luminae watching me, a stare that set my instincts bristling. She was somewhat of an aberration among her family—in looks as well as demeanor—but I had a feeling her cleverness showed itself in other ways; like her uncanny observation while I prepared and ladled up the cocoa, then whipped the rest of the cream by hand and dropped several generous dollops in each of the cups.

"Why can't *you* sleep?" Luminae asked as I passed her mug to her.

"That's not a good conversation for dark rooms like this." Beckoning with a tilt of my head, I led her out of the kitchen and up the stairs, back into the dining halls.

Each one was deeper than it was wide, a series of angled, stained-glass rooms protruding like claws from the side of the Fortress. The first one we entered was tiled pink; we passed through it to a green-tinted room, and finally, to a deep blue space that better matched the deep hour of the night. This was the broadest of the three—and, to my delight, it sported a series of lounging sofas and low tables. Perfect for sitting with a cup of cocoa.

Once we were settled in and sipping, I finally let myself answer Luminae's question: "All the soul-sender reports are driving me mad."

"I can only imagine." Sympathy silvered Luminae's eyes over the rim of her mug. "Death has never been my favorite part of the past."

"I wouldn't mind it so much if it felt like it was reaping *any* sort of return." Slouching with my neck balanced on the arm of the sofa and my knees drawn up, I craned my head back to peer up at the steepled pinnacle of the ceiling. "But it's hours of reading the same useless thing, over and over and *over* again."

"Sometimes, secrets hide in monotony."

I tossed Luminae a smile—and it widened when I saw she'd already drunk half her mug. *Another devotee.* "That must be one of the first lessons they teach you in Valorkeep. I imagine a place like that has more than its share of dry reads."

"Drier than the old bones of the bastards who built the place." Luminae's eyes sparkled with rare mischief. "But those are the best ones."

"The lessons worked, then."

"Oh, stop it, you!" She threw a beaded pillow at my legs, deliberately missing my mug.

"Well, why don't you tell me about it?" I urged, balancing my drink on my belly. "I'd love to fill my head with something other than those reports."

"Tell you about Valorkeep?" Luminae sat taller, her eyes lighting like stars.

I rolled a hand, motioning her on. "Absolutely!"

And for the next hour, that was all I held in my mind—a different sort of fortress built of lofty towers and jagged rooms, framed with shadowy stone and secret rooms drilled deep into the crust of this country. A place as different from the girl telling the story as anything I could possibly imagine.

Valorkeep sounded like a dark, imperious place, mysterious and ancient...a little like a blend of Harrow Hall and Fablehaven Academy. Maybe with a sprinkling of Erasure, Fablehaven's dark twin on a faraway island I never cared to see, judging by the tales Jaik and Audra had told us about it.

But it was impossible not to want to see Valorkeep—to *experience* it—after hearing Luminae talk about it with so much rapture. We'd drained our cups and settled against the arms of our respective sofas, heads leaned back, staring up at the stars by the time she finished telling me of the record halls where she did so much of her work.

"Every century or so, all the most important books in Hadrass-Drui are carted to Valorkeep to be copied," she explained. "Law books, important records, the Moraven family heritage tree...the chroniclers write them all over again with fresh ink on new paper, and the previous editions are stored in Valorkeep, while the newest writings are sent back to their respective resting places."

"I don't know how you do it," I admitted. "My hands ache just *thinking* about so much handwriting."

Luminae shrugged. "My hands are trained for it. It's my life...and the best way I can serve my country."

I dug my toes into the crushed-velvet cushions, pushing myself up a bit to peer at her. This whole last hour while she'd done most of the talking, I hadn't heard anything like the faint tinge of melancholy when she mentioned servitude to Hadrass-Drui.

It was a thin, familiar echo of a boy I'd known at fifteen...someone far, far away from carrying the title that now rested on his shoulders. A hint of wanting that would have to wait almost a lifetime to be fulfilled.

"Have *you* ever dreamed of ruling?" I asked quietly.

"Now and again." Luminae folded her hands over her middle, staring up through the paneled glass roof at the stars. "But some dreams aren't worth chasing. There are three people ahead of me in line to that title...even if my mother *and* Uncle Caspian abdicated once my grandfather and grandmother retire, there's still Phin. And he's much better suited for the role than I am."

"Why do you say that?"

"Well, the people love him." Luminae shrugged. "They've had *time* to learn to love him. He has a whole cluster of friends he refuses to let anyone stop him from seeing, no matter how paranoid Grandfather is about our safety. He goes wherever he pleases. He's bold, and confident, and he has charisma, and...that's easier to love than a recluse who likes books more than people."

"Maybe she just hasn't found the *right* people," I offered. "I like you plenty."

"Well, *that* will sway the country," Luminae laughed, laying a palm over her brow and shaking her head slowly. "Most of what I know about Hadrass-Drui is ancient history. But people won't follow someone because of what they know, they'll follow you if you give them something to believe in. I can't ever give them that...not the way Phin can."

"But is he ever going to know laws like you do? Be able to help people that way?"

"Does it matter?" Luminae tossed me a sideways smile. "If he can charm them into forgetting what they needed help with in the first place...they're better off that way."

I wasn't so certain of that; but before I could say so, Luminae pushed herself up, vulnerability softening the contours of her face

"My grandfather used to be afraid that my mother and her siblings would go to war for the Drui title," she confessed quietly. "Some of the annalists at Valorkeep believe that's the real reason he sent Aunt Callie to Mithra-Sha."

I sat up as well, stung with a tingling curiosity; I'd never heard this side of the history between our countries before. "*Really?*"

Luminae nodded haltingly. "I know he's frightened of plenty of things, but fighting among his children was always the one he was so...forthcoming about. Ever since I was a girl." She dragged her fingertips through the ends of her hair, jerking out knots with fretful tugs. "So, even if I wanted the Druaeva title badly enough to fight for it...I couldn't. I won't be the person who destroys this family with infighting. I won't make my grandfather's fears come true."

Regret hung cherry-tart on the corners of my smile. "I think that's really admirable, Lu."

More than that—it was how a leader ought to think. And it made me miss Arias so desperately, I wished there was some way I could contact him besides by letter...a way to tell him of all my frustrations and have his help sorting through them. Like I had for so much of my life, until Dalfi—until—

Somewhere out in the hall, a door slammed; voices shouted. Footsteps thundered on marble floors, jolting Luminae and I up from our respective couches. With a wide-eyed glance, we tore out of the dining room in our nightdresses, skidding out into the Fortress halls and almost colliding with a pack of sentinels dashing past.

And behind them, Caspian—grim-faced, yanking a weathered doublet over his bare chest. Judging by the red rim of his eyes, he'd just been dragged from sleep.

"Uncle Cass!" Luminae shouted as he swept past us, following the sentinels toward the next corridor. "What's wrong—what's happening?"

Caspian's focus bolted to us; and with the firm set of his mouth and the storm gathering in his eyes...even though I hardly knew him, I knew what was coming next before he even opened his mouth.

"The Poet Poisoner's just killed again."

CHAPTER 17
MAKE TIME

Aᴺᴼᵀᴴᴱᴿ ᴱᴸᴵᵀᴱ ᴹᴱᴹᴮᴱᴿ ᴼF the Drui's inner circle, dead by poison.

I couldn't help but feel like it was somehow my fault.

In some respects, that was absurd; I'd barely started my search, it wasn't as if I was ready to leap between the Poet Poisoner and the next blade—or dart, or dagger, or however in *Luck* he was doing this—and save a life.

But that still barely helped my smarting conscience when chaos descended on Fortress Ferregrand like a death shroud.

Luminae retreated back to her room, and stayed there...and I couldn't blame her. Her brother's almost-killer had struck again—right here in Amalgard, according to the whispers in the Fortress corridors—though it hadn't been as close this time. But what if next time, it was? What if he swung at Phin again—or another of the Moravens?

Anxiety nibbled on my bones, hearing the Drui had set Caspian to lead this particular investigation...and worse, that the carefree Druavas had actually taken it, apparently with little contestation. It was a mark of how dire things were, that all hands were being summoned to stanch the bleeding. That was the sort of call infirmaries dreaded—it usually balanced on the edge of death.

I couldn't let that happen. Not to Phin, not to Luminae, not even to Caspian.

That thought dropped me outside the Druavas's personal study three days later, directed by a handful of hand-wringing servants who were more than happy to point me the way I wanted to go, if it got me out of theirs.

Rocking on the balls of my feet, I reminded myself this was *why* I was here. I had every right to inconvenience someone as important as a Druavas...and I'd been pestering heirs for more than half my life. I wasn't about to back down from doing it again.

Nudging the door open without knocking, I breezed into Caspian's personal space.

He was as different today as I could ever imagine from the man who'd come in late to my first meeting with his family, draped himself in the chair, and encouraged me with a smile. Dark circles gathered beneath his eyes and a furrow dug permanently between his brows as he hunched over piles of papers and journals scattered across his desk, one of two opposing each other in the room's deep recess and bookcased walls. The other was peppered with plates and mugs and didn't seem as if it had seen much use otherwise.

Perhaps, a long time ago, that desk had belonged to Calten.

Tucking away my curiosity, I approached Caspian. "I need to speak with you."

"Busy."

"Make time." Swinging the chair out from behind the disused desk, I fluffed my skirts and sat, straddling it. "It's about the Poet Poisoner."

"Isn't everything these days?" He rubbed his brow. "He's really gone and done it this time. My father..." Breaking off sharply, Caspian drew in a deep breath; then he flung his fountain pen down and scooped another book toward himself.

When he didn't go on, *I* did. "This is the first murder he's committed since I set foot in Hadrass-Drui. I want to see the scene of the death."

"Do I look like an escort? I have enough messes to clean up at the moment, a funeral to arrange, a soul-candle to have custom-poured... I don't have the time to babysit you."

The words shouldn't have stung as deeply as they did; I should have expected them, even, from a Moraven. But from one of the few who'd seemed to see me as an asset, not a nuisance, until this moment...

I didn't let the hurt and fury make me cringe. Instead, they lifted me—up from the chair, shoving it aside. Leaning both hands on his desk, I yanked the book from under his hand; that forced him to look at me, his brows vaulting.

"Unless you want *more* important souls to send off," I seethed, "I need to get into that death scene, Druavas, so that I can do the task your family brought me here for."

He regarded me for a long, tense moment; then he rocked back his chair, snatched the cloak from behind it, and cast it over his shoulders as he rose, striding for the door. Only when he wrenched it open did he pause and glance back at me. "Well? Are you coming?"

Flipping Luck, was I ever.

CHAPTER 18
A HIDDEN HUNT

I T WAS IMPOSSIBLE TO pry my fingers out of fists the whole carriage ride across Amalgard to the outer burg where the latest murder had been committed. Every shadow that flitted through the streets beyond the curtain window, every rock of the carriage wheels through potholes, jostled loose another piece of memory from the night where I'd almost been killed in this city.

Where Kai had swooped in like a shadow himself to rescue me.

Though traveling in Caspian's company felt like the safest place I could currently be—he brought along seven sentinels between the two carriages, and lounged with a diffident sort of repose that suggested *he* wasn't worried about us having our throats slit—I was somehow more comforted remembering an absolute stranger's steady touch and his remark that he would be watching me for trouble.

Trouble felt like it lurked right ahead and a pace behind when we reached the section of the city where, according to Caspian, a good number of the wealthy elite made their residences. It was guarded by a piked wall—the most fortified plot of the capital I'd seen so far besides Fortress Ferregrand itself, though to be fair, I hadn't seen much. But what roused me from my terrified stupor was how impossible it should have been for an assassin to mount that wall.

The top soared almost high enough to touch where the low-bellied clouds met the fog winding in from the sea; even so, the razored edges jutting up and out like thorns were visible, as was the serrated wire winding between those pikes.

The wall itself seemed to be all one solid piece—no mortaring, no cracks. The gate we entered through was double layered with a pair of iron gates, the gaps far too small for anyone to slip through. And even though we traveled in an ebony-lacquered carriage with the Drui's own son, we were still rousted from the carriage, every seat flipped and searched, all of us patted down and made to turn out our boots, gloves, hats, and the seams of our clothing before they raised the second gate.

How in flipping *Luck* had the Poet Poisoner gotten inside?

The question was still rattling around in my head when we reached our destination—a manse on the edge of a manmade spring several streets deep into the walled district. Water bubbled up from the underground source and tumbled down to a pool surrounded by weeping willow trees, its gentle burble wafting in through the windows as the carriages climbed the inclined road.

The home itself was beyond impressive: paneled mosaic glass on both levels, decorating both the jutting half-rotundas and the doorway. The dark wood and stone that made up the surface of the manse itself were offset by flowerboxes blooming with riots of vivid purple and blue, the exact same shades as the glass. More flowers bunched along the edges of the steps and bordered the yard all the way to the spring.

It would've been idyllic on any other day; but the footpath to the manse's wraparound receiving lane was cordoned off by a dozen sentinels in full armor, fully armed. They watched us arrive with beady gazes gleaming beneath tooled helms; and even when the carriage halted and Caspian disembarked first, a pair swarmed us with enough suspicion to turn the chilly, overcast day downright icy.

"What's your business here, Druavas?" the older and taller of the sentinels demanded.

"Easy." Caspian smoothed a hand through the air. "Just escorting my father's guest to survey the scene."

The younger man scoffed; his superior eyed me with the same cool suspicion as Druella Serai had. "This is the Mithran healer, isn't it? What does she think she's going to find that my men haven't?"

"That's what we're all dying to know—if you'll pardon my turn of phrase," Caspian coughed.

The man's scowl deepened, still fixed on me. "These murders are no task for the inexperienced."

If only he knew just how experienced I was with death...even with poison. I let just a little of it seep into my saccharine smile. "I can promise you, I'm not going to vomit."

"And I can assure *you*, you won't find anything worth the coin they're paying for your upkeep, Healer."

Caspian nudged a shoulder in front of me, folding his arms over his broad chest. "Are you questioning my father's decision to bring a brilliant and tactical Mithran poison study into his confidences, to solve these murders you sentinels have failed spectacularly to bring to justice?"

The man stiffened. "No, I—"

"Really? So it's just his sanity you're calling to task?"

"Ooh, he won't like that." I whistled lowly.

The man crushed his helm lower over his eyes, sidestepping from our path. "Make it brief. The family will be here soon to collect their things."

"Much obliged." Flicking out his cloak, Caspian strolled up the footpath; I fell into step with him, chancing the smallest glance over my shoulder. The heat of the stares burning into our backs matched the narrowing of both sentinels' gazes.

"They're not overly fond of you, I take it?" I hedged as we mounted the broad steps to recessed door.

"Not many Hadrassis are." Caspian shrugged. "The price one pays for getting the job done as the mouthpiece of the Moraven family."

The groan of the door swinging inward punctuated his remark.

From our first steps over the threshold, everything about the manse screamed of a lavish lifestyle; floor-to-ceiling curtains that matched the flowers and glass for color and splendor. A fountain at the center of the foyer, fish flickering in its basin. Two pairs of staircases wrapping around to a mezzanine with a double doorway above, then branching off to the left and right and disappearing into vaulting, tapered stone archways I could only assume opened to a guest wing on one side and the family's quarters on the other.

Caspian led the way to the steps—past half-rotundas which housed a sitting room and a personal library respectively. Beyond the fountain, another set of double doors revealed themselves by an open seam: a glass-plated ballroom. The doors at the top of the curving stairwells must've led to a second balcony on the other side.

I could only imagine the kind of energy that must've surged through these halls...the parties, the laughter, the entertainment, the beauty and luster. But it was colder and darker than a mausoleum today, possessed with an eerie sort of quiet that made me think twice about the Mithran fables of souls that lingered after bodies decayed. It certainly felt like *something* was haunting us up the first set of steps and off to the left, up into the shadowy vault of the stairwell.

"Corylus Fletch was an exceptional nobleman," Caspian said as we followed the short spiral of a stairwell up to the residential wing. "Opinionated as all bones, and not afraid to challenge my father, but...a necessary challenger, and always respectful."

"The kind of council every ruler needs." For a heartbeat, my thoughts strayed—wondering just how much of that sort of council Arias regularly received. Reiko and Jaik would challenge him plenty, but was there a balance?

I shook away that notion—and the shiver of shame it induced—and focused on the rooms we passed. One appeared to be a nanny suite, coldly functional. Two rooms must've belonged to children, though they were oddly bare—not sporting anything that would hint at individual interests or unstructured play, just a pair of child-sized beds inside each. The windows caught my attention briefly as we hurried by—the only ones I'd seen in the manse not made of mosaic glass, but plain, clear panels crisscrossed by iron bars. Extra protection, perhaps, for the most valuable people in Corylus's life...though that didn't quite explain the doorknobs, fitted to lock from the outside, not within.

Corylus's own door loomed unmistakably at the end of the hall. It too was cordoned off, this time with a thick sway of velvet rope Caspian ducked beneath and held up for me.

Though it felt a little lawless, I followed his lead.

This suite was everything I'd expected after the rest of the house: darkly elegant and absolutely prismatic. One whole wall was taken up by another jutting half-rotunda, looking out over the front footpath and outer gardens; the opposite was furnished with a desk made of wood so sleek, it reflected the light spilling through the angled.

"You Hadrassis and your mosaics," I murmured, stepping deep beneath the lurid lavender-and-lilac hues. "Why the obsession with painted glass?"

"Honestly, I couldn't tell you," Caspian admitted. "Whatever its significance, it was lost before my time. Lu might be able to dig something out about it, if she cared to."

"I'll have to ask her." I slunk deeper into the room, looking over the desk, the flue behind it, the couch situated against the windows across the way.

It was a moment before I realized Caspian hadn't followed me; he leaned in the doorway, shoulder to the wood, running his fingers over the butter-smooth frame.

"Caspian?" I prompted. "Are you going to help me?"

His stare was a thousand miles away, fixed across the room. A faint crease formed between his brows.

"Caspian," I repeated, firmly.

"Hm?" His gaze darted from the corner, back to me. "What was that?"

The faint crack in his voice spoke words that didn't drift from his tongue: pain. Grief. I hadn't even considered that he might've known Corylus well...grown up around him, perhaps. They might've even been friends.

"You seem distracted," I offered gently. "I know this man was close to your family...would you like a moment?"

Sucking down a breath, Caspian rubbed a hand over his mouth. "That...might be best. Lots to think over. I'll be waiting for you out in the hall."

I couldn't help a puff of relief; with him gone, my mind expanded and absorbed more of the room's precise details—this place where Corylus had died.

It was as unremarkable as anywhere the Poet Poisoner had ever struck according to the soul-senders' ledgers, aside from its gorgeous architecture. I could almost see the newest report writing itself with every step I took, scouting along the parlor and then taking a turn through the bedchamber—finding no blood, no scuffs, nothing really out of place at all.

No sign of trauma presents itself on the corpse. No hint of a struggle, nor of a painful passing.

I examined the furniture...all of it in its proper place. No indication that anything had been moved. Nothing that suggested Corylus had gasped for breath or fought to save himself. That he'd ever known he was dying at all.

There was no hint that entry was forced. No trace of the poison left behind on any surface.

And nothing presented itself in my search; not in the bathing chamber when I swept every inch. Not in the windows when I tested them, or the door locks I jiggled uselessly. Not when I made another round through the entire suite and came back to the couch across from the desk. Sinking down on it, I rested my head in my hands.

I'd hoped to Luck that a *fresh* scene, rather than a report, would yield something new...something advantageous. But this confirmed my worst fears, *every* healer's worst fear when a death presented mysteriously—that there was no error in records, no detail missed. That the report actually *had* been thorough.

And in this case, the murderer had been, too.

This was what this flipping Poet left me with: untouched rooms. No signs of entry. No hint of a fight—between two men or one at the end of his life.

It was going to be a very long hunt here in Hadrass-Drui if I could only move forward by hints and crumbs.

And who knew how much time I had before the Poet Poisoner struck again?

CHAPTER 19
UNLIKELY ALLIES

W**HEN I FINALLY MANAGED** to pry myself from my fit of despair and wander back down the sweeping staircase and out through the front doors, I found Caspian perched on the steps. He rolled a stalk of lurid fuchsia flowers between his palms, his gaze transfixed far in the distance.

Sinking down on the steps and laying my skirt out around me, I bumped my shoulder against his. "Are you all right?"

He startled a bit, his focus swinging my way. After a long moment, his face cracked in a reluctant smile. "You know...you're actually the first person to ask me that."

"Today?"

"Since all this rotting chaos began."

"Oh." I wasn't certain what to say to that.

"You remind me of Callie that way." Melancholy touched his tone. "It was difficult for all of us when she left for Mithra-Sha, but I've always fancied it was harder for me than the rest. She's sharp, my sister...sneaky, but sharp. I suspect that plays into why she sent you to us." His conspiratorial gaze landed on me sidelong. "I also expect you're tangled up in this, at least in part, because Arias makes no secret you're one of his favorite people."

I couldn't think of what to say to that—I couldn't imagine a Calten like the one he remembered so fondly, that he had loved, and seemingly still did, with a brother's half-blind affection; nor could I bear the ache of missing Arias that rose with the mention of his name.

So I offered nothing but my silence.

For a while, that seemed to be all that either of us needed, weighing the emotions this place evoked in our own way. Then, finally, Caspian heaved a sigh.

"The more lighthearted a person is, I suppose, the less anyone thinks to check in with them. Difficult matters couldn't possibly touch Caspian Moraven...there's no chance he might be wrestling with things in secret." A puff of laughter, and he shoved a hand back through his hair. "Not even my family thinks to ask after me, most days. Except for Lu, but that girl sees everything."

"I've noticed that about her."

"Which doesn't surprise me...you're every bit as observant as she is." Caspian tilted his head back toward the door behind us. "So, what did you see in there?"

"More of the same." I blew out a frustrated breath, hanging my head in my hands again. "This Poet Poisoner...he's *good*."

"Indeed. But, according to the rumors, so are you." Caspian nudged a bit nearer to me, dropping his head—and his voice—to conspiratorial levels. "So, between us, Miss Weathers...why is such a prolific Mithran healer really wasting her time on these Hadrassi matters?"

I straightened sharply, prodded by the sincerity of the question, and he leaned back smoothly with me—his gaze never leaving mine once they locked.

"I know my sister," Caspian added quietly, "and I know she can be...*ardently* persuasive. I'll admit, I'm curious whether this assistance you've offered us has been out of the goodness of your heart, or something more."

"Do you ask because you think I might be some sort of threat to your family?"

The corner of his mouth quirked. "No, I suspect—given what Arias had mentioned of you—your loyalties are without fault."

He gave no other explanation for why he asked...and somehow, I didn't want to pry for one.

"I may have come for my own reasons," I admitted carefully, "but now that I've met all of you...and now that I've seen Phin...I'm putting my heart into this to stop this assassin from harming any of you. And that's the truth, I swear to Luck."

Caspian studied me for a moment longer; then his smile unfurled into something genuine, and he squeezed my shoulder. "That makes us allies of the highest order, then, Miss Weathers. And I assure you, I make a very good ally in dark times like these."

"I'm glad to hear that," I laughed for just a beat, the flare of humor withering when I glanced back at the manse. "I think I'm going to need all the friends I can find, if we're going to stop this assassin before it's too late for your family."

CHAPTER 20
OF LOST THINGS AND LEGACIES

Fortress Ferregrand was a somber sort of dark when we returned...a mourning pall I'd become familiar with immediately after the report of Corylus's death. The same blanket tugged halfway up the hips at my arrival after Phin's brush with death.

We were the only ones crossing the dim halls by torchlight in wall sconces that night, which made it all the eerier. As if we were carved out of time, moving through the Fortress a generation behind every other inhabitant.

"The mourning curfew's in effect," Caspian explained in a hushed undertone as we hurried through the abandoned corridors. "I'm surprised you haven't noticed it sooner."

"Is that a jab at my reclusive tendencies?" I laughed under my breath; anything louder would have felt disrespectful of the throbbing silence around us.

"Consider it more appreciative of your dedication. And likewise concerned that you apparently do not leave your chambers at all between sundown and sunup." He tossed a tired smile my way. "Except to sneak sweets with my niece, who is also willing to break the rules for food."

"Can you blame her? The custard here is excellent."

"I don't blame her in the least. Who do you suppose taught her and her brother how to dodge the sentinels' watch when they were hungry at night." Caspian rubbed his hands together. "Next, Mykos."

My next laugh burst out louder, echoing down the hall, and I clapped a hand over my mouth to smother it—which quieted things just enough that we both caught the whisper of a boot on stone around the corner ahead.

Caspian flung out an arm, barring me to a halt; my feet had already snagged on the marble, and I fell back another step by instinct, heart squeezing into my throat.

I had been almost *relaxed* on the carriage ride back from Corylus's manse, lulled by Caspian's promise of alliance—an ease that felt all at once foolish, like a hare forgetting to keep its ears on a swivel while it foraged near a fox's den.

What if the Poet Poisoner had used Corylus's death as a sneaky excuse to creep into Fortress Ferregrand and finish what he'd begun here?

The thought jolted me forward, hands digging into the spread of Caspian's arm; he pressed a finger to his lips, then crept toward the corner, bringing me along with him.

I wasn't at all sure what the lazy, arrogant Druavas thought he was going to do if we rounded that corner and found ourselves face-to-blade with an assassin's tools; I was of half a mind to yell for the sentinels we'd left behind at the last corridor.

But before I could muster the breath for it, Caspian had plucked a torch from the wall, wrapped his fingers backhand around the bend of my elbow, and jerked me behind the span of his back as he spun us both around the corner.

A piercing yelp jammed off the walls and straight into my eardrums as Caspian jabbed the torch aloft, shedding light over our mirrored image: Phineaus, tucking his sister behind him with one arm, Luminae clinging to his bicep as she peered around his shoulder at us.

Caspian lowered the torch at once. "Sullied souls, you two! What in the *grave?*"

Phineaus's brows leaped. "Late night tryst? Isn't she a little younger than your usual companions, Uncle Cass?"

"Phin, that's disgusting, oh my *soul*." Luminae shoved his arm down. "Ugh. *Ugh*!"

"I'll have you know your uncle just escorted me to Corylus Fletch's manse," I snapped good-naturedly; the twitch of Phin's mouth suggested the rise out of Luminae was the reason he'd made the comment. "And he was a perfect gentleman."

"Yeah, yeah...that's what he's known for." Phin rolled his eyes. "Put down the torch, old man, what are you going to do—set our hair on fire?"

"Don't put ideas in my head, you little maggot." Shaking his head, Caspian stabbed the torch back into its sconce. "What are you two doing out of bed?"

"Bored," said Phin.

"Hungry," Luminae added sheepishly.

Phin ruffled her hair. "Bad dreams."

She pinched his underarm. "Restless nights."

"Oh, dig a grave and bury me in it," Caspian grumbled, seizing them both by the shoulders and spinning them in place. "Kitchens?"

"Where else?" Phineaus slung an arm around his uncle's neck, leaning into him a bit as they walked. "You brought this on yourself."

"Blah, blah." Caspian knuckled Phin's hair, then pressed a sharp kiss to it. "Pain in my ass."

Luminae looped her arm through mine, tugging me into step with her. "That means you, too. We were going to settle for icebox cream, but I for one would prefer something warmer. And more chocolatey."

A smile tugged at my lips. "Don't mind if I help."

A half-hour later, Caspian had dodged us around every sentinel patrol and questionable watch to make our way to the kitchens, where he told Phin and Luminae of our venture to the Fletch manse while I brewed a pot of bone broth cocoa. Phineaus listened intently, never taking his eyes off his uncle's face even when I asked him to pass me four mugs from the cupboard.

"I just want to know how he gets in and out without a trace," he muttered. "He's like some kind of untethered soul, and he's better at dodging us than we are at the sentinels...no offense, Uncle Cass."

"That's what I'm here to help with," I reminded him as I took the mugs from his hands.

His gaze darted to my face, softening a bit when our fingers met around the glazed ceramic. "I know. Not sure if I've said it yet, but...thank you." He bumped his knuckles deliberately against mine before he relinquished the sleek, lacquered handles to my grip.

Luminae rubbed her arms, sinking back against the counter's edge. "It feels like he could be waiting around every corner of the Fortress."

"Which is why I'd prefer if you two heeded curfew for once in your lives." Caspian dropped an arm around Luminae's shoulders and hugged her against his side.

Wadding up the empty wrapper from the melting chocolate, Phin squinted one eye shut. "Ship..." He flicked the wad away with his thumb, landing it just shy of the wastebasket beside the counter, "sailed."

His tone dipped on the last word, a strange look contorting his face as he stared at the fallen scrap of paper...as if he wasn't used to missing that maneuver.

Luminae ducked from under her uncle's arm to pick up the wrapper, dropping it into the wastebasket and spinning a jig of silent victory. Phineaus cracked a smile at that; Caspian snorted. "Show-off."

With the cocoa poured, Phin lifted the mugs gently from my hands; I let him take them, with a warning scowl he parried by a wink. I was no stranger to patients—particularly men—who, after a near brush with mortality, seized every opportunity to prove themselves useful.

Better he do it here than by lifting something far heavier...or with something truly foolish, like trying to hunt the Poet Poisoner himself.

Caspian led us on a twisty, roundabout path to a corner of Fortress Ferregrand I hadn't visited yet; but Phin and Luminae seemed to know precisely where we were going, falling into step behind him. Phin balanced the mugs precariously and nodded while Luminae chattered about the latest chronicles she'd copied and ancient tomes uncovered in an excavation process to the west.

"It's incredible to think just how much history is buried out there," Luminae said wistfully as we mounted the steps of a corner tower, the skirts of her nightdress gathered in one hand. "So much about our past we hardly know a thing about, and so little coin allotted to excavating ruins like that."

"Make you a deal, Lu: you keep badgering all those stuffy scholars about it, and if I'm ever Drui," Phin swore, "you'll get all the funding you need."

"Phineaus, stop trying to make your sister swoon and fall down the stairs." Caspian halted at the crest of the stairwell, fiddling with the door at the top.

"Don't worry." I winked at Phin. "I'll catch her."

The boom of Phin's laugh in the stairwell told me we were safe at last from being caught outside of curfew as Caspian unlatched the door and swung it wide.

We entered a solarium—soaring, glass-walled and glass-roofed, the panes in deep, rich blues creating a muted underwater atmosphere. I nudged the door shut behind me as Luminae and Phin crossed the open space with easy familiarity, plucking pillows from the low sofas and ottomans, meeting in the middle to create a reclining area. Caspian lit a few candles on low tables, coaxing up just enough of a glow to complement the moonlight peering in and out behind tattered clouds.

Hugging my cardigan in the crooks of my arms, I padded after them to the heart of the room. "I take it you've all done this before?"

"Many, many times." Phin lowered himself with a groan, setting one mug by each pillow and keeping one for himself. "Your friend Arias, this is his favorite thinking spot. Uncle Cass used to drag the three of us up here to watch thunderstorms."

"Thunderstorms, stargazing, sunbathing..." Luminae hugged her mug with both hands, sitting with her back to her brother's. "Sleeping somewhere other than our bedrooms..."

"You can see danger coming from any direction up here," Caspian added, taking his space in the square; so I did the same, shoulders pressed to Luminae's and Phin's, back to Caspian's as I peered over the sprawl of Amalgard lit by night.

Somewhere out there, Corylus's manse lay dark, abandoned. I tried not to think of it.

We sat for some time, sipping cocoa, enjoying the moment. Phin broke the silence first with a staggered series of "Mm...mmm...*mmm*!"

Caspian snorted. "Grave's sake, Phin, it's cocoa, not a kiss. Keep the amorous grunting to a bare minimum, would you?"

Luminae burst into giggles; Phin dashed his mouth on his wrist. "Give me a break, this is...really rotting *excellent*." He smacked his lips. "Do I detect notes of cinnamon and maple?"

"You detect notes of *shut up and let us drink in peace*." Luminae elbowed him.

"You make me spill one drop of this sacred nectar and I will actually stab you to death, Lulu."

"I inherited the recipe from my mother," I intervened in their banter, a melancholy smile interrupting my next sip. "These were the kinds of nights she invented the recipe for, I think. She would have wanted a legacy where her recipes brought people together."

"I like that. Legacy is good," Phin mused. "Where you came from. Where you're going." Fabric chafed stone as he rocked his hips—chasing away a bit of lingering pain, perhaps. "I think about that a lot. The kind of legacy I want to leave, especially if I ever get to be Drui."

We sat with that for a soft, starlit moment...quiet, at first. Then Luminae murmured, "The linguist who uncovered stories no one else could."

"Hm?" I turned my cheek against my shoulder, studying her profile at my side; wreathed in strokes of the moon, her bright eyes and shining smile lit up from the outside inward.

"That's the legacy *I* want." She tucked her mug close to her belly, craning her head back to peer up through the solarium's angled roof. "I'd like to be known for unburying history. Bringing things to light that mattered, that would be lost without me. Changing the future by illuminating the past."

"A legacy that's about legacy," Phin hummed. "That's deep, baby sister."

"Thank you." Despite her pert tone, the satisfied lilt betrayed her glow at her brother's praise.

"You kids are my legacy." There was a shrug living in Caspian's tone. "No wife, no ankle-nippers of my own. But if I can drag you both over the threshold of adulthood in one piece, relatively unscathed, I'll consider that a memory worth leaving behind."

Luminae's hair swished as she leaned her cheek on his shoulder. "Love you, Uncle Cass."

"Yeah, love you, big man," Phin echoed with a resonate clap on Caspian's arm.

Heat pricked my eyes; all at once, I found myself thinking of Audra's family, who had created soft places to land when my harried father was too busy with my brothers' education and needs to notice mine. Mama Jashowin, who had talked me gently through my first bleeding, held me as I grieved my other mother in new ways, carried me softly over the threshold into womanhood. Papa Jashowin, who had listened in that quiet, intent way of his to all my stories about my family; who had offered Conor his first apprenticeship as an architect, gifted him his own toolset and sketchbooks, guided him with hand on his shoulder into a profession he loved.

Family *was* legacy. And it was so much larger than mothers and fathers and their children...it was aunts and uncles, siblings, and the people who filled those roles despite the different blood in their veins. Like Audra and Jaik—a sister and brother I hadn't been born with. Like Mama and Papa Jashowin, caring for me when my flesh and blood couldn't.

Like Caspian, with his niece and nephews.

Like Calten, risking my safety for the sake of seeing Phineaus's near-murderer brought to justice.

No wonder Caspian had let me go to the manse today—had escorted me himself, even. No wonder Luminae couldn't sleep with the threat angled at her brother, and Phin had snuck out with her tonight, risking trouble to be with her and show her he was going to be all right.

The Moravens stood on the threshold of a legacy bathed in bloodshed. I couldn't let it end that way.

"Naomi?" Luminae nudged me with her hip. "What about you? What sort of legacy do *you* want to leave behind?"

My thoughts strayed for a moment to a Mithran infirmary. To death and anguish. To a lonely road stretching between Vallanmyre and Dalfi, yawning like an uncrossable chasm.

I swallowed. "That I used my talents to serve and protect the people I cared for."

"That includes us, right?" Phin teased, thumping his foot over mine.

"If you don't stop crushing my toes, Phineaus Moraven, it will not."

Laughter from all of us brushed the solarium's roof, and Caspian said, "That's a legacy I could toast to, if I hadn't downed all that cocoa like a starved sailor at sea."

Carried on a single thought, we all raised our empty mugs. "Hear, hear!"

I let my arm tumble first, setting aside my mug and stretching out on my back with the pillow beneath my head. The others followed suit, Phineus with a hitch in his breath that held mine captive until he settled in some way that didn't ache.

We were all quiet in our thoughts of legacy and love...until Phin and Luminae's breathing deepened into sleep. Until Caspian murmured, drowsily himself, "Whatever you need to help keep these two safe, Miss Weathers...I'll be there to offer my aid, however I can."

"Thank you." Hugging my middle to keep safe the warmth his sincerity stoked in my belly, I gazed up at the stars winking through the glass.

That legacy I'd told them about, the goal Caspian and I shared, I had already begun shaping back in Mithra-Sha...but that was what had landed me in this mess with the Moravens.

And if I wanted it to be remembered as a protector, not a murderer, then I couldn't afford to let the Poet Poisoner slip through my fingers even one more time.

CHAPTER 21
AN UNMISSING PIECE

THE REPORTS FROM THE soul-sender about Corylus Fletch arrived by week's end—presenting every bit of the disappointment I'd feared and shriveling whatever tiny seed of hope I'd managed to grow.

No trace at all on the corpse. No hint at what the poison actually *was*. No skim of it left in the bloodpaths or organs, as if it had evaporated from Corylus's body. But certainly poison nonetheless, given the manner of death.

Nothing excavated from the house. Nothing found in the manse grounds. His wife and children—and maybe even Corylus himself—had slept through his death. It was as precise as a cut throat and as frustrating as a failed heart.

Another dead end. And another indication of a single variance in the Poet Poisoner's patterns—because none of what I read in Corylus's report and nothing I'd seen in his manse matched how Phineaus had almost died.

Bloody. In anguish. Bleeding internally.

None of those things were indicated in this latest report, or any of the previous ones. So he *had* broken pattern, though he'd kept the same deft precision and manner of killing that were making him notorious. And the only thing that linked Phineaus to any of the other victims was that they were all of similar status.

Wealthy. Influential. And most of them dear to the Moraven family...or they had been, long ago.

When I flipped to the end of the pitifully small report from the soul-sender, my stomach churned. Tossing the papers away from where I sat with my back pressed to the wall beside my room's dying hearth, I rocked forward, smoothing my palms over the silk handkerchief that tamed my curls and staring at the thick, woven emerald rug that swallowed up most of the floor.

"This can't be over," I hissed to the silence, digging my fingertips into my temples and kneading with all my might. "*Think*, Noni. You can outthink him!"

Of all the paths the Poet Poisoner had walked down, ending every one with murder...which one would I follow him down next?

Shutting my eyes, I leaned back against the wall.

One. This was just another diagnosis to make.

Two. I was trained to look for patterns.

Three.

It's often the least troubling symptoms that hide the answer.

The lesson from Harrow Hall reverberated in my skull, popping my eyes open and trapping my breath as I stared at the ledgers heaped on my desk.

One was missing.

Or...not *missing*. It had never been written, because a soul-sender hadn't been required.

If poring over every report and ledger on that desk had taught me anything, it was this: the Poet Poisoner was creepily detailed. Absolutely beholden to his patterns. Which meant I wasn't likely to find him through them, no matter how perfectly every attack matched. He would never allow it.

So I would have to find the chink in his armor to slip through. The report that wasn't written. A death that hadn't happened.

It was time to talk to Phin.

CHAPTER 22
MORAVEN FAMILY SECRETS

I T WAS ENTIRELY POSSIBLE I could've found my way back to the Moraven family's inner hall without help; but after so many days shut up in my room with only the occasional breaks to walk the halls, chat with the servants, or have a brief conversation with the few members of the ruling family who would bother to give me more than a cursory once-over...I was craving company.

"I'm surprised you found me so easily." Luminae's airy voice blended perfectly with the chilly light piercing through the mosaic glass today, throwing sharp fractals on our path as we wound through the halls. I had a feeling that summertime would've meant deeper, richer hues patterning the floor; instead, the early-autumn colors were so brilliant they almost hurt to look at.

"It was the *library*, Lu." I tucked my fingers into my cardigan's deep pockets. "I've been digging my closest friends like embedded ticks out of rows of bookshelves since I was a little girl."

"Fair." She shoved a strand of hair behind her ear; a glistening shell of silver and diamond studs framed it today, with a single gold chain draped from the gem at the top down to her earlobe. "I'm certain it devastates my mother that I prefer books over people, but—"

"Why wouldn't you? Books are less foul, less smelly, less prone to causing you harm—"

"Or at least, better at resolving it by the last page!" A giggle rolled behind her words.

"*Exactly*. Books make sense." I rubbed the heel of my hand between my eyes, where a perpetual headache had made its home these last few days. "*People* are a mess of contradictions."

"Even you?" Lu nudged me with her shoulder.

A faint memory tangled with the day's glow—death throes and the bite of my own fingers around an initiate's arm. "Even me," I sighed, hiding my hands in my pockets again. "How are you faring after Corylus?"

She shrank a bit at the reminder, rubbing her arms. "It's...well, stuffing my head in books helps. I'd rather be anywhere than here right now."

"I understand that." More than words could ever express.

"Mostly, it's Phin I'm worried for," she admitted. "If that rotting poisoner is still in Amalgard, close enough to strike the Fletch family...what's to say he won't try again with Phin?"

"That's what I'm hoping to put a stop to." I squeezed her shoulder, hoping one touch could convey all my determination. "So...tell me about the books you've been reading."

We chatted about the historical tomes she'd been buried in when I'd found her in the window reading nook in the Fortress library that morning. It turned out she had a particular love for the ageless past in our shared border at the Vensair Mountains—a range so broad and long, it was rumored not all of it had yet been explored.

"Imagine what could be lurking out there," she framed her thoughts with flying hands as we wound through the halls. "Ancient ruins, even *cities* unchronicled...creatures, beasts of legend..."

A smile prodded up my mouth. "The kind princesses tame?"

She knocked her hip against mine. "That's silly talk, Naomi. I'm not a princess."

"I never said you were." Wagging my brows, I lengthened my stride. "Just making small talk, is all."

Both of us were a bit more relaxed by the time we entered the dim central hall that housed the Moraven family's chambers; Luminae walked me to her brother's door, past the keen-eyed sentinels, then said shyly, "Thank you for letting me ramble in your ear."

"Honestly? I should be thanking *you*." I smoothed down my dress. "Luck, I've needed something to think about other than poisons and poetry for *days*."

"Well...you can always come find me." Uncertainty touched Luminae's tone. "I haven't had the chance to make many...acquaintances here in Amalgard since I started my training at Valorkeep. All of my childhood friends have sort of drifted off to their own lives, and—"

"And your grandfather doesn't like you to go out into the city to see them, anyway." A relatively blameless position on his part, given how I'd almost ben stabbed to death just walking through the city with a four-soldier escort.

Luminae hooked a strand of moonlight hair back from her temple. "Precisely. You can only hold onto so many friendships with people who don't understand where you are in life."

Memories of Dalfi pushed like a swollen bruise at the edges of my heart; I deftly ducked them, facing Luminae with my back to the door and my hand on the knob. "Well, if you'd like, you and I can be friends while I'm here. I have an *uncanny* head for how nobility works...growing up around your cousins and all that."

Her eyes widened slightly; after two swift blinks, a smile tugged up the corners of her mouth. "It would be lovely to have a friend while we're both stuck in this Fortress."

"You worded it *perfectly*." Winking, I knocked backhand on the door. "I'll see you soon, then, my starlight friend?"

That smile turned to a full-fledged grin. "You will, my healer heart-sister."

I found myself mulling over those words as I knocked again, and Luminae hurried down the corridor to her own door. Though I wasn't here to make friends—and though Hadrassi friends were dangerous in their own right—I couldn't help feeling a little less isolated and a little more at ease when the call came from beyond the door: "It's unlocked, let yourself in!"

"Is that really any way to conduct your affairs after almost being assassinated?" I asked by way of greeting, slipping into Phin's room. "The Poet Poisoner could just stroll right in, you know."

"Honestly, if he can find me in here, he deserves the kill." Phin glanced up with a mirthless smile. "Did you bring more of that *delectable* hot cocoa?"

"Not this time."

"Get out, then," he snorted. "No, just joking. Come on in." He waved me closer from his perch on the side of the bed, ruminating over what I could only assume were legal, official documents. I'd seen Arias doing the same tasks for his father as Shadran for years before I'd left Vallanmyre.

I toed the door shut, surprised by how relieved I was to see the Druavas working; between that and the midnight romp to the kitchens, his recovery seemed more than guaranteed. "You're really not concerned the Poet Poisoner could reach you here?"

"Not *here*, no."

His inflection prodded my head into a tilt. "So, this isn't the room where you were attacked?"

"Ah...no. No, all of us have a suite on the upper floors." I allowed myself an inner jig at that—I'd been right about the Fortress's layout, after all. "That's where I was, when...where, uh..." He trailed off, setting the papers aside and snaking a hand around the back of his neck, clearing his throat harshly. "Yeah. And then my parents had us all move down here, after. It's sort of a siege corridor inside the Fortress walls."

The stilting words was like an echo of a thousand patient assessments—men and women I'd talked to after we'd run blood back into their bodies or stitched together a dangling limb or restored them from the brink of death with a desperate blend of medicines.

Slowly, I crossed the room and lowered myself onto the bed's edge beside him. "Was this your first brush with your own mortality?"

A broken laugh cracked from his chest. "You could say that."

"It's terrifying when that happens." Pressing my lips together and trapping my hands between my knees, I stared at the dull wall opposite us; but across its surface, I watched a thousand memories play out. A thousand people I'd treated, asking through tearful eyes and bloodsoaked mouths if they were going to die. "It's that moment when you realize something that always happens to someone else, could really happen to you. Your armor cracks...you're not invincible anymore."

Phin was quiet for a moment. Then he rasped, "It happened to you?"

My mother's face darted across my mind—haggard, wasted from disease, her eyes turning opaque and her skin graying right in front of me. The phantom brush of her last breath raised the fine hairs on my cheek.

"Not *exactly* the same way, no." That was all I gave him...all I could bear to.

"Sorry," he mumbled.

Sucking in a deep breath, I shook myself free of that memory. "Do you mind if I search the rooms where you were attacked?"

"I mean, you're welcome to try." Phin shrugged. "I don't think you're going to find much that any of us missed. He didn't leave signs of entry, no footprints, not even a thread off his clothes. *Nothing*."

"What about the note? Could I examine that?"

"Well, you could...if I wasn't an idiot." He fingered the back of his neck again, grimacing. "When I saw it was just my name on a blank note, I figured it was an invitation that got missed. I didn't take it for a poisoner's calling card, since there wasn't a stupid poem line, so I just tossed it into the hearth and got busy unpacking my things."

"Unpacking?" I swiveled on the bedside to face him. "Did you just come back from somewhere?"

"Yeah, didn't...didn't my parents tell you?" When I stared him down, bewildered, his mouth corkscrewed with frustration and his head bobbed sharply. "See, *this* is why I should've been in that first meeting! Naomi, I just came back from Thrasmund...I've been training there ever since I turned sixteen. Just visiting home for important events, birthdays, that sort of thing."

The name pricked me with a needle's tip of memory; Arias had mentioned Thrasmund as a fabled city full of retired swordmasters and spicemakers. His aunt and uncle had offered him to stay there for a year, the same year Arias and I had met, to train and learn more about his Hadrassi heritage.

He'd declined...and to hear the rumor mill churn it out, that was the moment Arias had firmly chosen his Mithran blood over the Hadrassi shadows running through his veins. And it was the last time he'd been invited to spend the summer months with his cousins.

Swallowing, I blinked Phin's frowning countenance back into focus. "You haven't lived in the Fortress since you were *sixteen*?"

"No, just like Lu took off for Valorkeep. Every Moraven has that choice once they come of age, unless they're...you know, like my Aunt Callie."

Sent to Mithra-Sha at sixteen. "And you just came back this year. Why?"

His gaze shuttered a bit. He swung his face away, back to the wall. "I can't tell you that."

Something squirmed in my belly. "That doesn't inspire much confidence, Phin."

"Well, can you blame me? You've met my family."

"Then is this a *Phin secret*, or a *Moraven family secret*?"

His eyes flashed back to me; I held that stare, refusing to blink, refusing to give ground.

Perhaps I didn't have a right to know. But it didn't help my chances of bringing the Poet Poisoner to his knees if the family I was trying to save kept truths hidden from me.

"They really picked you well, didn't they?" Phin mused, his eyes tracing every angle of my face. "You're *sharp*."

His hand landed on the bedspread between us, and he bent my way—leaning so near, the smell of candied peaches and herbs brushed my face from his breath.

"Moraven family secret," he murmured.

Then he pushed up from the bed, striding to the door; I shook a trace of dizziness from my head, swiveling to track him. "Where in Luck are you going?"

"You said you wanted to see my other rooms?" He pulled the door wide, spanning a hand to the hall beyond. "Come on, I'll escort you."

CHAPTER 23
IN INK AND INSCRIPTION

PHIN WAS A MUCH more animated escort than his sister. Folding my hand into the crook of his elbow and moving like a man taking a jaunt with a suitor, he made a gregarious show of pointing out various aspect of Fortress Ferregrand he loved and missed during his years away.

Certain mosaics, and how the light fell through them. The tall panels of floor-to-ceiling curtains that required three servants on each side to pull apart every day. The heated pools and cascading fountains, the random assortment of seating beside fireplaces built into the walls. The viewing balconies and their lustrous view of Amalgard and the Fortress's inner gardens.

But even his outgoing charm dwindled when we arrived at his suite—the place that had nearly been his deathbed.

For the first time, he let my grip slip from the bend of his arm; he hid his hands in his pockets, shoulders hunching slightly as he took in the broad, high-roofed entry parlor with its three branching doorways...the rug still rumpled from where I could only assume the healers had tended him. The hearth blackened where the fire had been left to burn out. The furniture shoved off-center where sentinels must have rushed to reach their fallen Druavas at his mother's call.

Sympathy curdled my stomach. I laid a hand on his shoulder. "You don't have to stay."

A swift breath, and he pinched his nostrils, then rubbed swiftly beneath his nose. "No, it's...you know, I figured it wouldn't bother me, it's just..." A breathless laugh punctuated the words. "Rotting bones, you'd just think the servants would've cleaned it up by now."

"It's good they didn't," I reminded him gently. "I'll be better able to learn something if everything it still the way it was that night."

Phin blew out a tremulous breath. "I really hope you're better at all this than the sentinels have been, because this...this is beyond me."

"I suppose we're going to find out." I tilted my chin at the door. "You should go back and rest, before your uncle realizes you're gone."

"Yeah, he'll hit the roof. Fusspot." Affection laced Phin's tone as he backed toward the door; but he lingered in its frame, concern etching his brow. "You're sure you want to do this alone?"

"It's why your aunt sent me." I shrugged, then offered him a smile I hoped didn't betray my days of wearying, worthless searching until now. "I'll be fine, Phineaus. Go and rest."

He knocked his fist twice on the doorframe. "Well, if you need me...just send one of the sentinels."

Then he was gone, scurrying out and kicking the door shut behind him—the surest sign of just how deeply the trauma of his near-death had touched him. Maybe even deeper than he'd realized until he'd set foot in his suite.

So I took those steps for him...into the rooms that had every bit of the things he loved about the Fortress, all gathered into one place. Soaring panels of sheer crimson curtains blocking out mosaic windows with a dizzying drop to the Fortress grounds far below; vaults of arched stone supporting the parlor's rounded roof; the gleaming balcony with its cozy seating; more mosaics in the bedroom; and the workroom crammed with a desk, bookshelves, and various chests-of-drawers.

I found nothing there of interest—just a few displaced papers, stirred up dust, and Phineaus's cloak cast haphazardly over the back of his chair. A few indications of how the room had been searched by the sentinels and then put back together in honor of their Druavas.

Back out into the parlor. I combed every inch of it on both levels, but nothing in the shifted furniture, half-parted curtains, or clumped rug—or even the traces of blood on the floor—indicated the Poet Poisoner's movements here. All of this had been disarrayed by Phineaus's brush with death...not by what had preceded it.

Everything else seemed to have been left the way it was for quite some time, judging by the varying layers of dust everywhere. Phin hadn't even had time to disturb many of his own things after his return; when I wandered into his bedchamber, the canopy bed was still perfectly made, his satchel left on top of the covers where he'd started unpacking it.

The rest, undisturbed. Even the throw pillows were immaculate.

Giving up after several circles and searches through the room, I slipped back out into the entry parlor and strode for the door to what looked like the bathing chamber—then slowed.

Something brushed my nose from the ashy remains in the hearth, a tickle of a smell that had me swinging around on heel, peering into the cold, dark depths.

That can't be right.

Bittersweet. Assertive. A bit like anise and rosemary.

I'd only smelled that pungent odor once before, but it was burned into my memory forever.

Gripping the mantel with one hand, I ducked my head into the spacious hearth, breathing in with all my might—almost choking on a cloud of ashes stirred up by my movements.

But that scent, buried under the musky warmth of toppled kindling...I knew it. It sparkled in the corner of my memory like a dash of powerful spice in a good soup. It flared silver-bright, like infirmary walls...like bloodied final breaths and a man of the Mithran army, dead beneath my hands.

You will forget everything you saw here, Raynes.

Because the initiate who'd spilled my secret hadn't quite seen what she thought she had.

It was a death perpetrated by poison and masked as organ failure that had sent me on the run here, with Calten's bladed threats at my back. And the sharp stench of that same poison was inside this hearth.

My mind skipped and leaped, bouncing across everything I knew of the poison that *I* had once used—that had also been used against Phin, by the smell of it.

Mummer's Dance.

Luck, I should have recognized the signs from his report...but I hadn't been *looking* for it.

Mummer's Dance was extremely rare and incredibly expensive, something that affected the organs but could easily be cloaked as a luckless illness; a poison not mixed or even often found anywhere but in Hadrass-Drui. That was why I'd chosen it for my own purposes...a bit of extra cloaking over my steps when I'd made an unchangeable choice, years ago. The vain hope that if anyone looked twice, they would blame Hadrass-Drui for a bloody death on Mithran soil—not me.

And then, of course, the guilt of that—the implications that had only settled in after, when I'd realized that the Hadrassi murder of a Mithran general could be tantamount to an act of war—had been a hard shove between my shoulderblades, chasing me out of Vallanmyre.

I pushed my hair back from my temples with both hands now, blocking out those memories...choosing safer ones instead.

The woman I'd purchased the poison from...Hadrassi. The only known peddler who sold this poison. I'd had to import the sachet across the border, through contacts I'd made in Harrow Hall and in my continued poison studies after. I dimly remembered which city she'd lived in—a city which, apparently, the Poet Poisoner had also visited. Perhaps even frequented.

Dropping my hands, I slowly turned on heel to survey the room.

The question was still *how* he'd gotten the poison to Phin. My only experience with it had been by direct contact, but Phineaus had been alone in his chambers...chambers that had been searched and swept clean. There was absolutely nothing left here that was traceable...nevermind that none of the sentinels who'd searched the room had fallen sick with Phin's same symptoms. It seemed likely if they'd brushed up against even a trace of the Mummer's Dance, or if it had been fumigated through the flue, someone would have noticed by now.

"Think," I hissed, circling the parlor in another slow sweep. "If *you* were a poisoner—"

If?

Gritting my teeth, I shoved that thought away; it had made too many appearances today. "How are you *not* leaving a trace?"

Groaning, I spun on heel—and went back to staring at the fireplace.

I just tossed it into the hearth, Phin had said of the note left for him. And the ledgers I'd been laboring over from the sentinels and soul-senders all claimed they'd tested the notes at every death-place. The paper had been clean, not a trace of any substance on it.

But that wasn't all a note was made of.

A heady thrill twisted my lips up into a humorless, savage grin. "You clever bastard," I breathed.

They'd tested the paper...but not the ink itself. Because the properties of dry ink would mask themselves as they sank into the paper; how many times had Addie told me that? How many times as girls had she nearly bitten my fingers off because I'd dared to brush a hand over one of the stories she'd jotted in her journal before the ink was dry?

She'd been infatuated with ink's properties—with its semipermanence. How the written word could be altered until the ink bonded with the paper and took on its same qualities.

But, *wet* ink...

Wet ink could seep into fingertips.

Wet ink could hold secrets of its own.

Wet ink could possibly be imbued with poison that would vanish from all trace once the ink itself dried.

Gasping out a breath of disbelief, I tumbled to my seat on the sofa, staring into the hearth.

That was his angle...so perfectly fitting to his name.

This assassin was penning poison in his poetry.

And I knew where to start searching for him.

CHAPTER 24
MAKING TROUBLE

"WHERE ARE YOU GOING?" Luminae tucked her legs beneath her, leaning her weight into one hand half-swallowed by my plush bedspread. I'd invited her into my room as soon as I'd made the decision to leave Amalgard; as sure as I was of this next step, and the way I had to take it, I didn't love the notion of vanishing without at least one of the Moravens knowing where I'd gone.

For my own safety...but also so word wouldn't get back to Calten and make her think I'd gone on the run. The last thing I needed was to return to Mithra-Sha just to be clapped in chains and thrown in prison, my secret spilled to the entire country and all my closest friends.

"I'm going to Rastra," I answered after a brief wrestling match with my satchel, trying to fit my invisible ink comfortably back in its inner pouch. "To meet with someone who knows a thing or two about poisons." Folding the last of my new Hadrassi outfits carefully into my satchel, I buckled it shut and leaned both hands on top. "And I don't want you to tell *anyone* else where I've gone."

"Why not?" Luminae pouted.

"Because having your brother and uncle and mother *and* all of your grandfather's advisors *and* the sentinels tangled up in this business is making it absolutely impossible to get anything *done.*" Straightening, I swung the satchel across my front. "Especially since Corylus passed. I was sent to clean up this mess because I can think the way none of the rest of them can. That's what I've done now...Rastra is *my* lead to chase. Phin and Caspian and Serai can chase theirs while I'm gone."

"But...what if you run into danger?"

Swiping my palms on my thighs—clad in trousers for once, the cuffs stuffed in a pair of slightly-too-large travel boots from the closet—I lowered myself onto the bed across from her. "Believe me, Lu, I have no intention of looking for trouble. Even *if* this leads anywhere, I won't go dashing into danger. I'm not a..."

Troublemaker. The mischievous tease of a voice I'd all but managed to silence until now brushed against the back of my thoughts. I shook it fiercely away.

"I'm not an idiot," I amended. "I'm not going to go and make my intentions so obvious the Poet Poisoner would want me dead in the street. I'll just poke around a bit and see if I can learn what poison he's using...and maybe how he's acquiring it."

Now that I knew for almost certain that he was blending it into his ink, that narrowed down the possibilities considerably. But *narrow* wasn't *precise*—and I needed to be every bit as thorough as he was, if I was going to learn his secrets and trap him with them.

And, for the sake of the promise I'd made to Phin and Caspian...I needed to know if the woman who'd sold me the Mummer's Dance was an accomplice of his. Someone else to be dealt with before this whole ordeal could be laid to rest.

Luminae picked at the thick seams of the bedspread, tugging her lower lip between her teeth. "I just don't want to lose another person to this awful Poisoner." Her eyes lifted at last from the bed between us, searching mine. "Especially someone who's just become a friend."

Choked, I couldn't do much more than wrap my arms around her—and lean into the embrace when she hugged me back.

Because I absolutely understood...I'd been watching my friends walk into danger for too many years to count. Soldiers, Storycrafters, even the Shadran, always putting themselves at risk; it was just in the last handful of years that risk-taking had really fallen to me.

That first time—when I'd embraced it so wholeheartedly—it had set a pattern all its own. And this was just another step down a path carved out by that day. That choice.

"I decided a long time ago that it was a privilege to try to protect and save people who deserve it." I gave Luminae an extra squeeze before I pulled back. "And you, and your family, and their friends...you *all* deserve it. So I have to go."

Luminae sighed, rolled her eyes up to stare at the ceiling—then swiped away a tear. "*Fine.* But write to me...promise you will."

"Of course." I pushed up from the bed again. "What kind of friend would I be if I didn't provide you with some new reading material? Pity it's not historical, but I'll try to keep things exciting for you."

A damp laugh rattled from her chest. "You're impossible."

"That's why they love me." With a last smile and a wave, I slipped out into the corridor and tugged the door shut.

Then I leaned against it, blowing out my breath through rounded lips...attuning myself to the rattle in my hands and the knot of nerves in my belly.

This was it; my first time leaving the Fortress without a guard since I'd arrived. My first time really *alone* since I'd been saved from certain death. And with no real guarantee at all that some avenging shadow watched over me...a promise that felt especially empty now that I was striking off on my own.

But I had to do it; my contact in Rastra had been flighty enough the first and only other time I'd ever reached out to her. If I came tromping into that Hadrassi heartbeat city with an entourage sent from the Drui himself, that door would shut in my face forever.

To save myself, and the Moravens, and all of their established friends...I had to do this part alone. Just like when I'd fled to Dalfi; just like when I'd run back to Vallanmyre to plead for Jaik and Audra's lives after they'd stumbled onto my doorstep, hunted by a vengeful soldier and with a quest of their own to finish.

It turned out that of all the choices I ever had, *alone* seemed to work the very best.

Still, I let myself lean against the door and feel the nerves ransacking my courage for the count of three.

And then, just like I had so many times before, when the count was over...

I just *moved*.

CHAPTER 25
SMOKE AND SECRETS

I'D EXPECTED A BIT more of a fuss with leaving Fortress Ferregrand—but that, it turned out, was the easiest part of the whole expedition. The sentinels hardly looked twice at me when I breezed down the bridge and out through the second gate; I supposed they were more occupied with people coming in than those who were leaving. And after my excursion across the city with Caspian, I'd become somewhat better linked to the intentions of the ruling family.

A flash of the heirloom key around my neck to indicate my nearness with *someone* of Moraven blood...and I was through.

That was when the shaking started—and it didn't abate until I'd gone to the carriage station I'd spotted on one of the city maps, and purchased a ride out to the trade city of Rastra.

It was a long journey, but not an unpleasant one, thanks to the Hadrassi landscape. I was used to the sights up and down the Spine, the glass Storycrafted road that traveled the length of Mithra-Sha, and somewhat less so with the wilderness paths between Vallanmyre and Dalfi. But the road to Rastra was winding in the best ways; it detoured a bit toward the foothills of the Vensair Mountains that crested our countries' shared border, where even the lower dells were still high enough to allow for waterfalls and lush growth. Most of the way, we traveled near the steep dropoff to a meandering creek, its burbling journey a constant music to lull us to sleep when we stopped each evening.

I rode half the time up in the carriage seat with the driver, Seleni. A widowed mother of five grown daughters, she'd made the drive to Rastra more times than she could count; her stories of how the way had changed and improved over the years, and all the landmarks and historical sites she pointed out along the way, broke up the monotony that came with days of wagonriding.

The other half of the time, I sat inside the carriage, quieting my nerves with rereading the notes I'd taken in my journal from the soul-senders' ledgers and sorting my herbs and cures again and again.

Just in case.

Finally, after almost a week—a few days longer than expected, thanks to a chilly rainstorm that made portions of the road impassible for a time—we reached a place where the thick undergrowth peeled back on either side of the path. Where the road abandoned the hedge of trees and underbrush and rollicked over softer inclines and along a twist of river until homes and shops began to crop up, and then...

For the first time, I laid eyes on Rastra.

Amalgard had truly taken my breath away at first glance, with all of its mess of colors and sharp angles. But Rastra...

Rastra stopped my heart. Then sent it *racing*.

This city *lurked*. It lacked the soaring cathedrals and sharp steeples that had made Amalgard seem like a soldier warding off enemies. Instead, Rastra basked in secrets...the way it ushered us between the complexes of dark buildings with their steeply-sloped roofs and balconied sides, down roads lined in lampposts and along arched bridges over canals that flowed black like old blood.

Seleni drove us straight into the heart of the heartbeat city, through cobblestone ways that leaned desperately into floral fletching for the same bursts of color Amalgard made in mosaics. Moss hung from the swoops of most lampposts. Potted trees stretched as high as the second and sometimes third-level balconies of the housing complexes, where thick, climbing ivy in shades of burgundy and jade took over. Thick greenery wound up through the cracks everywhere in the city it could find, crowding in alleyways, tapering through the seams of the buildings, even winding up to the top windows of the countless mansard roofs—the preferred architecture around here, it seemed.

Boutiques and cafes, bistros and bookstores cornered almost every street. Plant houses and tea parlors spilled their earthy scents across the cobblestones. Carriages trundled past us in close quarters, and Seleni raised a hand to every driver.

I couldn't have loved it more if it had been made for me. Because it felt like it *had*—every clump of ivy and every drip of moss reminded me of my home in Dalfi, where I'd chosen the simplest but most beautiful plants for decoration. Where I'd thrived on surrounding myself with growing things.

We passed shops and businesses with round-topped windows still glowing despite the early evening hour; the road wound around gushing fountains with their ridge-lipped pools, past soaring buildings with four levels and steep, sharp corners buttressing their gated courtyards, past playhouses teeming with sweet melodies and eateries bustling with outdoor seating and braziers lit to ward off the cold.

I wasn't ready for the abbreviated tour of Rastra to end when Seleni drew back the reins and clicked her tongue, urging the horses to a halt. Leaning her elbows on her knees, she waved a weathered hand, dark skin kissed by a sharp line of well-lit buildings ahead of us. "Hostels. Take your pick...any one's as good as another."

"Then any one will do." I couldn't keep the smile off my face as I shook out a few extra coins for her trouble, shouldered my satchel, and started for the bush-lined curb.

I would never feel safe in Amalgard—not after what had happened there the first night. But Rastra...

Rastra, I might be able to love.

I even loved the room I secured—just for the week, keeping enough coin in my pockets that I didn't start sweating, but giving myself plenty of time so I wouldn't be rushed. The top-floor accommodation was stuffed with bookcases and sported a short, spiral staircase up to a tiny balcony above the bed, where even more books were shoved haphazardly into spots—likely the hostel-keeper's own collection, judging by the discordant titles and topics boasted by the spines.

Still, I had a feeling Lu would pout to the ends of the country when I told her about my sleeping arrangements.

Grinning, I dumped my satchel on the bed and went to the window, whipping the curtains wide and squinting at the view beyond. The arched glass offered a truly spectacular sight of the broad canal that backed this portion of Rastra, with just a narrow, tree-lined walking path separating the hostel grounds from the fencing at the water's edge. More lampposts lined the waterway itself, its track ribbed with bridges, hung with bunches of tapered flowers that somehow flourished despite the chill when they brushed their floral fingers over the surface of the water.

Felyx would've gone feral over a canal like this, almost as much as I wanted to turn feral over a whole *city* like this.

Gripping the halves of the deep olive curtains in both hands, I breathed in to the bottoms of my lungs—crinkling my nose at the smells of soap from the bedsheets, the peppery ashes from the small hearth across from it, and the ivy tendrilled around the bedposts and woven into the balustrades of the narrow balcony above.

"All right," I whispered on an exhale. "Let's find ourselves a Poet, shall we?"

CHAPTER 26
STOLEN GOODS

I T TURNED OUT THAT, freed of the suspicious glances from the Moravens and the everywhere-reminders of what was at stake, my mind flourished a bit more, easing into the task at hand rather than slamming itself against duties and deadlines like a trapped bird on a windowpane. Just like when I'd had my first room to myself in Harrow Hall, without a roommate's chatter or clutter poking at the edges of my concentration.

It didn't take long to review all my notes from the contact I'd made in this city all those years ago. A name, a place of business, the city of her operations...and armed with that, it was time to explore Rastra.

I went prepared: decked in a Hadrassi dress with my favorite beige cardigan tossed over it, my own pouch of poisons and tinctures at my hip, and my gifted dagger strapped on in easy reach—just in case.

By the time I located *Mistress Merrietti's House of Herbs*, I even had a plan cobbled together.

Break inside. Consult her sales ledgers. Copy down any names and herbs of interest...and begin to dissect which one could've been used on the Poet Poisoner's victims, and which buyer, by fault, could be him.

It wasn't the sturdiest scheme, if I was honest with myself. But it was *something*, and when I scouted the shop for several days—sipping a mug of disgustingly weak hot cocoa to warm myself and settle my nerves—I spotted the Mistress herself for the first time, and that sealed the choice for me.

Merrietti was just on the far side of middle-aged, tawny-skinned and perpetually dressed in deep, jewel-toned robes, with steely eyes, a strong jaw, and a shopfront that boasted in honest trade. I watched her chase out several people with an upraised voice when they tried to swindle her, wincing every time she slammed her door shut at their retreating backs.

So, she hadn't softened in the least; it had been hard work reaching her years ago, despite her reputation, and the sale had come with a signed agreement—that

I would never contact her again, and that, if I named her in any of my dealings with the Mummer's Dance, my signature proved me a fraud.

She was a woman intent on protecting the opposing sides of her life. I would never be able to convince her to give that up, even for the sake of solving murders or saving Phineaus Moraven.

I would just have to settle for stealing instead.

Picking locks was not one of my most used or proudest talents. But with four rowdy brothers and friends like Reiko—who had grown up in Mithran slums and survived off what people kept sealed up safely at night—and Jaik, who refused to accept a locked door as anything but a challenge to get inside—the knowledge rattling in my head was at least halfway inevitable.

So I tried not to feel too tremendously guilty when I fiddled with the complex convection of locks that bolted the back of Mistress Merrietti's shop shut, with only the slant of a glow around the edge of the sidestreet and a lonely lamppost bending from the opposite alley wall to light my way.

During the handful of days I'd spent at the teahouse across the plaza, I'd only ever seen Merrietti enter and exit by this door, never by the shopfront; and it always took her almost a full minute to do up the locks, which made sense given the nature of her dealings—both common and clandestine.

But, *Luck*, this was taking considerably longer than I'd bargained for. And the only other thing I had learned about this pocket of the city with any certainty was that the sentinels patrolled it in no particular pattern.

They might come at midnight. They might not come at all. Or they could stroll by any second and find me with one lock undone and the rest giving me more grief than a stubborn infection refusing every herb I threw at it.

Pitching my shoulder against the door, I blew a curl from my brow and wiped my sweaty palms on my thighs for the tenth time. "This is *not* working."

My gaze hunted both mouths of the alley again, speckled with just a few potted trees and, thankfully, unfilled with sentinels; but this time my attention snagged on a crooked pile at the base of the next establishment over.

A heap of disused bricks.

My gaze shot up to the window just to the right of the door, and my pulse doubled.

Strictly speaking, picking locks and breaking windows had the same means to the same end: thievery. But somehow, throwing a brick at the glass seemed far more degenerate. Lockpicking required talent, finesse; brutes broke windows.

But, maybe, so did desperate healers who needed to look at notes that would land them in trouble if they just strolled up and asked for them.

Easing my stiff legs out of a crouch, I slipped down the alley and snatched up one of the thickest bricks, tucking it inside the bundle of my cardigan. Then I padded back to Merrietti's side door, hesitating—but just for the count of three.

One.

I really hated to do this.

Two.

But I hated to have the Poet Poisoner running amuck even more.

Three.

I swung the wrapped brick with all my might, once, twice—and then the glass gave way with a crunch like sundering bone.

Scurrying back to replace the brick precisely where I'd found it, I let urgency overcome my conscience. The deed was done, so all that was left was the next step. Then the next one after that.

I surveyed the alleyway on both sides—still empty—then wrapped my hands in my cardigan this time and heaved myself through the windowframe. Dropping gingerly on the far side, I unlatched and opened the door, then kicked as many of the glass shards as I could over the threshold.

If Luck loved me, maybe the way it seemed like it had been broken from the *inside* outward would cast suspicion over my entry altogether.

Clinging to that worthless hope, I slunk inside.

The shop was oddly arranged, which I'd already surveyed through the front windows; crooked doorways led from the confined back entry room to the sprawl of the shop body itself, full of two-sided shelves stuffed to the brim with all sorts of tincture jars and bottles of various colors. The way the light from the streetlamps fell through the front windows painted the floor in mosaic stripes that reminded me of the Fortress.

With a pang, I wondered just how much trouble it would cause for Lu, Caspian, and Phin if it was ever discovered the Mithran they'd befriended was breaking into herbalist shops in Rastra.

I cared a little less what trouble it might cause for *Calten*.

Goaded on by the thought of her, I ignored the shelves themselves—with some effort—in favor of slipping behind the counter. Merrietti's logbook waited precisely where I'd seen her shove it at the end of every day, on a pullout ledge under the countertop. Unlatched and unattended, it was easy to hoist up, flip open, and read with my arms folded on the counter's edge.

Unfortunately, the sales pages didn't prove promising; everything recorded was utterly mundane. Curatives, tinctures, salves...not every name of every cure was familiar, but the body of evidence suggested a shop run perfectly on premise: a house of herbs for healing.

Which was a flat, flipping *lie*. Because this logbook dated back over a decade, well-kept and perfectly recorded; and there was precisely *nothing* to the date or page of when I'd contacted her to purchase Mummer's Dance.

Which meant there would be no record of the Poet purchasing it to use against Phin, either.

"You're a lying crook, Merrietti," I muttered, pressing my teeth around my thumbnail until it bent inward. "Where are you hiding the rest of it?"

Back to searching, though now it was starting to feel like borrowed time; I hadn't noticed Merrietti ever returning to her shop in the evenings, but trust her to do it on the day I decided to launch my plan.

Fingers scurrying at that notion, I tore through the counter below the register, searching for any additional logbook—anywhere else she might keep notes of her less-than-reputable transactions.

I was ready to acquiesce that she didn't keep that sort of ledger at all—or worse, that she brought it home with her for safekeeping at the end of the day—when, with my head wedged halfway into one of the cutouts and my frantic fingers scouting the inner recesses of the counter, a scent pricked my nostrils.

A fresh, woodsy smell.

Like sawdust.

Pulling back, I crinkled my nose, peering into the depths of the cutout. Then, slowly, I traced its edges again...and again. Over and over, until I didn't just smell the chipped wood...a sliver of it pierced my smallest finger.

Cursing, I yanked my hand out, pulled the splinter with my teeth, and sucked on the small puncture until the pain lessened. Then I tucked that finger in and used the other nine to feel at the inner edge of the hole.

And right there, so incredibly small I would've missed it entirely if I hadn't smelled the sawdust of blunted wood first...

A divot. A lever.

Grinning, I pressed it; the wood unlatched, and I fitted my fingers around its edge, grinding it back on a poorly-carved track—the kind my architect brother Conor would've cursed to the dark side of Luck's two-faced coin.

The space inside wasn't large enough for a ledger of any kind. Instead, my fingers encountered a small roll of parchment, four or so pinned together at the corner.

Frowning, I extracted it and slapped it down on the counter, studying it feverishly by the lamplight spilling between the bookcase rows.

This didn't look like any record of sales I had ever seen; there was no accompanying signature to any of the listed products. And the mark of cost was *exponentially* higher compared to the herbs and tinctures in her logbook—not only that, but it was subtracted from her earnings. Not added to them.

"Thefts," I breathed, trailing my finger down the list. "These are stolen goods."

She'd recorded every single time anyone had robbed her...of herbs, of sachets, of tinctures and brews. Even, apparently, of a stool that might've once sat behind this counter. Some had their full names written beside them—and those only appeared once, so she'd clearly run the thieves out of her shop after that. Others were accompanied by question marks or initials.

These thefts didn't seem to be an uncommon thing, which I supposed I could understand; given what I'd seen so far of Hadrass-Drui, plenty of people walked with tight belts and light coinpurses as well as bristled hackles. In the desperate throes of ailment for themselves or others, it was entirely possible they resorted to stealing.

Not that I would know anything about that. The rueful thought had me shaking my head as I pushed the parchment into a brighter slant of lamplight, flipping to the last page.

The ink here was the darkest and freshest of the four—and the bottom of the parchment drew my gaze immediately, the two words reaching for me like clawed hands out of a thornbush, hooking me in and raking me closer to the text.

Mummer's Dance. Dated several months ago—scripted in sharp, jagged slants, as if Merrietti had been struggling to control her temper while she wrote. Jotted into the margin beside it: *HOW?*

And then, next to that: *PP.*

I smoothed my thumb over the initials, mouthing to myself: *Poet Poisoner.*

Hastily, I flipped back to the previous page—and after a swift scour, found it again.

PP. Repeated again and again, next to a small array of varying herbs—but mostly the same one, again and again, poached from her once or twice a year.

"Got you," I hissed, drilling my finger into his initials; then I slid the tip across to read the name of the herb itself.

Lightbane.

Spinning with my back to the counter, I surveyed the shelf that backed it: bottles, jars, vials of what Merrietti likely considered her most valuable assets, always guarded behind her.

And one that had been stolen so many times, thwarting her again and again...that would be the most valuable of all.

Still, it took me another handful of minutes searching, reading labels, standing on my tiptoes and then crouching on my heels, before I'd moved far enough down the disorganized case to find what I was looking for.

A fist-sized glass jar of the Hadrassi herb in question.

The glittering, fathomless dark of the tendrilled plant floating inside the glass vial was no less of a beacon than the oddest symptoms. I couldn't help slinking around the side of the counter, reaching for them, running my fingers along the glass—

Freezing.

My reflection was wrong. My fingertips, pressed to the glass...they weren't bare.

They were *gloved*.

My gaze shot over the top of the jar itself, and for the first time I realized the shelving was hollow—backless, just like the rest. A whole other room yawned on the far side, soaked in shadows.

And a masked man stood wrapped in those intangible filaments, reaching for the Lightbane, just as frozen as I was. Both of us gaping at one another.

It took only one heartbeat for my mind to register why he looked familiar.

The dark hair. The deep cobalt shirt and slate trousers—Hadrassi core darks.

His black hair, one rogue lock falling into his eyes.

The metal mask and cowl. And those eyes, dark as pitch...fixed on me with startled familiarity.

A face that had featured in my dreams one or two or ten times too many to be respectable in the weeks since I'd met him...for what I'd been so sure was the first and last time.

I almost choked on the gasp of his name:
"*Kai?*"

CHAPTER 27
SHADOW-SOFT AND STEEL-SHARP

My savior from Amalgard...the man who had rescued me from a murderer, pulled me from my fears like a sea I'd been drowning in—this flipping *thief*—he just stared at me. Those dark eyes felt like they were laying me open layer by layer, peeling back skin to search beneath muscle and bone, right to the heart of me. To the stuff I was made of.

"You..." My voice cracked. Faltered. "Why are *you* stealing this herb?"

He went on staring, unspeaking.

I barely had enough breath to whisper the question that raged in my head—that would change *everything*.

"Are...are *you* the Poet Poisoner?"

The flicker of his eyes, the lowering of his brows, the sharp sideways cut of his mouth at that spoken title, were all proof enough.

Flipping Luck!

He eased a step toward me around the side of the shelf. I jolted back, my ribs jamming into the corner of Merrietti's counter. A hiss slid from between my teeth, and my hand shot up by instinct to guard my throbbing back.

The Poet Poisoner halted, one hand extended, his gaze flashing from the corner to my side, then bounding back to my face.

He took another step. I slipped sideways, giving myself space to retreat toward the shopfront without bumping into anything.

"I am not going to harm you." His tone was far from soothing; he wielded the words like an accusation. Like I was somehow ridiculous for thinking otherwise—for keeping space between us.

"Oh, says the flipping *Poet Poisoner*!" I hissed. "Can you even count how many people you've killed?"

He straightened a bit at that, as if it shocked him that I spoke the title without choking on it this time.

The title he'd earned from the people he terrorized with his murders. His *murders*.

No wonder he'd killed the man who'd stalked me in Amalgard without even flinching. They were cut from the same despicable cloth.

"Yes, as a matter of fact, I can," he grunted, "and I have no intention of adding your name to the list."

"You expect me to *believe* that?" No matter how desperately I wanted to, if it meant I was going to survive this encounter...survive what I'd just found out about him.

"It's a *precise* list." He paused when I retreated again, a frustrated breath bursting from his nostrils. "Stop, will you?

"Why? So you can jab me with something and end my life nice and slow?"

"Oh, for the love of every sullied soul!" He flung his hands out at his sides. "If I wanted you dead, would I waste my time and my precious little patience arguing with you?"

That was a fair point, almost the same one he'd made in Amalgard—and the entire trouble in arguing with someone more powerful than you. They could *always* kill you the next second; and it never made sense when they hadn't already done it.

"Fine," I muttered, stalling between a pair of shelves. "I'll bite. *Why* aren't you going to kill me?"

"Because, unlike the bedtime stories I'm sure your mother read to you until you were a belligerent adolescent, not all assassins kill for the pleasure of it." Another stalking step my way; this time, I refused the urge to give ground, testing his words—seeing if he would take the invitation to strike. "Just because one is trained to kill does not mean one must do it indiscriminately. Or do I really strike you as the sort of man so full of bloodlust, I would just rip your throat out here and now to sate my appetite?"

I sincerely did not have an answer for the sort of man he was. I'd barely begun to sketch an image of him in my head as the person who'd saved me, and I'd rendered him entirely differently as the person who'd nearly killed Phin and left a trail of bodies in his wake, and now...

Now I just knew the smell of fennel and pine was masking all the other scents in this shop, and that my mind had managed to forget the precise blend of shadow-soft and steel-sharp in his tone until I'd heard it again, and that he *wasn't killing me.*

I hadn't had enough time to make any of these mosaic pieces fit together. So all I managed to say was, "My mother died before I outgrew bedtime stories, you insensitive bastard."

Another swift blink. "Condolences."

How did *that* manage to sound more sincere than his promise not to harm me?

"So, if you aren't going to kill me," I eased back another half-step, "then what happens now?"

Any answer he might've intended was abrupted by the unmistakable rattle of iron keys jangling on an iron ring at the front of the shop.

My head whipped that way—and the Poet Poisoner struck.

He lunged before I even caught the brush of his boot beneath the creak of the opening door, wrapping one hand around my mouth from behind; I stumbled into his chest as he flung us back behind the herbalist's counter, pulling me between the sprawl of his long legs.

I snapped an elbow into his ribs; he grunted and bent away from the blow, tipping his head to hiss in my ear, "*Do not make a sound.*"

A muffled, pitchy squeak was all I could manage—reminding him of the gloved hand over my mouth that made *that* practically impossible.

He loosened his grip, but his other arm banded around my waist, hitching me tightly against him. "If you hope to survive this night, we're going to crawl into the back room. And then we are going to *run* like every sullied soul is chasing us. Do you understand?"

Huffing, I rolled my eyes, though he couldn't see. *I'm not an idiot.*

Or, maybe I was—because when he freed my mouth and unwound his grip from my waist, instead of shouting at whoever was opening the shop door for aid, I *did* follow him.

On our hands and knees, the Poet Poisoner and I wove between the shelves to the back room where I'd entered—then we lurched to our feet, taking opposite sides of the doorless frame, listening to mutters and clattering in the front room.

"Is that who I think it is?" I hissed.

"Yes, that would be the assassin who owns this shop—"

"*Stop.*" I shoved a hand out toward him, shock filling my mouth with sweat. I'd purchased poison from an *assassin*?

"Yes, the *assassin.*" He seized the hand I'd stuck out toward him, yanking me toward the back door I'd slipped through. "And it seems she suspected I'd returned to Rastra, if she's coming to check things."

"Oh, you mean this isn't your *first time* breaking into her shop?"

"Clearly not, because if I was here alone, I wouldn't have been found. Now *run*, will you?"

Against every better judgement...that was what I did.

With his fingers wrapped around mine, we fled for the back door—jolted by a venomous shriek from the shop behind us. The snap of leather. A steely whistle riving the air.

I moved by instinct, surging forward, shoving the Poet Poisoner a step faster; we stumbled out through the back door just as a throwing knife embedded in the edge, a hairsbreadth from the side of my head. The passing as it cleaved by stirred my hair and stole the wind from my lungs.

The Poet Poisoner caught me around the waist like a Mithran waltz, spinning me down off the back stoop and dropping me into the street; then he leaped after me, and together, we fled—pursued not only by Mistress Merrietti's curses and cries, but by the shouts of the sentinels she'd brought with her.

CHAPTER 28
THE PRICE OF INFILTRATION

WHEN CALTEN LOTHAR HAD given me the choice to serve her family or face trial, I had never once imagined myself running for my life from Hadrassi sentinels, step for step with the Poet Poisoner himself.

But here we were, tearing through Rastra's lamplit streets like a pair of mischief-makers who'd shoved over an applecart. Except my cheek was stinging where a knife had whipped past it, and my heart was in my throat, and I knew at *best*, if they caught us tonight, I'd be carted back to the Fortress with some impossible explaining to do.

At worst...they would stick their swords in both of us. Him for being an assassin thief, and me for the company I was keeping.

I wished that thought was enough to have me veering off from him, finding my own place to hide from the clatter of pursuing footfalls and the shouts from the sentinels—first to *halt in the name of the law*, then to one another to *find them* as we pulled further ahead in our lighter attire, devoid of any mentionable armor.

But some feral instinct had me keeping perfect stride with the Poet Poisoner, letting him guide me deeper and deeper into the heart of Rastra...until we'd passed the bulk of the playhouses, and the lights faded behind us. The gaps between the buildings widened, and amber tones paved the path below our feet....and I didn't dare take my eyes off of him. Now that I'd caught up to him, losing my mark was the last thing I wanted to risk.

Finally, we started to slow; the Poet Poisoner took to weaving in and around shops, taking branching streets like streams cutting through the forest of potted plants and trees until, finally, he sidestepped from the curb—lifting a dangling sheaf of ivy with one arm, revealing an alleyway tucked behind it.

I would have never even noticed it if not for him. The way the tendrils grew and climbed, they knitted the buildings so tightly together it barely looked like there was any space between them.

Ducking swiftly inside, I collapsed back against the overgrown wall on one side, gasping for breath; as much as a healer's work kept me on my feet, I just wasn't built for the unfair amount of running this country had demanded of me so far.

The Poet dipped in after me, letting the ivy tumble back in place after he tore down his cowl to free his staggered breathing; we were quiet for a long time, both of us tense, straining to hear the distant shouts and clamoring steps of the sentinels on the hunt.

After more than two full minutes, our eyes finally found each other across the narrow gap; and all I could do was free a huff of hysterical laughter.

Because I was hiding with a *murderer*, who I'd just fled with. And somehow I felt safer here than with those sentinels pursuing.

For a heartbeat—if even that—his lips twitched upward, like he was almost about to smile. Then they settled again, and his eyes drifted aside.

"Your face is bleeding," he remarked quietly.

Grimacing, I shoved my sleeve against my face. "Well, better that than the back of my *head*, which is what I'm sure Mistress Merrietti was aiming for."

"Most likely." That huff might've been the closest thing to a chuckle that a man like him was capable of.

I glowered. "Why did she have *sentinels* with her, if she's an assassin with that deft of a throwing arm?"

"Because that is not common knowledge," the Poet grunted, "and to this city, she is a well-loved herbalist, not a woman capable of some of the most painful murders you can possibly imagine."

Oh, I could better than imagine; I'd watched it happen.

I wished I could blame my violent shivers on the cool night and my lack of proper attire; but that was adrenaline burning hot on the back of my tongue, somehow making the Poet Poisoner's company feel preferable to slipping out into the streets and fleeing back to the hostel.

Luck, I wished I were in my bed.

Though...there was something beautiful about this space, now that I leaned into it; the forgotten alleyway was so overgrown, and the lamplight so diffused through the thick twine of branches, it felt like we'd left Rastra entirely and gotten swallowed up in the heart of the forests that lined the road from here to Amalgard.

I leaned my head back, breathing in the scents of hardy autumn flowers and the rich, compact soil that mortared the cobblestones of this city. Calm rode in the veins of those smells, until I could finally loosen my shoulders thanks to them.

It was only then that I realized how narrow the alley was...that my chest nearly brushed the Poet Poisoner's with every breath.

He seemed to realize it, too; he flattened himself back against the opposite side, deepening his respirations, pinching his nostrils for a moment and then glaring at me when he dropped his hand.

"Who are you, truly—and why were you breaking into Merrietti's tonight?" His tone held a warning all its own: my answer had better not be a lie.

As if I could offer him anything else.

I kept my head craned back, searching out the place where the evening mist rolling off the channels wrapped the ivy up in a veil...so it seemed like the world ended just above our heads.

One. My world—my life—could end tonight, depending on how I answered him.

Two. I had two choices: a lie that would let me escape this alleyway sanctuary with my life. Or...

Three.

Infiltrate.

Just like Phin had said.

There would be no better chance to do it than now—when we were both made vulnerable by our shared brush with capture. When we'd fled together. When he'd seen me on the run, just like him.

This hadn't been my plan...nothing at all like I'd prepared for. But this was what healers did: when new symptoms arose, when patients took a dire turn, we adapted. We pivoted. It was what made us so valuable, so talented.

And it was about to make a liar out of me.

I'm sorry, Luminae.

Because I was about to break my promise...and deprive her of things to read.

"I am *here*," I tilted my head down, scraping the back of my skull off the cushion of ivy, "for my own reasons, not because of *you*—you self-centered, egotistical—"

"What *reasons*?"

Biting off my well-deserved tirade, I pinned him with a glare. "I needed the Lightbane, too."

He folded his arms, leaning back against the brick. "Oh?"

"Don't *oh* me, you bastard!" I shoved into his space, my breath fogging the chilly air. "Do you really think you're the only one who needs to brew herbs into a poison that can cause a painless death...something that *looks* like the victim just went to sleep? You don't suppose there's anyone else who's clever enough to make those connections, who *needs* to use them?"

I let a bit of the desperation that had driven me to Hadrass-Drui at a Shadre's command, and a bit of the havoc born from the night's events, seep into my voice; and the Poet Poisoner shifted just a bit, trading his weight from heel to heel.

"I know how you do it," I added—pushing into that shift like widening a scalpel hole in flesh. "I figured out your secret. The notes, the ink...you blend poison into it, don't you?"

Before I could so much as blink, he was in *my* space—his hand pressed over my clavicles, backing me against the wall. A plume of heady moss and ivy filled my head as he pinned me gently by the slightest pressure over my collarbones—with a gloved hand so tense, it felt like it could crush my sternum in one thrust.

"How did you come by that information?" he growled.

"I figured it out on my own." A kernel of triumph erupted in my middle. *Got you.* "That's where a nose for trouble will get you."

His jaw tightened, feathering a muscle along his cheek. "Who *are* you?"

"My name is Naomi Weathers. I'm a healer from Mithra-Sha, and I am running for my life."

His eyes narrowed—just slightly. "You chose an interesting country to flee to. Hadrass-Drui is not kind to those with a healer's heart." When I said nothing—unsure of what words might incriminate me—he added, "Is that why you were bound for the Fortress Ferregrand the night we met?"

I scoffed, squaring my stance and folding my arms. "I was bound for the Fortress because I was being forced there...escorted by those soldiers who died in the street. I had no other choice. I was sent to serve the Moravens against my will...and I managed to escape. So I came here, looking for that herb, so that I could make a poison just like yours...so I could finally be free of the person who's coercing me."

"And who might that be?"

A test. A challenge.

"Calten Lothar," I spat, and his brows jerked up. "She's holding something over my head. And I need leverage in kind...something to stop her in her tracks. So I came to Hadrass-Drui looking for poison that could scare her off, or stop her permanently. And now, thanks to you, I don't have it!"

"Sympathies." He pushed up from the wall. "And not my concern."

"Oh, no, you don't. You are not—" I pushed him back with a flat palm to the chest—then hesitated. "Oh. Huh."

He stiffened, a guarded light in his eyes. "*Oh?*"

"You have a heart stutter." Fascination unraveled the rest of my rant; I'd rarely felt that cadence for myself, though I'd read about it countless times in my studies at Harrow Hall. It was just a slight clip in the steady *thump, thump, thump* of a regular pulse—like a child miscounting in a game of hopscotch.

"*Yes,*" he ground out through gritted teeth, seizing my wrist in a surprisingly gentle grip and removing my hand from his chest. "Ever since I was a boy. And that means what, precisely?"

"Nothing, I just..." I blinked, shaking off my intrigue, grounding myself again in where I was—who I was with.

The Poet Poisoner. Not merely a man with a stuttering heart—one who *stopped* them.

"You are not going *anywhere,*" I finished my thought from before, twisting my wrist from his grasp; he released me immediately. "Because now that I've found *you,* and I know how you kill, you're going to help me...or so help *me,* I'm going to make you wish we'd never met."

"I'm already wishing that."

"Oh, just listen, will you?" I snapped. "I need more than just poisons to protect myself...I need coin to start a new life. And you...you know the Moravens are hunting for you, don't you?"

"I would be incredibly shocked if they weren't."

"Well, I just escaped from their Fortress, where they are *very* close to finding you thanks to some recent mistakes you've made...like with the Druavas?" His eyes widened a fraction, and satisfaction bolstered my boldness. "So I can help you stay one step ahead , if you promise to give me the poison I need and pay my way out of this city."

"A woman being hunted by Calten Lothar is desperate to turn against her family?"

"What—do you think they treated me well?" I scoffed. "I was sent here to face justice for something I did...not for a little reprieve. So you are going to partner with me, and we'll keep each other out of trouble until I have the herb and coin I need to make myself disappear."

I pocketed the other threat that sizzled on my tongue—that I could tell them how he committed his murders, and use that as a bargaining chip for my own freedom. Believable, yes...but it was a bluff. And if he called it, that might well look like him killing me to protect his secret.

Better if we were partners than people with knives at each other's throats...especially when he was the better one at wielding them.

He went back to studying me, the same way he had in Merrietti's shop, and in the streets of Amalgard when we'd first met...a night I was beginning to wish had never happened, for another reason entirely.

Deceiving him would have been so much flipping easier if I hadn't seen another side to him first—a side that could save. A side that could scrape a stranger up from a city wall and bring her calm in the face of her near-death.

But maybe that other side—that sliver of something like *humanity*, an entirely absent note in all of the ledgers and reports I'd read about him—was what gave me the courage to hold that stare while he searched me. Until he finally said, "Fortunately for you, I find myself on a bit of a shortened timetable which does make an extra set of hands and feet...useful. But I'm not prepared to merely take you at your word." A sharp tilt of his head. "Prove it."

I blinked, and waited for him to elaborate; he didn't.

"What?" I ground out at last.

"Prove that the Lightbane is what you need." He straightened, and so did I, sidestepping when he did—ensuring I never showed him my back, in case he decided it was still worth putting a knife in. "Go back to Merrietti's and steal it. *Then* we will have a bargain."

A stunned laugh burst from my chest. "I'm sorry...did you overlook the bit where that woman is an *assassin*?"

"Yes, an assassin—a prolific poisoner. Someone with an herb which, it seems, we are both in need of." The quick tilt of his mouth suggested he still didn't believe that particular lie. "So, if you are truly as desperate as you claim to be—and as skilled as you would like me to believe, enough to be worthy of a so-called partnership—you'll chance it."

"Why don't *you* chance it?"

"Because, as you were so quick to point out, I have made...a miscalculation or two of late." The words emerged stiff—like he was chewing them up and spitting them out.

"And you don't think *I* will?"

"If you do, I'll be rid of you." A casual shrug. "And if you don't, well...then my taking time to spare your life in Amalgard will not have been entirely pointless, will it?"

"You're despicable."

"Says a woman extorting a man for her own ends."

"Says the man extorting *me* for *his*."

"Good. We understand one another precisely, then, don't we?"

Unfortunately, we did.

I'd always known that gaining any level of trust from the Poet Poisoner would require proving myself—likely more than once. At least Luck was on my side this time: my brothers and I had grown up filching things from one another so often, I'd run out of places to stash their shiny trinkets.

What was one more?

"Fine," I muttered, "I'll do it."

"Good." He brushed past me, then halted when our shoulders grazed; he didn't glance at me, but I didn't need to see his face to feel the irritation seething in his next words: "While you're there, you can steal something else for me: bitterroot, mallow, poppy, and a tincture of hot honey and arnica."

"What in Luck do you need *those* for?"

"Is the answer the prize you would like to claim for fixing what you broke tonight?" He tipped his head my way this time, and I couldn't help finding and holding that glittering, dark stare. "Or are you still committed to shaking off the shackles that bind you to the Moravens?"

I gritted my teeth. "*Fine*, I'll steal your precious remedy, too."

"If you manage it, meet me here again in three days," he said. "Otherwise, don't bother coming at all."

"Just don't be late, *Kai*."

It was a small victory, being the one who walked away first—but that didn't offer much relief to my swirling thoughts.

I couldn't believe I was going back into an assassin's shop—stealing *for* the Poet Poisoner, of all people.

Not any more than I could imagine why he was also making me steal a remedy for infected lungs.

CHAPTER 29
WHAT'S LIVING BENEATH YOUR FEET

I DIDN'T DARE RETURN to the hostel until morning—and then, it was just to change my clothing, tend my cheek, and retrieve my satchel and belongings; because if Luck flipped its coin my way today, I wouldn't be returning to my accommodations. I'd be sharing an assassin's.

And what had my life even become, that *that* counted for the smiling side of Luck's two-sided mask?

That question rattled through my head all night while I walked, putting as much distance as possible between my weary feet and Mistress Merrietti's shop; contemplating just what *precisely* I'd gotten myself into and how I could've chosen infiltration in a city where I had no help, no assistance from *anyone*—not even the sentinels.

And mulling over the Poet Poisoner, what I knew about him, or thought I had...and all the new mysteries he presented.

I stitched my own cheek by lanternlight at the washbasin by dawn's first golden rays, breathing deeply through every twist of the sutures, holding my own gaze until the determination that met me was enough to slow my racing heart. Then I dotted on cosmetics, hiding the wound, painting around my eyes and plumping out my lips.

And then I paid the rest of my board and went to do the same thing I'd done the day before:

Deceiving an assassin.

The bell tinkled musically above the door of Mistress Merrietti's shop when I entered, my heart stumbling almost to a halt while I surveyed her countless offerings from the customer's side of things.

She really was an impressive herbalist, regardless of what dark designs her business was a front for; those rows of shelves, studded in plant life between jars like a version in miniature of Rastra itself, were even more beautiful from this angle. I couldn't help brushing my fingertips over the bottles as I passed—some simple, smooth glass, others blown and twisted into artful seashell spirals. Some so thin, they were barely wide enough to contain the herbs stuffed inside; some smooth and bubbled, housing thick, syrupy liquids I couldn't find a name for even when I rifled through all my lessons from Harrow Hall.

If it was anyone else's shop, and if I were here for any other reason, I could've spent hours browsing; instead I made my way hastily toward the back counter, already braced for who I would meet.

Mistress Merrietti was every bit as intimidating up close as she'd seemed when I'd watched her from afar this past week; and now I knew that her sharp angles and smooth, ebony skin and the vivid tones of lilac and cerulean she wore were a sheath for the dagger beneath.

An assassin, hiding in plain sight.

When our gazes met, a chill skittered up my spine.

"Good morning!" I splinted my tone with an imitation of cheer, burying my ears in my shoulders and shuddering. "A cold one, isn't it?"

"Mmm." Mistress Merrietti waved a hand. "What can I do for you?"

"I was hoping you could help me with a few things...my mother is sickly, a lung infection, I think."

Merrietti grunted, leaning back from the counter. "I have just the infusion. One moment."

She swept around the counter, and I followed her—determined to keep things light between us. "You came extremely highly recommended by everyone

I've spoken to in this city. My mother and I, we live in a little village just to the north...Umbrah, have you ever been there?"

"I can't say I have." Merrietti perused the shelves, plucking up vials of this and that—bitterroot first, then mallow, then arnica.

A smile tugged at my lips. "I suppose you wouldn't have much time lately, either. This must be such a busy season for you, given the sicknesses that spread this time of year."

"Among other things keeping me busy," she muttered.

"Oh? Like *what*?" I stitched a gossip's tone over the quaver in my voice.

"Thieves." Merrietti pivoted on heel, brushing past me, hands weighed down with the ingredients the Poet had asked for—and then some. "Nearly caught a pair just last night, sneaking into my shop."

"In *here*?" I made a show of sweeping the shelves. "How did they manage that?"

"With far more arrogance than brains to back it," Merrietti muttered under her breath. "Someone's been pilfering my private stores for years, but as for how he gets in and out undetected...I wish I knew."

You and me both.

"But why would anyone *do* that?" I trailed after her, keeping what I hoped was more than a knife-throwing distance between us in these close quarters. "You run such a successful business, and you're more than helpful!"

"Lowlifes and cowards." Merrietti upended the ingredients into a mortar and pestle and started to grind them.

"Could we add sallow seeds to that?" I asked quickly; her gaze jerked up to hold mine, and I added, "If...if you've got any, of course."

"*If I've got any.*" She jerked her chin toward the shelves. "Listed by name, ordered by letter."

I dashed away, making the most of the escape from beneath her stare. Heart pounding so fiercely it felt like it would drag me out the door without the tincture in hand, I wove between the shelves, searching for the *S* labels, skimming my fingers in and around the plants and jars with their placards.

I could've spent hours perusing, if every second of that time hadn't felt like tempting Luck for Merrietti to somehow realize who I was. It was almost a disappointment to find the sachet of sallow seeds and make my way back to the counter, crisscrossing through the staggered rows until I passed through the aisle of *Ls*...

And then I slowed, my heart lunging up into my throat this time, my gaze darting down the row and coming to rest on a corkscrew vial full of shadowed herb stalks that glinted in the low lanternglow from the rafters.

Lightbane.

Did Merrietti usually keep it on the shelves? Or was this a test for the thieves—for the Poet Poisoner? For *me*?

If it *was* a test, then she would check as soon as I left; and then she would know I was to blame. She could have all the sentinels after me by sunhigh.

Did I dare risk it? Was the risk worth more than trying to swipe the other jar from the shelf behind her counter...if she'd left *that* one there at all?

I shot a hasty glance toward the counter, fingering the pouch of Mithran remedies at my waist when I called to Merrietti, "Could we use honey, possibly, as the base for the tincture?"

"What else would I use for a—?"

Whatever else she said, the roaring of my pulse in my ears muffled it; I swiped the Lightbane from the shelf and swapped it with one of the pain-relieving tinctures from my pouch.

It was done in a second; it felt like a lifetime before I was back at the counter, slapping the sallow seeds down, hoping my staggered breathing was only obvious to me.

"I'm sorry, I'm not used to finding my way around a shop like this," I lied through a smile.

"No, surely not." Merrietti eased the sachet from under my fingers; it was a heartbeat before I could pry my hand back and let her have it.

I watched with what I hoped passed for fascination, not nervousness, as she mixed a tincture I'd brewed myself so many times I could do it in my sleep; it was an effort to resist the screaming temptation to lay a hand on my pouch. I didn't dare draw any attention to it, to my thieving fingers.

Luck, let this be over with soon!

All the breath rushed from me in a gust when Merrietti poured the thick tincture into a bottle at last, capped it, then handed it to me. "Thank you! How much will that be?"

Merrietti's sleek brows arched. "Don't you want to hear the proper dosage? Or did you intend to just give it all to your poor mother at once?"

The tips of my ears burned; I stifled a curse. "I had just assumed you would tell me after I paid."

"Cures before coin." She tapped one finger on the stopper of the vial. "No more than fifteen drops at a time. As-is would be best, but she can stir it into tea if she doesn't like the taste."

"Perfect!" I slipped the vial into my cloak pocket—careful not to reveal the pouch strapped beneath—then pulled out my coin purse. "How does five silvers sound?"

"For a simple tincture?" she scoffed. "I thought villages were harder off for coin than all that."

I met her gaze, deliberating for a moment; then I let a small thread of honesty slip free, stitching over the suspicion of a few too many flounders in a row. "The truth is, Mistress Merrietti...I'm a bit of an herbalist in training, myself. That's how I knew of your name, I've followed your work for some time. I've even sourced things from you, now and again."

"Oh?"

"Your reputation stretches far outside Rastra." I slid the silvers across the counter toward her. "And it's because of you that I've learned to treat the people of my village myself. That's earned me plenty of coin...coin I've been saving to start a shop of my own. But when my mother fell ill, I just..."

A memory of a wounded stare, of eyes like mine glazing over in death, stuck in my head like a blade. Swallowing was difficult; I could barely gather enough breath to speak again.

"I didn't want to risk the chance I might brew the wrong treatment," I whispered. "Does that make me a fraud?"

Mistress Merrietti studied me for a long moment, clever eyes searching out the truths I'd handed over...the bits of me that were still so raw after losing my mother, and after everything that had happened to chase me out of Vallanmyre, that no one could mistake them for a lie.

At last, she said, "You came to the right place. All of us, even the proudest of us, have something in this world we're too terrified to gamble with."

"Even you?" I offered a weak smile.

"How do you think I've held onto this shop, no matter how many thieves have tried to rob me?" She cocked a brow. "That being as it is, I'll take the five silvers, since you're willing to part with them."

More than willing; I'd learned a long time ago that people with full pockets tended not to look as closely at where the coin came from. And I certainly didn't want Mistress Merrietti looking too long at *me*.

"Thank you." I stabbed one last shard of chipper gratitude into my tone. "For understanding."

"Thank you for the patronage, little herbalist." She scooped the coins into her weathered hand. "I truly hope it helps your mother."

If only something had. If only all the knowledge that made me proficient in spaces like this hadn't come far too late to save her.

"That makes two of us," I murmured; then I turned and wended my way back toward the shop door, batting off the tears that gathered on the corners of my lashes.

"Wait a moment."

I halted on the threshold, my heart wrenching in my chest. The stolen vial in my pouch suddenly felt as if it weighed as much as one of the anvils in my brother Patrik's forge.

"One of those thieves I mentioned, from last night," Merrietti called after me, "I caught them a mark on the cheek, I thought."

Laying a hand on the door's frame, I plastered on the smile I saved for the bedsides of the sickest patients...then turned back to pin it on the shop mistress. "You must be even more talented than I heard, then, if you could do that to a thief. Though, well-deserved, if you ask me."

Her gaze fixed on my face, just to the side of my eyes—on my powdered cheekbone. "Well-deserved, indeed."

Oh, flipping Luck. Sweat broke out beneath my arms; I hid it with a tight fold of them across my chest, guarding my middle...wondering how close her nearest throwing knife might be.

"Mistress Merrietti," I infused my tone with all the saccharine sweetness I could muster, "I'd like to be a return customer, so I hope you're not implying what I *think* you are with that look."

"And what might I be implying?"

She just had to make it a challenge, didn't she? "One would make for a poor thief indeed, if they came back and purchased with hard-earned coin what they could have just as easily stolen."

"Hmm," she hummed.

"Besides...if I were to rob anyone, it wouldn't be a woman who'd made a name for herself in this profession. I'd rather learn from you than steal from you."

"I should hope so." Merrietti laid her clasped arms on the counter—the same counter Kai and I had hidden behind when she'd entered the shop the day before.

The bangles on her wrists whispered like a threat from the shadows. "Because I am not fond of competition in this city, girl."

Oh, sweetheart, I almost laughed, *you have no idea who's already living beneath your feet, do you?*

"Noted," I replied instead—then dipped a curtsy and ducked outside.

Walking away from the shop with my head and shoulders tilted back felt like exposing myself to a group of lecherous soldiers; and I could feel Merrietti watching me go, trying to sort me out.

That made two of us.

I didn't breathe easily until I strolled out of sight, turning down the corridor of lamp-lined streets that led to the city's beggar district...keeping up the lie.

Then I fled as fast as my feet would carry me, barreling through those streets and down twists of alleyways until I burst out at one of the canalside bistros, where the bustle of foot traffic would hide me from prying eyes.

Even assassin eyes.

I stumbled through the nearest wide-open bistro doorway, paid for a steaming mug of chicory cocoa, then tucked myself away at an ivory-painted wrought-iron table behind a redflower hedge; drinking it calmed my nerves, but it didn't stop my darting gaze from seeking Merrietti's dark skin and beaded shawl among the crowd for hours after. I didn't stop me from brushing the pouch at my hip a dozen or more times, just to reassure myself my stolen treasure was still there.

If this was what *infiltration* was going to feel like for the rest of my time in Rastra...

Luck help me. I'd go gray before this assignment was over.

CHAPTER 30
A MOTHER'S ONLY PRAYER

FOR TWO DAYS, I slept in the same alley where the Poet had told me to meet him, slinking out just to find food and mugs of cocoa and to warm myself by the occasional brazier. Thank Luck it wasn't quite cold enough at night yet that I had to worry about freezing; the curtain of moss and ivy actually made things almost cozy, almost enough like my lichen-dripping walls back home in Dalfi to be a comfort. Considering the Poet Poisoner himself had thought this a safe enough refuge to hide from the sentinels, I didn't harbor too much concern that anyone would find me and rob me in my sleep—though I kept my dagger close, just in case.

And the outdoor accommodations certainly gave me plenty of time to take notes with Audra's invisible ink in my journal, and to list out possibilities for why the Poet needed the lung cure...and to speculate how he would use the Lightbane, precisely. Like the concoction for Mummer's Dance, it wasn't an herb we grew in Mithra-Sha; I'd never heard of it before I'd seen him reaching for it that night.

Dreams of the poison's properties—and the cold, killing prowess of the man who brewed it—stalked my dreams both nights I slept in the alley. It should've been a relief to wake from them...and the first morning, it was.

The second, I stirred to the sight of a pair of shiny, dark boots and wine-dark trouser legs tucked into them, an inch from my drooling face and the pillow I'd made of my cardigan.

Yelping a curse, I scrambled upright, shoving back against the springy wall of moss and ivy; and the Poet staggered back a step, buffeted by my flailing limbs, holding out both hands like he thought I might attack him.

Possibly correct, because—entirely without my own noticing—somehow my dagger had ended up in my hand, unsheathed, aimed at his middle.

"Flipping Luck, don't *do* that!" I snarled.

"I was standing there, making *no* sound—"

"*That's exactly what I mean!*" Jamming my dagger back into its sheath, I rubbed my trembling hands over my face. "Luck almighty. I could've stuck that blade in your eye!"

"No, you couldn't have." The cool certainty infused itself back into his tone, so smoothly I wouldn't have ever realized I'd startled him if not for his reeling footfalls still knocking against the inside of my skull. "Nor should you try."

Dropping both hands, I glared at him—and realized for the first time that he was maskless.

His sharp cheekbones, firm mouth, and deep-set brown eyes might have been pleasant to look at, if he wasn't responsible for the racing of my agitated heart.

"I am tired. I am hungry. I have not had a proper bath in three days—scrubbing at the canalside doesn't count," I snarled. "So forgive me if stabbing you holds *some* appeal right now."

Since you're the reason I'm in these conditions.

He didn't meet the abrasion of my words the way I'd expected; he frowned instead, surveying the alleyway...my satchel next to my cardigan, the moss and ivy crushed a bit where I'd leaned against them for hours, writing in my journal.

"How long have you been sleeping here?" he demanded.

"Ever since you crashed into my life and turned it sideways." I scurried to my feet, tossing my cloak around my shoulders.

"Have you ever heard of a hostel?"

"Have *you* ever heard of being *wanted by the sentinels*? Because I am, and *you* are, but do I look like I know all of the places to sleep without spending coin?" I scoffed. "Any room I rent, the Moravens could trace to me. I'd rather take my chances out in the open."

A flutter of a shadow darted through his gaze; then he cast himself back against the opposite alley wall, opening his hand to me. "Well? Did you succeed?"

Scoffing, I plundered in my pocket and pulled out the velvet sack I'd dropped the vial of cure into—for safekeeping, padded with a handkerchief I usually reserved for my hair.

"*Here,*" I snapped, slapping the sack into his hand. "Your lung infection remedy. Speaking of, you forgot the sallow seeds. Without them, the infection could easily come right back."

Silence as I stormed past him, making for the mouth of the alley; then he gave a short whistle.

When I whirled back, it was just in time to catch the sack he tossed back. "It isn't for me."

"You mean your *infectious* personality hasn't spread to your chest?"

"I am...aware of someone who needs it."

I stilled, staring at him; confusion clattered down every rib on its way to drag my stomach to my knees. A quiet scoff tripped over my lips. "And what does that matter to you? You're an assassin."

"So you've mentioned." He stepped toward me, tucking his hands behind his back. "A well-connected assassin...one such connection with a daughter whose failing lungs are creating a distraction for her mother." He jerked his chin at the heavy bundle in my hands. "This cure will ensure her mother remains useful, in time."

My gaze dropped to the cure—a child's last hope. A mother's only prayer.

It was an effort to look at him again. "And...the Lightbane?"

A feverish glint dashed across his eyes. "So, you did get your hands on it."

"You thought I wouldn't?"

"I wasn't certain if your particularities would get in the way of acquiring it." He strode toward me, filling up the alleyway like a shadow stretching wider at dusk. "After all, you know I will use it to kill."

I met his unblinking stare, comprehension cracking my heart wide open. "*That* was the test. You knew I *could* get it...you wanted to see if I'd go through with it."

"You broke into Merrietti's shop with less qualms and quibbling than most thieves I've watched in this city." The Poet halted abreast of me, still peering down into my eyes—searching them again. "Not desperate...calculated. And you struck a partnership with a prolific assassin, hardly batting an eye." He offered a hand between us, palm upturned. "I wondered just how far you would be willing to go...and I believe I have the beginnings of my answer now."

Another challenge. Because there was still a chance for me to bolt—to run away from this moment, this choice, and take his poisonous herb with me. Which would leave him stranded for Luck-knew how long.

But I didn't.

And somehow it felt like making a choice I would never fully come back from, when I laid that vial of Lightbane in his hand.

CHAPTER 31
THE LEAST AND THE MOST

To my surprise, we didn't stay in Rastra proper; from the moment we left the alleyway, the Poet walked like a man possessed with a singular mission. And nothing was going to stop him from carrying it out.

We strolled past rounds of sentinels on patrol, none of them ever looking twice our way; we hurried down bends and curves in streets I hadn't yet explored, or even seen when I'd arrived with Seleni. The Poet led me through a pocket of the city adjacent to the beggar's district; then he veered sharply through a series of alleyways less overgrown, until finally he pushed aside a thin, slatted wooden gate woven with ivy...and we stepped out into a field of grass.

The earthy smells of the wild outdoors washed over me, and I sucked them in as deep as my lungs would carry them: loam, moving water, late-season wildflowers, even animal manure. I hadn't realized how congested my nostrils had become with the smells of Rastra's food places and competing greenery until I stepped foot in nature.

The Poet didn't pause to enjoy it; he led the way to a footpath through the thigh-high grasses that bordered Rastra's outskirts. There were still homes here, but they were spread out and far more dilapidated. The roads that led to and past them hadn't seen much upkeep...grass shoved between the cracks and wildflower clusters had bloomed and wilted at the edges, spreading their brittle stalks across the crooked stones.

We crossed over a series of interlocking roads through the widespread plots, then started up a rolling hill fitted with stone steps speared deep into the incline. The ascent was punishing on the parts of my hips that were already sore from sleeping on the ground the last two nights, and the house at the top—narrow, two-leveled, a soft sage-green with flowers muraled up the sides by a child's hand—seemed an impossible distance away.

To distract myself, I lobbed a question the Poet's way: "Where are we going?"

"I told you—to deliver the cure."

So...either he was stretching out the time before he was forced to make good on our partnership and show me to his dwelling...or he deemed this more important than making use of the Lightbane that had vanished into his pocket the second I'd dropped it into his palm.

I didn't know which possibility unnerved me more.

"Who are these people?" I panted.

"Again, as mentioned, the mother is a contact of mine."

"But who are they to *you*?"

A beat of silence while we mounted several of the broad stone steps; then the Poet replied, with bladed reluctance like glass parting from skin, "Her husband was...a victim of my enemies. His death left her stranded with an infant daughter to care for. When word of how he perished reached my ears, it was an opportunity I couldn't let pass...his widow was desperate for coin, and her profession as a housekeeper made her valuable in fielding information for me."

That was all he gave me; then he pulled ahead with a surge of his long limbs, mounting the last two steps and pounding the side of his fist on the door.

No one answered the first summons; so the Poet knocked again, louder, more demanding this time. It set my teeth on edge as I drew up behind him and bent to catch my breath; I had to fight to straighten myself when, at the third round of knocking, the door finally pulled inward a crack.

I'd never seen the woman on the other side before—but I knew her face. The hollowness of despair, the dark circles scoured below her eyes, the dirty tangle of hair from days without washing or brushing. Even the stiffness of her movements as she drew further into the light, a testament to bedside vigils that never ended.

The faces of people who watched over their beloved sick always ran like a continuum in my mind; hers was just the latest in an endless ribbon unraveling through the channels of memory.

"You're back," she rasped, shoving a lock of limp, gray-streaked black hair from her creased brow.

"I am," was all the Poet said.

"I know I haven't delivered on my reports recently." She wedged her body into the door, blocking our way; her pleading gaze was fixed so earnestly on the Poet, it made me bristle. Did she fear he'd come to hurt her? "I've been writing what I can remember every spare moment, but I've been let go from the position because of my absences, and—Sofi is—"

"Worse. I'm aware." The Poet didn't explain how he knew—or how he'd found out so soon after returning from his rampage in Amalgard. "That's why we're here."

At the *we*, for the first time the woman seemed to notice me hovering in the Poet's shadow. Her mistrustful gaze fixed on my face. "And who is she?"

"She is the reason I have a cure to offer," the Poet replied curtly. "Now, would you like to stand in the doorway, arguing semantics? Or shall we see to your daughter?"

She held her ground, trembling with indecision, her focus flicking to the vial.

Did she think we'd come to poison her little girl?

"Let us help," I urged, slipping up to the Poet's side and nudging him gently out of the way. "I'm a healer, a talented one. I can tell you everything that's in the tincture we've brought...none of it will harm your daughter in any way."

"But what if..." The woman sucked in a breath, a silver sheen sparkling across her eyes. "What if it's already too late?"

I knew that precise blend of guilt, grief, and terror in her tone—the worry that she was being offered false hope. That she hadn't done enough. That this was all her fault.

"As long as she's still breathing, it's not too late," I urged.

"Nera." The Poet's voice was soft as night and firm as adamant. "Let us in."

A moment longer, she wavered; then, cursing all sullied souls, she wrenched the door wide. "Upstairs. You know the room."

The Poet dipped a hand into my pocket, took the velvet sack from inside, and crossed the small space faster than I could really take in more than the home's basic details—a sitting room and a kitchen in cramped confines, bisected by a dining table and arrayed with windows. Then he was clattering up the wrought-iron staircase, and I had no choice but to follow.

The upper level was squared to the lower—two small rooms set on either side of the arms-width landing at the top of the staircase. The Poet ducked through the doorway on the right, but I didn't need to see him go to follow him to the girl's room.

Sickness was *thick* here—a miasma that persisted even with the windows flung wide to usher in a cool, cleansing breeze. Nera's daughter lay heaped under blankets, but her shivering shook the shabby bedframe even so. The pillows that propped her up were yellowed with sweat; delirious murmurs whispered through her chapped, parted lips.

She looked to be seven or eight years old at most; but the way the dehydration and fever bonded her skin to her skull, she was almost more corpse than child.

The bed creaked as the Poet sank down on its edge and unstopped the vial, resting its thin edge on the girl's lips; the sight drew me from my stupor—my assessment—and I jolted into the small room. "Wait!"

The Poet stiffened, his gaze swinging my way. "You have some objection to this?" His fist tightened around the vial. "Or is there something in this intended for *me?*

"No, you idiot!" I hissed. "It's...with the thickness of the tincture...oh, just let me."

I clambered onto the foot of the bed, lifting the vial from his fingers; he let it go, watching with guarded wariness as I wedged into the sprawl of the girl's limp legs.

"Sit her up gently," I urged, "let her lay against your chest, and lean her head back against your shoulder. Then tilt her chin up."

To my shock, he did precisely as I asked—scooting behind the girl, settling her in his grip with an unexpected gentleness, angling her head. I filled the vial's dropper, measuring it by the sunlight that angled in through the windows.

"Ready," I said.

The Poet pressed a thumb to the corner of the girl's mouth. "Open, Sofi."

Fresh disbelief thudded in my veins as her tense jaw slowly unhinged; her tongue lolled out a bit, and I counted aloud in a whisper through the half-a-dozen drops I squeezed onto her tongue...a child's dose, rather than an adult's.

"You have to administer this sort of tincture slowly," I murmured, "and the right dosage, or the analgesic could overwhelm her body."

The Poet watched hawkishly as I stoppered the vial again; then his gaze swept downward to the girl's face, turned against his shoulder.

"Poisons are equally precise," he murmured, "but I never devoted myself to this practice."

"Of course not. You're too busy slitting throats." We shared a look over the girl's head—a memory of the Luck-cursed night we'd first met; then I dropped my gaze back to her sweat-stained face, monitoring the twitch of her eyelids, the labored rise and fall of her chest. "In Harrow Hall, where I was trained, they taught us that healing and poisoning are the two sides of Luck's coin."

"And you chose healing."

"Actually," I tossed him a trace of a smirk, "I chose both."

The satisfaction of the surprised tilt his brows was short-lived. Every thought of my poison studies led down the same road, to the same memory: to the blood on my hands, to the anguished death throes, to the threats. To running away.

And I ran this time, too; I ran from the curiosity in those night-dark eyes, slipping from the bed and escaping to the home's lower level, where Sofi's mother sat at the table, a forgotten mug of tea growing cold before her. Head in hands.

The sight soothed something in me, maybe in a way it shouldn't have; because this was familiar. Of all of the things I'd seen and done since that meeting with Calten Lothar, I knew this proving ground. I'd lived it hundreds of times, in hundreds of infirmaries. Even in my own home, where I'd once had to all but dump Jaik Grissom out of a chair to break through the fog of anguished concern that had kept him stuck at Addie's bedside.

I laid a much gentler hand on the back of Nera's chair, and leaned over her shoulder to set the tincture bottle beside her teacup.

"No more than six drops at a time," I instructed, "and once she's lucid enough and the fever has broken, she can drink it blended into tea."

Nera's hand dropped to the table—then she shoved back a bit and twisted in her seat, wrapping her arms around my neck.

"I don't know you," she gasped into my shoulder, "and I don't know why you're with *him*, but—thank you. On my husband's soul, on everything I hold dear, *thank you*."

I knew this proving ground, too; and somehow, after all of these years, it still brought tears to my eyes.

"You're welcome," I whispered, stroking a hand up and down her trembling back. "Really. It's the least I could do."

When I found my way back upstairs—after telling Nera to send word through her channels if Sofi worsened—the girl was sleeping propped up on the newly-fluffed pillows, the Poet nowhere to be seen. But the door to the narrow balcony hung open, the curtains stirring like an invitation.

I took it, slipping out onto the small spit of railed wood that hung over the grasslands. The forest was visible from here, and a slim, sparkling twist of the faraway river. It was the perfect place for a child Sofi's size to sit, to read a book...to daydream.

I prayed to Luck she would have countless more days of that as I lowered myself by the railing and slid my legs between the iron slats—mimicking the Poet's posture, both of us with our weight balanced back on our hands.

"The innocence of childhood always surprises me," he remarked after a moment of silence. "Sofi has no inclination of what I am...of what her mother does, to keep this home in their family, to keep food on their table." A quiet scoff, low in his throat. "She weaves flower crowns when I come to visit. So utterly ridiculous."

"But you care about them," I ventured.

"I care for the information Nera provides. And I care that this sickness may have been incidental...or possibly not."

Gooseflesh puckered on my arms. "A warning to you?"

The Poet didn't answer; he simply drummed his fingers on the balcony.

"I've left a note for Nera," he said—and when I stiffened, he went on curtly, "a termination of our agreement."

"I thought you wanted the cure so she could continue her work."

"That was before I saw Sofi." A beat of silence; then he brushed a hand back through his dark hair. "She won't be well before my timetable closes. Better if we end our dealings now."

I didn't dare ask him if that meant leaving the mother and daughter stranded without coin; somehow, I didn't think he'd have risked all of this, or sent me back to Merrietti's, if he was simply going to drop them into the gutter.

I settled for the safer question: "And the work Nera was doing for you?"

"Incidentally," his eyes landed on me sidelong, "it seems I've already stumbled upon her replacement."

I scoffed, turning my gaze back to the river. "You had it *all* planned, didn't you?"

"Not to associate with someone of your talents, no. But that may yet be in my favor." He was quiet for a time, watching the landscape ripple with the passing hand of the wind, too; then he cleared his throat. "You weren't lying. You have a skill for healing."

"Healing was my life for as long as I can remember."

"Was?"

Groaning, I swept my curls off my forehead and held them trapped there. "Oh, look at me. I don't know *what* my life is now."

"Perhaps not." After a moment, the Poet surged up from the balcony, offering his hand to me. "But I can show you where it leads next."

CHAPTER 32
MANSES AND MURDERERS

THE POET'S LAIR WAS nothing like I had ever imagined—and I'd imagined plenty, with all that time sifting through reports about the murders he'd committed. I'd built a home for him in my head of bleak, black stone strung with torture implements. Maybe a modest chamber where he bent hunchbacked over a cauldron and brewed his nefarious poisons, chuckling wickedly while he worked. No bed or washroom ever existed in those notions—because when was he finding time to sleep or bathe, if he was busy finding out how to tunnel into the most well-guarded places in Hadrass-Drui?

So it was surprising when—after hours of weaving through the city streets when we left Nera's, our pattern so staggered that I'd never be able to find my way back without some sort of map—the Poet Poisoner led me to...a house.

Or, more akin to a manse, perched on the opposite outskirts from the river, set back some distance from the nearest cobblestone road on the other side of a broken gate and down a long, winding, overgrown path. We had to pass below a pair of weeping willows to catch our first glimpse of it, and I almost staggered when I laid eyes on its face.

Admittedly, it was derelict at best; the right word might've even been *condemned*. Utterly choked with more of the same creeping ivy that made such a presence in the heart of Rastra, it was almost impossible to discern the shape of the exterior; but it sported apexes and conjoined rooftop angles in addition to the same mansard edges as most of the city, and its jutting central half-tower reminded me a bit of Corylus's manse.

I slowed at the sight of it, ears tingling with the echoing crunch of our feet on the gravel path. The Poet didn't hesitate, striding up to the recessed double-doors and meddling with the doorknob. His curt movements spelled out a clear message: keep up, or be left behind.

Hopping up the gently-curved edges of the cracked stone steps, I alighted behind him, tucking my satchel more tightly across my front. "Who does this house belong to?"

"One might assume it's mine," the Poet muttered down toward the handle.

"One might also assume an assassin doesn't purchase homes in his own name...for the purposes of anonymity."

He scoffed. "Plenty of assassins have things purchased in their family names." A beat of quiet, and in it the lock gave way with an audible grind; then he moved on to another, and another, dealing with them so quickly I didn't even see where they rested in the wood before the door eased inward on creaky hinges.

The Poet turned to me, that same guarded look in his eyes from when we'd stood at Sofi's bedside.

"It is not purchased in my name," he confessed, "but it is purchased, and private, and has remained undiscovered for more than a decade. And if any of that should change on your account—"

"You'll kill me?" Probably not the best moment to swing at humor, but the chaos of nerves rioting under my skin got the best of me.

His eyes narrowed slightly. "There are other methods of ensuring you never speak of this place to anyone."

Well, wasn't *that* reassuring?

"Threat received," I muttered under my breath, slipping past him into the house before he could see the fear stitching itself across my features.

The shellacked foyer was a strange blend of dusty and shiny, thanks to the treated wood under my feet. A crippled, crooked staircase twisted up on one side, leading to a row of shuttered doors above. A wraparound balcony fed from there into the central tower, but I could only catch a sliver of the wooden stairs meandering up through the heart of it. Who knew what waited up there?

The Poet latched the door with a series of bolts and twists, then led me beneath the foyer balcony, through a short hall, into the first really impressive thing about this place so far: the kitchen.

I wasn't certain which I loved most: the bricked walls with a bit of moss sprouting in the cracks, or the iron-and-wood table and matching chairs that looked like they would take a team of men to move. Or was it the beaded chandeliers dangling over the marble-sided, wood-topped butcher's block island? The glass-fronted, jadewood cabinets set on either side of the stove? The hearth across from it, or the wall of convex windows looking out over a completely overgrown inner space, open to the sky, that might've been a garden once?

"Flipping *Luck*." I let my satchel slide from my shoulder, plopping it on the table as I turned a circle, surveying the whole kitchen. My gaze landed on the sink, stacked with dirty pots and pans, then scoured the empty cabinets, and I wrinkled my nose. "So, you're more like Behn than Felyx."

The Poet frowned, leaning back against the edge of the butcher block, arms folded tightly over his waist. "I beg your pardon?"

"Nothing. My brothers." Waving off his confusion, I snatched up my satchel again and stepped past him toward one of the doorways angling off from the kitchen. "What's this way?"

"Ah-ah." His hand caught me beneath the arm, and he swung me back around to face him; he was so near, only my satchel in my hands armored me against the brush of his chest with mine. "*I* lead in this house."

"Then lead on," I challenged.

His mouth jerked, burying a furrow into his cheek; he released me and slipped past into a short hall beyond.

The inside of the manse was built around that inner garden, and I couldn't find a pattern to the pockets of it that saw use or neglect. Some doors were boarded off entirely, and some stretches of the hallway that linked all these lower-level chambers smelled so thickly of dust, I couldn't bite back a sneeze.

But others, the Poet seemed to have a use for—particularly the largest sitting room, directly across the courtyard from the kitchens, which he'd converted to a study.

He'd shuttered and bolted over the floor-to-ceiling windows, drawing the velvet curtains across them for good measure. Two levels of bookcases lined the walls, reminding me with a melancholic pang of the comfortable accommodations at the hostel; and, just like there, the Poet had shoved a bed under the upper level mezzanine, the sheets stirred and spilling off onto the floor.

Everything else was taken up with an array of worktables: one stacked with ledgers, one crowded with bottles, jars, and beakers, another that more closely resembled a desk. It might've been the most normal space in the room, if not for the skull on a lacquered pedestal in the uppermost corner.

"Why...why do you have a skull on your desk?" I asked slowly.

"That is Giddy Gus," the Poet deadpanned, "and he gives excellent advice."

I swung a wide-eyed look his way; he stared at me without a flicker of humor, and for the first time I wondered if he was a sincere madman—not just a murderer.

Whichever it was...best to play along.

"Well, pleased to make your acquaintance, Gus!" I called across the room, my voice catching oddly on the angles with the bookcases and shuttered windows and muffling curtains. "And aren't you a well-formed skull? I'm sure you were quite the head-turner when your own head was attached to your body."

The Poet raised a brow; I raised one back.

"What?" I goaded him. "I may be in need of some excellent advice at some point during our partnership. And I'm certainly not expecting it from *you*."

After a long, fraught pause, the Poet went to the desk, slid into the shabby wingbacked seat behind it, and scooped up a fountain pen. Tilting it between his fingers, he watched me cross the room and study its corners, survey the bed and the bookcases, and finally halt at a small recess between the shelves that I hadn't noticed at first.

It looked as if it might've been a reading nook, once...in happier times. Assuming this man with his soulful, dark eyes had ever seen a happy time in all his life. But now the place where a sitting bench ought to be was a gaping wound of jagged nails and paler wood, and strung up in place of a portrait or tapestry was a map.

A map of Hadrass-Drui.

My breath hitched at the detailed rendering—and at all of the notes and strings pinned and wrapped across it, tying one place to the next.

It was the Poet Poisoner's mind on a map. It was his schemes laid bare. And, *Luck*, I wished I had Mahalia's talent for sketching, so I could capture it all...so I could decipher it and stay a step ahead of him.

I would have to settle for committing it to memory. Which meant committing to the act.

Pivoting on heel, I found the Poet standing again—one hand braced on the desk, and still watching me. But his expression had shifted from guarded reticence to something that bordered on the verge of pain. Like a patient in an infirmary who knew something was *off*, but the ache hadn't quite manifested itself yet.

Swallowing, I fingered my satchel strap. "Why are you looking at me that way?"

His jaw shifted slightly. "This is..." A rasp of his hand along his bearded jaw. "You are the first person to set foot in this manse since it was condemned. Besides myself."

"You mean you've never brought any of your informants here?"

"No one." The round of his throat bobbed with a harsh swallow. "This is madness."

"Yes, it is." At least we could honestly agree on that—from both our perspectives.

"I do not accommodate *madness* in my line of work."

All evidence to the contrary, his skull considered. But I couldn't let him continue with that line of thinking—not when he'd already brought me here. If he decided this madness was a step too far...

Most likely, I wouldn't walk out of this manse with my tongue. Or mine would be the next skull on his desk.

"Fine. You don't do madness," I acknowledged. "But you need the help, and I need the coin. And I doubt if you're going to find someone *more* committed to eluding the Moravens than me."

He eased back into his seat, that brief glimpse of vulnerability vanishing from his face—a man in suffering, masking his anguish. "I suppose time will tell."

I turned back to the map, giving myself a chance to smooth over whatever had started bristling in my core at that look. A healer's instinct, I supposed...a reactive need to mend a wound when I saw it, because that was my sworn oath.

You've broken that oath before, I reminded myself, fisting my hands until the sweat in the creases felt like a dying man's blood. *If you were ever going to break it again, this is the time and he's the person to break it with.*

I couldn't let an assassin's secret suffering matter more than the lives he was Luck-bent on taking.

I wedged nearer to the recess in the wall, my gaze gliding along the familiar angles of the capital—including the district Caspian and I had visited by carriage.

"How did you manage to infiltrate the most guarded portion of Amalgard?" I wondered aloud, fingers hovering an inch from the detailed sketch of the outer wall; inside its confines were more than a dozen pins jabbed deep into the map's cloth weave.

Some I recognized from the soul-sender reports—marks he had already killed. And others he must not have struck yet.

The hair stood at attention on the back of my neck.

"It only takes so many years to chisel through a part of a wall where no one looks," the Poet scoffed.

I clapped a hand to my mouth, muffling a burst of untimely, half-hysterical laughter. Somehow, the last thing I'd expected from a man of his inherent elegance was that he'd chewed through the mortar like an incessant rat. But maybe that was why no one looked twice.

"And Mistress Merrietti's shop?" I demanded, once I'd regained my composure.

"I doubt if she realizes there's a loose stone in her storeroom floor, directly beneath the table where she brews her tinctures."

I pivoted back to him, letting a corner of my smile creep free. "More chiseling?"

"Everything worth doing and having in this world is merely a matter of time and patience, Miss Weathers." The Poet reclined, kicking his feet up on his worktable. "I happen to have an indulgence for both."

"And you learned that...where? At the Academy of Assassins?"

His eyes narrowed slightly; after a long moment, he said, "There are countless places one can train to be an assassin. You have The Guild Garrotet, the House of Thieves, the Menagerie of Madness—"

"And who do they hire to make up their names?"

"These names—and these guilds—are older than you and I. Older than much of Hadrass-Drui...possibly even older than the Moraven regime."

"Which one did *you* train with?"

Though he wasn't moving already, a preternatural stillness enveloped him; it reminded me too keenly of soldiers readying to fire.

A chill squirmed along my back.

"I am," he said at last, quietly, "self-made."

"Well, that's two of us." I wandered to the desk, risking Luck-knew-what as I leaned my hands on the opposite edge and bent toward him. "Does this city have an infirmary?"

The Poet dropped his gaze to the array of papers and books before him and twirled his fountain pen idly over his fingers, not even sparing me a glance. "If by *infirmary*, you mean the receiving room of the soul-sender's lair, then yes." He licked his thumb and turned a page with precision and grace. "But Rastra has no organized haven for healers."

Not surprising, given the general feeling of suspicion this whole city clung to like a rich woman's pearls. "The destitute, then."

He sighed through flared nostrils. "What of them?"

"I can't have you being my only way to earn coin, can I? That will raise attention." I straightened from the desk. "And more to *your* particular interests...if I'm tending the ill and injured, I'll be able to move freely all about the city. That way I can catch gossip about the Poet Poisoner and report back to you. Would that sufficiently fill Nera's position?"

The pen stopped twirling. He pinned me with that searching stare; I held it, and didn't dare show him the rest: that if I was going to be helping an assassin, I'd need to balance the flip of Luck's coin with some charitable work. It was the only way I'd be able to sleep at night.

"Clever," he said at last, finally breaking his stare. "And, yes, if your patients have loose tongues, it should more than suffice."

I bobbed a mocking curtsey. "Then I should get to work, shouldn't I? Are we sharing this study, or do I need to go build a blanket nest under the table in the kitchen?"

He dropped the pen on the desk, lurching back and folding his hands behind his head. "What is your obsession with sleeping in uncomfortable places? Were you robbed of common comforts as a child?"

"Besides my mother, you mean?"

He blinked—the only shift in his expression. But somehow a kernel of vulnerability slipped back across his eyes for that brief moment. "How did she die?"

Oh, Luck...were we really going to do this?

How much *was* I willing to do, to *give*, to keep him from suspecting all the truths about me?

I bit my lips together, but it was a feeble attempt to fight what I knew I had to surrender instead...to pay him back for the chance he'd taken in sharing this place with me. Even if he was doing it for his own ends as much as I was for mine.

"A wasting lung sickness." Even after all these years, the words came out shallow and raspy. "She was the reason I studied healing...the reason I excelled at it. Every person I've ever saved, it feels like I get to keep another piece of her."

He was quiet, studying me; a low brush of sound moved the air around him, like his thumbs were tapping against the back of his head.

At last, he said, "You'll find a bedroom one door further down the hall. I suspect it will suffice."

I settled on another curtsey to put things back the way they should be between us—purely professional. "Why, thank you, Your Murderousness."

Then I retreated into the room he'd pointed me toward—before I could catch fire under the heat of the glare he aimed at my back.

CHAPTER 33
THE ONES WHO DESERVE IT

THE ROOM HE'D GIVEN me was...lovely.

I hadn't expected it, given that he was making his own quarters in the study. I'd envisioned every other hidden chamber in this place must be decrepit and on the verge of breaking entirely, infested with spiders, spooky to the uttermost.

Instead, I found the room down the hall from the study dusty but charming in its own way; the thick corner posts of the bed married perfectly with the accents in the wainscoting and the thick beams that crisscrossed the roof. There was only one bookcase this time—indented above the mantel of the room's private hearth—and the rest of the walls were taken up with old canvas paintings and a window that would've had an impressive view of the grounds, if those had been anything to look at.

It also sported a locking door, which offered a modicum of comfort. Still, I undressed and redressed faster than I ever had in my life, relieved to slip into my nightgown and pull on my cardigan rather than my cloak. Then I wandered the room that was going to be mine for the foreseeable future, laying out plans with every step.

This whole manse would need work to be really livable—and the excuse of cleaning up for my sensibilities would give me permission to snoop and study most corners of it. Who knew where the Poet Poisoner was stashing his secrets in this three-level lair? But I was determined to find out.

Dusting, cleaning, repairing...I knew how to do a bit of each, at least enough to win my way behind closed doors. And that would just have to be how we danced, because every step now had to be precise. Every movement had to count.

I was deep in those thoughts—and still wandering the room, running my hands over the grimy mantel and its decorations for the third time—when a throat cleared behind me.

My stomach flipped and plunged; it was the first time in hours I'd heard even another breath besides my own. Something about the slumbering silence of this manse made it feel like the sound of anyone else here was forbidden. Unnatural.

A quick peek over my shoulder revealed the Poet standing in the doorframe, arms folded; he'd shed his dark coat and rolled the sleeves of his shirt up to the elbows.

He cleared his throat. "Admiring the view?"

I turned swiftly back to the mantel, my hand tightening to a white-knuckled death-throe-grip on its decorative supports. "I was, actually. These corbels must be two hundred years old. They're stunning."

Fabric strained against rough wood as he leaned his shoulder deeper into the doorframe. "You know architecture?"

"My brother Conor is an architect." Melancholy drilled into my middle, and I let my hand slip away from the sleek wood. "I used to help him study for his assessments. It's an easy way to pick up on the names of things you wouldn't normally remember." I returned to the bed, though the room was too small to dodge his following gaze; I settled for ignoring it instead, busying my hands with laying out and arranging my things. "Was there something you wanted?"

"You're...settled?"

"As much as I can be, with everything hanging above my head." Most of which he would never—*could* never—know. Not if I wanted to keep that head attached to my shoulders and avoid being the next skull giving grand advice from his desk.

"Good." A labored pause. "You'll find dry rations in the kitchens. Make use of them how you will."

"Delightful. I'll use them to hit birds for target practice."

This silence tolled on.

I rolled my eyes, jerking my journal from its special pocket and tossing it on my pillow. "Flipping Luck, they're *rations*. How else would I use them except to eat?"

"Well, the birds that call this place home *are* obnoxious before sunrise." His boot heels scraped the floor as he shifted his weight. "This is an unusual circumstance. Hosting *guests* is not my specialty."

"No, that would be *killing*." Something I had to keep reminding myself whenever he showed those flickers of humanity.

That wasn't something I had to worry about with his icy retort: "You speak of my choices with a startling amount of disdain for a woman who claims to desire a partnership with me."

"You'll have to forgive me if this is still new to me." The words were an effort to muster past the pounding of my heart. "An adjustment from the life I lived before."

"Likewise."

Whether that meant he hadn't always been an assassin—or, more likely, that my presence here was as trying for him as it was for me—I decided not to press it. That acquiescence felt like the closest thing to a certainty that he wasn't about to toss me out of his lair.

So I settled for another question—one stirred up by the thought of finding myself unroofed by our bickering. "You said this manse wasn't bought in your name." I kept my gaze on the satchel as I unpacked it, refusing to glance his way. "So, what name *wasn't* it bought in?"

The length of the silence suggested he was chewing over the question—most likely sorting out whether I could be trusted with the truth.

It seemed absurd that I wanted to know. That knowing *mattered* at all.

"You may continue to call me Kai."

I blew out a breath, stirring the curls off my forehead and chasing away the freckles of memory from the night we'd met...the night I'd thought of him more as *savior* than *killer*, even though he'd become both for my sake.

At least it was better than calling him *the Poet*. And maybe a name, real or not, would ingratiate me to him...it would ease down his guard, so that I could poke past it. So I could learn if he did have accomplices, or a guild he was starting in his own self-made image, and just what in Luck was happening here.

Another short, soft clearing of his throat; when I turned, he lurched up from the doorway. "I'll leave you to it, then. But I expect you to begin keeping your half of this partnership immediately."

"As soon as I'm confident Mistress Merietti has stopped searching for my face," I assured him.

The slightest upward tilt of his chin was the only agreeability he offered; then he turned to go, and all at once my curiosity got the better of me.

One question I had to know—because it mattered to what I was doing, and what *he* was doing, and why our paths had crossed at all. And because it didn't make *sense*...not with the man I'd seen holding a little girl so tenderly today. Who'd spoken of her family brusquely, but kept a strange sort of watch over them.

Just like he'd vowed to keep watch over me.

"Kai," I said, and he halted just over the threshold, one hand braced on the doorframe still. "I have to know, before we go any further with this. These people you've killed, as the Poet Poisoner...why them?"

He turned his head, just slightly—not quite enough to look my way, nor did he try to meet my eyes. His face half-obscured by the arch of his shoulder, he fixed his gaze on the floor off to the side of his feet...but that expression was chillingly remote and achingly weary. As if he was watching something awful play out in the cracks of the floor.

Like he was watching blood spill across them...so much blood he'd become numb to it.

"Because they deserve it."

And that was all he gave me before he slipped away.

The only consolation that I would win to soothe my conscience while I played house with the Poet Poisoner.

CHAPTER 34
PLAYING HOUSE

WELL. IF I WAS going to play house with someone, I certainly wouldn't live in a Luck-forsaken sepulcher.

The conviction goaded me out of a room I might've rather stayed huddled in the next morning, after waking from a surprisingly restful slumber in a shockingly tasteful bed. While the Poet Poisoner was, presumably, still sleep—or perched like a gargoyle on a balustrade somewhere, imitating mortal slumber—I slipped on my coziest cardigan and fuzziest socks, and went to do some exploring.

The manse he called his lair was beautiful in a forgotten, Luck-lost sort of way. It was clear someone had once put thought into the aesthetics of it, from the artful emerald paint on most of the walls to the gold-trimmed wainscoting and crown molding.

Sealed behind half-ruined doors all around the manse, I uncovered a slew of bedrooms in various states of disrepair; a marble-floored washroom I couldn't believe he'd neglected in favor of *washbasins*; an art gallery full of faded tapestries and sun-bleached canvases I had to stop and admire; two more sitting rooms in addition to the one he'd converted into a study, the first just off the foyer and the other lurking behind the balcony doors on the second level, both fully furnished and devastatingly silent.

I even found a sunroom jutting out into the garden, the glass grimed with a patina of dirt and bird droppings. Its wraparound pool was overgrown with algae, but the thick scent of overgrowth and rot didn't detract from the most beautiful piece of the sunroom: a large piano in moderately good repair, set on a dais overlooking the pool itself.

Sitting on the piano seat, heels swishing the air, I envisioned the potential of this place...what it might be like to sit here, sketching notes in my journal with invisible ink, soaking in the sunshine without the cold of being outdoors. Without having to look over my shoulder for trouble at a tavern or bistro in Rastra.

I could make this place functional. I might even be able to enjoy it here.

I returned to the sunroom that night, journal in hand, thoughts whizzing like puffs of breath-blown dust I'd stirred up—and sneezed through—all across the manse that day.

While I'd explored and wound my way back to my room, notions had pulsed to life...ways of moving around Rastra and meeting my ends without arousing suspicion with my ill-suited benefactor. Now it was just a matter of recording them for my own purposes...with ink even the Poet Poisoner couldn't stumble across.

A night not spent in streets or in a hostel, and uncountable days in a place like this...I couldn't have chosen a better place to do my work.

Grinning, I spun around the corner to the sunroom's outer hall—and collided with Kai.

Elbows and clavicles and knees all cracked together; a poignant bark of shock tore through the shadowy corridor, and he ripped backward just as I did.

And dark, rich-smelling coffee splashed a foot high, plastering the entire front of his slate shirt against his abdomen.

"Oh!" I yelped.

"Sullied souls!" he cursed, staring at the wash of coffee down his torso.

"Oh, flipping Luck...was it hot?" I inched toward him, hands upraised, mind cycling already through all the various treatments for burns. "Tell me that wasn't hot!"

He flicked his dripping hands clean, pinning me with a withering look. "Would I be this calm if it was?"

I froze, my hands just shy of his sopping shirt. "Well...fair." That was all the permission I needed to draw back, nose tickled by the scent of maple, cream, and deeply roasted beans. "I'm so sorry about your shirt."

He made some sound of disgust in the back of his throat. "You st—" Breaking off, he rubbed a hand over his bearded mouth.

Startled you? I almost teased—but sobered before the words had made it near enough to my lips to curve them into a smile.

He'd been alone in this manse for so long that even his particular talents hadn't prepared him for another person coming around the corner.

"I started to say," I intervened, "that I've toured the manse, and I think you have something truly lovely buried under all the grime here. So, to keep us out of one another's paths...and to spare you any more coffee-stained clothes...I intend to bring it into some semblance of cleanliness and order when I'm not in the city."

Plopping the cup on the broken banister, he folded his arms. "Why?"

I labored through several long breaths. *Patience. This man might murder you if you say the wrong thing.*

"Kai," I began carefully, "even someone in your position *must* have some sensibilities about your house."

"It's a manse. It's functional."

"I have quite honestly visited graveyards with more cheer."

Scratching his jaw, he darted his focus away...then peered at me from the corners of his eyes. "Bold of you to assume you'll have the time."

"I'll make it. I'll have the evenings, at least."

He was quiet for a moment, glancing down to wring out coffee from the hem of his shirt. When no more would come, he said at last, "Fine. If that's what you require in order to endure this partnership...do with it what you will." He raked a hand through the air between us. "But keep out of my study. And away from the third floor."

I eased out my breath. *That went better than expected.* "Thank you."

He regarded me for a long moment, shifting his weight. "Why are you *thanking* me? You know you're no prisoner here. If you don't find my accommodations befitting, you know where the door is."

An offer blandly given...which took into account nothing that Shadre Calten held against me, or what would become of the Moravens if I returned empty-handed.

So I spread those very aching hands in a shrug. "I have nowhere else to go. And it seems you don't, either, so...why not make the best of this time we have together? And why not be cordial, at least, while I'm here?"

He blinked at me. I dropped my shoulders from their shrug into an arm-cross, guarding my middle as that studious stare pressed against me. Seeking a way inside, like a scalpel breezing through flesh, still mindful of muscle and bone and organ beneath.

"You seem...remarkably cavalier about this dilemma we find ourselves in," he said at length.

"I'm a healer. Every day of my long and storied career has been imprinted with making the best out of poor circumstances and even worse outlooks."

A wandering scratch of his bearded jaw. Then, "In that case, you are...welcome, I suppose."

That unexpected sincerity struck like a kick to the chest. I wasn't certain what else to do...how else to close the stilted conversation, other than to flash him an awkward smile and slip past his elbow, journal hugged to my chest.

"Starting already?" he asked as I passed.

"Actually, I thought I'd spend some time in the sunroom." I pivoted back on the ball of my foot to face him. "It's a beautiful place."

"Yes, it is." Something remote stole the deep rumble of his voice...softened it. Quieted it, like a long-held memory.

It reminded me a bit of how my chest caved in when I looked at the mugs my mother had made for us.

I tapped my fingers on the upper edge of the journal. "The piano there. Do you—?"

"I dabble."

"Ah."

A pause ensued, as utterly unlikeable as the stretched-thin silences between a floundering patient's breaths.

"Is...that where you were coming from?" I ventured at last, just for some way to break it.

A hooded glower. "*Yes.*"

"Oh. Well, I'm sorry I missed it."

His lips thinned. "Is that so?"

"My father played. I have an appreciation for the art."

"How wonderful." His monotone suggested it was anything but; still, whatever he was hiding behind that level response and eyes that wouldn't meet mine, I couldn't guess.

Another strained silence, listening for breaths and heartbeats.

"So..." I scuffed my toe on the flagstones. "Why not the third floor?"

He shot me a look so cold, I let the subject fall immediately, whipped around on one foot, and scurried away.

But that notion wouldn't leave me. There was something up there worth guarding and knowing about...which meant I was going inside, somehow, one day. One way or another.

CHAPTER 35
FLIPPED IN FAVOR

The last thing I had ever expected to find in Rastra was some sort of...routine. A pattern that made sense, like being back in Dalfi. And I'd never *imagined* that part of this infiltration would really mean pretending as if the hair on my arms didn't stand on end every time I left my room and locked eyes with the Poet Poisoner himself, just about to enter his study, a steaming press of coffee in hand.

But...here I was.

And that was where I stayed, for days...then weeks.

Every morning, I left the lair and returned to the heart of Rastra by a round-about way—never letting myself decide which path I'd take until the moment my boots crossed the threshold and I clicked the locks shut behind me. That way, there was never a pattern for any prying eyes to follow.

Then it was down to places like the beggar's district, or to look in on Nera and Sofi, who made slow, slow progress in the direction we'd hoped. Though I never asked to go in and see her myself, the fourth time I dropped by to speak with Nera, I caught her peeking through the balcony railing at me when I left; feeble fingers wiggled in a wave when our eyes locked.

The tenth time, she was downstairs, peering over the sill while her mother and I chatted on the stoop; to my relief, Nera was better as well, her smile no longer straining, her hair washed, her eyes brighter. She accepted the herbs I gave for Sofi's lack of appetite like I'd offered her gold instead, and the hug she wrapped me up in was so sincere, it took my breath away.

Theirs was a happier outcome than most I saw; for all its floral frivolity even on the cusp of winter, Rastra seethed with plenty of infection below the surface.

The lack of infirmaries, I learned, was a matter of coin—or more accurately, of lining pockets with them. Places for the ill weren't cheap, and someone, some-where, had decided that coin was better spent elsewhere...possibly poured into their own coffers, if some of the grumbles from the ailing I treated were true.

That left me with *plenty* of avenues to listen in on; word spread like wildfire about a traveling healer who'd come to Rastra, and soon my services were being begged not just from the impoverished, but from those inconvenienced to journey to other villages or the next nearest town for healing help. And the people who needed those services were all too eager to talk filthy about the people whose greed put them in these dire straits.

My favorite craft kept me busy from morning to evening, most days; I barely noticed when a fortnight had passed, and it was a jolt when I realized I'd been in Rastra a whole month—a passage of time marked not by counting the days, but by a Hadrassi feast that marked the end of the harvest season at mid-autumn.

All that time, if Kai committed another murder...I didn't know it. Those whispers didn't reach me, and he didn't seem to leave the lair even as much as I did. Which made sense, I supposed...he was likely feeling me out. Waiting to see if I would betray him before he showed his hand—before he killed again.

Well, Luck's coin was flipping in *my* favor, not his. I'd treated patients with long-lasting illnesses; I'd sat beside friends and strangers fallen comatose before, holding their hands, speaking and even singing to them, knowing that everything was just a matter of time.

I could be patient without so much as batting an eye.

So I never let myself show a flicker of haste in Kai's presence; I greeted him every day with a singsong *"Good morning!"* when we met in the corridor that housed his office and my room. And I didn't know whether to be grateful or irate that he never asked for my direct aid with his schemes or invited me back into his study.

At least, not yet.

Slow. Steady. *Patient.*

One. Two. Three.

CHAPTER 36
LORE AND LOVE FORGOTTEN

"WHAT IN THE NAMES of every sullied soul are you *doing*?"

Disbelief fletched Kai's tone from the doorway behind me—possibly the first time I'd ever heard it reach that pitch.

I twisted around on my knees on the kitchen counter, cleaning cloth in hand, the cabinet door creaking like a sly snicker to my left. "Dusting. You'd know that's what I was doing if you ever bothered doing it yourself. And also, good morning to you, too."

"You've..." He dashed his hands back through his dark hair, sticking it up at odd angles, then swept his arms wide to indicate the room as a whole. "You've destroyed my kitchen."

Well, that was just unfair. I'd actually organized his pots and pans rather well, and grouped the various dry rations in likewise heaps. Which was more than I could say for how it had been when I'd decided to tackle the project this morning.

"Actually, you were doing that well enough on your own." I twisted to sit on the counter's edge, gripping the scalloped marble, knocking my heels against the cabinet door below. "It's terrible for your health, having so much dust and things just lying around."

"I only move what I need," he grumbled, bracing the heels of his hands on the doorframe to the corridor where he'd halted and leaning his weight into his forearms—which were bared as usual with his sleeves rolled to the elbows. "Right now, what I need is coffee. And you have made that *impossible* to obtain."

"Oh, don't be a sourpuss." I jerked my chin at the butcher's block. "I bought coffee for you, and cocoa for me—before all of *that* nonsense."

The flash of my hand drew his attention to the thing that was keeping me here, and out of Rastra's streets today: a blanket of snowfall that rocked the inner garden to sleep. I'd planned my usual day of healing and snooping, but I'd only made it to Rastra's first ring of shops—and a corner café—before the wind and cold had put that idea to death. Most of the people I tended to help would be hunkered down in this weather, and I'd have plenty more to do for them after the snow passed.

Better to keep busy in the manse and try prying a bit of information from my so-called *partner*.

A partner who currently looked as if he was chewing over an impossible problem while he snatched the takeaway coffee in a paper cup from the butcher's block and sipped it; his brows lifted and his mouth crooked down. Then he tipped his head and surveyed the pitiful array of items scattered on various surfaces around the room. "Why the kitchen?"

"Because good things happen in a well-tended kitchen," I retorted, hopping down from the counter. "But yours is so paltry, I don't think *much* could happen here. You know you don't have a single dish or cup?"

He studied me for a moment, forehead furrowing. "Why would I need any?"

"To *eat* from?"

A quiet scoff. "I've been the only occupant of this manse for more than a decade. Why in the grave would I make more work for myself by using dishes?" He flicked a casual hand at the two pots, the pair of pans, and the lonely coffee press I'd scrubbed clean that morning. "I can just as easily eat and drink out of the dishes I cook in."

"That's disgusting."

"One could say the same about your sensitivities."

"*Ugh.*" I wrinkled my nose. "I am *so* relieved I've eaten all of my meals outside this lair."

Which was, possibly, as foolish as it was devastating to my coinpurse; but this whole month, I hadn't been able to bring myself to eat anything prepared in this kitchen. It was a strange piece of prejudice stuck like shrapnel under my skin; logically, he wouldn't need to poison my food to kill me, nor was that his typical method to begin with. I should've been handling his books with more care than the cookware.

Besides, this much eating purchased meals simply wasn't sustainable. So, scrubbing all of the dishes and arranging the food myself was today's necessity...but Luck save me if he thought I was going to eat from them like he did.

I slapped the dusting rag over my shoulder and adjusted the handkerchief that held back my curls. "I'm almost done, anyway...I'll be putting everything back soon. Is there anything you need my help with, since I'm trapped in here with you today?"

How I managed to keep a faint quaver out of my voice with those words, Luck only knew. The thought didn't bother me as deeply as it might have if we'd been snow-trapped at the beginning of this arrangement, but...still.

Trapped in a lair with an assassin had not been how I'd seen myself spending any part of my autumn.

He regarded me for a moment longer; then he tilted his head, beckoning me after him. I snatched up my cocoa cup, pushed the cookpot away from the butcher block's edge with a kick of my heel, then followed him to his study.

Excitement fizzed bright like a stimulant herb in my veins the moment we entered the crowded room; of all the places I'd spent tidying up in the lair so far—when I had the time and energy between my runs into the city—this was the one that felt the most like it would be a step in the right direction. A means to my ends...so many layers to look beneath. So many little symptoms to diagnose. So many ways of finding out what Kai was doing, and why...and how to stop it.

And it was also the first time I'd set foot into it since the day he'd brought me to the manse.

Opportunities had presented themselves here and there—when he was cooking his food, or making coffee. But every time felt like a test of whether I would take the dare at all. So I'd restrained myself, for *weeks* now, and finally...

Finally, I was being led back inside.

I had to restrain my excitement and measure my paces—following him to his writing desk, where he stacked aside a cluster of thick books so ancient, their dusty, papery scent stormed my nostrils and invoked a sneeze.

His brows lifted. "Should you even be cleaning anything in your state?"

"Oh, shut your ramble hole," I muttered, plopping into the chair he pulled over for me from the nearest worktable. Muttering a *thank you*, I twisted the stack of books toward myself, gaze caught on the familiarity of the binding style. "Wait...these aren't ledgers."

"Don't touch those." He reached for the stack; I swiped the top book out of reach, letting it fall open in my lap as I settled back.

Surprise caught my throat in a chokehold; of all the things that might've been inscribed between the pages, this was somehow the last I'd expected.

"This is a book of *poetry*," I murmured, glancing up at him.

He dropped into his wingbacked seat like I'd kicked his legs out from under him. "Indeed."

"Are you...brushing up? For your next strike?"

"No. I read these for..." He trailed off, spanning a hand over the next book in the stack.

"Fun?" I guessed.

"It brings a sense of relief." He let his hand fall from the stack to the desktop with a muffled clap. "I've always been fond of poetry. All of the greats...Besmeth, Kilgrave, Gavinor. They were my professors of sorts, the ones who taught me rhyme and cadence."

"And you use those to write your own poems." Somehow, even after a month of this strange partnership, I couldn't imagine that side of him...secluded in his study, penning poetry. Even the lines that would kill his victims seemed so absurd in light of who and what he was.

"Everyone has their ways of passing the time." Kai offered his hand across the desk; slowly, I settled the volume back in it, reading the title and the poet's name upside-down.

"*Lore and Love Forgotten,*" I murmured. "*Kilgrave.*"

"Tragedy makes sweeter poetry than romance." Kai set the book carefully back on top of the stack.

"So I've seen."

He was quiet for a moment, watching me...maybe hoping I would elaborate. When I didn't, he settled back in his chair.

"Well?" he prompted when I indulged a little too long in enjoying the fragrant steam rising from my cocoa cup, "what word have you caught around the city this past month?"

"Nothing particularly out of the ordinary," I confessed. "Watches are more vigilant than ever on the road between here and Amalgard, though people can only speculate as to why. There's been a few mentions of the Poet Poisoner being the reason, but that's only conjecture."

"Mmm." A nonchalant response—urging me on.

"Some people are wondering if the assassins will go into a lull during the winter," I added, plucking through the various gossip and rumors that I'd teased from my patients while I'd stitched wounds and treated infections. "There's been talk about the Moravens—"

"What of them?" Kai straightened, a bit of a gleam tracing the darkness of his pupils.

"I don't think it's anything worth mentioning. Just gossip about Athicus getting older, and what that means for Serai and her children."

"Hmmm." Less nonchalant now...a little too interested, for someone who had the capability and the lack of conscience to usher death along more quickly if he so desired.

"There's also talk about various balls and fetes upcoming," I changed the subject hastily. "It sounds as if Souls Day at the end of winter is something the elite love to celebrate in Hadrass-Drui, so the poor have been talking about it, too. Apparently they toss out plenty of scraps, whole spreads of food, and—what? Why are you looking at me that way?"

A slow smile crawled across Kai's mouth as he regarded me across the desk.

"Because that," he said, "is what I have been waiting for."

CHAPTER 37
A TREASURE OF ASSASSINS

For a heartbeat, I wondered if I'd given something away—something that doomed me. If he was going to lunge across the desk and slit my throat right then and there for some offense I'd unknowingly committed.

Instead, Kai shoved back from the desk and rose, striding to one of the three curtain panels along the study's back wall; he took the one furthest to the left and whipped it aside, but it didn't scatter dust like I'd expected.

Behind the curtain, there wasn't another window that never saw use—there was a door, plain and unassuming, with scuff marks on the stone before it that suggested it had been opened often.

Kai unlatched it and slipped inside, leaving it wide. An invitation.

It was more curiosity than anything that compelled me to hop up and hurry in after him.

The room beyond was windowless and dim, six feet across and twelve feet deep at most, and barely touched by lanternlight swaying in the shallow rafters. The stone walls gave off a chilly, abandoned odor, but that staleness was cut by the spicy licorice scent wafting from the worktable at the far end.

I glanced at Kai; he gave the slightest jerk of his chin, inviting me to investigate.

I didn't even have to step below the lanternlight to recognize the bottle swaying on a balanced pendulum atop the room's only worktable—a self-mixing stand. Its properties were given away by the other jars lined up beside it, waiting to be filled.

Glass inkpots.

"This...is your poison?" I whispered.

The poison that had killed Corylus and so many others, their names scattered across stacks of ledgers I'd left behind in a far safer place than this.

Kai nodded slowly. "I've almost finished distilling the Lightbane into a fresh batch. It's taken longer than usual this time, but with the amount you stole, I shouldn't have to pay Merrietti another visit...possibly ever."

Nerves chafing at my skin, I wrapped both hands around my cup of cocoa. "You...you're that close to being done?"

His eyes cut sideways to me. "What is it you suppose I have to be *done* with, Miss Weathers?"

"Whatever *all of this* is about." I gestured to the worktable and its brewings. "Or are you just planning to keep killing forever?"

He trailed one knuckle along the edge of the desk, his gaze remote. "If that's what it requires...yes."

I hid my shiver in a sip of cocoa, and didn't respond. How would *anyone* respond to that?

But when the silence stretched on past the point of pain, I couldn't help the next question that leaped from my tongue: "Where did you learn to make this poison?"

He stroked a finger along the pendulum, lightly mimicking its whirling track. "I invented it myself...with a bit of help from a friend, long ago. Crafting a new poison was a requirement of our adolescence."

Well. That wasn't the least bit terrifying, knowing he'd been brewing this poison since he was practically a child. "Has Merrietti always been your source?"

"Only since my friend and I were forced to part ways." After a moment, Kai pivoted from the worktable, leaning on its edge and snorting into a sip of his coffee. "I can still hardly believe you had the audacity to stroll through her front door and steal from beneath her nose, knowing what she was—and the very *day* after you first attempted to rob her."

I shrugged, mollified by the lilt of his tone. I liked praise when I heard it, even delivered as a backhanded insult from a murderer. "It was foolish, I know...but that was why it worked. She was looking for a thief to break through her back door again, not to come walking through the front."

Kai shook his head. "You are certainly the most interesting fool I've ever worked with."

"But not the *first*," I prodded.

"The first in a very, very long time."

I hid a grimace in my next sip. I'd been poking at the edges of that subject for a month now, and it always evoked the exact same reaction: he had his contacts like Nera, who were few and far between...people who reported things to him, likely because of extortion or fear. But none seemed to classify the sort of partnership Phin and Caspian had speculated about; and there was no trace around the lair of an accomplice, apprentice, or assistant.

Stitching together the scarcity inside the manse and Kai's patterns as I'd noted them so far, he truly seemed to be working alone. *Mostly* alone. But we needed to know the rest of his contacts before the Moravens swooped down on him—and them.

I brushed that thought aside before it could take root, focusing on the mixing pendulum behind him. "So, once it's finished distilling, you mix it with the ink?"

Kai nodded. "And then the work begins again."

"What you've been waiting for."

"In part." Kai's gaze drifted back to the pendulum as well. "You may recall I mentioned to you, your first day here, that there are numerous guilds of assassins in this country."

"Yes, thank you, that notion has haunted my nightmares ever since."

He cast me a look askance; I batted a hand, urging him on.

Turning, he folded his arms, reclining against the worktable's edge again. "They are often the ones who host these fetes and balls you've heard mention of. And there is one I am particularly interested in this winter."

"Which would be—?"

"The Jester's Jubilee." Feverbrightness flashed in his gaze with the next stroke of swinging lanternlight settling above. "It's to be hosted by the Guild Garrote at year's end, at the manse of Solomyn and Katia Degrace. And you and I will be attending."

The paper cup almost slipped through my fingertips when a jolt of numbness overtook them. "What? Why would you want *me* to go along?"

"Because you have proven yourself proficient at breaking into places, and stealing things—and deceiving people." Though his earlier praise had made it clear he meant Merrietti, I still couldn't suppress a shiver; I sipped my cocoa, hoping he would blame that reaction on the chilly room and not my raw nerves. "And we will be doing precisely that at the Jubilee."

Popping my lips away from the cup's rim, I studied him—struggling to think past a flare of panic. "You want to *steal* from a guild of assassins?"

Kai dropped his hands back to brace on the worktable, drumming below its edge. "There are other whispers in this country to which a healer wouldn't be privy. One is that the Guild Garrote has finally accomplished what *countless* leagues just like them have been attempting for decades…perhaps more than a century."

Oh, Luck…why did that make my stomach quiver with excitement? This was like living in one of Addie or Reiko's stories…I couldn't help the bounding of intrigue at the notion of a treasure like that, even if it was a treasure of assassins. "And what might *that* be?"

"They've concocted a truth-telling serum." His fingers stilled all at once, tightening to white-knuckled fists around the worktable's ledge. "And I am in need of it."

A puff of breath ghosted over my lips—it couldn't even pass for a chuckle. "You…you want to steal something that forces people to tell the truth?"

It isn't about me. It can't be about me. He'd clearly been planning this for a long time—and besides, he didn't need a serum to make me tell the truth. If he started carving into me, my weak constitution would give him anything he asked.

He had to know that, after this last month together.

Kai turned his head aside again, peering over his shoulder at the Lightbane. "Death, when wielded indiscriminately, becomes more harm than help." He spoke the words so softly, I wasn't certain they were meant for me; then his gaze snapped back my way, focusing again. "My marks have been chosen carefully over the years, compiled of two lists. Unfortunately, both lists are incomplete…and to craft a comprehensive ledger, I require truths that will not be given up easily."

"So you're going to steal this serum and force them?"

"No. *We* are going to steal it." Kai strode for the door, brushing shoulders with me in passing—a clear sign that I should follow him. "The other reason I agreed to this partnership—besides the need to replace Nera—is that the assault on the Jubilee will require two pairs of hands. And you've begun to show yours are at least modestly capable."

"I'm not a thief!" I argued, banging the door shut behind me as I followed him back into the study.

"Oh, but you are." He turned to face me as he backed away, lifting the curtain out of my way and studying my face in the shadow it cast. "A clever, capable thief…but you exude a sense of guilelessness that most at the Jubilee will find irresistible."

"You mean I'm *bait*."

"I mean that you are capable of whipping masks on and off, and that is precisely the sort of distraction we'll require at this celebration." Kai let the curtain fall, its drape whispering against my back—coaxing another shiver down my spine. "And, given the value of the serum to my purposes, I am willing to make you a deal."

"And what deal could *possibly* make that risk worthwhile?"

"I will let you name your price for coin," he said, "and I will show you the best way to disappear from this country."

Luck help me.

I'd never felt so cornered in my life—not even by Calten.

If I had been telling him the truth—about who I was and what I was fleeing from—that offer would be irresistible. And even though I *could* have resisted it, given I didn't need his coin or his help...

That truth-telling serum would allow me to learn everything I needed from him, all at once. If I could just slip him some, then his plans, his schemes, and the people who helped orchestrate them...

I would have it all.

And all it would cost me was possibly my life.

Swallowing, I edged out a nod. "All right, fine...*fine*. But we're going to practice and prepare for this, because I refuse to go unschooled into an assassin's jubilee."

He dipped his head. "Fair."

And that wasn't all; I was going to need a way to give him that truth serum without taking in any that would slip *my* tongue.

Fortunately, after all the work that had occupied my hands today...I knew *precisely* how I was going to give the Poet Poisoner some of that serum.

CHAPTER 38
POTTERED PLANS

THE SNOW PERSISTED FOR two days—two days cooped up in the manse, fixing what I could, dusting every room I could access and the sunroom twice. Two days of repairing the staircase in the foyer, with the begrudging assistance of the Poet Poisoner, who at first held posts and wood boards in place while I hammered in the nails I'd found stashed in a kitchen drawer; then, while I struggled to grip the banister and nail a board at the same time, he silently plucked both from my hands and effortlessly replaced me, his broader fingers fitting and aligning and affixing with ease.

Two days before I learned he *had* been seeing to the upkeep of this place...he simply didn't have a vision for its potential the way I did. He'd kept it coldly functional; I wanted it to be homey as long as I was going to be trapped here, keeping up this ruse.

Two days that weren't quite as unpleasant as they could have been, since Kai never said *no* when I popped my head into his study to ask for help with this or that.

But staying inside was the last thing I wanted to do when the third day after the storm's arrival dawned bright with sunshine again; the moment it pricked the sliver of my still-opening eyes, I was *fully* awake.

Hopping out of bed, I dressed in a flurry, barely paying attention to which Hadrassi dress I slipped into. I tugged my cardigan over the thin straps, then my cloak over that, spritzed on my signature perfume, and snatched my coinpurse and dagger before I stuffed my feet into my boots and all but ran from the Poet's lair.

It was time to put my latest scheme into motion.

The intoxicating dazzle of sunlight on snow put me in a mood so cheerful, I was humming in cloud plumes when I wound my way through the outskirts and into Rastra proper. And it seemed I wasn't the only one; there were flocks of smiling shoppers everywhere, people just as sick of being stuffed inside the same four walls for two entire days as I was.

Another throwaway cup of cocoa in hand—and with a wave to the owner of my favorite café that served it—I was off to spend my first day in this country entirely for myself.

There were more than a dozen potters up and down the various avenues I'd acquainted myself with in the last month; I'd always admired their wares through the bay of windows that displayed the best , although I'd never had any need to actually visit...until now.

It was time to put deception and other talents to good use.

It was time to be my father's daughter.

The day consumed itself in an array of window-shopping, dipping in through the occasional doorway and haggling like the peddler's grifting, gremlin child I was. The fact that Rastra was a city built one-third of honest folk and the rest of scoundrels and thieves—a truth made clear not only by the rumors from the people I treated, but the company I'd chosen to keep—made bartering a much less guilty pleasure.

It was even almost *fun*—a delightful way to use the charming smiles I'd perfected on grouchy patients for my own benefit. A chance to flaunt the kind of skills that used to make Addie roll her eyes and tell me I should've gone into theater, with how good I was at flashing on and off both sides of Luck's two-faced mask.

And maybe she was right; because by the time I left the last potter's shop in the city—which I'd been eyeing the longest and had the most hope for—all the intelligence I'd gathered on pricing and design from the others throughout the day had paid off handsomely. My coinpurse felt remarkably heavier by far than it should've, considering the beautiful hand-potted dishes wrapped up in the bag that bumped against my hip.

Those dishes would more than settle my squeamishness about eating after the Poet Poisoner; they would provide a vessel to slip him the serum without ever risking coming into contact with it myself.

That was only one portion of my relief. The other was the giddy, smug thought that if Calten managed to still strip me of my healer's title after all of this, somehow, then at least I might have a paying future in the theater.

The notion had me laughing as I stepped off the curb, bracing myself to be swept off in the stream of shoppers still packing the streets despite the dimming daylight—

And a hand closed over my arm, wrenching me off-balance, dragging me stumbling backward under the shadow of potted trees overcasting the nearest alley.

CHAPTER 39
CAREFUL STEPS, CRUEL INTENTIONS

THE SHARP SMELL OF fruit and leather jammed itself into my nostrils with the next staggered breath that tripped into my lungs. Somehow, I managed not to scream; instinct flashed into place faster than fear could take hold, and I whipped out my dagger from its perpetual place at my side, spinning and aiming it at where I expected my assailant's chest to be.

I had to aim higher. He was *tall*, and—

And his face, cast under the glow of the lamplights in the alley as he released me and jerked back out of reach of my knife, was *familiar*.

Painfully, horrifically familiar.

"*Phineaus*?" I choked.

"Easy!" the Druavas pleaded, hands still extended. "Hey—no stabbing, all right? I'm sorry I grabbed you, I just know how the foot traffic gets in the city, and I didn't want to lose you again...I've been looking everywhere for you!"

Lightheadedness made me fumble as I stabbed for my sheath and finally slid the dagger in; realistically, I wasn't going to impale the Druavas, even if he'd been asking for it with the way he'd revealed himself.

Luck, every *blink* had me seeing the murderer who'd chased me in Amalgard—the one Kai had killed to save me—

Kai.

I flattened my palm over my clammy brow.

They were both here. In the same city.

No, no, no. This was not supposed to happen. This was *my* mission, not Phin's.

"How did you *find* me?" I snapped.

Phin smiled sheepishly, dropping his hands and stuffing them in his pockets. "Lu spilled. She was worried about you...you disappeared over a month ago, and you stopped writing almost as soon as you got here."

Ugh, Lu. Not that I could blame her—I'd made the choice not to write to her, not to draw attention from Kai or from the Moravens, but I should've known *that* would draw more attention in itself.

I just hadn't expected *Phineaus Moraven himself* to come looking for me. And that he'd managed to sort me out in a city this large at all was a different concern entirely. "But how did you find me *here?*"

"Oh, that. Right, so...my family has some contacts here in Rastra, and one deals in herbs, so I thought, you know, you being a healer and all..." He flashed a lopsided grin. "Anyway, Merrietti said she'd met someone fitting your description, she'd been keeping an eye on you and she saw you went up and down this street a few times a week—"

Noted. Change routines.

"—and I've just been keeping an eye down it the last few days." Phin searched my face with anxious eyes. "Where've you been staying? You've been all right, with the snowstorm and everything?"

"I'm *fine,*" I muttered through gritted teeth. "You didn't have to put yourself out on my account."

"That was my choice. I volunteered."

"And I'm sure Lu is singing your praises about how you're the noblest brother in all the countries of the Wellspoken World." I snorted. "But you can go back and tell her I am *fine*, and I'm handling—"

"Naomi...*I* was worried about you." Phin's brows knitted, and he took my shoulders gently. "I know what this city is like, the kind of people who call it home...nevermind the rotting *Poet,* right? But you're here because of my family...because of *me.* And I know how much you mean to Arias." The mention of him lobbed a heavy lump into my throat, and Phin's mouth curled up gently to one side. "Don't worry...I wrote to him, told him you were fine, since I'm figuring you haven't been in touch with anyone if you haven't been with Lu."

"Thank you," I rasped—because he was right. I hadn't written to *anyone* in the last month...I'd been too focused on what was happening in the manse.

"Don't mention it." Phin's thumbs brushed against my shoulders. "Now, if your goal here in this city is to save me...you should probably know I'm never going to live with myself if something bad happens to you."

Flipping Luck, did he have to make it *this* hard to argue?

I tightened my fist around the woven twine of the purchase bag's handles, letting the chafe of fabric ground me a little. "I appreciate your concern...I do. And that you agree any danger I'm in here is at least partially your family's fault."

I waited for the fresh bud of a smile to bloom across his lips before I added, "But I can't manage this alone."

"Really? A trained assassin? *Alone*?"

"It's not..."

Not like that.

That trained assassin hadn't done me any harm; quite the opposite, in fact. And yes, perhaps I was being foolish, or feeling too comfortable in his presence...but I'd never once felt incapable of handling myself there.

Not until Phin gave me that *look*.

"It's not that simple," I amended carefully. "I've made strides since I came here. I did what you and Caspian suggested, I infiltrated—"

His fingers squeezed once, then fell from my shoulders; disbelief sketched his brow. "Wait. Are you serious? *Already*?"

I whacked him on the chest with the back of my hand. "See? I told you I was handling it!"

"You call this *handling it?* You infiltrated with an *assassin*, on your own, without telling any of us?" His hands smoothed down his stubbled cheeks. "Sullied *souls*, Naomi! We've got the sentinels looking for an accomplice for him, after what happened to me...what if they thought it was *you*?"

"If they were close enough to him to see me, they would already have him in chains," I argued. "But that's my point, Phin, he's let me in. He's starting to trust me. Having you here could ruin *everything*."

A slow, uncertain blink. "How *much* does he trust you?"

Discomfort wrenched through my gut; I shifted my weight, edging it away. "Enough. Why?"

A scathing laugh scraped from his throat. "I mean, I think we need to know how much we can wring out of him at any given point."

Something foul bubbled in my throat. *I don't like this.*

Careful steps had gotten me this far with Kai, stepping just over the edge of his confidences, letting me into his study...into his plans for the Jubilee. Phineaus had barely set foot in Rastra, had *just* found me, and already he was making plans for how to maneuver this scheme. *My* scheme. He was taking over without even asking, a smooth transition of power.

The exact kind of inevitable politicking I'd come here *alone* to avoid.

"I don't think you're being objective about this." I tightened my grip, hefting my bag more securely into my hand. "Not after what he did to you. And I still think it's best if I handle this on my own."

I turned away before those pleading eyes could trap me, stepped back toward the mouth of the alley and the bustling street beyond—then yelped when Phin snagged my arm and wrenched me back toward him.

"Sorry!" He freed me at once when I shouted, and I spun back to him, clapping a hand over the pulsing, painful circle his fingers had made around my arm. "Rotting bones, I'm sorry, Naomi, hey—are you okay?"

"Don't you *ever* grab me like that again!" I snarled—my head thudding with the reminder of a handsy soldier who'd liked to snare me the same way.

"I won't! I won't, sorry." He held up his hands again, then dragged them back through his hair. "I just...you can't leave. You can't play the game like this just for the sake of your pride. I *know* my family chose you for a reason, but that doesn't mean you have to handle this all on your own. You *can't*. Lives are at stake."

Including his—for reasons the Poet hadn't yet disclosed, no matter how much I prodded.

And even knowing that—but not knowing *why* he was targeted—Phin had come here himself. To protect me.

I focused on that—not on my surprise, or the feeling that I was being herded by the Moravens, or on the pinched skin all around my bicep—and I rubbed the tingling shock and irritation from my cold-nipped cheeks. Then I let my fingertips come to rest over my mouth, watching Phin's face...the play of concern and disbelief in his eyes.

"I know lives are at stake," I murmured through the cage of my fingers. "I'm not wasting time."

The last two days didn't count. Nor did the bag bumping against my leg.

"I know that," Phin insisted. "I also know this is dangerous, and two heads are better than one. Look, if he trusts you...can you slip out from wherever he's got you staying?"

Why did that question prick like a splinter sliding under my skin? "Whenever I want."

"Okay, good. Then don't shut me out, promise?" Phin urged. "We can meet up, talk, come up with a real plan for how to protect the people he's trying to hurt while you keep moving with the infiltration. Sound good?"

It didn't sound *awful*. But the thought of sharing this mission with anyone, especially the Poet's sloppiest mark, filled my mouth with sourness. "I'm not sure about this, Phin."

"But *I'm* sure," he insisted, stepping nearer to me again. "I'll be your contact, I'll be the one sending word to my family so they know you're all right. And I'll stay in touch with the sentinels on the city watch...I can make sure they stay out of your way until you've pushed him for everything he's got. Fair?"

Well, that *would* be helpful...particularly if Merrietti was watching me and ever decided to pursue the matter of her missing Lightbane and the thieves she'd run out of her shop.

I gritted my teeth against the feeling of being backed into a corner. "Fine. I'll meet with you at the tavern. But *I'll* decide what course of action we take to stop him, because I know his schemes best. Agreed?"

"*Agreed*," he echoed fervently. "Listen...give me two days, then meet me at *The Saffron Sachet Tavern,* all right? I'll have proof I moved the city watch, that way you'll know I'm serious about this."

"You had better."

And that was how I left him in the alley—blinking back my tears, relieved he didn't try to follow or accost me again, and fighting for breath against the feeling that I had stepped on thin ice, tumbled through, and started drowning before I'd even realized the surface was cracking.

I'd left the manse today for dishes and a breath of fresh air.

Somehow, I was coming back with a new secret...and one that could easily and imminently send me to my grave.

CHAPTER 40
LIKE A LOVER'S KISS

I TOOK A ROUNDABOUT way back to the Poet's lair—just in case Phineaus decided his chivalry outweighed his common sense.

Thank Luck, it didn't seem anyone had followed me. Still, I made sure to lay several false trails of footprints around the city, stopping and shopping here and there, waiting for dusk to muffle the world and mask my steps before I finally wound through the decaying verge of Rastra. Hopscotching from one clump of brittle greenery to the next across the manse's grounds, I scrambled up to the door from around the side of the crooked stone stairs.

Winded, panting, with sore calves and cramped haunches, I finally tumbled in through the door and shut it, latching it behind me. Then I peeped through the curtains that veiled the high, narrow, arched windows on either side of the door, watching for any hint of movement on the manse grounds.

Nothing. But, Luck, I couldn't *wait* for this snow to melt.

Swiping the knit hat from my head, I shook glistening drops of snowmelt off of my curls and ducked into the kitchen—then drew up short.

Kai was stooped over the butcher's block, arms outstretched and hands clasped, head bowed. It was a deathbed posture—the way loved ones bent over their dying family and friends, tossing prayers to Luck and whatever else for just one more day together.

I'd never seen him take that pose. Before now, I couldn't have even imagined it.

"Is something wrong?" I asked, letting the bag drop from my hand to the floor with a soft *swish*.

Kai's head jerked up, his attention cleaving my way so sharply I almost took a step back. A whole month and then some, and I still wasn't used to the quick cut of his movements, like a blade being drawn—or how breathtaking it was to bear the brunt of it all at once.

Palming the block, Kai lurched up from it. "You're back."

"What, did I surprise you?" My laughter sounded off-beat to my own ears. If only he knew why I'd been gone so long...I'd be a dead woman.

"Not as surprised as I was to realize you were gone."

Oh.

Well, there was that. I hadn't told him. And I supposed he *could've* been under the impression I'd left—fled—betrayed him, somehow—

I shivered; that thought felt a little too close to the truth today.

"Where have you been?" Kai demanded. "Leaving the manse after a snowfall is foolhardy—your tracks could easily be followed."

"Yes, I realized that," I huffed, shedding my cloak and biting back a wince as the skin where Phin had grabbed me gave an uncomfortable throb. "Why do you think I'm so late? I had to retrace my steps and make everything confusing, so now I'm soaked to the bone and footsore. *You're welcome.*"

"You would be neither if you'd stayed here today."

A tendril of the foul mood I'd been in ever since Phin's question about being able to slip away escaped now in a burst of coarse laughter. "You don't think I've had enough of being cooped up in this lair with you? Maybe I just wanted a day of something more than monosyllabic replies and the occasional murderous glare."

His brow tweaked upward. "You're in a mood."

"*What tipped you off?*" I pivoted with a scoff, my cardigan slipping down my shoulders and pooling across the crooks of my arms in my haste to snatch up my bag and stomp for the doorway. "I've never needed your permission to take care of my business outside this manse, and I'm not about to start asking now. So, if you'll excuse me, I have some drying off to do."

A tender pressure slipped under the crook of my armpit, so featherlight at first I didn't even realize it was there—not until Kai snagged me to a halt midstep, turning me gently back to face him.

But he wasn't looking at me; his gaze was riveted on my upper arm.

Marks of the passion that seemed to fuel Phineaus Moraven's every breath—a passion almost entirely absent from Kai—was stamped around my skin in a ring of blossoming purple-blue bruises.

"Oh." I hadn't even realized that was starting to show.

Kai's thumb traced the circlet of marks, so lightly it was like a whisper. Like a lover's kiss.

It raised every little hair along my body.

"Is there someone I need to deal with for this?"

Luck, I'd been asked that before—by my brothers over boys who'd broken my adolescent heart. By Jaik after he'd found me in the infirmary once, my eye blackened by a delirious, drunken patient who'd taken a swing at me while I stitched him up. By Arias, when he'd found me hiding in a broom closet, dodging the eyes of a malicious, harassing soldier.

When Kai asked, it was...different. A more permanent solution by far promised in the quiet seething of his tone. A ferocity I expected from an assassin, but not like this—not angled *my* way.

Or rather, angled at the person who'd bruised me.

A person I had to protect from him.

"No, it's..." My voice wavered, cracked; I cleared my throat. "It's icy still, in the streets. I tripped, and someone grabbed my arm to keep me from falling." I shrugged, but it didn't break his grip; and I hadn't really meant it to. "If bruises are the price to pay for not landing on my face in a crowd of shoppers, I'll pay it gladly."

Kai went on studying the bruises for a moment longer; the set of his mouth shifted, downturned. His jaw stiffened and his cheek ticked.

"You're a clever woman, not a fool." His gaze tracked slowly up from my shoulder, along the side of my neck, to latch onto mine. "You should be more cautious. You never know what you might be stumbling into in these streets...in this *partnership*."

"Is that a threat?" I searched his eyes for a hint of one—and wondered just what in Luck I would *do* if I finally found it there.

The shimmer that darted across his dark irises wasn't that, though...it was something else, something unfathomable that made my stomach twist and plummet. "I don't believe you need to be *threatened* to understand the threats you face."

"Kai, talking in riddles isn't actually helpful." I rested my hand over his, surprised by how wonderful the coolness of his palm felt against the warm, thumping bruises. "What is that supposed to *mean*?"

His thumb brushed against the bruises again, grazing the edge of my fingers and jolting a soft tingle through every one. "No one can be trusted in this city—in this country. My enemies are murderous ones, Miss Weathers. Most would consider the prize of my capture of far greater value than your safety. Remember that when you're alone in the streets...use that quick wit of yours, and stay out of trouble."

He dropped his hand from under mine, leaving me gently clasping the bruises, careful not to press. My palm was much, much warmer than his, almost to the point of discomfort against the pain banded around my bicep.

"But then I wouldn't be your little troublemaker, would I?" It was the only thing I could think to say—even when it sounded so ridiculous tumbling off my lips.

His eyes widened a fraction. His throat bobbed with a harsh swallow.

He turned away, spreading his hands on the edge of the butcher's block; then he lurched back up again just as swiftly, striding for the wraparound corridor. "There's warm water in the kettle."

Well, what did he expect me to do with *that*—make him coffee?

He was going to be sorely disappointed, then; because I took that kettle to warm the rest of the water coaxed through the pipes into the bathing chamber's clawfooted tub.

I'd be flipped on the dark side of Luck's coin if I was going to end the day cold and shivering—especially when I didn't know which shivers were from the cold and which were lingering from the way Kai had touched my wounds.

CHAPTER 41
AN ODDBALL AND A THREAT

I T TOOK ME AN hour to stop the shudders.

Not only because the water was just on the uncomfortable side of luke-warm—though it was—and not because of the extra hours I'd spent traipsing through the snow—though that was part of it. It wasn't even the memories of my unexpected encounter with Phin clashing against the argument with Kai or his warnings about this city.

It turned out that plain, old-fashioned nerves were responsible for my quivering muscles—because they were still tight and trembling when I finally left the bath, toweled off and treated my curls, pulled on my thickest pajamas, and went to let myself into Kai's study.

He jerked back in his seat, surprise stitched all across his wide eyes and parted lips when I slipped inside without knocking.

Maybe the fear and indecision from before had made me bolder. Or maybe it was the way he'd looked at the bruises now hidden beneath my cardigan and long sleeves that made me absolutely confident the worst he would do was glare me out of the room.

And that was if I *chose* to retreat, which I didn't. I had something to deliver.

"You may have plenty of enemies," I plopped my merchandise bag on his desk, nudging aside stacks of poetry to make room for it, "but I'm not one of them. So consider this a gift, from one partner to another who is in dire need of something to call his own."

Kai's gaze flicked to the bag handles, then back to my face. "If I stick my hand in there, is something going to bite me?"

"Has anyone ever told you that you are *entirely* too suspicious?"

"Suspicion has kept me alive all these years." But even as he spoke, he was tugging the bag closer, parting the handles, peering inside.

He went incredibly, incredibly still.

A kernel of unease budded in my gut—then bloomed into an odd blend of anxiety and satisfaction when he pulled out one of the matching pairs of plates and mugs. They dripped with shimmering blue glaze, patterned with silver speckles like a starry night—so utterly smooth, I caught the corner of his reflection in the surface as he turned the mug in his hands.

"These must have cost a small fortune," he said at last.

My breath whooshed out all at once. "No...well, they weren't precisely *inexpensive*, but...my father is a peddler. I know how to haggle for things of value."

"And what of saving your coin to start a new life somewhere, free of the Moravens?"

Weeks ago, that question would have felt dipped in suspicion...like he was searching for a reason not to trust me. But now...

Now it felt different. Like he was truly curious why I'd made this choice.

Why did he have to ask it that way *today*, after what I'd promised to Phin?

Wrapping my arms around my middle, I shrugged. "You don't have any plates or cups. It seemed ridiculous to keep eating and drinking out of the same pots and pans. And, besides...after the Jubilee, I'll have plenty of coin. It made the expense worthwhile."

"Fair." He went back to studying the mug, turning it around in his hands.

A small sliver of anxiety—almost *vulnerability*—scratched the base of my throat like the beginnings of a headcold. I eased a step nearer to his desk. "Do you like it? I thought the glaze and pattern would go well with the décor in the kitchen, but—"

"It's quite nice," he interrupted gruffly, setting the mug gently before himself on the desk. "Possibly the...nicest mug I have ever personally owned."

"Oh. Well." I settled back on my heels, warmth spreading through my middle—finally putting to death the last of those pesky shivers. "In that case, how about if I make us supper? Something we can enjoy on these new plates."

He pushed back from the desk and rose with an odd reluctance in every movement. "I don't have anything here but the usual rations."

"You may not —but I made an extra stop on my way back through the city." I slung my arm through the crook of his, drawing him out from behind the desk. "And we are going to have a proper supper. Dishes like these deserve to be broken in the right way."

Propped on our elbows before the fire in his study, Kai and I polished off a tavern-bought meal of potted roast and whipped potatoes from the nicest plates either of us had eaten off of for quite some time.

Tired as I was of meals purchased from markets and bistros, I had to admit, if only to myself, it had been nice to plate the already-prepared food in the kitchen, and brew cocoa, and bring it all into the study to eat in front of the fire.

Certainly warmer than a hasty meal on the way home from visiting the people I treated, or rations consumed in my room while reading and taking notes.

It seemed Kai's thoughts strayed the same way; after he stacked the polished-off plates to the side, and we both settled back on our elbows, sipping cocoa, he was the first to break the silence.

"Thank you for this." The words emerged husky, grudging—not as if he didn't mean them, more as if he wasn't used to saying them. Or having a reason to.

"You're welcome." I grinned, tugging a blanket off the sofa beside the hearth and pooling it across my lap. "Though I did it for both of us, if I'm being honest...I really didn't want to eat after you out of your pans."

"I didn't mean the dishes." That confession seemed to cost him less, though he still didn't look away from the fire. "The meal. The company. The conversation. It has been...lonely here," he said carefully, "for quite some time."

I pushed myself up on one palm, studying his profile in the firelight. "Do you do anything besides dream up poisons and new ways of killing? Anything that would help you actually *see* people?"

"I read and write poetry," he reminded me curtly—almost a touch of offense in his tone. "I visit Rastra proper when I have time." He gestured vaguely toward the study door. "We've already discussed my dabblings with the sunroom piano."

"All hearsay until you prove it," I teased.

He turned on an elbow, studying me with his head cocked. "What of you? What does a Mithran healer do in her spare time, besides mending broken manses?"

"Does a Mithran healer *have* spare time after all that?" I bent over my knees, smoothing the blanket flush to my thighs. "Honestly...my work is my life. If I'm not having meals with friends, or shopping sometimes like I did today, usually I have my head in healing books. Or poison studies."

I chanced a glance his way at that quiet admission—one that had earned me a few uneasy sideways looks from friends over the years. But he met it without fazing, one brow angling up only at my stare.

"Is that meant to frighten me?" A crooked tilt to the corner of his mouth. "A woman who is capable of healing as well as destroying...I find that magnificent."

I blinked, taken off guard at the sincerity of his tone; I'd expected something mocking, but the way he was looking at me—

Hastily, I turned my gaze back to the flames. "Well, you would be one of the first. My proficiency in both has always made me one of two things: an oddball, or a threat."

And, at one time, for one man...worse than that.

"I've just learned not to mention it to most people," I admitted. "Even around my friends and family. Fascination with poisons can only go so far before it's...troubling. Concerning. And if that ever tainted the way people see me, I could lose the chance to heal."

"Which would you rather have?" he asked. "The chance to poison, or to heal?"

"Healing, obviously. Poisons are intriguing, but healing is so much of who I am." I shrugged, resting my chin on my bent knees. "I see a hurt, and I mend it...even if it's someone I don't like, or who may be a threat to me."

Like an assassin I'd bought plates and cups for, with my own coin.

He twisted to look at me again, a strange angle to his brows and the turn of his mouth now. "Would you heal me, if I came to you injured?"

Holding his gaze, it was such an easy answer—possibly easier than it should have been. "Of course I would." Even if the Moravens might skin me alive after.

He nodded faintly, then settled back, draping one arm across his middle to turn his mug with both hands. "Healing was never a possibility for me. Poison is all but in my blood."

"Would you choose differently, if you could?" I ventured. "For a chance to heal?"

"Healing is for good men—and women." He tilted his head my way. "I left that light for the shadows long ago."

We sat with that for a time, which left me with an ache in my middle I didn't quite know what to do with.

In one sense, he was right—I had seen that about him from the first time we'd met. Most good men didn't slit throats without hesitation. They didn't poison countless people and rob families of mothers and fathers—or brothers, nephews, sons.

Still. The truly ruthless and terrible people I'd met didn't steal herbs for dying little girls, either, or hold them tenderly while they took them. They didn't agree to partnerships with runaways or give them places to stay...beautiful bedrooms in charming, discarded manses.

They didn't look at people the way Kai had looked at me tonight, when he'd seen those bruises...with genuine concern and a muted sort of fury at the injustice of an injury, accidental or not.

That was what the good men did.

He was such a contradiction, this poisoner sitting beside me; but maybe I was, too. Because I was a liar carrying a new secret in my pocket today. And because I felt no fear being beside him in spite of that, only intrigue...a warm, quiet curiosity that made it possible to stretch out my legs and lean back against the edge of the sofa behind me, almost perfectly *content*.

"Given our differences of view, we would make quite formidable opponents, I think," Kai muttered at last, sipping from his mug.

I went to follow suit—then hesitated, struck by a thought that had my fingers flexing tight around the handle. That had me lowering it, then turning from the flames to stare at him. "We could use that."

"Hm?" He cast a distracted look my way.

"Being opponents." The notion swirled like a diagnosis taking shape in my mind—symptom after symptom aligning into a mosaic all its own. "You were talking about a distraction being necessary at the Jester's Jubilee. What if we used our opposing talents to create a diversion?"

Kai pushed himself up from his sprawl, paying me his full attention now. "Explain."

"You're a poisoner. I'm a healer." The worlds spilled out more quickly as the notion built up on itself. "What better way to captivate an entire room than by someone almost dying—and someone saving them?"

Kai's lips parted, a silent rush of breath swelling his chest. "Strike them a wound, then close it."

"And while I'm closing it, you strike another one." I nodded vigorously. "Stealing that truth-telling serum."

His wondering gaze searched my face for a moment; he crooked a knuckle, sliding it deftly beneath my chin, tilting my head back just a bit. "As I said...*magnificent.*"

Then he bolted to his feet and hurried to his desk—most likely to start jotting notes for whatever poison he thought would do the trick for that sort of diversion. I stayed huddled by the fire, hugging my mug with both hands, watching him work...and struggling with another contradiction altogether.

My own head, which shouldn't have even come up with that idea...and my heart, beating out of tune, warmed by the Poet Poisoner's praise.

CHAPTER 42
WALTZING WITH TROUBLE

Another two days in the manse was not long enough to quiet all the havoc inside me.

Not knowing Phineaus was somewhere in Rastra. Not knowing I wasn't alone anymore. And not knowing either that I'd slipped more deeply into planning this mark on the Jubilee than I had ever imagined...and that it was *empowering*, somehow, to have cobbled together a scheme that impressed an assassin.

Havoc wasn't just inside me, either...it was all around me. It greeted me when I slipped into Kai's study the third afternoon since the storm passed and found it in disarray.

The furniture pushed to the walls. Even his desk eased back several feet. And the Poet Poisoner himself, fiddling with a hand-carved Hadrassi gramophone stand.

I strolled to a halt, frowning. "I thought that was in the sitting room on the second floor."

"It was." He dropped to a knee, tweaking and turning things within the wood casement. "And I appreciate the reminder that you've snooped in all of my rooms."

"Not all of them, I kept away from the third floor." Folding my arms on one of the wingbacked chairs scooched off to the side, I surveyed the wide span of open flagstone he'd laid bare. "Has my cleaning inspired you?"

He waved a hand without looking, indicating the mess around me. "Is this your definition of cleaning?"

A silly smile stitched up one corner of my mouth, and I pillowed my chin on my folded arms. "It is, in fact, my definition of *Kai has lost his mind,* which can be found just after *Kai has gone tripping down the stairs with a gramophone table in his arms.*"

"I did not—"

"Shh." I squeezed my eyes shut. "I'm enjoying the image."

Wobbly, deep strings and woodwind notes pealed through the room, setting me wincing at first; then, half-buried under them, the pad of stern footfalls.

I peeked one eye open and found Kai across the chair from me, one hand extended. "Come."

I straightened, comprehension dawning as I took in the space he'd cleared. "Oh. *Oh.*"

Lessons. Preparation for the Jubilee.

My good humor vanished, transplanted with a writhing ball of nerves as I took his hand. He guided me effortlessly around the chair and into the center of the broad span he'd cleared; then he set about arranging our hands and feet with calm efficiency, giving me less than no time at all to think about what we were doing. Or who I was doing it with, and *why*.

His touch was light on my arm—reluctant proximity. His jaw strained a bit as he looked down at me from the rims of his eyes, dark lashes casting feathered shadows on his sharp cheekbones. "What experience do you have with waltzing?"

I shrugged, then fought back a wince; the motion pressed the bruise on my bicep against the stiff ridge of his palm, lancing a brief bolt of pain into the muscle. "I went to more than my share of cotillions hosted by Harrow Hall." Though those had been rowdier and more impish than anything I suspected Hadrass-Drui to throw.

"Formal dances?"

"Only a few." Most had been at the Shastah, fumbling the steps with Arias and laughing until we were both in stitches. I wasn't an incapable dancer...just an inexperienced one.

Kai snorted, pivoting his hand to adjust my grip on it. "All assassins are versed in waltzes."

"You're joking." Laughter snorted from me, a bit harsher than I'd intended; but that was his fault, bringing me in closer with a smooth tug that set our feet a proper distance apart.

"Not at all. Waltzing teaches grace. And..." he shifted his weight, centering his stance in a way that felt almost...precipitous. Like I should prepare to be swept off any moment. "It allows one to canvass a room for threats while keeping one's back turning."

"Ah. So no one can put a blade in it."

"Precisely." With a roguish tilt to his mouth, we were off.

There were some similarities between Mithran and Hadrassi waltzes—how could there not be, with our shared border? The square and the steps were enough alike that I managed to avoid crunching the Poet Poisoner's toes as we turned.

But there was also something...sharper about it. The pivots, the angles, the brace of hands and the swivel of feet. It reminded me sharply of play-wrestling with my brothers...a surge of one-upmanship that caught me off guard where I was used to two dance partners melding into one another.

We stumbled several times when I was too slow to keep up with the harsh turns, Kai yanking me along a hairsbreadth before I could drag us both down. I bit apologies behind my gritted teeth, pushing myself to anticipate the pivots.

We staggered through a humiliating half-hour before Kai had enough. Releasing me with a scalded abruptness and stepping back, he dusted his hands on his trousers. "We'll make this a daily practice."

Luck help me. "Is that your very subtle way of suggesting I'm in desperate need of lessons?"

His eyes narrowed. "Subtlety is my way in most things, Miss Weathers. But since you prefer the blunt touch *surprisingly* often for a healer, allow me to paint it in crisp terms." He angled his head, measuring me from feet to eyes. "You, more than most, will be made vulnerable at the Jubilee. These people are my kind, they are not yours, and they are trained. So, yes, you will require more lessons...and more practice, to ensure that you can deceive some of the greatest deceivers in the Wellspoken World."

Sweat broke out in the small of my back. Flipping Luck...did the Shadre have *any* notion what she'd gotten me into?

"Well, then...what's next?" I demanded.

He studied my face a moment—which was longer than I liked. Then he jerked his chin toward the sofas and seats we'd pushed to the walls. "Blades."

Flipping *wonderful*.

I retrieved my knife from my room; when I returned, he'd retrieved his own, whirling it between his fingers as he leaned against the desk.

"Show-off," I muttered; but it was effective.

It reminded me exactly whose back *I* was putting a knife in.

Kai stilled when I came to him, knife gripped backhand in fist. "You have some training in this already. I saw as much the night we met."

"Life isn't always safe and simple for a healer." Not just the slums we occasionally visited to help the sick who couldn't find us themselves; but the people who feigned illness for a chance to get us close. To rob us.

And…because of the blood already on my hands. I had been looking over my shoulder longer than he could imagine.

"Indeed." He circled me, assessing my posture. "Talented, then. But untested."

He eyed the clench of my hand around the knife when he came back to stand before me; then his long fingers closed over my knuckles, his thumb pressing my wrist until my grip loosened of its own accord. His gaze hooked mine and held it with a primal steadiness; a reminder that these things that shook me didn't even sway him.

"We are doing all of this to ensure that nothing goes wrong," he reminded me. "That nothing happens to you."

I rooted around in the depths of my heart for a quip or a sharp retort, and found none. All I could manage was a faint nod.

Then we began our paces.

Kai beckoned me to show him what I knew first…so I did. The parries and blocks and strokes that Jaik and Wyat had showed me; the steps that put me in range and out of range again.

I was still nothing against him; if the Poet Poisoner had wanted me dead, none of these motions would have made me a match for him. Just as they hadn't been enough against the man who'd massacred my escort that first night in Amalgard.

But Kai had patience as much as predatory might; and while he didn't abound in praise, he was coolly efficient. Noting the places where my posture and movements reflected the talents I'd learned from those who might have actually been a match for him; assessing the places where my form lacked grace and function.

Gaps that could get me killed.

It must have been more than an hour of shifting, adjusting, correcting, practicing before he pulled his blade back from mine the final time and announced we were finished for the day.

"That's all?" I demanded. It felt like we could have gone on forever at that rhythm.

Kai's cheek flexed—possibly burying a smile before it could claw itself to life. "Crucial as this training is, I can only assume we both have other matters to attend as well."

He was right. Time was impossible to track in this study, and I…

I had a meeting to make.

Flashing him a quick grin, I hurried to the door and threw it wide, sticking my head out into the hall. My stomach somersaulted at the wash of light bathing the inner courtyard through the windows. It was almost time to meet Phin—and I still had a swath of Rastra to cross before I reached the tavern.

Hastily, I ducked down the corridor into my room, snatching up my cloak and leaving my knife belted on for good measure. I made sure to poke my head back into Kai's study as I passed. "I'll see you in the morning, I'm sure."

He was back at his desk already, poring over his notes; but his gaze flicked up at my return, assessing the drape of emerald fabric in the crook of my elbow. "Somewhere to be?" he asked mildly.

"Appearances to keep up." Swinging my cloak around my shoulders, I knotted it at my throat and cast him a smile. "Thank you, for today. I'm looking forward to our next lesson."

He scoffed. "If you're anticipating it with anything but insurmountable dread, I haven't worked you hard enough."

"Is that how *you* were trained?"

He waved a hand, bending back to his work. "Goodnight, Miss Weathers."

I could have left it at that; but I couldn't help studying him a moment longer, even when the press of passing time ticked against the beat of my heart.

He made an excellent point; he could have been cruel, commandeering, barking orders. He could have been like Galan Fiordona, a soldier wielding his brawn like a jagged weapon, making my days as a healer-in-training a living nightmare. He could have pushed me, berated me, taunted me...*hurt me*. And I might not have questioned it, given the gravity of what we were facing.

But instead, he'd been gentle and driven. Firm, but yielding. And I was leaving feeling like I *had* learned—my confidence bolstered a bit in this mad game Calten was subjecting me to—without any new bruises to show for it.

Subtlety *was* his specialty. And today, it had made me feel less like I was bait to be slaughtered.

"You're a good teacher, Kai," I offered.

When his gaze jumped to me, I offered a smile—then ducked away before I could make myself any later.

CHAPTER 43
DILUTING THE DRINK

THE BRUISES ON MY upper arm had stopped throbbing from the training session by the time I joined Phin at *The Saffron Sachet Tavern*, which I was endlessly grateful for. It would've made it harder, somehow, sitting across from him at the ale-swollen table in a remote corner of the raucous, seedy place, if my arm had still been sore from his pinching grip.

But it was obvious *he* was thinking about it; his eyes kept straying to my arm while we waited for our food and drink. And as soon as the barmistress shoved the platters of stew and tankards of mead before us, then sashayed away, Phin blurted out, "Look, I'm sorry about the other night. *Again.*"

"So you've said." I offered what I hoped was a reassuring smile, but the anguish in his eyes just brightened.

"No, see, that's the thing...I feel like you're trying to make *me* feel better, and you shouldn't. I mean, you shouldn't even have to." Folding his arms on the table's edge, he leaned toward me. "I can't stop beating myself up about that. So I've decided I'm not going to say *anything* tonight, I'm just going to listen. You tell me your plans, you tell me every brilliant thing you're doing, and I'm just going to shut up. Starting...now."

He sat back in his seat, scooped up a spoonful of stew, and gestured me on.

A tiny grin tugged at my mouth; it was a relief to talk to someone who did more than mutter or keep secrets or try to undress my soul with his eyes.

Rubbing a flush of nerves from my arms, I bent toward Phin. "So far, I've gathered a few things about the Poet Poisoner. I know the herb he's using for these murders and how he's preparing it. And I know how he's delivering it."

Phin's mouth popped open; he slammed it shut almost at once, rolling an eager hand my way.

My smile widening, I shifted in my seat and sipped my mead; it was no hot cocoa, but it certainly warmed me on the way down. Which I appreciated, with all the cold rain hurling itself at the windows tonight and all the tension that came from knowing what we were doing here. What *I* was doing—betraying one of the most prolific assassins in Hadrass-Drui.

I just had to hope the man I was betraying them *to*, with the might of his family name behind him, could somehow protect me if my actions ever came to light.

And even then, somehow, telling him about the Lightbane and the ink and the notes...it wasn't myself I was thinking of. It wasn't the fear of a knife across the throat if Kai walked through that tavern door and spotted me sitting here with Phin.

No, what kept repeating itself over and over in my mind—in the tingles dancing across my skin—was the way Kai had brushed over my bruises the night he'd first seen them...how gentle he'd been with them today. And the way he'd been hunched at the butcher's block when I'd walked in after my first encounter with Phin, before he'd asked where I'd been. And the things he'd said, when we'd eaten dinner together off the new plates I'd bought.

I didn't tell Phin all of this despite those things; I told him *because* of them. Because I couldn't afford to let a few quiet moments shared in a cozy manse—a few concerns, a few earnest praises, a few glimpses of humanity behind the assassin's mask—deter me from what I'd come here to do.

So I talked myself hoarse about what I'd learned of the Poet's methods; Phin listened raptly, sipping his soup in louder and louder slurps until the bowl was empty. Then he moved onto the ale, slurping at the same volume, his gaze fixed on me...full of wonder.

Finally, I'd told him everything I dared tonight—everything I could be certain wasn't enough for him to choose to end this mission and swoop in on Kai right now. I still needed more time, to learn more. And that decision needed to be mine.

So I gave Phin just enough; and then I sat back, a pit yawning in my middle, wondering why doing my duty felt like a betrayal.

Maybe it was good the Druavas had come to Rastra when he had. Maybe things were becoming just a little too entangled for my own good.

"You *can* talk, you know," I mumbled at last, trying to lighten the weight that had settled in my gut. "You have my permission."

Phin held his breath a moment longer; then it all came tumbling out in a rush of, "The thing is, with what you've learned so far...I think I have an idea for how we can get ahead of him."

Curiosity tilted my head as I helped myself to a spoonful of room-temperature stew. "How do you mean?"

"Well, since you're infiltrating, it's too soon to show your hand...to turn on him." Phin drummed his fingers on the tabletop. "But we can't just let him get away with killing innocent people."

"*Precisely*." Relief gusted out my breath, too—that he was touching on the fear that had kept me awake more nights in the lair than I could count, worrying about what I would do when the Poet Poisoner *did* come back from a kill.

"So, here's what I'm thinking." Arms crossed on the table, Phin leaned toward me again. "You're a good healer. You think you could dilute the poison?"

I settled back in my seat, struck by the thought—and surprised I hadn't considered it myself in the last handful of days since Kai had let me through the hidden door in his study.

Had I just been so stricken that he'd let me into that private confidence at all, and that we'd begun conspiring together about the Jubilee, that I'd missed how I could use it to my advantage?

"I...I think so," I hedged. "I'll have to do a bit of research on its properties, but...it's entirely possible, since poisons aren't entirely different from medicines. And we dilute those all the time, for different constitutions, for children—"

"Great!" Phin clapped a hand on the tabletop. "If you can take the edge off the poison, then maybe we can trick the Poet...make him *think* his victims are dead, while they're really just unconscious."

Holding his gaze, the realization dawned—his plan conferred in the moment of quiet that hung between us.

"Then you send sentinels to swoop in," I murmured, "and they make the people disappear."

"Exactly." Phin snapped his fingers and pointed my way, leaning back in his chair. "He thinks they're dead...we keep them safe."

"And the Poet is never any the wiser I altered his recipe."

"Can you do it?" Phin's eyes flashed with concern as he cocked his head. "I know it's asking a lot. If he catches you—"

"I can do it." I had to—if it gave us a chance to spare innocent lives, then my nerves weren't reason enough not to try.

"*Excellent*." Phin's grin was brighter than the lanternlight glowing on the edge of our table. "I know this will keep you busy, so I won't pry...I'll be working with the sentinels in the meantime. Just, whenever you need to get in touch, or want to meet with me again…go to Merrietti's shop and give her a note. She'll get it to me."

Oh, the inescapable irony of all of this. It was going to be the death of me.

If the mission didn't get to me first.

CHAPTER 44
LIFE BEHIND CLOSED DOORS

THERE WAS SOMEONE ELSE besides us in the manse.

That was my first thought a week later when I padded down the hall to Kai's study, steaming mugs of coffee in hand—and caught the rumble of indiscernible dialogue hovering beyond the door.

I might've thought my groggy mind was mishearing things...if I hadn't already been awake since before dawn, fiddling with my herbs and tinctures and reading through my books on poisons and healing to perfect the recipe I'd determined to dilute the effects of Lightbane. It would require another visit to Mistress Merrietti's shop—something I felt much better about knowing I had Phin's connection to her stashed in my pocket—and until now, the notion of brewing the dilution had been the most unpleasant part of my day.

Until I heard the muttering.

"I'm aware it's not conventional." That was Kai's voice—that unmistakable, shadow-soft growl I'd come to recognize over the last several weeks. "And none of it is according to plan. But it does make things...easier."

Silence. Like he was waiting for a reply.

My heart pounded so hard my sternum ached as I tiptoed to the door, leaning my ear against it. I heard no reply, but that didn't mean someone else wasn't speaking; especially when he went on, even more quietly, "It makes things so much easier, it terrifies me."

My hackles bristled a bit.

What was I going to do if I nudged open this door and saw precisely what Caspian and Phin had feared—an accomplice in there? Someone he actually *did* trust enough to let into the manse...someone he trusted as much, or more, than me?

I gripped the handles of our coffee mugs so tightly, they bit into my palms. *Best to get it over with, then.*

"Good *morning*, Kai!" I twisted the knob with my elbow and pushed inside. "Good morning—"

I halted.

There was no one else here. Just Kai, sitting at the desk, drumming his pen on its edge while he surveyed a small map splayed out before him. He didn't even look up when he said, "You didn't knock."

"I...just brought you coffee, I didn't think it required knocking." I eased the door shut with my haunches, peering around the room. Not a whisper of a moving curtain...no hint some other occupant had fled before I entered. "Who are you talking to?"

He raised his gaze just enough to lock eyes with Giddy Gus's empty sockets; after a long, silent moment, I was absolutely convinced he was going to admit he'd been conversing with the skull.

So I wasn't prepared for his quiet reply: "I have been alone for much of the latter half of my life." A strained swallow punctuated the confession. "Sometimes, the silence is...too much. Even for me."

His gaze flicked to meet mine, a silent, lethal glare—daring me to mock him. To call his sanity into question, even.

Luck, if only.

"I know exactly what you mean."

His slow blink was the only sign I'd surprised him.

I eased into the chair across the desk—which he hadn't moved back after our last conference here—and settled the mugs on the desk.

"Back home, in Dalfi," I explained, "because of what I did, the thing that put me on the run, I...I could never afford to let people close. Not my family, not even my dearest friends." I paused, breath catching, waiting for him to ask the inevitable *why*—the press into what I'd done.

He only watched me, silent and still.

Relief pushed the tumble of words from my lips: "I was alone in my house most of the time. I'd greet people in the street, and talk to my patients, of course, but it never felt safe to let anyone in past my front door. The only reason that ever changed was because my oldest and best friend was dying, and I was the only one who could save her."

My hands spasmed into fists around the rag, remembering that treacherous day and the ones that had followed—when Addie had been clinging to life, and Jaik and I had held on to her with all our might. And when it had been a struggle even to see her, to have her under my roof, knowing she was *so close* to my secrets. My painful choices.

"It's...incredibly lonely," I added softly. "Living behind a closed door, terrified of anyone knowing the truth of who you are."

For a moment, the tap of his pen on the edge of the desk was the only sound between us. Then, equally soft, "Yes, it is."

I offered him a tenuous smile. "Maybe it's not the worst fate in the world, that we're stuck with one another. That we have no choice but to be behind the same locked doors."

Kai leaned against the edge of his desk, folded his hands together. Sighed. "I can imagine worse."

We were both left silent, pondering what *worse* and *worst* might look like, until finally Kai sat tall again.

"Speaking of worse things," he added gruffly, "I have business to attend tonight."

"Business—?" I began—then broke off at his pointed look. "Oh."

There it was. The thing I'd been anticipating and dreading for over a month.

"There is a convoy passing nearby," he said, scraping his cup of coffee nearer and taking a careful sip; his mouth tilted down at the corners, chin wrinkling and brows rising. Then he helped himself to a second, longer gulp. "An unlikely chance to pass along a note."

I gripped my own mug so tightly, my knuckles strained.

I wouldn't have time to dilute the poison before he left...I hadn't even gone to Merrietti's shop for the proper agent. But tonight, when he was gone...

Tonight might be the only chance I had.

"I have you to thank," Kai added, tugging me out of the heart-pounding spiral that notion sent me sliding into. "If not for the gossip from your contacts this week, I wouldn't have known Raversen's convoy was passing so near Rastra."

Raversen. He'd been mentioned by a woman I was treating for necrotic toes; a prolific businessman traveling from Hyraith, the most abundant spice-farming city in all of Hadrass-Drui. With feverbright eyes, she'd asked if I was planning to see him when he passed through—and mentioned the business he was better known for in gutters and slums than at the fancy tables where he did his twice-annual reporting to the Moravens.

She, and many others I'd treated that day, knew him for spices that didn't go into food. Things better suited to Merrietti's shop than a cooking rack.

Judging by the state of the patient—and the lack of any coin to pay me with, any of the times I'd treated her—she'd been one of his frequent customers.

So it was difficult to muster up a respectable amount of sorrow at the notion that this man, though a friend of the Moravens, wouldn't be experiencing the gentle sleep Phin hoped for the Poet's future marks.

Still, I would make sure he was the last.

"When do you leave?" I asked with false brightness—as if none of this business bothered me at all.

"Just before dusk." Kai sipped from his coffee again, tapping his pen against Giddy Gus's skull. "And what do *you* have planned for the day?"

Thwarting the rest of your marks, if I have any say in it.

"I have a few errands to run," I offered vaguely. "I'll need to buy more food, if we're going to honor those plates."

Kai swirled his coffee, a groove carving into one side of his mouth; then he set his mug aside and jerked open a drawer beside his left leg. Pulling out a thick, velvet coinpurse, he plopped it onto the desk and shoved it my way.

"For the food," he said, "and whatever else you deem us in need of."

I reached for the bag, gratitude scorching the tip of my tongue—then hesitated with my fingertips kissed by silvery crushed-velvet softness. "How do you know I won't take this and disappear from the city tonight while you're gone?"

"I don't." He watched me over the rim of his mug as he took another sip.

I contemplated the test before me, wondering how it was possible to pass—or fail.

But with all the lies I was weaving—particularly now, with Phin hiding in the city—I decided a morsel of truth would be best.

Sliding the bag across the desk, I let it drop into my lap. "Any food you would prefer?"

"I've always been fond of potato and leek soup."

"Family recipe?" I guessed.

"Rotting bones, no. My parents both were terrible cooks."

"My father was, too...I think we ate nothing but tavern food and the meals from my mother's friends who took pity on us for a full year after she passed. I almost wept when I moved to Harrow Hall and accessed their dining hall." I snorted at the memory now, though at the time the lack of home cooking had felt like a whole new dimension of missing my mother. "I've never been a proficient cook, either, but at least I can follow a recipe."

Kai leaned an elbow on the desk, pointing around my shoulder. "Recipe books, over there."

I swiveled my gaze from him to the shelf and back.

He lofted a brow. "What? Did you really expect I've been buying *my* meals from taverns?"

"I suppose I just assumed it's been the same jerky, bread, and cheese all this time."

"I'm capable of cooking," he said, with a touch more defensiveness than I'd expected. "I simply lose the inspiration after a while when I'm only cooking for myself."

"I was the same way in Dalfi," I admitted. "I mostly ate the same few things over and over, until my friends arrived on my doorstep. *Then* I started cooking and baking again."

We both looked away, lost in our own thoughts of food and friendship and the beauty of having people to share those things with.

Finally, Kai cleared his throat. "Mutton. And goat-cheese toast, drizzled with honey. That seems like a meal worthy of new dishes."

My mouth watered. "That sounds worthy of eating off the *floor*."

He drowned a chuckle in a final swig of coffee, rising to his feet. "It was my brother's meal of choice, for every birthday." He lifted his chin toward the shelf. "The cookbook my mother used for it should be there somewhere."

"Well, I can't promise it will taste the same...but I promise I'll try."

The mug *clumped* heavily onto the desk; he flexed his fingertips on the rim, peering into its empty depths. "We should do this again."

"What, the coffee?"

With a curt nod, he drew back his hand. "I'll return tomorrow before midday."

He let the study door creak shut at his back—and suddenly, unexpectedly, for the first time I was *alone* in his private space.

Alone with all his stacks and ledgers. His poetry books, his cot, his workroom.

Alone with the ink.

Downing my coffee in a searing gulp, I hooked the coinpurse to my belt and raced to retrieve my cloak.

It was time to get to work.

CHAPTER 45
CONTAGIOUS MADNESS

I T WAS PAINFULLY LATE, the moon silvering my steps like a dream and the floorboards creaking like ominous secrets whispered in the dark, when I finally picked my way back to Kai's study—dilution in hand.

I wasn't entirely convinced of the recipe, though I knew the properties of its contents like I knew my own name. And the counterpoison I'd purchased from Merrietti's shop was meant to be wide-reaching, effective against a long list of powerful poisons...it had to be, for the price she'd made me pay.

If she hadn't been a friend to Phin, I would've assumed she was selling me something useless for top coin. She certainly had been no friendlier to me, in word or in charge...but whether that was because she believed me an angst of the Moravens who'd lied to her at the first, or if she still thought I might be some competition encroaching from the outer towns who'd gotten starstruck by Phineaus Moraven, it hardly mattered. She hadn't run me out of her shop, and the solution—while it had cost half the coin in the velvet purse—was the final piece my own antidote required.

The contents had looked right, and certainly *smelled* right—an earthy, bittersweet aroma that had thankfully mellowed while I'd had it steeping under my bed all day. Now it was just a matter of adding it to the ink, and hoping—*praying*—it would do the trick.

When I stole into Kai's office, the silence and solitude struck like a blow. I'd just gotten so used to seeing him around the house, it was strange to hear and see and feel *nothing* while he was out chasing Raversen today; but that was safest for me as I picked my way across the study to the drape, and tested the knob.

Part of me still expected to find it locked; but it gave way under my hand, easing inward on ancient hinges, and when I lit the lantern in the low rafters everything looked exactly how it had the last time I'd been here.

Except that the pendulum no longer swayed. And the three inkpots were full now.

My mouth dried at the sight .

Luck, help me. This should have felt like the perfect choice, the easy thing...a triumph, even; but doing it *tonight*, when Kai had just left me unaccompanied in his study and this whole manse for the first time, felt like a betrayal instead. Even though there was nothing *to* betray.

Nothing but a tenuous thread of trust. No one but an assassin with a taste for mutton and goat-cheese toast, who wanted to share coffee with me.

I swatted myself on the cheek. "Get out of your *head*, Naomi."

Oh, joy. It seemed talking to oneself was a contagious madness around here.

Grimacing, I tiptoed to the table where the inkpots waited. I bent close to breathe deeply of the scents of each—and sure enough, though all three held the pungent odor of the Lightbane muddled with the richness of the ink, just one had the smell of fennel and pine, faint around the bottle lip.

I had decided already this morning that I would dilute two and leave one untouched; that way, just in case Kai discovered the anomaly, it might look like his mistake rather than my sabotage.

At least, I hoped to Luck it would. All of this was guesswork...even whether the dilution would be successful.

But I had to try.

Slipping the vial from my pocket, I gently thumbed it open and tipped it against the edge of the first inkpot.

Just one drop. The familiar mantra echoed in my head.

I tapped the side of the vial—and watched the diluting droplet plop over the edge into the first inkwell. Its spread was only visible for a moment, spiraling out in hazy tendrils...then absorbing, disappearing like a shooting star lost across an endless night.

But its impression was burned on the back of my eyes when I blinked...an unwashable stain. A wound I couldn't heal even if I'd wanted to take it back.

One drop can destroy everything.

CHAPTER 46
HIS CURSE, HER CURE

A NEW ROUTINE MANIFESTED after Kai returned from slipping the poisoned letter to Raversen's retinue, like an unexpected symptom developing in the midst of a malady.

It...wasn't entirely an unpleasant one, as strange as it was.

It started the way most mornings did: an encounter in the hallway outside my door and Kai's study; me, still rubbing sleep from my eyes, bundled in my cardigan and nightpants, tousled and yawning. And Kai, put together as ever in his deep emerald shirt with the cuffs rucked up to his elbows—the way he always wore them—and black trousers tucked into boots, looking as if he'd been awake and working for hours even though I knew sometimes he slept later than I did...still snoring on the cot inside his study when I tiptoed by.

Not that morning, though. That first morning after his return, he was awake, bright-eyed, hair combed...and hands full of two starlight-glazed, steaming mugs.

I stopped in midstep, socks whispering on the shellacked wood, eyes leaping from the mug to his inscrutable face.

He tilted his head. "Join me."

And that was how I began taking coffee with an assassin in his study each morning—and working alongside him while we drank.

Some days, he brought the mugs; some days, I did. But it always ended the same way: with us in the storeroom, working at separate tables on our separate recipes for the poison and cure to use at the Jubilee—sipping coffee and bickering over the finer points of our concoctions.

His curse. My cure.

It was the first time in so *long* that I could speak to someone—and trade barbed banter—about both sides of my interests. Ribbing about poisons had never been considered in good taste, especially under the reproachful gazes of our ever-serious professors at Harrow Hall; and those of us who had embraced the study to its fullest had always looked at one another a bit out of the corners of our eyes...and learned not to accept a drink from our fellow students.

It wasn't like that with Kai; something about knowing precisely what he *was* made it so much easier, so much more relaxed in that workroom...so that I didn't even mind kicking his haunch occasionally when he mentioned how he hoped I was up to the task, as this poison was going to be potent, indeed.

"Please," I'd scoff, "my antidote will be so effective they'll forget they were ever poisoned at all!"

Sometimes, the jabs about our separate brews and how we would infiltrate the Jubilee moved to the kitchen, continued over platters of eggs and sausage; sometimes it stretched on so long I was late for appointments, late to the beggar's district, late to meet Phin.

I was late to hear the Druavas's report about how Raversen's death had rocked Hyraith to its roots and upset the entire applecart of spice trade across Hadrass-Drui. I was late to endure his mutterings about how furious his grandparents were. I was late to learn from my fidgeting, fretting, furious patients about how their supply to the more dangerous spices had been cut off as well.

I wished I minded. I wished I cared about the death of a notorious spice-trader wearing a two-faced Luck mask more than I looked forward to the feeling of a routine shared with another living, breathing person—something I'd barely had since my abrupt replanting in Dalfi, and dreaded whenever I'd returned to Vallanmyre.

But that routine was a safeguarded part of my life, something I wrapped my heart's armor around. Because mutual habits were vulnerable things; the moment you couldn't maintain one, it called everything into question. It stoked friends' concerns; it made acquaintances wary. It gave enemies a place to slide in a knife.

Kai and I existed in a comfortably hazy place where we were none of those things to each other; and the routine born of that was something I could enjoy without the fear of what would happen whenever it inevitably came to an end.

So I let myself embrace it—wholeheartedly, for as long as I could have it.

"Good morning, Kai! Good morning, Giddy Gus!" I singsonged one morning, stepping inside the open study door and toeing it shut behind me; Kai greeted me with a flick of the hand, his focus trained on the work he was poring over.

Giddy Gus, predictably, said nothing. Secretive little bastard.

I joined Kai at the desk, setting his mug in front of him. "Coffee with milk and molasses sugar. And what are *you* doing this—?"

I hesitated, heart catching in my throat.

There was a smell drifting around him I'd never caught in this place before; a zesty floral aroma like potpourri or incredibly expensive perfume, pressed into the collar of his shirt, wafting like a taunt in my nostrils when I bent near to set down the coffee.

My insides curdled; I drew back swiftly, and his head rocked up, our gazes meeting.

"Where did you go last night?" I whispered.

He was quiet for a moment, his focus straying from my face to Giddy Gus's eyesockets; I'd wedged a pair of winter blooms in them just to try and get a reaction from him—after I'd shaken the seeds loose from them for my antidote. But he gave absolutely no sign he loathed or liked it.

That was not the most pressing mystery today.

"Visiting another mark," Kai said at last.

I dropped my weight back on my heels, jolting a splash of hot coffee onto my knuckle; hissing a curse, I sucked on the offended finger, and Kai's focus lunged back to my face—his features all tightening slightly at whatever he saw in my expression.

"Oh," was all I could bring myself to say.

The squirm of relief in my middle had to be because I knew what he didn't—that the diluted poison hadn't killed whomever he'd struck last night, his first mark since Raversen. That Phin would be pleased, not furious and fretful this time. That the Moravens wouldn't be lighting another candle for another beloved soul lost tonight.

It had absolutely nothing to do with the fact that the first word that had crawled into my head at that pungent scent had been *brothel*.

"Who, um..." I swallowed, shifting my weight. "Who is it this time?"

"The landlady of a town half the night from here," he said dismissively. "Nellatrix Glas."

There was no effect in his tone at all; no concern for the life he thought he'd taken.

He truly despised his marks *that much*...though I'd seen by now he was capable of compassion. Concern, even. I could hardly wrap my mind around the thought that the man I shared coffee and conversation with every morning, and meals with most nights, was the same one who spoke without inflection about a woman he fully believed he'd killed.

"How do you choose them?" The words tumbled over my quivering lips. "Who dies?"

Kai said nothing; his focus trailed past me, lingered for a moment, then returned to my face. And just when the hair began to rise on my arms, he dropped his head and resumed his work.

I turned on heel to see what he'd indicated with that flick of his eyes: the map pinned in the recess of the wall.

I darted a swift glance at Kai; he didn't lift his head, scribbling notes in a ledger, turning the page to reveal several long stanzas inked on the back of the binding—line after line after line crossed out.

Sipping my coffee, I padded across the room to study the map—more closely now than any other time I'd been here. Until now, I'd always been too nervous he would catch me staring...that it would arouse suspicion if I did. But now, with the silent invitation of his glance, and without his attention riveted on my back, I allowed myself a closer look.

Tacks. Threads. And note after note after note, each one a small square penned in a neat, elegant script—which matched the perpetually neat, often-gloved, elegant hands that must've written them.

They were pinned all across Hadrass-Drui—many obscuring Amalgard, many more spread out, some clustered to overwhelm in places like Thrasmund and fewer pinned around Rastra.

I fingered the edges of a few I recognized—from soul-sender reports I'd read through feverishly in the Fortress. "What are all of these?"

"Names in a ledger," he said briskly. "And their crimes."

I jerked my fingers back, sliding a swift glance his way; he didn't glance up from his work. As if he was baiting me—waiting to see what I would do.

Luck, I loved and *hated* challenges.

I eased nearer to the map again when he didn't so much as spare a glance my way, observing all the tacks and the lines that joined them to one another. Those, I couldn't make sense of; but the notes pinned beneath them...

Corylus Fletch. It was easy to find his name, stuck above the rendering of Amalgard; my eyes darted to it almost immediately. And scripted beneath:

Fraudulent coffers.

Brothel—twice weekly.

Violence—bruises.

And the names of Corylus's children, crossed out.

My breath hitched, my attention darting back to Kai, then springing to the wall again. Gently, I smoothed my thumb over the names rendered in dark penstrokes after that word: *bruises.*

Kai was not a murderer of children...I'd seen that in the way he'd handled Sofi. I'd seen it in all the soul-sender reports. Those crossings-out were not a sign of work he'd finished.

They indicated a father's brutality.

The way Caspian and the people in Fortress Ferregrand had spoken of Corylus, he'd seemed like a fair but challenging friend to the Drui. But who knew what happened behind closed doors? And with my next blink, I recalled the children's rooms in Corylus's manse—the windows barred, the settings devoid of personality and play.

Cold dread puddled in my stomach; my gaze leaped down to Rastra, searching the nearby towns and villages until I plucked Nellatrix's name from beneath another scarlet tack:

Nellatrix Glas.

Extortion—taxes funneled to private interests.

Sentinels on bankroll.

Votes for personal gain.

I gripped the edge of the bookcase in one hand, my mug in the other; breath struggled its way down into my lungs.

I was no stranger to corruption at the heart of governing; it was why I was *here*, why there had been anything in my life for Calten to extort that would force me into this mess. But seeing it all laid out in script, all of these wrongdoings pinned to names on a wall—

A veritable list of deaths dealt, and deaths determined.

Pressing nearer, I hunted across Amalgard—the greatest contingent of gathered names—but among them, there was one markedly absent.

No *Phineaus Moraven*.

"Incredible, isn't it?" Kai's voice just over my shoulder made me jump; I twisted to peer up at him beside me. He sloped one arm against the other bookcase that boxed in the recessed wall, leaning his weight into it, fingers flicking the air in a silent beat as he surveyed his map—his *work*. "That first drop of corruption is all it takes. The next thing you know, the whole batch is tainted."

The hair on my neck prickled—not just because of how those words echoed the teachings of Harrow Hall, but because of how keenly they reminded me of what I'd done in his private workroom, days ago.

"This is what you meant, isn't it?" I murmured, pulling my gaze back to the map before he could look my way—before he could find the guilt in my eyes. "When you said your marks deserved it."

A deep breath in through his nostrils; he held it for several moments before he said, "This is one part of it, yes."

Disbelief rattled my mirthless laugh. "Do I *want* to know the other parts?"

This time, his gaze drew mine like a lodestone; we stared at one another for a long moment, that intrusive curiosity in his stare leaving me breathless and almost entirely sure he knew *exactly* all of my secrets, too. That they were just waiting on a note somewhere, possibly next to be tacked to the wall.

He rocked on his feet, dropping his hand to rest on the bookcase and pushing off as he pivoted, striding back to his desk. "I have an assignment for you."

All my breath whooshed out as I turned to follow him—though I didn't think I would ever fully leave that map behind. "Oh? Something the esteemed Poet Poisoner can't do for himself?"

"Something I am *choosing* not to, for the sake of our partnership." He slid in at the desk, and I finally joined him in my usual, comfortable, *familiar* spot. The first part of the morning that didn't feel like treading on foreign ground. "The Jester's Jubilee, as I've mentioned, is hosted by the Guild Garrott. But they are not the only ones in attendance."

"Naturally. Or else if anyone found out who was attending, they would also know everyone who was a member of the guild."

Kai hesitated a moment; then he scooped up his mug and shook his head. "Observant."

"I don't just diagnose illnesses, Kai, I diagnose people." I grinned. "That requires knowing a bit of how they think."

His mouth opened and shut swiftly—a question unspoken perishing in the air between us before it had even been given life.

"Well, your diagnosis is correct—as I gather is often the case with you," he muttered after a beat. "Yes, the Guild are all in attendance, but they frequently invite unfamiliar faces to their fetes. It helps them blend in."

I frowned. "Aren't they worried about inviting other assassins by mistake?"

"That is a perpetual risk in everything these guilds and leagues do...which is in part why I refuse to associate with one," Kai said. "However, the Guild does make their choices carefully...usually they select from well-to-do businesspeople and those of humbler station."

"Offering them something that looks like a glitter-wrapped daydream," I murmured. "They don't know they're only invited in to keep up the ruse."

"Precisely." Kai folded his hands on the desk. "Attendance, thus, is by invitation only." He bobbed his head several times, holding my gaze—watching the comprehension rise through me on a surge of cheek-stinging warmth. "You can see where I'm going with this."

"We're not getting into that Jubilee without an invitation."

"Precisely."

"Well, flipping Luck!" I crashed back in my chair, rubbing the heat from my cheeks. "How *are* we getting in, then?"

"By stealing one."

Shoving my heels into the floor, I pushed myself up from my slouch again, meeting his calm, unaffected stare.

"You want *me* to steal one?" I rasped.

"You've stolen twice from Merrietti, once successfully...and she is herself an assassin." He tilted his head. "Don't lie to me that you aren't capable, Miss Weathers."

"It's not a matter of capability—I wouldn't even know where to start!"

"Yes, you would." Kai reclined, propping his elbows on the broad arms of his seat, resting those interlaced fingers over his middle this time; his thumbs tapped restlessly against the shadowed green silk of his shirt. "Diagnose your mark."

I shot him a glare; we'd been practicing this on and off over mugs of starlight coffee and meals on star-glazed plates—the notion of *thinking like an assassin*. Kai insisted it was necessary to move through the Jubilee undetected; more often, it felt like he was testing me to see if I was a match for his wit.

And that was one challenge I vehemently refused to fail.

I mirrored his posture, leaning my head against the back of my seat, peering up at the lofty rafters of his study. Turning the problem—the symptoms at hand—over and over in my mind.

Silence dominated the room for several long, *long* minutes; but it was an oddly breathable kind of silence. It didn't feel like when a professor was waiting for your retort to a trick question; when someone like Calten was goading you to make the right choice, *their* choice.

Kai's quiet didn't push itself against me, didn't test my boundaries. No sense of expectation came from it; he was just waiting for me to sort out what he assumed I was clever enough to deduce.

Well, he was right.

"We're not thinking like an assassin in this case," I said at last. "This would be a commoner who's just received a once-in-a-lifetime invitation."

"An honor," Kai agreed. "Absolute esteem."

"They wouldn't think of hiding it." I straightened in my seat again, my thoughts racing the way they always did when symptoms started to connect—when the illness at hand began to crystallize. "They would flaunt it, they would tell all of their friends—"

"And if they were foolish enough—"

"They wouldn't dare leave the invitation at home," I finished, biting my lower lip to temper my smile. "The right person would keep it on them at *all* times, as a bragging chip—"

"And to keep it safe."

Excitement shot me up from my seat, my nerves tingling like someone held a flame to my skin. "If you'll excuse me, I have gossip to go chase. We'll have to save the workroom for another day."

"I look forward to it. Happy hunting." Kai scooped up his fountain pen, tapped Giddy Gus three times on the round of the skull, then returned to jotting notes in his ledger.

Maybe it was my own giddiness making me bold; maybe it was the feeling that, for the first time, we were *truly* partners in something that didn't have to end in murder...just in theft. But when I snatched up my mug and backed away from the desk, daring words tingled on the tip of my tongue.

And, Luck, why not—I set them free.

"I'm glad you came back safe, from your mark yesterday."

His head shot up; I flashed him a smile the moment our eyes met, blunting the edges of my shame.

No one had died last night—not him, not Nellatrix, even if he thought otherwise. So there was no harm in being glad he'd returned unharmed for morning coffee, since she was alive today, too.

After a long moment, he said, quietly, "So am I." Then his attention dropped back to his work. "Go stir up trouble, will you?"

"Your Murderousness." I curtseyed—then ducked out before he could throw his pen at my head.

CHAPTER 47
RAISE A GLASS TO THE GRAVE

IN LESS THAN A week, I had made my first real mark as partner to an assassin.

The initial thread to stitch it together came with an unplanned visit to Nera and Sofi, after a note came to me through a chain of beggars about Sofi needing a bit of extra herb to stimulate her appetite. When I delivered it to their house—and sat on the front steps with Nera, drinking tea—she mentioned the new job she'd taken up since Sofi had begun to recover: a few hours here and there at a local bistro.

She mentioned it—and had reached out to me in part, she told me with twinkling eyes—because the owner had let slip something Nera was certain our mutual friend the Poet would want to hear: that the bistro's owner been awarded quite an honor to attend some lavish and secretive event. And she liked to rattle off all the reasons why she assumed she'd been noticed and praised and invited.

For the next handful of days, the sutures wove themselves together; an extra cup of cocoa here and there at a particular canalside bistro, a meal on its brazier-edged patio every day. The owner, Beris, was more than eager to chat with me while I enjoyed the same unremarkable sandwich each visit; and, like Nera had hinted, it didn't take long for the repeated remarks about her popular, infamous, and eye-catching establishment to stray into more interesting matters.

Like who had noticed it—the elites of the city. And how they were rewarding her. And how this would change everything for her.

I almost felt guilty for the reason I was prying, what I was going to take from her...but that dissipated like a sudden headcold the day she tugged a thick square of cardstock from her pocket in the middle of her predictable, proud tirade and flashed it under my nose.

"Look!" she belted out in singsong. "This is it, right here—*my* invitation to the *Jester's Jubilee*!" She stashed it back in her apron pocket before I could do more than ascertain the silvery overlay of the paper, the gold-leaf lettering, and the seal on the corner...likely stamped on there to ensure no false invitations at the door.

But possibly also the mark of the Guild Garrote itself—a thought that gave me shivers.

"Remember to tell all of your friends," Beris added smugly, "that when they eat at *Beris's Bistro by the Canal*, they're eating at an establishment beloved by the *elite*, not just the common."

I caught Nera's gaze around her back, where she brushed another table's half-eaten sandwich and lukewarm soup into a bucket for washing; it was hard not to match the roll of her eyes.

"I'll be sure to tell everyone who's important to me in this city," I replied sweetly, pivoting my focus back to Beris. "So, I was wondering...as someone who knows both the common *and* shakes hands with the elite, could you tell me some of your favorite places for finding entertainment in Rastra?"

"I've got her," I announced, sliding into my chair across the desk from Kai.

He'd been reclining in his seat, hands folded in his lap, eyes closed; now they popped open, gliding down to glance at me though he didn't lift his head. "Is *she* someone who fits in your pocket, or is this a metaphor?"

"Ha, ha. You'd need even bigger pockets than *that* to fit your hilarity in," I deadpanned, drawing my feet up onto the edge of the seat. "Beris Barclay. She insists she's thirty-five, though the prominence of the veins in her hands suggests *that* is a lie. What's not a lie is that she was invited to this year's Jester's Jubilee...and that it's made her absolutely insufferable and a real torment to all the other bistro owners who weren't deemed *deserving* of that honor."

Kai's lips twitched upward. "She irritates you."

"People always irritate me when they mistake Luck for merit," I grumbled. "Anyway, that's not the point. I've seen the invitation, Kai...I almost swiped it right from her hand."

"I'm proud of you for resisting the urge. Clandestine matters dealt with in daylight will more likely lead to a knife in your throat than a celebration of success."

"Is that supposed to be poetry?"

"Prose, actually. Kilgrave, from *Raise a Glass to the Grave.*"

"Mm. Sounds like a riveting read." I arched my brows. "Anyway, back to Beris. I managed to coax some information from her, so I know what her favorite activities are when she's not haranguing her customers or making the most mediocre sandwiches I've ever had the displeasure of paying three coins a piece for."

"And those are—?"

"Well, I think it's supposed to be ham, though the pig she butchered for it must've been close to a thousand years old. And the lettuce gave up its soul *weeks* ago, judging by the texture of—"

"The activities, Miss Weathers. Focus."

I rolled my eyes. "Focusing would be easier if I could stomach more than half a sandwich. I'm famished."

Scoffing, Kai rose. "Let's continue this in the kitchen, then."

To my relief, he was sincere; and my thoughts did sharpen once I'd made my own sandwich, mutton slices on goat-cheese toast with honey drizzled on top.

Sitting on the edge of the butcher's block, I plucked crumbles of cheese from the bread and popped them into my mouth; Kai leaned his elbows on the block beside me, watching me eat with a muted fascination I could only attribute to him wondering how I could keep the secret of Beris's favorite activities to myself for this long.

"Well?" he finally prompted, an entire five minutes after we'd left the study—a new record for the Poet's patience.

"Mmm, yes. So," I polished the last of the honey from the plate with my smallest finger, licking it clean before I replied, "she's especially fond of the performing arts."

Kai leaned back, bracing his hands on the edge of the block—which made the corded muscles and stark veins of his forearms stand out more prominently than usual beneath his rolled-back sleeves. "Is she?"

I nodded absently, watching the muscles flex from his wrists to his elbows. "Operas, stageplays, poetry readings, reenactments—"

"Aerial acrobatics?"

I paused, focusing again. "Well...that wouldn't surprise me, although it's oddly specific."

"Because it is *quite* specific. So specific, in fact, she may find it irresistible." He tapped his thumbs on the edge of the block. "Which also makes it the perfect trap."

Excitement nudged me to the edge of the counter, catching me up in the moment. "What are you thinking?"

"Another of my contacts owns a playhouse," he said, "and his sisters' troupe performs there whenever they tour Hadrass-Drui. They bring news from across the countries whenever they visit, and through him, that news finds its way directly to my ears."

"So, if he could convince his sisters to perform at his playhouse—"

"Beris could be tempted by another private invitation," Kai finished. "And that will be your moment to apprehend the one that truly matters."

"Do you have the plans for the playhouse?" I asked. "I'll need to know what I'm getting myself into once we're inside."

"I do...the originals, in fact." Kai folded his arms and settled his weight, head ducking slightly as he studied me through his lashes with that piercing, searching curiosity I was slowly growing used to. "Can you lure her there, is the question."

"Give me a little time to poke at her," I grinned, drumming a discordant tune on the edge of the butcher's block with my heels, "and I think I can have her doing whatever I want."

CHAPTER 48
A FUTURE LIKE THIS

I T WAS A JOINT effort between Nera and me to play up the unexpected performance slated at *The Hall of Majesties*—a lovely but modest playhouse that straddled the edge of the beggar's district and the affluent portions of the city. Several conversations between us within earshot of Beris about the performance's small attendance opportunity, and how the show was by invitation only, and suddenly Beris couldn't wait to tell us how *she* had procured seats—by marching down to the Hall herself and flashing a different invitation altogether in its owner's face.

Funny how that worked out.

A fortnight later and with a handful of late-night visits to other marks notched into his map, I finally convinced Kai to leave the manse for something other than delivering poisoned poem lines. And that was how I found myself crossing a plaza framed in evergreen trees and two-armed lampposts well after dark, the smell of pine wafting more strongly from their boughs than from Kai's shoulder-cloak, off to see a performance with the Poet Poisoner, of all people.

Matched step-for-step, we hurried toward the place where the plaza ended and the road dipped down into a broad sidestreet—where *The Hall of Majesties* awaited.

"Remind me again why *I'm* here," Kai's voice barreled out around a muffled yawn, "rather than sleeping off last night's activities."

And by *activities*, naturally, he meant his latest supposed assassination.

"Because, despite what you may think about how clever and capable I am, I know I've occasionally diagnosed wrong, or drawn blood when I shouldn't have." I stuffed my hands into my cardigan pockets, shivering as I wrapped it tighter around myself; I'd dressed for swift movements and concealment, not exactly for the cold. "This is too important to risk the invitation slipping through our hands if I fumble something. So you're here to make certain we get our hands on it, no matter what."

Our bootsteps scuffed stone as we descended toward the dimmer districts of the city. Then a sudden snap of cloth nearly had me jumping out of my skin; before I could begin to pivot, the familiar scent of fennel and pine washed over me, and a trapped, bodily warmth snuffed the chill that not even my favorite cardigan had cut.

In one swift movement so smooth I still couldn't trace it, Kai had freed the shoulder clasp of his cloak and tossed it around my shoulders.

"The beauty of partnership," he said when my gaze found his, limned golden in the lanternlight.

Heat plumed fresh from the thick threads, scampering up my cheeks and making a nest in the very roots of my hair.

I should have handed it back; I should have scoffed that it hardly fit my lightweight attire. But instead I banded it tightly around myself, hunkering my chin in the collar and breathing in the scent from the folds.

Another reminder that I didn't do this alone. That, if I misstepped, someone was there to pivot the dance

Flipping Luck, how long had it been since I'd been able to trust anyone to do that?

We slowed when we reached the halfway point of the avenue, where *The Hall of Majesties* jutted from the flatter building fronts on either side of it and lit the cobblestone way like daylight. It wasn't as lofty as the playhouses I'd passed in other corners of Rastra; tucked midway down the wide sidestreet, it lacked the broad milling space out front, settling instead for a small, circular courtyard across from another bistro, with shared tables and chairs between them.

But there was warmth and welcome in the tawny glow that spilled from its four-level façade, and the illuminated kiosk dazzled with the name of tonight's performing group—drawing me in just as helplessly as it had Beris.

Four Brothers, Four Brides.

"Wait—I know this troupe!" Excitement had me bouncing on the balls of my feet. "They perform across Mithra-Sha...Addie and Jaik love them!"

"And now you're about to have a night to hold over their heads." Kai pressed a broad hand to the small of my back, herding me along. "Shall we?"

We entered the foyer, red-and-gold striped velvet lining the walls and low roof and carpeting the floor between several potted fabric plants. The entry space was all but deserted, with the show having already started ten minutes prior; strings plucked and shimmied in an enticing chorus beyond the pair of gilded double-doors straight ahead, with only one other door in sight—plain, drab brown. The way to both was guarded by a long admittance counter and the tall, slender man with dusky skin who hosted it.

His bearded face broke into a grin when he caught sight of us, and he slapped both hands on the counter. "Kai, what in Ahim's name are you doing here? I didn't expect you to come yourself!"

"Dashian." Kai dipped his chin. "That makes two of us."

"Ah, Kai!" The Ameresh man rounded the counter to clap both hands on Kai's shoulders, shaking him gently. "It's so *good* to see you. Everything is ready for your business tonight."

"*Her* business." Kai flicked a glance my way. "I'm only an escort."

Dashian turned to me, his eyes brightening as they swept over me in a way that almost made me blush—something I wasn't especially prone to but seemed to be a victim of tonight. "Such an honor to meet another of Kai's contacts." Dashian took one of my hands from the folds of Kai's cloak and pressed a delicate kiss to my knuckles. "I have only one rule: make no trouble for this place, and it will always be welcoming to you."

"I'll do my best to manage that," I laughed a bit breathlessly. "The woman who flashed that invitation in your face a few days ago...she's here, isn't she?"

"Just to the left of the front, as requested." Dashian's brow furrowed as he drew back a bit, still gripping my hand. "She's quite unpleasant, isn't she?"

"That's putting it one way." I squeezed his fingers lightly. "Would you have your servers ply her with plenty of sparkling wine? I'll pay, of course."

Kai eyed me sideways as I unhooked my coinpurse and shook out several coins into Dashian's palm.

"And have them spill a bit on the *left* side of her coat, just after the intermission," I added.

"These are very odd requests." Dashian shrugged, pocketing the coin and pressing another kiss to my knuckles. "But not the oddest we've ever had. It will be done."

"We're short on time," Kai hinted, nudging Dashian back from me; he finally released my hand and straightened, sidestepping and motioning us around the counter.

"The back stairwell," he said. "You know the way up, Kai."

"Oh, do you?" I prodded lightly as we slipped through the plain door; it opened to a narrow stairwell, the walls so thick they all but completely masked the strains of string music from the Hall itself.

"I've done my share of surveying marks from here," he murmured as we climbed. "But I've also come occasionally simply for the shows."

"Really?" We pushed out into a small box with a half-wall framed by a wraparound velvet curtain; I suspected this seatless balcony had been built at first for the Hall's workers, or maybe even for someone to watch over the assembly for a hint of threat. Now it was our perch, just wide enough for us both to fit in as we slunk to the edge. "You like the theater?"

"Now and again." Kai tugged the curtain back on its fastening. "I have an appreciation for poetry in motion."

And that was precisely the sight that awaited us beyond the veil.

Though I'd heard plenty about *Four Brothers, Four Brides* from Addie when we were girls, I'd never actually seen them perform; to the tune of the small orchestra filling the pit below the stage, the eight acrobats spun cyr wheels and tied themselves expertly in twines of silk strung from the rafters. The gold paint on their skin—mostly bare apart from light, breathable shifts—shimmered like sundust as they twisted and turned. The accents on their flesh were the perfect backdrop to the deep jade curtains that lined the arched walls and padded the velvet seat settings below.

I sank down cross-legged, folding my arms on the edge of the half-wall and nuzzling my cheek into the warmth of the cloak that bunched around my shoulders. "This place is *beautiful*."

"Dashian has always had an eye for beauty." Kai settled next to me, one leg drawn to his chest, the other tucked behind his ankle. "Occasionally too much of one."

"But not in this case." I shook my head, breath snagging as one of the women dropped, unraveling from the length of silk rope and catching herself by the arm just inches from the stage; one of the men swooped in with arm bound in his own trappings, scooping her up around the waist and lifting her off in an aerial dance around the edge of the stage. "Luck, that's incredible."

We watched in silent awe, as caught up in the performance as the two levels of audience gasping and cheering now and again when the music fell to allow for it. I'd expected nerves to gnaw away at me while I waited for my time to act, to perform my own part; but somehow, sitting here on this secluded balcony with Kai at my side, nerves were the furthest thing from my mind.

There was almost a part of me that wished we could be down there, among the crowd; not a liar running in so many ways, not an assassin stalking the shadows. Just another part of the blend of common and noble, distinguished only by the finery of their clothes, enjoying something absolutely normal. As simple as it came.

"Do you ever dream of a life like this?" I blurted as the show reached intermission; a hum of chatter started below, masking our voices that otherwise might've echoed from the box.

"Life in the theater?" Kai asked.

"No...a normal one." I rested my chin on my arms, risking missing something marvelous—or even the mundane—among the people below to glance at him instead.

And that was something marvelous, too—the way the golden light caught on his stubble and the dark thatch of his hair. The way it danced like gilded motes in his eyes as he stared at the deep green velvet drapes through which the troupe had disappeared to rest.

"That has always been far, far beyond my reach," he murmured; a deep groove dug in around his mouth, and his focus flicked to me. "But certain things lately have made me wonder, if I ever could...what that would be like."

"And?" I prompted softly. "What *would* it be like?"

"I think it may be...morning coffee. Card games in the evening," he said, slowly—as if speaking it might shatter every hope of a future like that. "Or waltzes. Or mutton sandwiches."

A giggle scraped from my throat. "Or just having someone waiting for you when you come back."

Our gazes met, and held; Kai's throat heaved in a hard swallow, and his voice was husky when he rasped, "Why are you looking at me that way, Miss Weathers?"

"How am I looking at you?" I really didn't know; I'd grown so used to masking the heat that crawled through my veins when he touched me, to glancing away when he held my stare too long, but...

Tonight, I didn't want to look away.

"Like you see something the rest of the world can't," Kai said after a long moment.

"Well, maybe I do." I let my arms slide from the balcony edge, twisting to face him. "Maybe I'm the only person who knows the Poet Poisoner thinks about a different life."

He scoffed, tearing his gaze away. "Hardly a secret worth knowing."

"Actually, I think it may be the most precious one you've given me so far."

His head slowly revolved back my way, and I found myself inclining, breathing in the scent of fennel and pine, spicing my veins with curiosity, with courage—

A clatter. A curse. A high-pitched *scream* from the seats below, so violent in its profanity it sent Kai and me both lunging up to our knees, peering over the balcony edge.

Beris Barclay was unmistakable, from her coiffed silver-blonde updo to her too-shimmery dress to her shrill swearing as she swiped frantically along the stain of sparkline wine spilled all down the left-side front of her coat.

"You absolute, useless fool!" she shrieked at one of Dashian's green-vested servers. "Don't you know *anything* about how to treat a guest at your establishment? Look what you've done—my nicest coat!"

"Here it comes," I breathed.

"This is absolutely horrendous service," Beris snapped. "This sort of mistake would never happen at *Beris's Bistro by the Canal*—and none of you should forget it! I'll be speaking to your employer...come dawn, you won't have a pot left to piss in, you *idiot*!"

She shoved past the server and stormed blindly down the aisle, tossing up her hands with another profane shriek when the lanterns began to dim again, signaling the start of the show's second half.

"You should leave a bit more coin with Dashian, for that poor server's sake," Kai suggested.

"*You* handle that." I shook out two more of the coins he'd given me and slapped them into his palm. "And then meet me outside."

I didn't know if it was relief or nerves that made me slip from his cloak with a shrug and all but leap two-at-a-time down the steps to escape that balcony box.

And maybe I never would.

The washroom door, of course, was locked; but a brief brush past Dashian, and the key was in my hand—with a final kiss to my knuckles and a savage grin that made me fully aware all at once why this Ameresh man had the privilege of being in Kai's inner circle.

I slipped inside the washroom already knowing what awaited me inside—a sketch from the plans I'd reviewed in Kai's study countless times over the last handful of days. The room was long and narrow and cornered at the end; the length of it was lined with mirrors, so I could look down to the corner and glimpse Beris hunched over the washbasin beside the gilded chamberpot on the other side, furiously scrubbing a cloth against her soiled dress. Still muttering and cursing to herself.

A pivot on heel, and I found her coat hung on the hook behind the door.

Shaking with anticipation, I dove into the right pocket—the same pocket she always reached into on her apron when she was preparing to flourish her supposed new status beneath the nose of another bistro customer. Or when she just felt like touching it while she talked.

And there it was—the first brush of that silvery cardstock almost dropping my heart clean out of my chest.

I actually did it.

I whipped the invitation free and slipped it into my cardigan pocket, then glanced over my shoulder hastily at the mirrors—and froze.

Because I caught Beris's gaze fixed on mine through the mirrors...seeing me around the corner down the row of glass, just as I was watching her.

She threw the cloth against the mirror—against my reflection, I assumed—with a loud, vicious *splat*.

"Stop!" she howled. "Stop—*thief!*"

But I was already out the door, slamming it, locking it with a twist of the key and sprinting across the foyer—tossing the key to Dashian in passing and yelping my thanks as I bolted for escape.

Beris's screams still strung across the air when I burst outside and sprinted for the light of the broad plaza above the crest of the street, arms pumping, legs throbbing at the uphill slope.

Barreling into the open, I crashed straight into Kai's waiting grip; before his lips could even begin to frame a question, the Hall doors ricocheted open behind us, and a whistle-shrill cry shot our way. "*Don't you move!*"

"I think we've just overstayed our welcome." Kai's hand banded around mine, and then we were running for all we were worth—with a furious bistro owner in sharp heels chasing after us.

It was the oddest fleeing I'd ever done; almost comical, fringed with only the barest sense of danger, all while knowing that if Beris Barclay ever got her hands on me, she'd likely claw my eyes out and render me incapable of ever being a healer again.

But somehow I was *cackling* as we jogged over bridges and sprinted through familiar streets, losing her tinny wailing and sobbing curses on the wind behind us. We ran until we skidded into a pocket of Rastra I knew like the nose on my face; then I wrenched at Kai's arm, pulling him in a pivot with a bark of shock through a hedge of overgrowth, into the same alley where we'd ducked to escape the pursuing sentinels after we'd broken into Merrietti's shop.

I tumbled back against one wall, him against the other, still puffing with laughter from the run.

"Well, it's safe to say you can never return to her bistro again," Kai panted.

"Oh, no...robbed of the worst sandwiches of my life." I crushed the heel of my hand over my pounding heart. "What *ever* will I do?"

Then we were both laughing again, the hardest we ever had together, tipping dizzily toward each other until my brow landed against his chest and his face was buried in my hair.

And the truth I didn't even want to admit to myself was, this small heist had been daring, and thrilling...almost *fun*. The triumph of clutching that invitation in my pocket was headier than almost any diagnosis I'd ever sorted out, even the most difficult ones.

And...I didn't want to leave this small, stolen space that belonged just to the two of us.

I never wanted to forget how this warmth felt, or the man who laughed with me in it, his hand wandering up to rest in my hair and hold my head against him. The same way my arms looped around his narrow waist, holding fast to his solid presence.

I never wanted to forget *him*. A man who was starting to dream about a different life...

Or how a life like that might look just like tonight.

CHAPTER 49
STOLEN SKULLS AND LESSONS LEARNED

Our victory at Dashian's playhouse brightened all of the days that followed. Even with the weather chilling worse by the day, warmth played at the tips of my fingers like a mug of cocoa that never lost its steam.

Success would do that to a person. And after so many years of running, of disquiet rioting in my core, *triumph* felt like a homecoming. It made my steps float through the manse; it invigorated me through tasks like sweeping the inner courtyard and treating the water in the sunroom to clear away the algae.

I felt...unstoppable.

It wasn't only me—Kai seemed lighter, too. More easygoing, quicker to laugh, swifter to smile. Maybe that was just the result of leaving the manse for something other than missions of murder; but I suspected he was relieved by how I'd proven myself at the playhouse.

Capable...of upholding my part in the task at hand, and also of escaping afterward.

"Do you think Beris is still mourning?" I snickered as we made another sharp turn in our latest waltz around the open span at the heart of Kai's study. The movements were coming more naturally now...my head twisted pertly at every step, on a constant swivel for danger.

Not that there was any here; but I was imagining shadows, anticipating the Jubilee. And after the mission at the playhouse, my instincts felt sharper, somehow...as if whetting them on true experience had made a better liar of me.

Kai's low chuckle whisked against my ear as he led us through the next pattern of steps. "You truly despise that woman, don't you?"

"You saw how she treated the server at the playhouse," I pointed out. "That's how she treats Nera...and everyone who works for her. No, I don't like bullies...and I don't mind teaching them difficult lessons."

"Something we have in common."

My gaze strayed toward the map in its alcove on the wall; Kai's hand drifted up from my waist for a fleeting instant, guiding the line of my jaw until my face aligned with his.

"Eyes on mine, Miss Weathers."

My stomach decided to practice its own arial acrobatics to rival *Four Brothers, Four Brides* as we took our next turn; desperate, I hunted for some way to return to the conversation...and to escape the focused intent of his gaze.

The wall...bullies...Beris.

Ah, yes. Beris.

"You know, I was thinking that perhaps we could make it up to her." I waggled my brows mischievously as Kai spun me out from him. "If things look like they aren't going to plan at the Jubilee...let's just have Beris's Bistro cater. Plenty of coin in her pockets, by way of apology—and with any luck, all of the assassins will choke on the Luck-flipped dry bread. Death by sandwich."

He spun me in, and I crashed into his grip, my back to his chest, laughter erupting from my throat; he squeezed it out of me as his arms tightened, pinning me into the curve of his body.

"You are trouble incarnate," he hissed playfully in my ear.

"I know. Isn't it *fun*?"

This time he spun me with both arms, lifting me off my feet as he whirled—then gave me a shove toward the mantel. "Weapons."

I kicked a foot back at him, but hurried to do as he said; I was actually beginning to enjoy the lessons in knifeplay, once the waltzes loosened my muscles and carried me out of my thoughts. And the deeper I traveled into this mission of Kai's—the more it became *mine*—the more I looked forward to these sessions.

Daggers in hand, we walked through the warmup pattern of thrusts, jabs, blocks, and parries that had become another routine; it was such a smooth, practiced part of the training that we could talk while we did it...talk about next steps and past ones. Talk of his marks, if I dared broach the subject.

But today, I didn't; not as I watched the refrained calculation burn in Kai's gaze...some haven of thought he wasn't letting me all the way into. Not yet.

"Was there a moment you were afraid, in the playhouse?" he asked abruptly.

I reflected on the night again, sifting and sorting through the tangle of nerves, the elation, the tension...and that quiet moment on our private balcony. And the pulse-thudding minutes we'd spent in the alleyway after.

"Not...not really," I admitted—surprised by that truth even though I'd *lived* it. "I never felt out of my depth with Beris. Not like I would with an assassin."

Kai nodded curtly. "She presented no physical threat. But that does not diminish the triumph."

We carried ourselves more swiftly than usual through the warmup, and almost before I'd caught my breath from dancing, we were moving into the unpredictable parts of this battle-dance. Places where Kai corrected my form or warned me to brace before he landed a flurry of blows, forcing me to look for openings to block and escape.

Attacking was less our focus these days; at the Jubilee, I wouldn't be a match for anyone regardless of how much was practiced, even if it was sunup to sundown every day for weeks on end. The point was to make me proficient enough to keep myself alive until I found an opening to bolt through.

Today, he changed the patterns; after several attacks, he stepped back and spread his arms, knife hanging casually in his fist. "I'd like you to practice something different today, Miss Weathers. To win this round, slip past me and make it out into the hall."

I eyed the empty span of the room around him, cleared for our dance. "That's...that's all?"

A flicker of a dimple grooved his cheek on one side. "That's all."

Well. He wasn't going to make that *easy* for me, naturally; but just how hard it would be, I wasn't going to be made aware until I moved.

Centering my stance, I breathed deeply and released the air again from the very bottoms of my lungs.

One. Two. Three.

I lunged to Kai's left; he tossed the knife to himself and caught it, and as he moved, I feinted, slipping right. But he spun with sinuous, serpentine speed, bringing his knife in an easy-blocked stroke toward my shoulder.

When I caught his dagger with mine, he *shoved* with brutal might...forcing me back to the desk.

"Again."

Licking my lips, I tried for a simple approach...a hard lunge without preamble. He caught me with the brace of his arm and slung me back toward the desk again.

Cursing, I heaved his arm away, smashing my hands into his chest; he backed off, eyes gleaming. "Again, Miss Weathers."

It was the most infuriating training he'd put me through so far; wild dashes and calculated slips both met the same end. It was always Kai, right in my way, forcing me to block, parry, retreat. I wasn't gaining ground…I was losing it so much it felt like the door was slipping away.

Frustration bubbled hot and thick, tarring my insides after an hour of failed attempt after failed attempt. Sweat stuck my curls against my forehead as I paced before the desk, measuring Kai with his ridiculous, unbothered face and his ridiculous, casual stance.

Luck flip it all.

Clenching my grip around my dagger, I broke into a charge; and when he rose to the tips of his feet, prepared to leap one way or another when I dodged him, I didn't give him the chance.

I barreled my whole weight into his offset balance, shoving him back and plunging my knife in a downward thrust.

Kai caught the blow overhand; his smile flared, baring a sharp cut of teeth. "Yes!" he barked. "There it is!"

"There *what* is?" I snarled.

"Even if you have no interest in using your weapons, your enemies *will*," he said. "You will never survive the Jubilee unless you *think* as they do…think like them *first*, and then *act* as yourself."

He bore down against the knife, backing me up swiftly. My hips smashed against the edge of the desk, jarring it with an ear-splitting screech, sending his chair tumbling and papers floating across the surface. Kai pressed in, one hand jammed against the wood beside my waist as he bent me backward over the desk, his blade shoving mine down above my head.

"Fight back." His lips flared around the words. "Find a way to slip free."

Difficult, with his leonine frame pressing me down, with the brunt of his knife arm deadening mine—

But I still had one free hand.

I cast across the desk, feeling, fidgeting, finding, scraping…

There it is!

Grabbing a poetry book, I clapped it against his ear; he ducked and cursed, one hand flying to the side of his head, and I seized my chance. Slithering out from under him, I nicked the drape of his sleeve in passing—then spun back to him, keeping one arm behind my back. I drilled my boot into the back of his knees, tossing him down against the desk; then I drove my weight into him, pressing the tip of my knife above his kidney.

Stretching up on my tiptoes, I breathed against his ear: "*My* round."

"Yours," he yielded, panting; when I drew back, he turned to face me, still scrubbing at his ear. "A handy trick."

"I'll never be quite strong enough to break a man's skull with a book," I said, "but the resonance from striking the ear..."

"Indeed." He winced as he drew his hand away, and my stomach tumbled over itself.

"Kai, I didn't mean to—"

The instant I stepped nearer, his blade touched my throat.

"*My* round," he murmured, softer and more serious than he had been all day. "Compassion is a strength your opponents will not hesitate to twist for their own ends. You should have gone for the door."

"Noted," I gulped.

The dagger spun back into its sheath behind his back before I'd drawn my next breath. "Well done. That will be all for this afternoon."

"Well done? I never made it to the door."

"But you acted with your knowledge...of what I would do, and what you could do to best me." He tossed me the poetry book, and I caught it by instinct. "The door was not the lesson."

Grinning, I crossed the room to the furniture we'd pushed against the walls that morning. Draping myself across the nearest chair, I played with my sleeves and watched him, metering my breath carefully. Waiting.

Kai shuffled through several papers dislodged by our knocking into the desk. He straightened the fountain pen and stood the chair back to its feet. Then his gaze slid across the array of books, papers, red thread...and the teetering tower of poetry that was so rarely disturbed.

A predatory stillness coursed over his body...awareness stoked like a fire.

I wrinkled my nose. *Flipping Luck, that was fast.*

He leaned his fists into his desk. "Naomi?"

"Yes?" I purred, schooling my features into the image of innocence.

His gaze shot to me, a smile wrenching the corners of his mouth. "Where is Giddy Gus?"

I rolled my eyes up to the vaulted ceiling. "How in fickle Luck should I know?"

"Naomi, please."

I wagged a finger his way. "No, no. I will not take responsibility for you misplacing an entire human skull, Kai."

Slowly, he pushed up from the desk. "Take your left hand out from behind your back."

A demure swivel of the wrists behind my waist, and I wagged my left hand his way. "Satisfied?"

"*Both* hands."

Plastering on the most pronounced pout I could muster, I swapped the skull to my other hand, then bared both before him. He dragged in a deep breath, pursing his lips, peering down his nose at Giddy Gus, crossing his arms and flexing them as he settled his weight.

Then he pinned his dry look on *me*.

"What?" Mirth bubbled under my tone; I could barely keep my giggles at bay. "He was lonely. You haven't been rambling at him as often...he needed a friend."

"Put the skull back, Naomi."

Sticking out my tongue, I sashayed to the desk and lowered Giddy Gus gingerly back to his post. "You, Poet, are precisely no fun at all."

His hand flashed out, swift as a dagger strike—but possibly I was growing too used to his presence, to his movements, after all of the hours we'd spent training in this room. Because I didn't even flinch when he seized my wrist; I simply deposited Gus and then straightened, watching Kai's face.

He watched mine; then his focus trailed down the length of my arm, to where his hand held my wrist. "You stole him without my notice."

"Cardigan sleeves." I jiggled the free one. "They cuff at just the right place."

"Your sleight of hand is improving."

A flush dappled the bridge of my nose and flared across my cheeks. "Well, I didn't think I should stop practicing after we stole the invitation, considering we still have one *more* thing of importance to steal."

"You do recall that I will be doing the stealing, and you the distracting."

I shrugged, tugging a bit at his grip—and oddly enough, wishing I hadn't when his hold loosened. "I'd like to be adept at both. Just in case."

Sharper heat flared in my veins as, for just a brief instant, Kai's thumb grazed the pulse at the inside of my wrist. "I am...very proud of the progress you've made, Miss Weathers."

What in Luck was I supposed to say to *that*?

Nothing at all, it turned out; because before I had wrangled my tongue into a respectable response of any sort, Kai released me, leaning back over his desk, all splayed palms and bowed head and focus fixed on his work. "I have a mark to plan for. I'll see you at dinner."

I mimed his least-favorite curtsy. "Your Poisonousness."

"Naomi, I swear on my own grave—"

"Blah, blah." I mimed a flapping mouth with one hand. "Tell it to Gus."

The levity had yet to fade from my footfalls as I flounced to the door, drawing it open; I slipped through, then hesitated as I swept it shut...as his low voice swiveled through the narrow gap behind me.

"Lonely, are you?" A tap of a fountain pen on bone. "I'll give you something to think about, you empty-headed, cavernous creature."

Grinning, I shut the door.

CHAPTER 50
THICK AS THIEVES

M Y NEXT MEETING WITH Phin, arranged through a note handed to a scowling Mistress Merrietti, was in a dark market tucked away over the edge of the beggar's district...somewhere I could be fairly confident Kai wouldn't find us.

There was an odd thrill walking through the city with the stinging cut of a contraband invitation still pulsing on my fingertips. No one looked twice at me while I tended my patients or when I made my way afterward to the corridor of shadowed awnings where less expensive—and often less reputable—wares were sold.

I'd felt like a match for Rastra in many ways since my arrival...especially after I'd stolen the Lightbane from Merrietti. But this was different, this success Kai and I had wrangled together at Dashian's playhouse.

I couldn't quite explain it; I just knew I was smiling and confident in every stride while I wandered down the tunnel of the market between potted trees so overgrown, their branches tangled overhead in a brittle, woven dome. No one had bothered replacing the deciduous plants with cold-hardy ivies or lichens, either, so there was no new growth here, strung like Mithra-Sha's *Spirited Sunrise* garlands among the bare branches.

This corridor of the city felt the dimmest, the closest to winter's death. But that didn't wipe the grin off my face when I spotted Phin casually perusing a stand of necklaces and charms woven out of thin wire and what looked suspiciously like broken glass shards sanded down into imitation gemstones.

I knocked my shoulder against his back in greeting, leaning over the wares beside him. "What do you suppose—beryl, or lager bottle?"

"Eh, it's never really a question of quality." Phin pocketed his hands, shooting me a grin. "It's whether you can convince the person you're buying it for that it has value."

"Oh, so *sly*," I teased as we both straightened.

"I prefer to think of it like this: if they think it has value, whether it does or not, doesn't that *make* it valuable?"

"Unless they're planning to pass it down as an inheritance...or unless they fall on hard times."

"Ah, ah, shh-shh-shh." He pressed one finger to his lips, the others cocked at half-mast while he made a show of peering around the numinous shadows lurking beneath the entangled boughs. "Not the best place to talk about *hard times*."

"Fair enough." I beckoned him with a sway of my head, and we wandered down to a fruit cart selling produce past its prime; deeply discounted, but not moldering yet.

"You look tired," Phin remarked as I browsed the fruits and vegetables.

"Mmm, well, being this city's only affordable healer will do that to you." I neglected mentioning that my exhaustion had more to do with preparing for the Jubilee...scheming with Kai about all of the things that would make us both sharp, make us blend in...but also not betray us as anything other than humble bistro owners awestruck at the invitation.

The double deception required late nights now in addition to my already-early mornings. And I had a feeling Phin wouldn't take kindly to how much time I was spending in close proximity to his almost-killer.

"This city needs an infirmary, Phin," I added—rescuing myself from that dangerous thought-path. "Luck flip the cost. This is *much* more need than any one person can possibly meet."

"I hear you." He stuffed his hands into his pockets. "I'll look into it, if I ever become Drui—maybe when I'm about eighty-five."

"I meant that you could speak to your grandfather about it. Or possibly your mother."

A rueful smile coiled up one corner of his mouth. "You think I haven't? Lu and I—even Uncle Cass—we've talked about all kinds of reform with them until we're blue in the face." He bobbed a helpless shrug. "Doesn't change anything. They have their own ideas about what's worth the cost. Nothing's going to change during this regime."

"Well, not with that sort of pessimism, they won't." I knocked my shoulder against his again. "You look tired, too."

And he did; there were darker circles under his eyes than I'd seen since the day we'd met, when he was recovering from his brush with death, and he dragged his feet a bit as we wandered from one vendor booth to the next.

"I am. It hasn't been easy, moving these marks faster than the soul-senders can get to them." He yawned, ruffling a hand through his hair. "That last run, out to the dam for the bridgekeeper? I didn't even sleep that night...feels like I haven't caught my breath since."

Sympathy twisted in my middle. "But at least these people are alive thanks to what we're doing."

"There is that." Phin pinched and rubbed at the corners of his eyes, then shook his head fiercely and focused on me again. "So, what have you got for me?"

"I know who the Poet is going after next," I offered. "I caught the name on the notes he was going over this morning: Vespertine Craley. But you should have the rest of this week to recover before it's time to move him."

Phin's pallor turned ashen in a heartbeat—so swiftly I laid a hand to his chest and halted us both, fearing he might buckle down to his knees.

"Are you all right?" I demanded. "Do you know him personally?"

"Yeah...yeah, I...Vez is around our age, he's a friend." Phin's tongue swiped his lips. "He's *my* friend."

And we were about to consign him to an indeterminate slumber—in the hopes of saving him from a far worse fate.

"I'm sorry, Phin," I croaked. And I was—for the necessity of all of this. And for what I knew it cost, to stand by while your friends struggled, and to do nothing...because you knew that intervening would be worse for everyone.

It was what made my visits to Vallanmyre so awful lately.

"I am, too." Phin swallowed, rubbing a hand over his eyes, then pinning me with that hopeless, pleading stare. "You're sure you don't have enough that we can just move on him *now*?"

I shook my head. "No, not yet. I haven't copied all the names of his marks, I can only do that in batches when he's distracted—and there's something he's working toward right now, something important. I have to keep going."

"Fine, fine, all right...I know," Phin grumbled. "But I don't have to like it."

I scooped up my bag of produce, offering him a fleeting smile. "Neither of us do."

I left him with that—a warning of what was coming and the hope of what I was uncovering—and ducked from the side-market.

In solitude, I found some of my cheeriness had blunted; with Phin, there was always the feeling that I wasn't doing *enough*, that I wasn't moving as quickly as I should. That I wasn't being as helpful as he expected.

It was part of why I'd given him the name—penance and a peace offering; but that didn't stoke my joy again as I put distance between us, crossing a pair of bridges back to the more populated parts of Rastra.

The longer Phin was here, and the more times we met, the more my mission in Rastra felt like borrowed time.

I sidestepped the crowds pouring out of various sidestreets to one of the city's arterial avenues; foot traffic was heavier this way, and while I preferred the concealment, the road wound past Beris's bistro—and I was going to have to avoid that like a plague from now on.

Ducking down an alley instead, I meandered past wrought-iron seating arrangements and apartment windows buttressed by flowerboxes and hung trellises; I skimmed my fingers along evergreen leaves and pine boughs, unwinding a breath of relief when I found the street on the far side much less crowded.

It would be an easy trek back to the manse from this way...and I couldn't deny I was looking forward to a night of routine again. Practicing Hadrassi waltzes. Playing cards and talking about assassin fetes.

Things that would erase the weariness in Phin's face from my mind. And my guilty heart.

"How many lives did you save today, troublemaker?"

I jumped halfway out of my skin, shrieking and spinning and swinging my bag like a battering ram—and Kai still batted it aside like an afterthought as he straightened up from the alley archway, where I hadn't even seen him lounging.

"That isn't a weapon," he pointed out. "Where's your dagger?"

"Give me a moment, and I'll pull it out and stick it in your eye!" I smacked the bag against his hip this time, and he bent with the blow, raising a brow.

"An assailant wouldn't give you a moment."

"When did this become one of your *lessons* about surviving assassins?" I hissed.

"Everything is a lesson about survival. Haven't you learned anything?" The upward stitch at one corner of his mouth was the only sign that he was teasing me—and possibly enjoying it *far* too much.

"Ugh," I snapped. "What are you *doing* here?"

"By all accounts, meeting a friend." He raised a brow—a silent reminder that, behind the mask he wore as the Poet Poisoner, he was nothing but an innocent citizen strolling Rastra's streets. "You haven't answered my question."

"About what I've *learned*?"

"About saving lives, Miss Weathers."

Oh. Right. That.

"I don't know about saving lives." I brushed a corkscrew curl from my forehead. "But I did help a little girl's seasonal cough, and I pulled a tick from an old man's beard—and I convinced a shopkeeper that her teeth would be in much better repair if she ate a piece of fruit every once in a while."

I raised the bag for evidence—and he lifted it lightly from my grasp, pivoting smoothly so my upraised hand tucked itself neatly in the crook of his arm.

"What are you *doing*?" I laughed; this was a lighter, airier side than I've ever seen to him. And I wasn't entirely sure I minded it.

"You must have heard the rumors." He bent his head conspiratorially my way. "A local bistro owner is in absolute fits, offering a full year's worth of free meals to anyone who can help retrieve her mysteriously missing invitation to a certain Jubilee at year's end."

"Scandalous!" I pressed a hand over my heart, frowning at the racing cadence of it.

Quiet, you. No one knows who really stole the flipping thing. The invitation was hidden in my satchel back at the manse; unlike Beris, I knew better than to carry it on me everywhere.

"With such blatant thievery afoot, it seemed ill-mannered to let you walk home unescorted. After all, who knows what they might set out to steal next. Handkerchiefs, anklets..." he peered into the bag. "Cabbages."

So he had crossed the city, and found me...to walk me back to the manse. Not to protect me from thieves, but to keep me from being found out as one.

Maybe I should've been more worried he could have found me with Phin—that he still might, if he insisted on making this a habit. But for now, nothing but gratitude warmed me, like a sip of the richest cocoa ever made.

I grinned, bumping my shoulder against his. "Well, I was going to decline the offer, but I couldn't risk anything happening to my precious cabbages."

"Then you understand my concern." Kai slipped his arm from under my hand only to curve it behind my back—leading me off the road and down a footpath nearer to the canal. "But we'll be taking a small diversion. There's someone I need to see before we return to the manse."

CHAPTER 51
BENEATH THE FIRELIGHT

KAI'S WAY THROUGH THE city was one I hadn't taken often—through the darkest streets my patients had warned me not to travel alone. Hurrying along the shadowy edges of the canals, where figures slunk with the glint of knives at their belts, seemed in direct contradiction to what Kai claimed we were trying to avoid: detection. An attack. Retribution for what we'd stolen at Dashian's playhouse.

Kai ushered me with a hand perpetually behind my back—mostly to herd me when I hesitated, but there was a warning in the set of his shoulders and the lift of his head that anyone with ill intentions would be foolish to ignore.

Still, I didn't breathe easily until we reached a lighter path...a narrow twist of cobblestone that edged the side of the canal to our left, the water eddying several feet below the artful iron railing. To our right were short complexes of apartments bisected by alleys in neat, narrow rows. Neighbors could have called to each other across those gaps, or thrown a ball back and forth from one rooftop to another.

"Where are we, precisely?" I asked.

"The sort of place one finds lodging when they have coin they don't want anyone to know they're in possession of." Kai turned me suddenly down one of the alleys, and I slowed when I realized it was occupied: by an elderly woman in a wheeled chair, and a flock of children she seemed to be watching over.

"Who—?" I began.

"Another of my contacts." Kai fished in his deep pocket and drew out a small sachet wafting an unmistakable scent—the one that permeated his workroom every day we worked in there.

I shot him a look of reproach. Lips twitching, he held the sachet up between two fingers.

"Not poison," he assured me. "When distilled of its harsher properties, the scraps left over from the Lightbane plant become brittle. Powdered, they can be used to treat a host of ailments...including those that come with life spent in a wheeled chair."

Tossing the sachet with a flip and catching it in his palm, he sauntered down the alley toward the back of the woman's chair; I watched him go for a whole count of three before I managed to shake off my shocked stupor.

"I never heard about *that* in Harrow Hall," I muttered, trotting after him.

Kai had just reached the chair when I caught up; he rested his hand on the occupant's wizened shoulder, giving it the lightest squeeze.

Knobby fingers gripped the wheels and pivoted the chair so quickly, it almost crushed Kai's toes.

"Don't you creep up on me in the dark, you—! Oh." She paused, her gaze dancing between us. "Well, hello there, handsome."

"Valessa." His dipped his chin.

"Kai." The old woman shifted, folding her hands over her lap, bright blue eyes twinkling with mischief. "Come to flirt?"

"Ah...no." A slide of a smile on one side of his mouth, and I could've sworn a blush warmed his cheeks, soft in the lamplight before he extended his palm. "No, I came to bring you the usual."

"Oh, my herbs!" Valessa twined her gnarled fingers over her heart. "Look at the *size* of that sachet...you spoil me rotten, you swarthy fool."

Kai bowed low, extending the sachet of scraps to her. "Only the best, for the best eyes and ears in Rastra."

"And you said you weren't *flirting*." The old woman shot me a cheeky smile and dipped her voice to a conspiratorial whisper, "Don't let jealousy get the best of you, love. He only likes me for my body."

Kai and I sputtered at the same time, shooting wide-eyed glances at each other.

"There's nothing to be jealous *about*—" I protested.

"I said your *eyes and ears*, you ridiculous—" Kai snapped.

Valessa burst into laughter, settling back into her seat. "Certainly, there's not. And certainly, you did." She winked at Kai. "Then who is this lovely woman, if not your escort for the night?"

"She is my..." Kai veered another glance my way, then rubbed the back of his neck. "Partner."

"Naomi." I offered my hand to Valessa. "Aspiring herbalist."

"Valessa." She tipped her head as she clasped my hand, looking me up and down. "Still sharp as a knife, so you're welcome to drop the herbalist lie, love. We both know Kai's soul is stained with the worst of them...he's got no need for an herbalist to assist him."

"I don't believe that." I jerked back my hand, tucking it around my satchel strap. "I don't think a sullied soul would bother bringing herb scraps to an old woman for her comforts."

"Old, but not deaf!" Valessa reminded me with a grin. "These are payments."

Kai tucked his hands behind his back, flashing her a charming smile. "Very few people pay an appropriate amount of concern to a nosy old woman."

"And few old women know precisely where to stick those noses." Valessa tapped the side of hers—then all at once, her brows knitted together. "Which is how I caught this particular rumor, Kai. You ought to be careful."

A chill darted down my spine; Kai crouched beside her chair, draping one wrist on the armrest, his other hand settled on his thigh. "Tell me."

Valessa bent nearer, but I still caught her whisper: "Phineaus Moraven has been spotted here in Rastra."

My hand clapped to my mouth, trapping the yelp that wanted to set itself free. Kai tensed, his hand curling into a fist that knocked against her armrest. "You're certain those rumors are true?"

"Not proven yet," Valessa admitted. "If he *is* here, he's keeping low to the ground. But that should concern you, too."

"Because if he were here on official business, it wouldn't be mere rumor...he wouldn't slink through the shadows, trying to keep his presence secret." Kai was quiet for a moment; then he lurched to his feet. "Thank you for your time...and the information. We should be going."

"You don't want to stay for the show?" Valessa gestured to the children, unpacking what I could see from this distance was a crate of Ameresh fireworks. "They've been saving for these for months. It'll be a beautiful display, no doubt."

Kai glanced at me; I struggled to marshal my features into something bland before I shrugged. "I don't have anywhere else to be."

It was a relief when he took the lead, ascending a staggered heap of old crates to the low rooftops lining the alleyway—it gave me time to gather my thoughts, to calm my racing heart. To adopt a neutral tone when I asked, as we edged down the alley line to find a gap between the boxes of winter greenery, "Do you really think the Druavas is here?"

"Entirely possible." Kai settled himself on the edge of the second roof with an enviable amount of dispassionate ease. "The only question is *why*?"

"As in, did his family send him?"

"More to the point...could he be here for one of us?"

I opened my mouth, then shut it, gnawing at the corner of my lip as I braced both hands on the scalloped edge of the roof, bending to peer down at the children lining up their fireworks in the alley below. "Luck, I hope not."

Kai's gaze settled on me, dark and heavy as the fall of night; then he braced his hands on either side of his thighs, his smallest finger crooking up to brush the back of my nearest knuckle.

"If he is," he rumbled, "I will never let him drag you back to that Fortress."

My gaze jerked to him; he met the twist of my head with the flick of his other hand, tucking a wayward curl behind my ear.

"You're safe with me."

But was *he* safe with *me*?

Blowing out a slow breath, I moved my hand from beneath his under the excuse of gesturing to Valessa and her grandchildren. "So, these are all of your contacts?" I teased lightly. "A widow and her daughter, a playhouse owner, and a crippled old woman?"

Kai waited through the lurch and burst of the first firework setting off—a vivid blue spiral launching and exploding high above our heads—before he answered.

"Nera was a housekeeper for Rastra's governor, before Sofi fell ill...her husband once led the sentinel forces in this city. He took ill and died of a lung infection a fortnight after he refused the governor's command to have the beggar's district plundered and its inhabitants run out or killed." His fingers tightened around the rooftop's edge. "Dashian's first playhouse burned to cinders with no obvious cause after he tore up a contract requiring him to cater to only the elite—his life's work and all of his coin, plundered. And Valessa once served as a spy hired on behalf of the Moravens by one of their closest allies." His jaw shifted before he added quietly, "Her crippling was not accidental...though it wasn't the killing blow intended when she resigned her services."

I blinked, choked by those horrific truths, and twisted to stare at Valessa—her face painted in the glow of the small Ameresh fireworks, her gap-toothed smile broadening by the moment as she watched her grandchildren frolic in the sparkles like a rainstorm.

These were the people he chose to surround himself with...the contacts he made. Not the most powerful, the wealthiest, those with bone-quaking talent...but the people hurt by those who had those things. The people cast off by them. The ones lost in the lurch, and with a grudge to hold for it.

And maybe that was what he cared about most…that they'd been wounded enough to turn against the same people Kai hunted. And that they had ears and eyes in places that could turn a profit for his plan.

But that didn't explain the cure for Sofi. The business he brought to Dashian. The powdered herbs set aside to ease an old woman's aches. Or why we were sitting here, on this rooftop, watching the fireworks sizzle and explode overhead, striping the alleyway walls in emerald swaths; why we were stealing a moment that earned us absolutely nothing but the beauty and joy of it all.

And maybe it was Valessa's assumptions, or how Kai had spoken to her—or the way he surveyed the alley and its occupants like a man with something to protect—that made me feel suddenly bold enough to rest my head against his shoulder.

He stiffened, for a moment; and then, when he could've shrugged me off, he simply shifted…sliding a hairsbreadth nearer.

"There are people in this city who would be dead or worse if not for you," I murmured. "You may not think that counts for much, but I happen to think it's admirable."

"That never used to concern me."

I tilted back, searching the silhouette of his face painted in fireworks. "But now?"

Before he could answer, one of Valessa's grandsons skipped up to stand beneath the rooftop, holding an unlit firework our way like a knife to a throat. "Hey, up there! Kai! My grandmama says she's going to marry you…that true?"

Snorting, Kai sprang lithely down and caught the boy under the arms; he swooped him up on the perch of his shoulder, plucking the firework from his hand. "Let's go have a *word* with your grandmother, shall we?"

Then he sprawled the boy over his back and sauntered down the alley, toward a cackling Valessa and the rest of her hooting, giggling grandchildren.

I just stayed, and watched while Kai bent over the old woman's chair, planting a kiss on her hair; laughing with the children when they chortled and gagged. And grinning when Kai snatched the flintrock from one of the girls and crouched, helping her set off the largest firework—sending it bursting in a haze of green-and-gold sparks above, lighting up the depths of Kai's eyes when they found mine.

And then he smiled, and, *Luck*…I'd never seen him grin like that before. It crinkled the corners of his eyes almost shut; it altered the shape of his mouth, baring his teeth in a silvery slash, and wrinkled the sides of his nose a bit.

It transformed him from the scowling recluse built of shadows into someone who belonged here beneath these glittering lights. As if, for one moment, the assassin was consumed in a shower of dazzling emerald stars, and a different man was looking back at me.

A man I almost wanted to walk me home every night for the rest of my life.

A new note joined the rest in my journal that night, after we returned to the manse, before my racing thoughts would let me sleep; a task scribbled in invisible ink in the margins...a secret pressed between the pages like a petal. Like a kiss. Like a promise.

Make Kai smile like that again.

CHAPTER 52
UNRAVELED AND UNDONE

"A**H-HA!**" M**Y TRIUMPHANT SHOUT** was the perfect herald to the slap of cards on the table in front of Kai's study hearth. "A full suit of blades! I win!"

He frowned at the cards—the fifth round I'd won of the popular Hadrassi game of Suits—then shot a reproachful look at me. "You must be cheating."

"I mustn't, to beat you." Smiling smugly, I settled back in my seat, arms folded. "You lost, fair and final. *Admit it.*"

Gathering both our hands—and the last two rounds we'd played—Kai shuffled the deck, tapping the corners lightly against the tabletop. "I refuse to admit defeat to a Mithran cheat who *claims* to have never played Hadrassi cards before."

"You really think I could have acted how badly I was losing when we first started playing?" That, in itself, was almost a backhanded compliment.

"I believe you are clever enough to be capable of anything, Miss Weathers." Kai dealt the next hand with the precision of throwing blades. "Even deceiving me."

I hid my wince in a sip of cocoa.

We were tucked into opposite chairs with the hearthfront table between us in his study; we'd been playing this game of Suits for hours, just like every night for the past several weeks—when we weren't practicing the quick draw of my dagger, or learning the steps of a Hadrassi waltz, or spending time out in the streets together, reading crowds while he walked me home from the beggar's district as he had every night since I'd last met with Phin.

That change had ground my series of clandestine meetings with the Druavas to a screeching halt. I wished that bothered me more than it did, when the exchange was nothing more than time spent preparing for the Jubilee with Kai.

But tonight, like all the others, I didn't find myself dreaming of other places to be; not while I scooped up my cards and peered coyly at him over the fan of them. "So, what do you suppose? Am I almost ready to play at the card tables of *assassins*?"

"Nearly." He offered a wry, one-sided smile. "If only to gamble and lose my coin."

I rolled my eyes. "Flattery will get you *everywhere*, you know. Just ask Giddy Gus—I'm sure that's why he hasn't left after all these years."

"How many compliments do you suppose I pay to that skull?"

"You tell me—I still hear you mumbling in here with him some mornings before I bring coffee."

So much so that I didn't even find it troubling anymore. We all had our ways of coping with the unimaginable; and an assassin could do far worse than sating his loneliness by talking to himself...or to the skull on his desk, Luck forbid.

But the more we settled into our routine of morning coffee and work in the hidden room before we began our daily tasks, the less I heard him talking when I arrived; like he was storing up the conversation for my arrival.

I didn't mind that, either.

We played through two more games of Suits before Kai cleared his throat—always a troubling prelude to something I wasn't likely going to be happy about.

"You should know that the Jubilee will not only be well-attended," he said, shuffling the latest hand back together again, "it will be a show of status. The Guild Garrote flaunt like peacocks...you can expect the most lavish of the lavish from them. Fine dress is also expected of whomever receives an invitation." A scoff chafed in his throat. "Many commoners have gone from modest to poor just to pay for one night's revelry."

For better or worse, we'd spared Beris *that* fate. "So, we'll be expected to dress fancy, is what you're wanting me to know."

His eyes darted to mine, and a grin slipped across my lips when I caught the reserve lurking behind that stare.

"I don't know whether you're afraid to ask me if I could afford a nice dress already, or if you're worried about asking me to buy one," I teased, taking the cards he dealt me right from his hand. "But you should know I love pretty dresses as much as the next woman, and, no, I didn't precisely have the time to pack for parties when I fled from Fortress Ferregrand."

"Then you know where the coinpurse lives." He skipped a glance toward his desk. "Remember, the purpose here is both to impress and to blend in."

"Stand out, and disappear." I was already having ideas; I'd encountered my fair share of cloths and fabric cuts thanks to my father's peddling business, and my brief time rooting through my closet in the Fortress had introduced me to several Hadrassi styles.

I could manage this part of the infiltration without embarrassing—or out-ing—us both.

"One more game?" I pleaded when Kai shoved back his chair and stood, gathering our plates and his empty cup. "I promise to let you win this time!"

His mouth quirked to the side. "Is that meant to entice me?"

I scrunched my nose. "I promise to also make it look like an accident?"

"You absolutely spoil me." He paused as he circled behind his chair, tapping his thumb along its swooped back. "Truly, you...you've made this manse a more bearable place by far, these last few months. I hope you're aware of that."

Heat bloomed along the back of my neck and climbed into my cheeks. The laugh I forced was a bit breathless. "If you don't stop complimenting me, I might just catch fire."

"Well, we certainly can't have that." Relief touched his tone as he leaned back from the chair. "Only insults from now on."

Somehow, I doubted that.

And somehow, I was already looking forward to another dinner in his study—whether it led to dancing, or card games, or something else entirely.

I managed to bury the thought of compliments and future dinners deep in soil I hoped would *smother* it when I curled up in my bed an hour later, poking through the pages of a poetry collection by the infamous Kilgrave. I'd never had much use for rhyme and fancy notions as a girl; I liked things to be plainspoken, straightforward, like the facts of healing and poisoning and even the recipes I'd inherited from my mother or read from the cookbooks here in the manse.

But the more I read Kilgrave's particular style of poetry—more like prose, Audra would've called it, tangential thoughts that somehow made sense in the havoc of the human head and heart—I found I was developing an appreciation for it.

Something I would never in a hundred years share with my murderous host.

But, as fickle Luck liked it best, that was where he found me anyway: blankets puddled around my hips, hair tied up and pajamas donned, propped back against my pillow and thumbing through another of Kilgrave's nondescript volumes of prose. This one contained the fevered longings of forbidden love, and entirely against my will, a few of the lines had already made my toes curl.

You wrap me up in your promises, in the seat of your affection, you try to stitch me together with it...I'm undone.
We're running with all our might toward the inevitable, love, and I'm unraveling, unraveling...how long are you going to drag the threads of me after you, tangling your feet, stumbling, falling, rising again?
How long until you let me go?

A throat cleared in across the room; I jumped, flattening my toes against the mattress, peeking over the rim of the book at Kai.

That shy glance revealed him, not dressed in his bedclothes the way he was most nights when he popped his head into my doorway to say goodnight; instead he was decked in shadow-dark linen and black, seamless trousers, donning his cloak that pinned to one shoulder...cowl and hood in one seamless piece.

"I'm leaving now," he announced.

I dropped the book facedown in my lap, a lie about how I wasn't enjoying Kilgrave's work at all tangling on my tongue. "I beg your pardon?"

I hadn't bothered peeking between the drapes for the last hour, but it had to be long past dusk. This was the time we usually said our goodnights, occasionally lingered in each other's doorways for a chat about the poetry he was reading or the Hadrassi history books I'd pulled off his study shelves.

Kai never left at night unless I was going with him. Unless—

"Vespertine's manse." He knocked his fist lightly on the doorpost.

Every semblance of peace I'd sunk into since our card game evaporated in a foul rush, like having the air sucked from my lungs. I scrambled upright, shoving the blankets aside. "That's tonight? *Already?*"

"It is."

I flattened my curls against my scalp, willing myself for calm; he'd gone on five marks since I'd diluted the inkpots, and I'd never felt this churning in my gut before.

But then...before...he hadn't walked me home. He hadn't taken me to meet Valessa. He hadn't gone to Dashian's theater with me, stolen the invitation with me, laughed breathless in that alley with me. Given that same cloak to me, to keep me warm.

Why did the Kai I'd last said *happy hunting* to—and fallen asleep right after he'd left to slip a poisoned note to the bridgekeeper at the nearby dam—feel like a different Kai from the one tipped against my doorframe now?

Why did my chest feel so lucking *tight*?

When I didn't say anything, Kai pushed himself upright with a shove of knuckles to the door. "Sleep well, Miss Weathers. Steep the coffee strong in the morning...I suspect I'll need it."

"Kai?" I called after him, jolting to the edge of the bed but freezing when my bare feet touched the cold floor; and when he glanced back, I found myself still lost for words.

What could I ever say to an assassin I should've wanted to fail? To a man whose fate I realized all at once I cared entirely too much about...someone I would really miss if he never came back at all?

His gaze softened by the slightest degree. "Naomi."

Swallowing shouldn't hurt like this; holding his gaze shouldn't feel so impossible. "Just...watch out for yourself."

The faintest dip of his head. "I'll see you soon."

Then he was gone, the door whispering shut behind him...leaving me alone in the rumpled sheets, my book forgotten, feeling as if it would be a very long time before I could take a full breath again.

CHAPTER 53
THE POET'S PAST

THAT NIGHT WAS ONE of the longest I'd lived in Hadrass-Drui. And I couldn't find my calm, no matter what I did.

I tidied up the manse. Sequestered myself in the study and flipped through Kai's poetry books until my temples hurt. Checked and rechecked my antidote, which was currently on its fifth of seven days steeping in a curing oil. Paced in the same track that Kai himself had worn into the shellacked wood around the corridor that looped the inner courtyard; traced my fingertips over a pale path on the wall that he'd worn down into the paint with the brush of his hand.

I sat in his chair for the first time, admired its cushiness, then drummed a tune on Giddy Gus's head—the only time I smiled all night.

I made two mugs of bone broth cocoa in starlight mugs, and sat at the dining table, sipping mine though my queasy stomach rebelled. Chin resting on my folded arms, I watched the steam drift from his mug, then taper off, then vanish altogether.

The next thing I knew, I was waking to the slam of something heavy against solid wood—so close that at first, I thought I'd knocked my mug off the table. I fumbled upright, my back aching from lying against the table for too long, my heart jamming into my throat as I slipped off the seat; blinking wildly, I struggled to orient myself to the early-morning light nudging through the windows looking out into the courtyard. To the pair of mugs on the table, one absolutely cold and undrinkable, the other empty—neither one broken, thank Luck.

Then came the rattling, axing grind of metal on metal. Of latches fumbling and grating together like bone against bone.

Cursing, I flew through the short hall to the foyer, tugging at the locks from my side and succeeding in sliding them apart after several sweat-slick seconds. I wrenched the door open and found myself faced with—

Blood.

So much blood. Blackening wine-dark clothes, dripping from leather boot tips, turning the ends of sable hair tacky and sticking them to the sides of a neck where the pulse fought and fluttered visibly.

Kai slumped his shoulder against the doorframe, panting, one hand pressed over his side. Blood puddled between his fingers and spilled over his knuckles, plopping on the floor.

"I need your help," he panted, dragging his gaze up to meet mine.

Then he sagged down to his knees.

"Flipping—*Luck*!" I lunged, catching him by the collar, an odd, tenuous stillness sweeping through me when blood squeezed from the fabric and slickened between my fingers.

The healer's calm. The poignant and precise inner quiet that came with knowing I was someone's only hope—and to be that, I also had to be the strongest person in the room.

So I smothered the shrill teakettle whistle of panic singing in my ears; I twisted, ducking under Kai's arm, drawing it across my shoulders and wrapping mine around his waist.

"Lean on me," I urged.

He had no choice; I was doing most of the walking for both of us, his feet managing not much more than a stumble through the foyer and to the left, into the sitting room. I'd just finished liberating it of cobwebs earlier that week, so I was relatively confident of its cleanliness compared to the rest of the manse...and I wasn't certain Kai could make it any farther than the sheet-draped sofa taking up the middle of the room.

I whipped the pale cloth off the swooped back and bowed us both; Kai took his weight on the bend of his forearm, slumping into the cushions as I crouched before him. My fingers were shockingly steady against the racing of my heart as they flew through undoing his buttons and pushed the halves of his shirt apart; I hissed a breath in through my teeth at the array of lacerations and punctures and bruises that lurked below, all masked under a film of blood.

"What *happened*?" I demanded, my gaze shooting to his face.

He watched me through half-lidded eyes, a thatch of dark hair falling across his brow. "Ambush. At Vespertine's manse."

My stillness had nothing to do with calm now; it was horror that rooted me in place.

Phineaus.

I'd told him about Vespertine—his friend. The first mark I'd shared before Kai struck them.

No, no, no...

All this blood couldn't be on my hands. Phin couldn't be responsible for this—he *knew* how much was at stake.

Kai's anguished groan jerked me from my thoughts; he swatted my hand away, wrapping one arm around his middle, struggling to lift himself upright along the seatback with the other. "I'll handle this."

"Absolutely not!" I straightened, taking his shoulder gently, pushing him back down. "No. I'm a healer, I can fix this."

I *had* to fix this.

Kai crumbled back under my touch, pinning a glare on me. "I have been stitching my own wounds for—"

"More than half your life, I know." I caught his head when it bobbed and started to sink, his bearded jaw softened by the dampness of blood caught in the stubble. "But I'm here now. You don't *have* to."

He gave no more protest—maybe saving his strength for what we both knew was coming.

I had never run faster in my life than I did through the halls of the manse just then, to retrieve my satchel and the healing supplies inside. I was winded by the time I skidded back into the parlor where, to my relief, Kai had managed to shift himself around. He sprawled on the sofa now, one arm braced along the swooped frame, his back propped to the armrest.

The calm settled like relief the moment I laid eyes on him again—breathing and awake, though his eyes were pained slits, fixed on me as I crossed the room.

I knew these steps—a dance I'd performed so many times, I'd lost count more than a decade ago. Slinging a chair over from against the wall, I dropped into it beside the sofa, peeling back the tacky halves of Kai's ruined shirt again.

The metal-and-meat smell of blood clawed its way into my nostrils, and heat stamped my eyes. I blinked it back, stifling a curse against fickle Luck.

I *never* cried over blood. *Ever.*

One. Two.

A shudder rocked along the length of his body; without thinking, I brushed a clump of bloodstained hair from his brow, and his eyes opened wide, shooting straight to my face.

Three.

I ducked nearer, gliding my fingers along his toned abdomen, feeling for distension that would suggest internal bleeding—finding none. *Good.* A bit of swelling that hinted at contused organs, but it didn't seem as if his attackers had struck to kill. Only to inflict as much pain as possible in a short amount of time.

A boiled cloth and a cleansing solution, tipped out of my bag; then I started to wipe, cleaning the blood from his body so that I could see exactly what needed mending.

With a grating hiss, Kai knocked his head back against the arm of the sofa. "At least do your usual rambling, will you? I despise when you're quiet."

He almost made it sound too caustic to be a plea.

Almost.

"Most of these lacerations look superficial," I told him, plucking gently at the edges of one and ignoring the way my stomach swooped when he flinched. "But judging by the curve of them, I'm thinking...sentinel blades?"

"More than a dozen," Kai confirmed through gritted teeth. "An assassin can be a match for many men, but our work is...best done in the shadows, not in outright combat."

"Sentinels are the opposite."

"Precisely." The word was a groan itself, his head rocking against the armrest.

"Kai." I abandoned his wounded middle for a moment, sliding a hand behind his head and lifting it until our eyes locked. Every angle of his face was cut with the agony he bit back behind his gritted teeth.

Focus. Focus.

One. Two. Three.

"I've got you," I whispered. "I'm going to take care of you."

After a long moment, his chin dipped.

I let his head down gently against the armrest, and this time he kept it turned—watching me as I cleaned the blood from his body, as I fought not to notice the flutters that moved his muscular abdomen with every flare of pain.

"Tell me," he croaked, "tell me about your Harrow Hall. About where you learned to do this."

So I did.

While I flushed the lacerations and puncture wounds, I told him everything I could remember after all these years since graduation—about the gardens full of healing plants and poisonous ones. About being the youngest in my class, the smallest, and the most afraid...and how I'd never let that stop me.

While I rubbed a numbing salve around the edges of each tear in his flesh, I told him about the times I'd been bullied...about my Storycrafter friend who'd stood up for me, time after time. I told him about a soldier who'd stalked and harassed me until I'd feared for my safety. For my life.

He caught my wrist when I was about to delve into my bag for my faithful needle and suture thread; bladed ferocity cut through his pained gaze, so brutal it stopped my breath.

"Is he dead now?" he growled.

"Yes," I whispered. "Years ago. My friend blew his head off with a rifle."

His grip loosened, his arm swaying back down to hang from the edge of the sofa. "*Good.*"

While I stitched his wounds—beginning with the most concerning, the ones along his gut and sides—I told him about graduation. About everything I'd done to climb and claw my way to the top marks of my class. How everyone, even my detractors over the years, had cheered my name that day.

How it had all rung hollow in my empty ears.

"I realized I'd been trying to become good enough for one thing, all that time," I murmured, fixing my gaze on the familiar dip and swivel and tug of the suture needle. "To save my mother. And when I graduated, it finally struck me that I'd learned so much, I'd even learned how to treat a wasting lung sickness like the one that took her from us, and...I still couldn't bring her back."

Kai's eyelids had settled to half-mast again, but his gaze hadn't left my face all this time—most likely to avoid glancing down at the needle winnowing in and out of his skin. "So, what trouble did you cause next?"

A smile dug itself into one side of my mouth as I snipped the thread and reached for my bandage roll. "I went back for more."

A tandem year of poison studies and sacrificing every bit of my spare time in Vallanmyre's most prestigious infirmaries—and spending the few hours every day I should've been sleeping cheering my Luck-loved head off at Audra instead while she'd completed the Master Storycrafter trials.

"Drink this," I added after I finished that part of my story, offering Kai one of my Mithran tinctures. "I invented this myself...a poppy and valerian brew, with analgesics and arnica."

"Potent?" I'd never heard him sound so hopeful.

"The strongest I could legally make in Mithra-Sha."

He tipped back half the vial before I jerked it from his fingers and stoppered it, shaking my head; then I went back to dabbing on infection-fighting salves and pasting bandages over his injuries, picking up my story where I'd left off—after Audra took up the scarlet cloak.

Finally rid of my soldier shadow. My status rising in Vallanmyre, my poison studies continuing, my life becoming inextricably linked with Audra's, with the rest of her friends'...though I didn't mention how close I'd been to Arias and Mahalia. He didn't need to plumb the depths of how complicated everything really was when it came to me and the Lothars.

"And then, several years ago...I left. To start my life in Dalfi." Gently, I took the back of Kai's neck, helping prop him up while I moved to sit on the edge of the sofa, so I could wrap the bandages around his back and middle. To protect his wounds, and also to brace his bruised organs.

I shivered at the thought of one becoming too damaged. Bursting. Having to operate on him in this city with no infirmary.

I wasn't certain either of us would survive that.

His forehead bowed against my shoulder as I worked my arms under and around his, again and again...binding and bracing. "You have lived...a far different life from what I imagined."

"Well, so have you," I snorted. "When I first heard the Moravens talking about you, I assumed you were an arrogant bastard lounging in his shadow lair, just enjoying picking your way through the elites for fun. I never expected a man with a skull for a companion and a house so lovely."

"I don't...enjoy killing." A sharp grunt escaped him when I jostled just below his left ribs; his hand leaped to fasten over my hip, gripping so tightly my breath caught, too.

Heat crept up my neck when I resumed binding...more tenderly this time. "I've gathered that about you."

"It's a necessity."

"Every name on that map is *necessary*?" I tucked the bandages down and leaned back, forcing him to lift his head from my shoulder—to meet my eyes while I smoothed a hand between us, down his bandaged torso. "*This* is necessary?"

Agony still stamped the downturn of his mouth, the dampness of his weary eyes. "Every bit of it."

Wretched laughter burst from me—a fingerlength of the emotion blistering in my chest finally working its way free, piercing through the place where I'd kept it tamped down for both our sakes. "Kai, what could *possibly* be worth all of this?"

"They killed my family."

Nausea twisted my throat almost all the way shut.

I couldn't breathe. If my lips parted, I would be sick; so I pressed them tight, forcing air through my nose in trembling puffs, holding his anguished, utterly *sincere* gaze.

"My mother and father," he went on, brows cutting low over his eyes. "My sister. My brother." His arm, draped along the sofa's back, twitched; his dangling hand flexed up to grip my shoulder. "They were all taken by...by these people I am hunting."

His fingers fell from my waist to grip his side instead, a cracked groan seeping from between his gritted teeth; I clasped his wrist and pulled his hand up to hold the back of my head, then shifted closer, wrapping my arms around his chest. Supporting him, tugging him close—so close the heat of his skin and mine blended into the same cocoon of warmth.

"Hold on to me," I whispered. "The tincture I gave you will help you sleep...just hold on a few more minutes, Kai. Tell me about your family."

Fingers buried in my hair, chin resting on my shoulder, he rasped, "My sister was the first...until her, we had no notion we were in any danger. A blade to her heart, and it put us all on the run." His hold tightened, tugging at threads in my curls, strands coming undone...the same way a piece of my heart unraveled with every word he spoke. "I never saw my mother and father fall...but I heard their screams when they were gutted. My brother and I fled together, pursued...we almost escaped."

I hated that *almost.* I hated that there could be no hope of any happiness in the outcome...not for a man who'd been alone for so long, he'd taken to talking to himself in this lonely, empty house. That he'd befriended a skull, of all things.

That he was used to bandaging his own wounds.

"They caught him...a dagger to the back." Kai's voice had lost an edge of its strength—whether to pain or exhaustion, I was too afraid to wonder. "It was most likely meant for me. But he kept himself between me and our pursuers, and...I heard it strike. He fell against me, so I pulled him onto my back. And I carried him."

"While you were being *chased*?"

"We lost them in a stream, in the woods behind our family's home." His forehead settled more heavily in the crook of my neck. "It concealed our trail. I carried him...all that night. Past dawn. I couldn't bear to put him down even when he begged me to leave him, to save myself...or when he stopped begging. Or when I no longer felt his breath on my neck."

Like I could feel *his*—staggering and shallow and ravaged with grief and pain.

I squeezed my eyes shut; tears budded along my lashes and slipped down my cheeks. "I'm so sorry, Kai."

For his family. And for tonight—and the things I'd done that had made him vulnerable.

For all the ways this was my fault.

"I left him," Kai rasped, "when I no longer had a choice. When a friend found us, and...for a time, he and I fled together. Until we were forgotten, until we were thought dead ourselves. But then he went his way, and I came back."

"To avenge them." I turned my head, burying my face in his hair. "*Kai.*"

"The truth-telling serum is for them. To learn every name connected to their deaths—every last one. So that no one who had a hand in it escapes the justice they're due."

His fingers slid from my hair to grip the back of the sofa again; he pulled away, and I found his eyes were closed. He eased down on the plush cushions, and compulsion needled me to my feet.

I ducked around him, to sit against the armrest; and I guided him down to rest his head in my lap.

He didn't fight, didn't protest—most likely because that tincture was spinning his head into a muffled whirlwind. He didn't even swat me away when I stroked the hair from his brow, determined to rinse the blood from it in the morning. After he'd slept off the first wave of pain.

"Your brother," I murmured, "what was his name?"

"Geovany."

"And your sister's?"

"Cerene."

"Those names are—"

"Mine is Malakai. Malakai Kane."

I froze, my hand dropping from his hair to rest over his unsteady heart; his eyelids tugged upward, his drowsy gaze searching for mine. His breath passed over half-parted lips, struggling faintly with the pain—and struggling against the lull of unconsciousness.

Those lips still painted with his full name.

Malakai Kane.

"Why are you telling me this?" I stroked my thumb over the bare skin that quivered with the throb of his pulse beneath.

"Well," a husky laugh shuddered through him, and he dug his feet into the opposite armrest, shifting his sprawl...settling his head deeper into my lap. "If it turns out you're a poor healer after all, it seems a tragedy that I would die with no one left to remember my name."

I pursed my lips, considered at least flicking his nose in rebuke...then decided against it.

I'd done enough damage already.

"Malakai...why *your* family?" I murmured instead.

"Because we knew entirely too much about the wrong things," he answered, voice soft, distant. "Less than I know now. But enough that...I knew a night like this would be inevitable. For me."

A sluggish blink; then his eyes drifted shut. He turned his head against my thigh...and after a moment, his right arm rose, his hand inching across his chest to grip my wrist. Holding my hand above his heart.

"I'm glad you're here, Naomi."

His breaths steadied out into slumber only a few minutes later; so I was finally free to prop my elbow on the armrest, and bury my face against my knuckles.

And *cry*.

For this awful night. For him. For all of it.

They killed my family.

Corylus, Raversen, Nellatrix...Vespertine, tonight...and all of those ledgers and reports I had read, all of those names that blurred together—people I'd thought of as *victims*—

All of them, murderers.

Even Phin?

The thought stopped my heart mid-beat. My eyes popped open. My gaze fixed on the scuffed wooden floor.

No.

I couldn't believe that about him. That he might be connected to the others, yes...that Kai had a reason to despise him, yes. But the chaos of all of it, and the different way he'd lashed out at Phin, and that Phin's name wasn't on the map...

There was something there between them, some grudge slashed into the Druavas's body. But it wasn't the same as the rest.

I wished to Luck that I could ask Kai for the *truth* of what it was. But if I revealed how much I knew about Phin's near-death—that it had been a different poison, the messiness of it, all those small details I'd gleaned over time—it would reveal me for the fraud I was fast becoming.

The fraud who didn't want to know what was truly happening between him and Phin. And the fraud that didn't even bother to question the delirious truth he'd given me in the throes of agony tonight.

I believed him. Luck help me...I knew *he* believed in what he was doing. That there was a purpose to it. That this was truly about his family, and about avenging them, not about dealing hurt without gain.

And maybe I was starting to believe that, too. To believe in *him*.

Because, when I should have been leaving—slipping off the sofa, jotting a note to send to Phin, preparing to share these truths, to break Malakai Kane with them...

Instead, I was carding that rebellious lock of hair from his brow, monitoring his breathing, keeping one arm wrapped across him. My hand over his heart, his fingers tight around my wrist. My tears falling soundlessly from my jaw into his bloodstained hair.

Tears of regret. And shame. And *relief*.

Because Malakai understood something about me that no one did...not even him.

How alike we were.

Both of us had poisoned and killed in the name of family. Mine...Arias, Mahalia, the family I'd chosen for myself. And him, the sister he couldn't save, the parents who had perished while he escaped. The brother he still couldn't put down, even after all these years.

For the first time since I'd fled to Dalfi, a stranger in my own skin...a stranger to my family, my friends, even if they didn't know *why*...a piece of the loneliness perished while I held Malakai through that dark, tumultuous night.

Because I had found someone just like me.

CHAPTER 54
FURY UNFORGIVEN

I T WAS DAYS BEFORE I left the manse again.

Days before I felt comfortable enough with Malakai's condition to even let him sleep alone; though he staggered and grumbled his way off the sofa and trudged to his study—and the cot there—after the first day, I didn't go back to my own room. I slept in the chair by the desk, keeping watch over his breathing; I monitored every shift of his prostrate form and every slow, sore movement when he rose to use the washroom or to snatch a poetry book off the desk, watching for a hint that his bruised insides might be worsening.

And maybe it was that I didn't trust a man Luck-bent on revenge to wait around for measly things like *healing wounds* and *not making his organs perforate and bleed*…but I watched him more closely than I'd ever watched another patient. Even Addie, when she'd come wounded to Dalfi—though to be fair, I'd left the bedside vigil business to Jaik.

This was so much different. A personal concern hummed along the twists of my muscles and the lines of my bones, anchoring me at the desk even when cravings for sunshine and city streets enticed me through the convex windows in the kitchen while I made cocoa every morning.

I could have been jotting names in my journal with invisible ink. I could've been searching his desk, working on my antidote, tampering with his poison for the Jubilee if the urge struck me…I could have had my way with the study. He slept so much, he wouldn't have noticed.

But I just read poetry, too; and I sipped cocoa, and I stared at the soaring curtain panels and reflected on everything he'd told me…about his family's fate. About these people he hunted and killed.

And every day, my confusion crystallized into a sharper and sharper fury. Until, finally, I couldn't bear to be in the manse anymore.

So, while Malakai took his first bath in days, I whipped on my cloak and strapped on my dagger; and when he returned, a slow plod and a heavy lean in the study doorway, shirtless, his damp hair mussed forward over his brow, I was waiting, arms folded. Fidgeting.

And not even because he'd decided to come back without a shirt—baring the lacerations stitched with ugly, dark thread across his middle.

Some of my best work. Something I wished I didn't have to see.

"Where do you think you're going?" he rasped.

"Out." I tapped my foot on the flagstones. "We need food. Supplies. Fresh bandages."

Frowning, he slowly levered himself up from the doorway...familiar grace forsaken for shuffling agony as he entered the study. "If you're going, then—"

"Stop." I flared a palm his way. "If the next words out of your mouth are *then I'm coming with you*, so help me, Malakai Kane, I—"

He winced as he caught the hand I held outstretched. A tremor rattled his forearm...one of a hundred familiar signs of weakness, of a body on the verge of collapse.

"Then you convince me you will go safely," he finished roughly. "Look into my eyes, and convince me, troublemaker."

I *did* look into his eyes...hazy from exhaustion, red-rimmed and stamped with shadows. He trembled, his skin that special sort of warm that came from a hot bath...the kind of heat I wished I could sink into.

But there was no bath awaiting me. Just a cold confrontation that I all but itched for under my dancing nerves.

"The only thing I am concerned with right now," I said, "is going, and coming back to make certain you're all right."

His fingers flexed gently around mine; then he brought my knuckles up to his mouth, pressing a swift, searing kiss to them.

"Remember I'm waiting."

I wasn't certain whether he meant I shouldn't dally...or whether that was intended to comfort me.

But it did both, as I finally did was what I'd wanted to do since that long, sleepless night I'd spent just watching Malakai take one breath, then the next.

I went to confront Phineaus.

The note I delivered to Mistress Merrietti came without my usual attempts to play nice as the secret thief she'd run out of her shop; I held her gaze like grabbing a dagger aimed at my chest across the counter between us.

"You leave and go take this to him *now*," I snarled, "and you tell him not to wait."

Her brows lifted as she yanked the note from my hand. I pirouetted on heel and stalked through the front door—knowing she wouldn't dare heed that order until I was off her premises.

I circled the streets of Rastra several times while I waited, but for once, its winter florals and charming architecture did *nothing* to soothe me; in fact, the temper I'd tried to tame with a crisscross walking pattern bloomed and crawled even higher when I finally made my way to the cathedral where I'd ordered Phin to meet me.

He had somehow beaten me there despite my sharp, swift stride, kneeling to light a new candle among the hundreds clustered on one side of the ancient stone steps—maybe a show for Vespertine, just in case anyone else like Valessa spotted him here in the city and wondered what he was doing here.

I was beginning to wonder the same flipping thing.

"*Phineaus*!" I barked as I crossed the short bridge leading over a hoop of water to the cathedral's private plot.

"Hey, there you are!" He straightened and turned, hurrying to meet me, his usual affable smile sutured in place. "What was so important you couldn't wait to—?"

"You *lied* to me!" I met him with a shove of both hands to his toned chest. "After everything you promised, after I told you I had it *handled*...you warned Vespertine, didn't you?"

Phin staggered harder than I'd expected with the force of my blow; when he recovered, it was with his shoulders pulled in and jaw gaping slightly as he rubbed the heel of his palm over his chest. "*Ow!*"

"Don't you even start with me!" Barreling forward, I shoved him again. "You told me this mission was *mine*, but I didn't agree to have sentinels waiting for him!"

He only retreated a step and a half this time before he planted his heels in the grass that edged the cathedral's sides; a smaller smile unfurled at the corners of his mouth. "All right, all right...guilty as charged." When I snarled a profanity, he flung up his hands. "Well, rotting bones, Naomi, what'd you want me to do? Vez is my friend! We've known each other since we were kids!"

"We have a plan in place for that, for him—for *all* of them! The *watered-down poison*, remember?"

"Yeah, I remember, all right." Fury fell across his features, thick as a funeral sheet. "I remember the five people he's already hit since we put that plan in motion, the friends of my family's that I've dragged away from this city and others just like it. They're all sleeping under that poison still, so forgive me if I couldn't stand the thought of watching one of *my personal friends* go under like that!"

"Ugh, you're impossible!" I jerked my hands back through my tangled curls, snagging after only a few inches; I hadn't brushed my hair all the way through in days. "You're going to ruin everything!"

"Why, because the Poet got a little scrape?" he scoffed; when I didn't answer—when I couldn't unstick my tongue from the roof of my mouth or breathe the stench of Malakai's blood from my nostrils quickly enough—Phin hesitated, lips twitching. "Was it *really* bad?"

Bad wouldn't begin to touch what I'd dealt with...the new blood on my hands, staining far worse than the old. The way the pain had cracked him in half...or how his trust in me that night had knitted something in me so close to him, it was almost terrifying.

"That's not the point," I seethed. "Hurting him endangers *me*...something you were so quick to tell me once that you couldn't live with."

Phin blinked. He rocked his weight from his heels to the balls of his feet and back again. Then he averted his gaze, rubbing his neck.

"Look...you're right," he sighed. "That was stupid. It wasn't even really about Vez...I mean, it was, but it wasn't. It was more about me." Dropping his hand, he offered a guilty glance from the corners of his eyes. "It's killing me, being in the same city as the assassin who almost got the best of me, knowing he's with *you* every day, and not being able to do anything about it."

The confession set me back on my heels, too. A strange, not entirely pleasant consideration uncurled in my middle, twining itself into the way he was looking at me. The way he'd come to this city for *me.*

I didn't dare ask. And to my relief, he didn't elaborate on that, just laughed gruffly. "I guess I'm not built for sitting on the edge of things. I just wanted to get one over on him."

A petty, proud swipe. I understood it, given what he'd gone through.

But I didn't forgive him for it.

And I wished my rage and disgust were only because of the mission that was at stake, because of how it could've affected *me,* but...

Malakai was back in the manse, injured, just now beginning to rally...all because of Phin's malicious grudge.

I'd tried for days to let that go. And I just *couldn't.*

"If you can't keep your hands *out* of things," I snapped, "then go *home,* Phineaus. You're doing more harm than help."

His eyes widened a bit. "Whoa, let's not...let's not get ahead of ourselves. It's still not smart for you to face this alone—"

"I was doing fine before you pushed your way into things!"

"Not from where I'm standing! Diluting the poison was *my* idea—those people would be dead if not for me!"

I bit the tip of my tongue, swallowing a harsh retort—a retort that would betray the unsteady ground where I stood now.

Because I wasn't entirely sure anymore that those people were better off alive. Not with the blood of a whole family on their hands.

But what did Phin have to do with that? What did he *know* about it?

"Phin," I rasped. "If there was something more between you and the Poet...you would tell me, wouldn't you?"

He frowned, grabbing my elbows and tugging me close; it wasn't the first time I'd wanted to squirm from his grip, but there was a new awareness in every nerve now of where he touched me. *How* he held me...like he wanted to hold tighter.

Or hold me differently, maybe.

"Naomi...of course I would," he rasped. "Sullied souls, what kind of friend would I be if I kept letting you go in there without all the information? I swear, I've told you *everything*...and I know that hasn't been much, but at least I can promise it's all been the truth."

I shrugged him off, relieved to be free of his heated touch; then I swiveled to sit on the steps, resting my head in my hands. "Do you suppose there could be nuance to why he does what he does?"

Slowly, Phin settled himself at my side, shoulder bumping mine; a peek between my fingers showed him with wrists hung on his knees, hands loosely clasped between them. "I'm sure in his mind, there is. I mean, like Uncle Cass always says, most assassins you'd ask probably wouldn't say they kill just for sport...for the thrill of it." He shrugged. "Doesn't excuse what he's done."

Even if it was vengeance for his family?

"Hey." Phin ducked his head to catch my eyes; his were earnest, his tone faintly pleading. "I'll stay out of it from now on...I swear. Just promise me you'll be more careful. Don't let him into your head."

I didn't know how to tell him it wasn't my head I was worried about.

It was my heart.

CHAPTER 55
A SLOW DANCE

THE FIRST TIME I drew breath without a stitch of worry after my confrontation with Phin was, ironically, the day Malakai asked me to dance again.

The request came without preamble when I slipped into his study two mornings later; my heart somersaulted when I spotted Malakai upright already, perched on the frame of his cot, slowly working a loose linen nightshirt down over his head.

"Good morning to you, too," I snorted, toeing the door shut behind me. "We've been over this."

"*You* have…brooking little argument from me, I might add." Malakai arched a brow. "I feel stronger today than I have since the incident. And we have precious little time to waste."

I wrinkled my nose, leaning my forearms crossed on the back of the chair I had occupied for days at his bedside. "Healing is not a *waste of time*, Malakai."

A muscle in his cheek ticked; it did that sometimes when I teased out his full name on my tongue. "I'm well aware. But remaining bedridden when one has the strength to return to one's former tasks—"

"*No* training," I reminded him sharply. "No duels, no blades, no stabbing, no straining your stitches."

His nostrils flared. "Very well. No *training*." His gravelly voice curled unfairly around the emphasis. "But I think we can agree that *dancing* poses far less of a threat to my health."

"Debatable, at least for your toes."

He favored me with a look so dry, it almost chafed. "Do you mind?"

"Not at all." Grinning, I offered him my hand; I couldn't really deny that he was fit for dancing, even if I selfishly wished he'd rest longer, just to put my nerves at ease.

But I knew him better than that.

It was impossible to miss how slowly he moved still—or the brunt of his weight I had to take when I helped him up, or the way his other hand snagged my shoulder for a brief moment while he steadied himself. But it was fleeting, and with a squeeze, he let go. "The gramophone, Miss Weathers, if you please."

It gave me enough time to quiet the faint tremor in my hands, to chase the tension out of my forearms.

We didn't take the form of a waltz—frankly, I wasn't certain his arms or innards could withstand the strain of the precision those movements required. Instead, we slipped effortlessly into the rhythm of a slow dance...closer, a bit more intimate, without the brace of our arms keeping us a respectable distance apart.

It was...nice. Strangely relieving, to be this close to him, to be able to track his breathing and his pallor without feeling like I was hovering.

Fickle Luck, that's exactly what I was doing. But I had an excuse for it now, at least.

"You tell me the moment your stamina wanes," I warned. "No dance is worth making your condition worse."

"Though I tend to agree, the argument could be made—"

"Not with me, it couldn't."

A chuckle rumbled in the base of his throat, and he twisted his head, lips brushing my forehead; I could almost *feel* him rolling his eyes. "As a healer, I understand your concerns. But this is necessary...the Jubilee is coming, whether either of us feels prepared or not. The more we practice now, the less likely we'll repeat the unfortunate incident from Vespertine's manse."

My nerves sputtered at the thought. "All right, fair enough, let's *not* repeat that. If we can."

We swayed in several quiet turns around the same patch of worn-down rugging between the desk and cot. The music was quiet, but somehow the air around us felt quieter still—a lull that wrapped us in its arms. That moved us to its own rhythm.

It made me miss the way we'd danced and trained after Dashian's playhouse. I would have given almost anything for Malakai to have the strength to lift me off the ground with both arms, to spin me...to hold me down against the desk.

I wasn't certain if he could right now. And with the Jubilee looming on the horizon, that thought jabbed an icy needle of fear through my gut.

At my shiver, Malakai's arms tightened just a bit, shifting me deeper into the breadth of his chest. Giving me somewhere warm and safe to settle.

"I haven't asked," he ventured, "how you've been faring."

"Do you mean with preparation for the Jubilee while you've been—?"

"Not the preparations. How have *you* been faring?" He drew back a bit, meeting my gaze when I tipped my head to peer up at him; there was the slightest, deprecating curl to his mouth at whatever look of blank confusion he found on my face. "It was not *easy*, I suspect, treating me in the state I was in when I returned."

Startled, I gnawed the tip of my tongue. I couldn't remember the last time someone had asked me how *I* was after treating a patient. Had it been my schooldays in Harrow Hall?

Most healers were expected to shuttle things off to their appropriate places. To deal with them precisely, logically, so that we could continue putting one foot before the other. Continue to shove our hands into more gaping wounds, to grip more dying fingers, to pronounce more and more fatalities and misfortunes.

Most healers also didn't treat their friends. The people they...

I shook off the thought, curls springing against my cheek. "I've been sorting through it, when I can. Plenty to keep me busy."

Though I lightened my tone, his gaze darkened. "And now the truth."

My breath whipped in, then tumbled out in a rush. "I can still feel your blood on my hands. And I see you hanging in that doorway, begging for my help, every time I close my eyes."

The lines around his eyes shifted...a ripple of regret that rearranged the angle of his brows, the angle of his mouth, the angle of his gaze. He drew near again, resting his cheek on my hair. "I would have spared you that, if I could."

His nearness—the warmth of his body, the scent of his clothes, more linen than woodsy today—teased out a stitch of daring in me. Slipping my hand from his upper arm, I looped it around his shoulders and teased my fingers through the hair at the nape of his neck. "In spite of everything...I'm glad I was there."

I'm glad I'm here—with you.

Another slow, swaying turn. And then his hand dipped from beneath my shoulderblades, down to the small of my back. He drew me nearer, his cheek settling more heavily against my hair. "So was I."

My eyes tumbled shut as I rested my head in the crook of his shoulder; with my body pressed to his, I felt every place where he leaned more heavily into me. Where exhaustion and weariness prodded against the tight fetters he held them with. Where he was not as healed as he wanted to show—maybe even to believe.

So I did what I knew best: I slipped my arms around those places. From around his shoulders, to his waist; I took the pace of half the turns and left him the other half; one of us leading, then the other. And Malakai met the new pattern without a stumble, following and then guiding.

Turn after turn, as the music swelled to a poignant ache around us. Strings strained and woodwinds piped, and for the first time it truly struck me how near I'd come to never having another moment like this with him. No more dances or duels or card games. No more cocoa or coffee or time spent with poisons and cures.

He had almost died because of me. And he was still *here* because of me.

A tear slipped from my eye, soaking into the folds of his cotton shirt.

Malakai brought our entwined hands nearer, brushing the damp path from my cheek. His long fingers tightened around mine. "Naomi."

A thin seam of pain splintered his voice; I poured myself into that, fleeing from my own fears. My *almosts* and *nearlys* that drove me mad if I looked at them too long.

Tugging back a bit, I searched his face—haggard, framed with exhaustion, and lines of anguish bracketing his mouth.

Planting my feet, I pulled us both to a halt. "We're finished."

His throat jerked. "Miss Weathers—"

"*No*," I gritted the word out—because gritting and fighting and being stubborn felt better than sinking beneath the tide of what had happened. And what could have, because of me. "You're lying back down, right now. Or else you can practice dancing by yourself."

He grumbled under his breath; but he let me guide him back to the cot, and then he tumbled into it of his own accord. His mouth went taut at the impact, and he pulled himself up to the pillow far more slowly on one elbow, shielding his middle with his other hand.

My fingers hovered an inch away from his abdomen, ready to test the stitches when he finally pulled back. They hadn't given, thank Luck; but the muscles around them fluttered with the same tension that carved his features.

"Why are you doing this?" I choked. "Look at you, you can barely stand. Why won't you just lie down and *rest*?"

"You know why," he grunted, easing onto his back and folding one arm behind his neck.

Because of his family. Because of the people who had taken them away.

I shook my head, helpless to reason with a man so Luck-bent on vengeance. "Kai..."

"Our days until the Jubilee are numbered." His eyes sank shut, a groove digging between his brows. "I don't know...how many more dances I'll have with you."

My heart squeezed so swiftly, I sucked in a breath to keep it from faltering entirely.

"We have to prepare," he mumbled, pinching the bridge of his nose. "*I* have to be ready for..."

"We *will* be ready." I captured his hand and brought it down from his face, squeezing it with both of mine. "I've trusted you, and you've brought us this close. Now trust *me*...go at my pace, and I'll carry us the rest of the way."

His fingers flexed in the cage of mine...then wrapped one of my hands and squeezed back.

He was still holding my hand when he slipped away into sleep, those pinched, pained breaths easing, his head lolling against the pillow of his arm.

I held his hand—and held myself together by wisps and silk thread, while tears scored relentlessly down my cheeks.

What a hypocrite I was.

He had trusted me...and look where it had gotten him.

There was no telling, after my argument with Phin, where it would take us now.

CHAPTER 56
NAMES AND CRIMES

To my absolute disbelief, Malakai Kane actually listened to me.

And after a fortnight of careful bandage changes, doses of Mithran herbs, and as much rest forced on him as I could muster between slow dances and card tricks, he was moving almost without a trace of pain; whether that was because he didn't feel any, or because he didn't want me to see that it lingered, I couldn't be certain.

I was still grateful he might even be well enough to put on airs.

And it was a relief to be back to our routine—back to coffee in the mornings and cocoa most evenings, and our time in the workroom perfecting and bottling our separate brews. Only now, there was new things...small truths sprinkled like healing powder over a wound.

He told me about the names on the wall now. Not just what the cards claimed, but what he'd learned about them, and how.

Elites all across Hadrass-Drui. Officials within the ruling ranks. People who had the Moravens' ears, and in some cases, their personal friendship...like Vespertine and so many others.

All capable—and possibly guilty—of horrific crimes.

Swindling whole cities. Forcing their will on the people under their charge. Razing entire villages to build their complex manses. Trafficking in stolen flesh. Bribery. Coercion. Terrible threats that left innocents living in terror. A list that grew and grew, and planted and watered and tended my horror until it bloomed thorny vines that almost strangled me.

"Do the Moravens know *any* of this?" I demanded one day, leaning my folded arms on top of Malakai's desk—my cocoa for once completely forgotten.

"That question has no easy answer." Malakai wagged his pen between two fingers in a constant, steady *swish*. "Some of it would be impossible without their knowledge. But whether they realize the depths of the depravity, or they choose to be ignorant...that remains to be seen."

My thoughts strayed to Phin. "If someone brought it to their attention, do you think it would change anything?"

He peered at me over the fast-tilting pen. "Do *you* think, if such recourse were possible, I would've settled for a life in the shadows for all these years—killing in secret?"

"Revenge might be sweeter than justice by law." I frowned, gnawing my lip. "But if these people are this well-connected, this high in the ranks, it stands to reason that if you tried to bring this to light, it would mean more lies, more deception, trying to bury it again. And as for proof...it would be your word against theirs." I knew the precise hopelessness of that path...I'd edged down it a ways myself before I'd known it would get me nowhere. "So vengeance for what you know is cleaner, quicker, and less likely to end with them getting away unscathed."

With no warning whatsoever, Malakai bopped the tip of my nose with his pen. "Now you're thinking like an assassin."

I pushed back, crinkling my nose. "Was that a compliment, or an insult?"

"That depends entirely on your perspective, Miss Weathers." But his smile gave him away.

The more Malakai told me about his plans, day after day, the greater something nagged in the back of my mind. Something I knew I had to do, regardless of risk. Regardless of sentiments or the tempting tug of a Druavas's solemn, pleading eyes. Something I knew couldn't be a deception Malakai was weaving, because he didn't know I'd deceived him in kind.

I had a mistake to make right.

And that necessity was what finally gave me the strength to slip into Malakai's workroom alone for the first time in more than two weeks. But even once I was inside the windowless chamber, lantern kindled...I still hesitated.

Squinting at the jars of ink...two diluted. And one not.

I couldn't will myself to move, to make the choice. Not even when I counted to three, over and over and over again, knowing I was supposed to *move* when the count ran out.

I just stared at those jars of ink, heartbeat after heartbeat tolling on. Willing my feet to unstick from the floor...willing my hands to do *something*, instead of standing here uselessly for entirely too long. Long enough that Malakai could come in at any moment and find me just staring at the jars, hearing his broken confession again and again as the tides of pain pulled him under.

They killed my family.

What was I doing? Did I even *know* what I was doing?

All I'd had to guide my hands in this meticulous, surgical process was the word and loyalties of the Moravens toward their friends—and my sensibilities against justice dealt without trial. Something Mithra-Sha had outlawed long ago.

Except when people were stabbed in the heart and left to die in gilded halls. Except when vicious soldiers needed to be dealt with in the moment. Except when worlds shattered because of deals done in the dark.

No, absolutely none of this was simple. The politicking, the protection that came with status, the cruelties that couldn't—*wouldn't*—ever be solved through lawful recourse. That was why Malakai was doing what he did. That was why there was a place and purpose for this kind of justice.

I used to know that. It was that certainty that'd guided my hands to write my first correspondence to Mistress Merrietti. That had put my feet on the path to Hadrass-Drui long before I could've ever predicted things would go this way.

Some things had to be handled through unconventional means.

Like men with Mithran military ranking and protection and too many contacts, who dreamed of murderous schemes.

Like people with blood on their hands who were so well-connected, they would never face their due at the hand of the law.

The question was no longer about sensibilities—I had no higher ground to stand on when it came to that. It was simply a matter of this: who did I trust more? Malakai, or the Moravens?

The Moravens—who called me a pet poisoner and scoffed at the aid their daughter and sister had sent me to offer. Who couldn't answer plainly when I asked how well they knew their own friends.

Malakai—with half a lifetime of work tacked up on his wall. With ledgers and notes and a lethal precision that still aimed for a higher road than inflicting suffering...even against those he claimed to be his family's killers.

Malakai, who had struck a partnership with me, and helped heal a sick girl, and walked me home through dangerous city streets. Malakai, who saw the value of my talents...the ones I showed in the light and the ones I kept in the shadows.

Malakai, who'd had no strength left to trick me when he'd given me the truth...about his family. About the people who had orchestrated their deaths.

Names and crimes, listed on his wall.

Thieves. Intimidators. Child-beaters.

The prejudiced. The cruel. The ones who could only be stopped by someone willing to do what no one else would.

We'll see about that.

That vicious echo from the past struck me like a shove between the shoulderblades—and I lurched forward, swiping two of the inkpots from the table. Sending them shattering across the floor.

My breath caught as I stared at the last remaining jar—the only one I hadn't diluted. Knowing what I'd just done could never be undone.

Knowing what it meant. And absolutely not caring in the *least*.

Footsteps thudded on stone; the workroom door wrenched open, spilling light across the inkstain spreading along the stone floor. Malakai materialized in the doorway like shadow made flesh, his shirt partially unbuttoned, baring his still-healing wounds, and only one sleeve rucked up.

Our gazes met—he took in the sight of me, standing in the manifestation of the absolute mess I'd made—and then he was across the cool chamber in two strides, taking my wrists and turning my palms out toward him.

"*Are you harmed*?" he asked roughly—almost desperately.

"No, the glass didn't cut me, I—"

"Did the *ink* touch you?"

Oh. *Oh.*

That. I'd almost forgotten he always wore gloves when he handled the ink, because...

Because he didn't know the ink in the jars I'd shattered would only put me to sleep if it touched me.

He thought it would kill me outright.

"No, no, I don't think..." I quieted, watching him turn my hands this way and that, examining them for a trace of poisoned ink.

And it struck me all at once how gently he always touched me...not like I was fragile, breakable. But like he'd never held anything so important, and he was afraid of doing it the wrong way.

Even before we'd struck our partnership, his touch had never been bruising. Possessive. That just wasn't how he conveyed his thoughts and feelings...he always handled me with restraint. Like he knew how capable those hands were of killing, and he refused to let a single drop of that prowess brush up against me.

A ball of emotion lobbed into my throat; I flipped my hands, taking his wrists instead, sidestepping us both out of the mess.

"It didn't touch me," I said firmly. "I was just checking my antidote, and I thought something was wrong with it, so I got distracted—I didn't notice how close I was to the jars, and I caught the ones at the end with my elbow trying to brighten the lantern."

I'd expected the classic clench of Malakai's jaw at that, the narrowing of his eyes; so it wasn't until his whole face relaxed and his gaze brightened slightly that I realized he'd already been tense, already watching me that closely.

Not because of what I'd broken, but because he was afraid his poison had broken *me*.

"Well, thank your Mithran Luck there's still one left." He edged around the spilled ink, scooping up the last inkpot and flashing it in his palm before he tucked it away in his pocket. "But you'll forgive me if I keep this in my desk from now on."

I blew a straggling curl off my forehead. "Most likely for the best. The closer we get to the Jubilee, I just feel clumsy all over."

"You still seem graceful to me."

Flipping Luck, why couldn't I think of anything to say to that?

"Your antidote," Malakai added while I fumbled with my useless tongue. "*Was* there something wrong with it?"

"No, thank Luck," I muttered. "Though that makes me feel worse about the broken inkpots, all for nothing."

We stood there a moment beside the spray of mortal ink; then Malakai swept an arm at the door. "After you."

I scampered out, and he shut and locked the door for the first time since he'd first let me inside. But before I could dwell on the implications of that, he turned to face me, tugging the curtain shut at his back.

"I'll clean that mess myself." The smallest dimple carved into his cheek—a hint of that smile I'd been trying to coax out ever since our night beneath the fireworks. "It's not the first inkpot that's been broken. I've grown adept at blotting it up without poisoning myself."

"Well, thank Luck for that, too." I leaned against his desk, rubbing my face with both hands. "I'm really sorry, Kai."

Not for breaking the inkpots, though he could never know that; but because I'd possibly been sabotaging something truly meaningful here, and I'd never paused to question it in any depth until now.

He shrugged. "It's only ink. Nothing of real value was harmed."

The way he held my gaze when he said it...the way his hands curled into fists at his sides, as if they still held mine—

My mouth dried out. I hunted desperately for something to say—and of course, my focus landed on his shirt, undone to the middle of his chest. On the pinking lines and the few bandages still plastered over the puncture wounds.

"It's a bit early to be undressing for the day, isn't it?" I blurted.

His lips twitched. "It would be, if I were changing into sleep clothes."

And when our eyes met this time, I understood; my heart jolted, pulse thundering so loudly in my ears I barely heard my own whisper: "You're going out again tonight."

He nodded. "There's still work to be done."

Work that he would be doing now with the undiluted ink.

Work that had brought him back to me bloodied the last time he'd gone.

Work that we wouldn't know if he was even well enough to do, until it was done...or not done.

I didn't know which thought was the one that stitched my throat shut—that made breathing almost impossible.

When I'd decided to break the inkpots, I hadn't expected him to go out *tonight*. And I hadn't expected that the thought of him going at all would tie my stomach in such horrific knots, I wanted to be sick.

"Oh," was all I said.

Malakai frowned, searching my face for a long moment; then he stepped nearer to the desk. When I didn't put space between us, he offered his hands; it was less an effort to take them than it was to do it slowly, to not latch onto his grip and let it root me in this moment so I wouldn't start drumming up scenarios. Thinking of all the things that could go wrong.

"I will come back," he said with a quiet, certain strength I wanted to wrap up in like the warmest cardigan. "I will come back to you unharmed this time."

"You can't promise that."

"I can." A firm squeeze of my trembling fingers. "Because this is the first time in all my years of this work that I have something worth coming back to."

My fingers seized so tight around his, I was shocked he didn't hiss—didn't pull away.

Oh, this was dangerous. The most dangerous precipice I'd ever stood on. Something my mind was *screaming* to run away from, so loudly it was like another echo from the past—from when I'd put Vallanmyre and everyone and everything I'd ever loved behind me, and just *run*.

Run from the uncontrollable, the unpredictable...the things that could only end in tragedy.

This was not supposed to happen. Not this. Not between Malakai and me.

But I was still holding onto his hands; and he was still looking into my eyes.

And nothing kept me from stretching up on my tiptoes and kissing his cheek, filling my nostrils with the smell of piney beard oil and Mithran tinctures and the heat of his skin...a nervousness seething below the surface that his cool demeanor couldn't mask.

"Be careful," I whispered—to him. To myself.

He turned his head toward mine, and for a moment his brow pressed to my temple. And we just stood there like that, tangled in thoughts we couldn't share. Tangled hopelessly in each other's lives.

Then he stepped back, doing up his buttons with swift fingers, tugging down his opposite sleeve. "I'll return by dawn."

"Kai, wait." I pushed up from the edge of the desk before he could walk away, my tongue fumbling again around useless words.

So useless. *Be careful*...when had that ever been enough to keep anyone safe?

And I needed him safe. I didn't know if I could stand stitching him, of all people, back together again.

Out of everyone I'd ever treated—even Audra, and Jaik, and Arias...even my own brothers—that was the one that still haunted my dreams.

He needed more than well-wishes for what was coming. We both did.

So when he turned back to me, expectation and impatience cording the line of his shoulders beneath his shirt, I crouched and undid the Luck-charm anklet I'd worn every single day since Audra had given it to me for graduation...even for all those years when I hadn't really remembered where it came from. My thumb traced the thin circle of paler flesh beneath it, my steps so odd in their quiet when I went to Malakai; I took his hand and pooled the small silver chain in his palm.

"Mithran Luck coins," I explained at his mystified glance. "This was a gift from the best friend I've ever had. Maybe it will help keep you safe."

Maybe it will help bring you back to me.

Malakai stared at the thin chain for so long, I started to wonder exactly what I'd do—and how hard I'd hit him—if he gave it back to me.

"I am going to need a rotting awful lot of luck," he muttered at last—almost to himself.

Then he slipped the chain around his wrist, tucked his sleeve over it to silence its jingling, and strode from the study without another word.

Leaving me there with my naked ankle, and my empty hands, and my heart still crying out uselessly after him.

Be safe. Be safe. Be safe.
Come back to me.

I waited up for him again; though I hadn't been sleeping well the last fortnight, it didn't matter. My body simply didn't succumb to exhaustion at all until I heard the familiar twist of the locks on the front door.

And I knew something fundamental had changed the moment our eyes locked down the short hall between the foyer and the kitchen, where I sat at the table again, just like the last night he'd gone; because it used to be nerves that kept me awake the first several times he'd gone hunting. Imagining what was happening to his victims. Envisioning the poison taking hold, pulling them under. Worrying and wondering if I'd done enough to dilute it, so that they would be safe.

Not this time.

When Malakai met my gaze—when he tossed me a small, lopsided smile in greeting as he shed his night-dark coat, baring a muscular wrist still banded with that silver, coin-studded chain—I realized what was different. What had been realigned by him stumbling broken and bloody through that same doorway after he'd paid a visit to Vespertine.

I wasn't waiting up for them anymore. I was waiting for *him*.

And only when I knew he was safe and unharmed could I tumble into my bed...and fall right to sleep.

I couldn't even keep my eyes open long enough to reflect on the fact that someone had been killed tonight.

All I knew was how grateful I was that it hadn't been him.

CHAPTER 57
BENEATH THE EMERALD BRIDGE

I AVOIDED MEETING WITH Phin as long as I could, biding my time with the gnawing unease in my gut, busying myself cleaning and repairing things around the manse...and preparing for the Jester's Jubilee with Malakai. But distractions and delays could only last so long; and when the report of surveyor Edelena Rothfor's death spread through the streets of Rastra like poison, I knew a confrontation was inevitable.

Even if the people of Rastra were rejoicing over the removal of a corrupt elite who tended to snap up parcels of land and divide them in favor of her fellow wealthy and well-paying clientele...that wouldn't stop the reckoning on the horizon.

Still. The last thing I really expected was for Mistress Merrietti to corner me after a day of tending to the latest batch of ill to catch a nasty chest cough in the close quarters of the beggar's district, my ears humming with their relief that, now that Edelena was gone, they might be able to afford housing within the year. The simmering triumph in the herbalist's tight smile as she handed me a note was all the proof I needed: their joy aside, trouble was barreling my way.

That still didn't prepare me for the twist in my gut when I read Phin's curt script on the heavy cardstock:

Meet me by the canal. The Emerald Bridge, waterside. Midnight tonight.

Not my preferred meeting place...I would've liked a bistro courtyard or even an alleyway better. Maybe the empty plaza outside of Dashian's playhouse, somewhere a sympathetic ear could hear me scream if some sort of conflict broke out between us.

But I didn't have a choice. Not if I wanted to stop things from escalating another step further from where they had after Vespertine's manse.

Phin had enough information to meddle in my plans if provoked—and my choice with the ink had clearly provoked him plenty. Better I meet with him now, acquiescent to his terms, before he decided to tell his family where I was and ruin everything.

So I prepared as best I could—mentally, cladding myself to lie and argue. Physically, dressing as warmly as I could after dinner, with an extra-thick shirt beneath my cardigan protecting the memory of bruises around my upper arm.

I tossed out silent prayers and hoped to Luck my choice hadn't ruined everything; and wished with all my might I cared more if it did.

When had all of this become so *confusing*?

"Going somewhere?"

I almost jumped out of my cardigan, spinning away from my bedside where I'd been applying a spritz of perfume to my wrists—bolstering my strength with the scent of the familiar.

Another familiar scent crowded my senses now, soothing the edges of my nerves; fennel and pine, and that coupled with the sight of Malakai in my doorway, still dressed well though the day should have been over for us both. His damp hair was slicked back from his brow, suggesting he'd just bathed.

Luck. Don't think about him bathing.

"I have a patient who refused to meet me during the day today," I lied, shrugging my cardigan up around my shoulders. "He's a little paranoid, but he needs my help."

Malakai frowned. "Would you like an escort?"

That innocent offer brought tears to my eyes.

"No." Another lie, and I averted my gaze, sniffing and swiping under my nose. "He's not the dangerous sort of paranoid."

At least, Luck, I hope not.

Malakai crossed the room in a few short strides; he flashed his palms, and when I didn't brush past him or tell him I had to leave *now*, he took my elbows, drawing me a single step nearer to him.

That one step put me close enough to feel the radiating warmth from the bath still seeping out of his skin. Close enough to catch the flecks of silver here and there along the dark growth that lined his jaw. Close enough that I wanted to sink into him and completely forget what I had to do tonight.

"I'll wait up for you," Malakai murmured.

A gust of relieved breath tumbled from my lungs. "Thank you."

An unspoken vow that if I was gone too long, he would intervene; that he was still watching over me, just like he'd promised that first night in Amalgard, even after things had become so tangled between us.

He tugged me an inch nearer, and for just a moment, his nose brushed the crown of my head—maybe his lips did, too.

Before I pull could away—before I could search his face and see if my shock had any merit—he released me and turned, striding from the room.

I toppled back on the edge of my bed, burying my face in my hands.

Luck, help me.

The scrape of chilly wind past the panes of my room seemed like laughter—like Luck was mocking me.

Like Luck couldn't do *anything* about this mess I'd gotten myself into.

No, only I could do that.

So I did; standing again with heavy joints, shoving my feet into my boots, slipping out of the manse to meet the fate I'd crafted for myself.

And for the first time since the first day he'd accosted me on the street, I strapped on my dagger when I went to meet Phineaus Moraven.

CHAPTER 58
THE UNRAVELING THREAD

Lamplight along the curved bridges, tumbling bunches of winter ivy sported in flowerboxes on their sides, and the trailing, frondless arms of the weeping willow trees on the bank painted a picturesque view of Rastra. Like something out of one of Mahalia's watercolors, or the storybook she and Reiko were making.

I had never loved that beauty less than when I trudged through it on my way to Emerald Bridge, one of the several named arches that crisscrossed the canal; the prettiness felt muffled somehow tonight, like an illusion one breath away from shattering. Like the last burst of energy that often preceded the swift decline into death.

I still wished we were somewhere within screaming distance.

I hated thinking that way about *Phin*, of all people. But when I caught sight of him ducking out from below the bridge as I approached, striding through the snow to meet me, I wondered if maybe my reservations had merit; because, in all the time I'd known him and all the times we'd met in various parts of this city, I'd never seen real fury on his face before.

Not until now.

It transformed him. It darkened his eyes. It made him feel like a stranger.

"What *happened*?" His shout plumed thick on the air, a man spitting fire as he stalked toward me.

Hands shoved in my cardigan pockets, I halted and shrugged my elbows out from my body. "Things didn't go how I expected."

"Yeah, I'll say!" He loomed in my path. "Naomi, sullied *souls*—what did you do? What went wrong?"

"Nothing went..." I broke off, dragging my lower lip through my teeth. "He...the Poet was growing suspicious about the lack of funerals for the dead, about...about *me*. I had to give him *something*."

"So you let him *kill* Edelena Rothfor? The woman who was responsible for making sure every city has enough parcels to fit people into?" Phin barked. "That was life or death—life! Or *death*! You know we can't get that back once he's taken care of? She'll still be *gone*!"

The feverish light in his eyes, the impassioned, heartbroken strain of his tone, stoked the shame that had lain nearly fallow within me ever since I'd sent Kai off with the undiluted bottle of ink.

Whether his victims were murderers or not, their deaths still had impact. They hurt the Moraven family, the people they were responsible to rule.

They hurt *Phin*.

All of this was so messy. So much of it complicated. There was no way at *all* to do any of this where someone didn't get hurt. And the trouble was, I couldn't really tell anymore who deserved the hurt, and who was trying to stop it...and who was just caught in the middle.

"I had no *choice*, Phin." My tongue stuck a little against the half-truth. "He was getting suspicious. Do you understand what I mean by that? I had to decide if I could thwart him, or keep my cover."

Phin stepped back from me, hands flexing in fists at his sides; then he dragged one through his hair, flattening the messy strands to his scalp. "*Yeah*. Well, your choice cost a good family their wife and mother," he rasped, turning away from me to compose himself. "So, I hope you can live with that."

Could I? It felt less and less like I could survive *any* of this. I had no prayer to Luck of knowing how Malakai would react whenever he found out the truth about me...a truth I felt less inclined to tell him as the days went on. And, staring at Phin's hunched shoulders and hung head, I couldn't begin to fathom what my latest choice would do to us...if I could still count him an ally after this.

I was severing tethers and burning bridges and snipping the sutures that held this plan together every single time I moved. Sooner or later, it was all going to unravel.

"Phin," I murmured, stepping nearer to him, "how well do you actually *know* these friends of your family's?"

"How well do you think?" He swung back around to face me, a faint silver sheen budding along the lining of his eyes. "They're my friends, too...most have been around since I was born."

"But do you *know* them?" I persisted. "The way they conduct business, the things they do when the rest of Hadrass-Drui isn't watching?"

"Better than you do! Why?" Phin's gaze sharpened. "What did *he* say about them?"

"Nothing!" I lied in a shout. "Do you think he's willingly giving me *anything*, Phin? This is the Poet Poisoner we're discussing...I have to wrestle every scrap of *everything* out of this by myself!"

Every single lie tasted sour on my tongue.

"I'm just trying to understand *why*." I softened my tone—and tried to soften the bladed desperation knifing at the insides of my lungs. "Why these people, why *you*...why all of this is happening."

"Because he's a bastard murderer, Naomi!" Phin snarled. "What more do we need?"

So much more.

Because that wasn't Malakai Kane. The man I'd shared my life with these last few months; the man who'd entrusted me with his schemes, and his home, and the fates of his family. The man who saved children and old women and destitutes. The man who killed with precision, but not with cruelty. Whose path was vengeance, not injustice.

Did I know him better than Phin knew these family friends? Or did Phin know *everything* these people were capable of, every note on Malakai's wall...and was he turning a blind eye?

"Look." Phin stepped nearer again, tearing me out of those stomach-churning thoughts and drawing my focus back to him. "No one is perfect. Have these people made mistakes? Absolutely. Done things they shouldn't have? Sure. But that doesn't justify murdering them without a public trial, a chance to defend themselves. Countries can't be run like that...I should know, I'm a rotting Druavas!"

And maybe that was why Malakai despised him; because Phin stood for the rule of law, and laws could let cruel people continue their cruelty with enough strings pulled. With enough coins poured into the right coffers, the right backs rubbed. With a bought or inherent lack of impartiality.

That was precisely why I had the kind of blood on my hands that had landed me in this mess; that left me tongue-tied, stuck between two impossible outcomes, staring into Phin's gleaming eyes and feeling unconvinced of his argument.

"I need you to give me *something*, Naomi," Phin begged.

"I gave you Vespertine, and look what happened!"

"I know, but that...that was my mistake, and I already told you, nothing like that will happen again!" he argued. "Just...please. I'll let you choose what it is, but I need something to get us out ahead of him. Somewhere we can hit him that *hurts*."

My tongue darted out, swiping my lips—stopping a reply in its tracks.

I could give him some of what he wanted...contacts. Associations.

I could give him Nera and Sofi, desperate for survival, their husband and father stolen from them by doing the right thing. Their care now provided for by a man who still sent them coin even when their contract was done.

I could give him Valessa, withered and all but spent in the eyes of everyone she knew...everyone except for an assassin who saw her sharp mind and keen ears as a tool; an assassin whose generosity kept her pain at bay.

I could give him Dashian and a playhouse that made space for the impoverished to forget their troubles for a night and belong among the elite. A man whose dreams healed hurts not even my herbs and medicines could touch...a man funded by a Poet's coins, which gave him a place to escape, too.

I had them. Maybe not all of Malakai's contacts, but enough that we could wound his operations...and possibly break them, if I did what I'd come here to do. If I gave Phin every truth I'd dug up so far.

The choice was in my hands, just like it had been when I'd broken those inkpots. When I'd left one undiluted in the first place.

"It's still too soon," I rasped, and when Phin swept his hands back through his hair, folding them behind his head this time, I persisted. "He's paranoid, he hasn't told me much yet...there are too many potential loose threads. If we start scraping in his contacts now, he'll either turn on me, or he'll disappear. We'll lose the rest."

"Not if we move fast enough." Phin edged nearer, gripping my shoulders until they throbbed, then smoothing his hands down my folded arms until he shoved his fingers through the limp gaps of mine. "Not if I keep you safe."

Safe. Was that really what I wanted to be, anymore?

Why was it that the only times I felt *unsafe* in this city anymore were the times when I was meeting with him?

I tugged out from his grip, stepping back. "Phin, your family trusted *me* with this task. I know what I'm doing...I know it's too soon." When his brows mashed low and his mouth leaped open, I added hastily, "But I think we're close. There's something he wants my help with...something that has to do with the rest of his plans. I think after that, his guard will be down enough that I can pull the rest of the truth out of him."

Phin's eyes widened; he crossed his arms at his waist, shifting his weight from foot to foot. "Something like—what?"

"Something he wants me to help him steal."

"From my family?"

"No...I don't know," I lied. "He hasn't told me yet."

Frowning, Phin rubbed his jaw. "You *really* think this is the thread that's going to unravel everything?"

"Yes." I could at least be certain of that much. Whatever happened at the Jubilee, whatever came after it...it was going to change everything.

Phin peered off across the channel, still smoothing his palm over his face, then running it down the side of his neck. Finally, he let it swing loose at his side, his other arm still banded around his middle when he pivoted his focus back to me.

"Look...I just hope you're right." Unease and a tinge of accusation laced his tone. "Because the last time you made a call like this, a woman lost her life."

Shame pricked the backs of my eyes. "I know, Phin. And I know this is messier than either of us wanted, but...we're so close. Just trust me a little while longer."

"I did trust you," he muttered. "Look where that got Edelena."

And with that, Phin walked away from me; he strode up the slope and vanished into the floral gaps of Rastra without a backward glance.

No urging from him for me to be safe, no promise from me that I'd be in contact soon. This wasn't like any of the other times we'd parted ways, when it had still felt like we were a facing this together, somehow.

And that thought, more than Edelena's death, more than *anything*, truly shook me to my core.

It was nearly dawn when I finally returned to the manse; I didn't dare make the swiftest way back, not with the terms Phin and I had parted on. I wove and wound through the streets and outskirts just like I had that first time we'd met in Rastra, checking over my shoulder at every curve for a flirt of familiar clothing—any sign at all that he or his sentinels were following me.

Nothing showed among the shadows; but I was still so tense my joints *ached* by the time I slipped into the manse, slammed the door, and leaned against it for a moment, hiding my face in my chilled fingers.

Then I spun, fumbling at the locks as quickly as my trembling hands could manage. But the shaking and the cold made me clumsy, and the frigid metal resisted me so fiercely it was like struggling to strap a delirious patient into their bed.

"Come on!" I cursed, yanking one of the latches toward its fastenings. "Come on, you *stupid*, useless piece of—!"

"Here."

Warmth surrounded me from behind; steady fingers slid over mine, jamming the bolt home as one, then moving on to the last latch.

I slumped against the door, burying my face in the wood, squeezing my eyes shut—until those calm fingers fastened around my shoulder, turning me with an insistent, steady pressure.

Malakai's sleepless face swam in the pool of tears obscuring my vision—and then his body, dressed for the day. His mask, slipping from his fingers, falling to the floor between us.

He'd been leaving. For a mark I knew nothing about, or...?

Distress gleamed in his shadow-stamped eyes as he watched me...as he stretched a hand toward me, and when I didn't flinch away, slid his palm along my cheekbone, tucking my curls behind my ear.

"Did your patient follow you?"

A twist of my head scraped my frigid cheek against knife-grip grooves on his palms...as if he'd been clenching a dagger in his fist for hours, leaving marks on the flesh.

His throat jerked, his lips barely fluttering around the next words. "Did he *hurt you*."

How simple it would have been to say *no*. To resign myself to the easiest answer: that Phin hadn't laid a bruising hand on me since that first passionate exchange in the streets when he came to Rastra.

But what slipped my lips was a different, half-whispered, shaky truth. "He scared me."

Malakai's jaw shifted left, then right. "Do you want me to hurt *him*?"

I wasn't certain I would ever want that. But it seemed more inevitable with every moment that passed between all of us...even the ones Malakai knew nothing about.

How long was left before it all came crashing down? Before I lost this game I had never dreamed of playing?

Before I lost *him*?

Not tonight. I couldn't lose him tonight. I couldn't watch him walk out that door and confront Phin.

For both their sakes. And for mine.

"I just...I just want you to stay with me."

His hand was so *warm*, it almost hurt after the cold that had bitten my cheeks ever since I'd left the manse well before midnight. I couldn't help myself leaning into it when I spoke...into the heat, into the comfort of his touch.

So when his hand left my cheek, sliding around the nape of my neck, and he guided me toward him at the same time he stepped nearer, meeting my incessant trembling with his sturdy strength, the smell of fennel and pine wrapping around me like a blanket...I didn't resist.

And when he released my neck to wrap one arm around both of my shoulders, I didn't pull away.

When he braced his other hand on the door, and leaned both of us into it...I wasn't afraid.

I wasn't afraid of this assassin who held me so carefully, with that calm restraint...tenderly, like he could see all of the places I was hurting. And with so much protectiveness, in the grip of his arm snugged around my shoulders, his hand tight against my bicep, that I felt safe for the first time since I'd spotted Phin walking to meet me from under Emerald Bridge.

I fisted both hands in his rumpled shirt, and buried my face against the uneven cadence of his heart.

And I finally, finally stopped shaking.

CHAPTER 59
VENOM BLADE

I DIDN'T WRITE TO Phin again.

Weeks passed; then an entire month. Time after time when I should've reached out to him, should've conveyed something, should've asked after Vespertine and the rest of the victims...the still-living and the newly-dead.

Instead, I consumed myself with preparations for the Jubilee, barreling nearer as the year slipped toward its end. *Spirited Sunrise*—usually my favorite Mithran holiday—skipped past with barely a nod in its general direction. I couldn't bring myself to hang a single wreath or garland.

Not that they would have been easy to come by; I never went to the market anymore. Malakai took over those tasks again, and any flicker of guilt I felt at making him live as if he was alone in the manse was easily buried when I imagined knocking into Phin in the city streets.

I read through all of the books I'd brought with me—once, and then again. I wrestled with whether or not I should tell Malakai about the batches of tainted ink, or let him continue what he was doing now: leaving Rastra at least once a week, sometimes for days at a time, armed with lines of poetry penned in poison.

As if I'd never stepped in his way. As if I'd never tried to sabotage his work at all.

Cowardice kept my tongue tied and kept me mostly in my room, doing what I could to pass the time before the Jubilee...trying desperately to feel useful, and less like I was being ripped in half by a contention I really had no place in.

Except I'd made my place. I'd made my choice.

And it was right here, in this room where I sat cross-legged, huddled in my cardigan, reading the last of my book of poison studies for the second time in as many weeks.

Luck. I'd never felt so low...not even when I'd been dragging myself weeping out of bed every morning my first several months in Dalfi.

A clearing throat in my bedroom doorway had me picking my head up from my fist; as usual lately, it felt like it weighed a hundred pounds. But at least I managed a halfhearted smile when my eyes met Malakai's, lounging in the doorway, arms folded and weight tipped into the frame.

"You're quiet," he remarked.

I held up the book. "I was reading."

"No." He shrugged up, gliding gracefully into the room. "You've *been* quiet for weeks now."

"Mmm." I sighed, clapping the book shut. "Well, I have more than a lot on my mind, and unfortunately tired old books about poisons that I've read a thousand times aren't much of a distraction."

He settled on the edge of the bed, facing me, frowning as he scooped up the discarded book. "You haven't been going out for your healing sessions. Or tidying the manse."

"Oh, I was wondering when you'd notice I was shirking my duties." Teasing was easier than thinking of a truth I couldn't even tell him; that I'd stopped my services for fear they'd lead me into Phin's path, too, somewhere in the city. Whether by accident or—worse—because it would turn out he had Merrietti and his family's other friends keeping watch on me.

I didn't want to talk to him. I didn't want to hear more accusations, or have my motives questioned, or be judged by a man who'd taken pleasure in outwitting Malakai just so he could hurt him.

Maybe Phin had considered all of that just repayment for the Mummer's Dance. And maybe it was. But after the incident at Vespertine's manse, my stomach turned queasy at the thought of someone cornering Malakai again. At the thought that I might somehow give away *something* that would empower Phin to dispatch the sentinels like that.

It was a conflict best avoided altogether; I had enough to think about already.

A brush of fingertips to my knuckles jolted me from those deprecating reflections; Malakai's eyes were on mine, searching me out with such intensity, I wasn't certain he even realized his hand had grazed against mine.

"You've made it no secret you love this house," he said. "To see you neglecting it is...such a strange thing, after all these months." His head tilted, gaze dropping to my lips. "I wonder where that smile's gone you used to carry around here like a shield and sword."

I tried to muster it up, but my lips just flattened. I shrugged my shoulders deeper into my cardigan. "I haven't felt much like smiling these days. Too nervous about the Jubilee." And a hundred other things, not the least of which was the way my heart had stuttered all over itself when he touched my hand.

Malakai regarded me for another moment in contemplative silence; then he pushed up from the bed. "Come here." He bent the book in a gentle gesture of beckoning. "I want to show you something."

Well, he knew by now that my curiosity would handle the rest.

The cool air floating through the cracks in the manse whispered against my bare legs between the hem of my cardigan and my thick wool socks as I padded after him. We neglected his study and the workroom—my first guess for a rendezvous—and the kitchen, though the smell of freshly-brewed coffee begged for attention.

My heart actually leaped out of its miserable, muttering rhythm for the first time in weeks when Malakai led me to the staircase we'd repaired together—the one that led up to the second level. And it turned from stumbling to *racing* when he passed the doorway at the top and continued on through the bricked archway to...

The rotunda staircase.

I nudged his arm up and ducked beneath it in my haste to reach the one part of the manse he'd always insisted—this entire partnership—that I stay away from. Daylight poured through slim, high windows notched into the curve of the protruding wall, painting the buttercream walls with stripes of gold.

Catching myself on the railing, I peered over the edge. The staircase corkscrewed down to a small staging area on the first floor; disused furniture was heaped in the space below, with no other ways in or out that I could see.

So I craned my head back, peering up.

The twist of the staircase climbed up the turret from the second level to a third, disappearing through a chink in what looked like the ceiling. But I could guess otherwise: there was a landing up there.

"Come." Malakai tilted his head and started for the stairs; I all but lunged after him.

We climbed the steps entirely too slowly for my liking; my legs wanted to gobble them two at a time, and I was practically itching with impatience by the time we stepped up through the small gap at the top of the stairs and arrived in a small, windowless room at the top; it was only lit with the glow from below our feet, sunlight edging up through the stairwell.

Malakai slipped a key from the inseam of his trouser leg and slid it into the lock; but before he turned it, he peered at me over his shoulder. The slash of vulnerability in his eyes was so much like the way he'd stared at me the night I'd mended his wounds—somewhere between a plea not to betray what was coming, and a warning of what would happen if I did—that it strangled my curiosity and replaced it with somber attention.

"All of the most valuable things in this manse lie beyond this door," he said. "I trust their existence will remain between us."

"I swear on my soul." A Hadrassi vow I intended to keep for the rest of my life.

He studied me for several moments more; then, with a trace of a smirk, he unlatched the door and pushed it wide, letting me enter first.

I barely made it over the threshold before wonder halted me in my tracks.

Whatever part of the manse this turret was sinewed to, I suspected it encompassed most of the upper levels. From the turret, another stairwell stepped down to a broad span of open room beneath a chain of lofty vaults. The ceiling was reinforced with stone arches—likely to prevent collapse—and painted between those veins were celestial scenes, constellations and galaxies. Just like the starlight glaze on our mugs.

And on the walls...shelves of valuables.

Half of them were bookcases, overflowing with volumes just like in Malakai's study...but these appeared to be books on poisons, some ribbed in steel latches, some buckled shut and facing outward. Across the brilliant emerald runner that spanned the hardwood floor, curio cases of bottles, jars, and décor lined the opposite wall.

All of it was lit with a strange, ethereal silver-blue glow I'd never witnessed before—a light that didn't come through any window. It emitted in soft pulses along the line of every bookcase and from every shelf of the curio cabinets. It even dripped from the ceiling in hair-fine garlands.

"What *are* those?" I breathed.

"Storycrafted light chains." Malakai slipped in after me, shutting the door at his back. "They cost a small fortune to procure, but they never lose their glow. And I find they add a certain charm to the room."

"A *certain charm*?" I choked on laughter, clattering down the stairs and spinning on the balls of my feet as I stepped deeper into the room. "Kai, I want to *live* here. I can't believe you gave me that room next to your study when you knew *this* was lurking above our heads!"

"As I said...everything of value is now in this room." He crossed his arms, leaning back against the winged banister at the base of the steps. "That isn't a secret easily shared."

Winding my fingers together over my heart, I pivoted back to face him. "But you're sharing it with me now."

"Because I trust you."

Four simple words. But they couldn't have struck harder if he'd aimed a punch at my gut.

Would I ever really be worthy of that trust? After the meetings I'd held with Phin behind his back, after the ink I'd sabotaged, after...everything?

I blinked a shimmer of heat from my eyes, pressing my lips tight against a trembling breath.

I couldn't change anything I'd done until this moment. But, starting now, I could make it different. Starting with keeping this place secret, no matter what.

"Thank you," I croaked.

With a curt nod, Malakai lurched up from the banister; the brush of his arm against mine guided me to the first curio case, where he pointed through the artful, swooping face to the contents in various glass bottles it contained.

"Rare poisons," he explained. "Some I've found, others I've brewed myself. A few are Mithran, bartered at the markets in Amalgard."

"You give us spices, we give you something deadly," I laughed.

A twinkle of mischief lit Malakai's dark eyes. "Let's settle to say that these are not the common imports for which spices are traded."

We walked side-by-side down the row, casual as a couple browsing at a marketplace while he showed off his treasures: the most valuable books of poetry ever found, not recreations of the chroniclers and scribes in Valorkeep but hand-penned by the poets themselves. Gilded busts and small blown-glass figurines. Skulls—human, animal, sea-beast. Books in languages lost to time, or that came to us from across the oceans that neither of us could even read.

"Why do you collect all of this?" I asked as we neared the last cabinet. "At least half of it you can't even use."

Malakai shrugged. "Things can be beautiful and intriguing without serving any inherent purpose. I lived much of my life in a world where things—people—were only valued for what use you could make of them." Darkness dashed across the light that sharing these things had stoked in his eyes; but he blinked it quickly away. "I prefer to surround myself with beauty that's beautiful for its own merit."

"Like this manse?"

"That's part of it, yes." A sideways glance my way; then he halted before the last cabinet.

It was the most stunning of all…hand-tooled wood, six arched glass windows on the front, and only a few contents inside: a necklace crafted of lace and teardrop diamonds, a journal, a beryl ring, a set of silver knuckle-knives. But one item in particular caught my attention, dragging me nearer to the glass, my nose almost brushing it, my breath fogging the surface.

"Flipping Luck," I breathed.

I'd never been one to think weapons were particularly *pretty*. Functional, yes. Absolutely necessary, of course—if I hadn't accepted that before my visit to Hadrass-Drui, that first night alone would've made a believer of me. But I'd never thought them aesthetically appealing the way people like Jaik and Arias did; they were simply a means to an end.

This weapon, set on blackwood mounts, its sheath propped off to the side—this was a work of art as beautiful as any canvas or sculpture or well-tended plant I'd ever seen.

Not just because of the pale purple-pink gemstones set into the brilliant silver handle, bound in twists like hand-forged ivy. Not even the elegant crossguard, hammered out of what looked like shards of rainbow metal.

But the blade itself was glittering, gleaming with streaks of color like black opal. It was almost *mesmerizing*, from hilt to serrated edge to tip.

It was the first time a weapon had ever put me close to *swooning*.

"A Navarian venom-blade." Reverence touched Malakai's tone as he propped a hand against the edge of the cabinet above my head, leaning so near his next exhale brushed his chest against my spine. "There were only a handful ever forged…I won't tell you how many throats I slit to lay hands on this one."

"Good, because I don't want to know." I skimmed a finger along the glass, imagining the texture of those intricate silver swoops beneath my touch. "Navar-Bane is famous for their blades, but I didn't realize they were so *beautiful*."

"And deadly," Malakai warned. "This sort in particular. Venom-blades are cured with poison laid into the steel. The wounds they deal are all but entirely unhealing. Almost a certain death-sentence."

I pulled my finger back. "Ah. Well, that explains why you keep it locked in this case."

"Yes. Highly valuable and highly dangerous...and I would make myself a target of countless assassins if they knew I'd come into possession of one."

"So, you're saving it for a special day," I joked.

"Or a particular kill." His hand dropped from the edge of the cabinet, and he pivoted, turning me with the slightest curve of his arm around my back and his hand brushing my shoulder.

It reminded me of the night I'd stumbled back into the manse after my last meeting with Phin; I almost wished he'd leave his arm there as he guided the way across the room, to the bookcases.

"This," he said, halting before the lower of the two-level shelves with a rolling ladder stretching up the vaults, "is what I most wanted you to see. The poison studies." He set the book he'd taken from me on the shelf, outward-facing, and tapped the cover. "I've watched you pore through this cover to cover more than once since we struck our bargain. I suspect you're in need of more scintillating content...something you've never read before."

I had to swallow the water in my mouth before I croaked, "You're setting me free in an entire *library* of Hadrassi poison studies."

It was the sort of content my professors at Harrow Hall had *dreamed* of; but these books were kept so sacred and secret by the Hadrassi assassins, most humble academia would never lay hands on even a small recreation of a single text.

Judging by the age and tooling on some of these covers, Malakai had the *original* copies.

"Read as much as you like," he offered. "It will help pass the time."

Until the Jubilee. Until everything changed again.

Suddenly, I wished everything would *stop*. Rather than racing toward the next turning point, the way I'd been begging time to flow since I'd last seen Phin...now I wanted to hold it fast in its tracks.

I wanted a hundred days to read the books in this sacred space. To study the curios and even the poetry. To brush up on my knowledge of poisons before I tangled with their wielders; to understand *Malakai* better, everything he did and *how* he did it.

I couldn't stop time any more than I'd been able to rush it along before; but, *Luck*, now I knew how to spend it *wisely*.

I snatched the nearest—and oldest—book from the shelf, then clapped it against Malakai's bicep. "You need to go away. I have *reading* to do."

"And quite a bit of it," he snorted. "If you need me, I'll be—"

"Brewing poisons, killing people, the usual." I waved him off like it didn't matter—because, for once, it didn't. I was more interested in what lay between these pages than what he was writing in his. "I know how to scream like a damsel if I somehow lock myself in. *Go, go, go!*"

Chuckling under his breath, he herded me—groaning and protesting—toward a long table that took up the back portion of the room. He drew out the chair at the head of it for me, and I was about to sink into it when something else caught my attention: a standalone stone pedestal at the very back of the vaulted attic space, topped with a glass case.

"Wait." I batted his arm again with the book. "What's *that*?"

He was slow to follow as I ducked around him and hurried to the pedestal, setting the poison study gently on the floor so I could smooth my hands over both sides of the glass.

Its contents were simple, framed with another strand of that Storycrafted light: a scroll of parchment, stained and splotched in several places by small, spider-veined droplets. But the ink was as stark as if it had just been written, and when my eyes soaked in the first few lines, familiarity roared through me like a deluge of blood.

"The poem," Malakai murmured, halting beside me. "*My* poem, in its entirety. I penned it during the first year after my family's deaths...while I grieved them the most painfully. While I planned my vengeance."

I traced my fingers over the glass casement, my heart wrenching into my throat.

I'd read most of the lines before, scattered across the various soul-sender reports and ledgers. They'd gotten a few out of order, and by now he must've finished another entire stanza, with how often he'd been in and out of the manse.

My gaze snagged on a few lines as I read along the way, hooking my attention like a suture needle snaring in thick, leathery skin.

Some were penned in diluted ink. The line that had delivered Vespertine's poisoned slumber. The line that had severed things between Phin and me. They'd run a bit, as if they'd been splashed with water.

Or with the tears of a young man mourning the deaths of his family.

"How many lines are left?" The warm breath of my question fogged the glass.

Malakai's fist unfurled, his thumb and smallest finger tapping a muffled tune against the case. "Not many at all." His gaze tapered my way. "But, if things go according to plan at the Jubilee, I may have a few stanzas to add."

"And…what happens when the poem is finished entirely, Malakai?"

Something like ecstasy dashed across the surface of his eyes; he sloped forward, leaning his chin on the crook of his arm, his lashes fluttering shut as he drew in a deep, calming breath.

"Absolution, at long last."

CHAPTER 60
A VISION OF TROUBLE

T HE BEGINNING OF THE end came with snow.

Fitting, somehow, that that was what ushered in the close of the year: a silver, sparkling storm that whirled against the windowpanes while I dressed for the Guild Garrote.

Anticipation and reflection danced like those powdery flakes, all of the things Malakai and I had practiced and prepared for spinning a gale in my head while I faced the new, full-length mirror propped against the bedframe...and tugged on the dress I'd bought in the same shop as that, on the same day.

It had been difficult not to walk out with something finer...something that better suited my own style. But I had to think like a bistro owner who had a shop to upkeep after tonight's Jubilee...not like a woman whose purchases were personally financed by an assassin.

Even so, I did love this dress. The pine-green layers sported modest skirts and long sleeves in a blend of sheer and silken fabric that cuffed at the wrists. The bodice was the truly eye-catching feature, crusted with false gemstones and lace that gathered across the shoulders and bound at the nape—leaving the rest of my back exposed through long drapes of silk, all the way to my waistline.

Of course, it would be cold—but that was what my healer's cloak was for. And besides, I was fond of the message it sent...exposing my back at a gala of assassins felt like precisely the sort of joke they would make with each other.

Clipping the small clasp at my nape into place, I swiveled this way and that, smoothing and fluffing and adjusting things...all of which felt like halfhearted attempts to keep the trembling in my fingers from finding a way out into the rest of me.

I breathed in deeply, blew it free through rounded lips—then jumped in place when I caught a flash of movement reflected in the doorway behind me.

Malakai, as usual, arrived like the first shadows at sunset...unannounced and not at all unwelcomed. He leaned in the doorway, dressed even finer than his usual attire: all core blacks this time, a high-collared shirt, trousers tucked into formal shoes, a tooled leather belt sporting his only pop of color in a circular silver buckle. A well-tailored coat hung across the lean frame of his body, the flaps holding perfectly to his chest, his hands tucked in his pockets and his mask fixed in place.

Not the usual mask he wore for his marks, but a silver, skull-like shroud that hung as low as his upper lip, the edges winged in bone-sharp spurs; somehow, it wasn't enough to hide the way he was looking at me, our gazes caught in the reflection of the mirror.

Impossibly soft. Incredibly captivated.

I swallowed. "Was Giddy Gus your inspiration?" I gestured to the mask.

For once, he didn't take the bait; instead, he shrugged up and stepped into the room, his husky murmur trailing like fingertips up my spine: "*In a garden of words, she blooms like a rose...petals of ash, in grace she glows. But beneath the surface, thorns lie unseen. A fierce protector, in shades of shadow and green.*"

"More Kilgrave?" I rubbed the heat from my cheeks.

"My own work, in fact."

"You're ridiculous," I laughed, finally wrenching my gaze from his. "Hand me my dagger sheath, would you? It's over there on the bed."

He disappeared from the mirror's view; straps whispered and buckles jangled as he fiddled with the long leather wrappings. I busied myself pinning up my hair, because the act of combing and sticking the curls in place gave time for the heat in my cheeks to finally make its long overdue escape.

Malakai appeared behind me in the reflection again at last, touching my shoulder lightly. "May I?"

I almost told him I could handle it myself—almost cheated myself out of what I truly wanted.

So for once, I was glad when my nerves peeled down my defenses like stripping a bandage from a tacky wound: "Please do."

He crouched, bunching my skirt up nearly to my hip; I snatched it and held it clear for him, closing my eyes so that I wouldn't have to watch him binding the sheath around my thigh. But, Luck, I felt every bit of it...every graze of his fingers on my bare skin, the way gooseflesh reared all the way down to my ankle and refused to settle while he tied and buckled things into place.

"All finished." His gloved fingertips floated down the back of my thigh, past my knee, falling away finally from my ankle when he clasped his own knee and pushed himself up swiftly from his crouch. "I have a last piece to complete your ensemble."

"Oh?" The question came out absolutely strangled; there was no hope to Luck he hadn't noticed, but thankfully, he didn't remark on it. He just fished in his pocket a moment and drew from its depths...

The most lovely necklace I'd ever seen—a pure silver chain strung with two bottles. The first was a simple stopper bottle of amber liquid, innocuous but familiar, because I had been looking at it almost every morning for weeks on end.

My antidote.

But the second...I'd never seen it before: an opalescent, teardrop vial strung on a coiled metal fastening and a leather cord. It straddled the line between breathtakingly beautiful and unassumingly plain.

"This one is for more than decoration," Malakai murmured, touching a finger to it. "This is protection. I would like you to wear it tonight as well, if you're willing."

I flattened a hand over my breastbone, where the vial would hang—then edged out a nod.

Difficult, not because I didn't want it...but because everything felt so alarmingly *intimate* about all of this that I wasn't exactly certain how to react to his offer. This gift.

It was almost a relief to turn my back on him so that he could fasten the pendant in place.

"Is this your subtle way of saying Mithran jewelry would give the ruse away?" The joke felt a bit weak on my lips as I watched him tuck the vials around my neck in the mirror—his knuckles brushing both sides of my throat when he drew the chain back.

"On the contrary...consider this a nod to it." The tapered ends of the bottles whispered along my sternum like the tracing of his fingertip as he draped the cord behind my neck. "It suits your style, but it contains a poison I brewed myself."

"Do I want to know?" I mock-groaned.

"A contact poison." The chain settled against my clavicles, and his fingers brushed my nape, setting the fine hairs on my arms on end as he worked the clasp. "The same properties I use in my ink. If you ever feel threatened, a drop of this poison to any bit of bare skin will paralyze your enemy."

"But not kill them?"

His touch vanished for a moment; then his knuckles glided down my spine through the bare swoop of my backless dress, rattling my insides with a pleasant, uncontrollable shiver.

"I'm aware you hold death more lightly than I," he murmured against the shell of my ear. "So, no, this poison will not kill them...only incapacitate them so that you may decide whether you wish to end their life on your own terms. Or not."

I squeezed my eyes shut, wrestling down the impossible urge to turn and tie my arms around his neck and *taste* the dark rumble of his voice for myself.

Flipping Luck, I am in so much trouble.

I had to count to three *twice* before I could bring myself to turn and face him, hooking my hair over my shoulder to keep my hands from rebelling and carrying out my secret wishes. Thank Luck, Malakai stepped back when I pivoted, giving me a bit more breathing room—and making it so I would have to practically fling myself at him if I really wanted that taste.

Composure. That was going to be my armor tonight.

His gaze trailed up the length of me, the round of his throat bobbing in a swallow. "You look magnificent in that dress...the absolute vision of trouble."

"How did you guess that's exactly what I'm angling for?"

"Naomi." He took my hand and brought my knuckles to his lips, glittering gaze fixed on mine. "You are *beautiful*, do you realize that?"

I hadn't exactly been *unaware*, but the way he said it made it feel like something sacred...like art. Like *poetry*.

"None of that." Breathlessness undercut my teasing tone. *Ugh.* "We have a job to do tonight, Poet."

"I won't deny that." He was quiet for a long moment, his eyes scouring my face in a way they never had before...less of a search, more of a plea. As if he was asking me to look back, look deeper. To see *him*.

"But I think," he added quietly, "you are the first thing I have ever wanted to be selfish with. Even if it's only stealing a moment more of your time."

I dared to step closer, tucking my head under his chin—breathing in the comforting, spicy aroma of fennel and pine from the hollow of his throat. "So, take it."

We stood there a moment, his hands cupping my lace-capped shoulders, mine settling over his waist. Sinking into a heartbeat of all that waited ahead of us...the danger. The reckless hope. All the trouble we planned to stir up tonight, with the unfathomable belief it somehow wouldn't come back to haunt us for the rest of our possibly short and agonized lives, if anything went wrong.

And that thought was what pulled me away from him...what had me turning for the bed and scooping up my gold mask, stringing it hastily beneath my upswept hair and then letting a portion of curls tumble down to hide the strap.

It felt safer to be hidden now. Hidden from every assassin—even the blush on my cheeks hidden from Malakai when I spun back to face him.

"Well?" I situated the mask more firmly onto the bridge of my nose, then spread my hands slightly at my hips. "How do I look?"

His smile cut somewhere between anticipation and a strange heartache. "Every inch the assassin."

Well...that was good.

Because tonight, I'd be surrounded by them.

CHAPTER 61
THE JESTER'S JUBILEE

THE HIRED CARRIAGE RIDE to the Jubilee was even more fraught with nerves than the one I'd taken with Caspian across Amalgard, fearing an attacker in every shadow.

Shockingly, going straight into a hive of them did not make me feel any better.

What *did* numb the edge of my nerves was Malakai; he gripped my hand on the cushy, crushed-velvet seat between us, thumb stroking my knuckles in a gentle, reassuring rhythm. And though that was mostly for show—we were meant to be a humble bistro owner and her husband, after all—it still cocooned me in a sense of safety more potent than I'd thought possible.

Even so, my stomach dipped when we trundled away from cobblestone roads and over a slicker, smoother sort of byway; when shadows closed around the carriage, erasing the last of twilight's glow, I tilted forward to peer around Malakai through the carriage's curtained window.

Dark tines of spired rock and harsh, hardy trees rambled past. Snow fell in swirling gales, dusting the winding road that looped through a thick neck of forest well beyond the outskirts of Rastra, until we reached an iron gate and its finialed fence carving the landscape in two. Its defenses were helmed not by sentinels, but by a cluster of armored men and women watching dispassionately as we passed.

Whether they were assassins or simply hands hired for an illusion of protection, I didn't know; and I didn't know which possibility grated worse on my nerves.

Another stretch of forest drank us down deep like a cure-all; then lanternlight flickered ahead, popping through the trees like bursts of Ameresh fireworks. And before I'd fully caught my breath from passing through the imposing iron gate and into the lands of the Guild Garrot, we were trundling up to the manse itself.

I hated to think it, but the place put Kai's lair to shame. It was all stone, the most lavish, sleek, expensive kind I'd ever laid eyes on, opalescent and gleaming in the light of the lanterns set in every window. And there were *dozens* of windows, framing the east and west wings, and the steepled spans that joined them to the foremost turret; that turret itself was capped in a spired dome and ribbed with a balcony halfway up its height.

Soaring, sloped roofs, birdcage gazebos on the willow-heavy grounds, and a fountain shaped like a tree pouring water from its branches at the center of the hooped road outside the doors all seethed with riches. Someone's daydream; another person's nightmare.

We weren't the first carriage in line, and I wished it was easier to tell who was an assassin and who was common while we watched the attendees glide through the glass-paned doors circling the rotunda base in streams of three. But they all wore the same lustrous gowns and fletched core-darks, and carried themselves with a similar haughty air. Everyone was trying to blend in…whether to seem lower or higher than their true station.

I just had to hope that the indistinguishable difference worked both ways—that the Guild wouldn't be able to tell us apart from the rest of the commoners, either.

Before I was really ready, our carriage came to a final halt abreast of the turret's center. Malakai popped the door open and slid out, but I couldn't unstick my haunches from the seat and make myself follow him.

I'd been preparing for this for…months now. But it still felt like laying my head on the surgeon's table and inviting a first-year initiate to carve into my skull.

Malakai turned back, peering into the carriage. "Coming?"

"I don't think I can do this," I choked.

No reprimand came; no rebuke, no pushing and prodding. Just his gloved hand offered back into the carriage…steady. Confident.

"This is my world," he reminded me, shadow-soft. "And you have become an indispensable part of it. I will keep you safe, even if it means shedding blood tonight."

Maybe I shouldn't have found that as comforting—or as knee-quakingly attractive—as I did.

But at least it was enough to push me up from the seat, to set my hand in his.

And the rest…the rest was just pretending. Like I'd been doing ever since I'd fled to Dalfi.

Hand-in-hand, Malakai and I mounted the two shallow steps that wrapped around the rotunda's face and stepped through the prismatic wooden doors into the heart of the rotunda.

The etched and muraled ceiling—which ended where that balconied second level began—caught the chatter of the occupants with an echo like a rainshower. It hammered in tune with the pounding pulse in my ears as Malakai led the way to the first greeter, a man in gold-and-crimson livery holding ground in the swirl of bodies only a few steps from the door.

Producing the invitation from the inner pocket of his well-tailored jacket, Malakai extended it between two fingers. "My wife and I are eternally grateful for this opportunity."

"Mmm." The greeter surveyed the cardstock, turned it this way and that, then pressed his finger against the seal and lingered there for a moment.

I couldn't imagine what he was feeling for, but he must've found it—which made me all the more grateful we hadn't tried to forge our way into this Jubilee. Nodding faintly, the man tore the invitation to shreds before us, tossed the scraps into a bucket at his feet, then sidestepped with a sweep of his arm.

"Welcome to the Jester's Jubilee."

Malakai's fingers tightened and twisted, lacing between mine as we stepped into the crush of bodies flowing through the turret, toward the wide-open doors at the back...toward the revelry that waited beyond.

Vivid light strained my eyes as we swept in with the crowd to the upper mezzanine of a recessed ballroom and entertainment parlor, which seemed to dominate the heart of the lavish manse.

The tapered ceiling was plated with mosaic tile—a nod to the sort of finery found in Amalgard—which strengthened the blush-and-gold-glow that held the room in a dreamlike fist. Card and dice tables lined the windowed walls, the games already well underway, while servants twirled like dancers themselves along the ballroom floor, handing out flutes of sparkling wine and platters of the most delectable-smelling food I'd ever scented...buttery, rich, spicy, *decadent.* Pastries, finger-sandwiches, chicken skewers, seafood, truffles. And aromatic enough to tickle my nose even past the layers of perfumes and colognes lingering around every body that shoved past us, hurrying down the steps to begin their night of fun.

Every so often, bursts of glitter plumed from the sides of the rooms, scattering across the attendees like the snow falling outside. It gave everything a starlight quality—celestial. Otherworldly. Sparkles on skin and silk glittered beneath chandeliers the dripped in gemstone rows three across and six deep all the way down the room's impressive length; they shed a warm glow over knots of dancers performing a Hadrassi waltz in perfect step. It was halfway beautiful and halfway eerie, all of those masked faces twirling around the floor together.

And one of those faces was our mark.

I glanced sideways at Malakai, who canvassed the space with a sort of casual indifference I had been trying to learn through our sessions practicing and preparing for this night; but it was hard to hide I was a little starstruck, a little wide-eyed, a little nervous in this room full of would-be killers.

Just play your part, I reminded myself.

A gentle, clearing throat behind me; I jerked my head to the left to find a well-dressed man in the same gilded crimson uniform as the greeter's extending his arm to me, and by instinct, I drew a bit closer to Malakai.

The man raised a brow. "Your cloak, madame?"

"Oh...yes. Of course, I'm sorry. I'm not used to..." I fumbled to release the tie around my throat.

The man raised a silver brow almost to his well-trimmed, equally-silver hairline. "Yes. Quite."

Flushing, I shed the cloak's weight, passing it off to the man and watching him whisk it away; and when I turned back to the room, several sets of eyes snagged on me from the sunken chamber below.

On my dress, my exposed back...a perfect place to dig a blade in.

Maybe I'd chosen wrong; maybe I was showing I didn't belong here, after all.

Well, I'd meant to make a statement. And here it was.

Kai escorted me by the hand, down the steps, past clusters of commoners and assassins who peered at us even after we'd breezed through their midst. As if they had as keen noses as I did—as if they smelled the trouble on us. The chaos we'd come to create.

In the middle of the dance floor—which Kai took like we belonged there, rather than keeping to the fringes—we faced one another. I barely fought the urge to wipe my sweating palms on my thighs.

Many of the attendees had gone back to their conversations, but several watched us with hawkish curiosity; most likely because, no matter what lie we clad around ourselves, we just didn't give off the impression of a bistro owner and her husband. And they didn't know that was who we'd come disguised as, anyway.

The invitation had gotten us through the door on those merits. But it couldn't change who we were—and who we were drew attention, in this palace of killers and unwitting guests.

I hadn't had this many eyes on me since graduation from Harrow Hall—if even then. I'd avoided being noticed for so long, ever since I'd fled Vallanmyre, that this felt more than ever like a death sentence.

Malakai's smile twisted upward, his eyes flashing within the holes of his mask; his movements were the essence of confident ease when he gripped my waist and slipped his fingers around mine. Only the faintest clench of his hand on my hip and the feathering in his jaw told of the agitation lurking below...that he was as unused to the attention as I was.

That, in this sea of potential enemies—in the whole world that reviled the parts of ourselves made necessary by our survival—all we had was each other.

"Don't look at any of them," he murmured. "They don't matter. Look at *me*, Naomi."

"Difficult." The tie of my sheath felt heavier than I'd ever remembered it hanging before, like it was trying to cut off the circulation below my thigh, and I was keenly aware of every rub of lace against my sensitive skin—and his molten gaze was almost impossible to bear. "Kai, they're all *staring*."

Mischief darted across the upturn of his mouth. "Then let's give them something worth looking at, shall we?"

And he swept me off into a dance.

My feet found the paces we'd practiced in his study with surprising ease, considering this felt *nothing* like those times; not with the way his fingertips brushed my exposed back just past my hip, or how he held my stare unblinking as we spun in perfect synchrony with our fellow dancers.

This was just a mission, a smaller one within the larger work I'd been sent here to do. But it was hard not to feel caught up in the moment...in the softness of his gloves, warm against my skin. In the heady strains of the quartet echoing from the recesses of the room, so perfectly captured by the sloped roof and drizzled back over us, sweet as honey. In the floatiness of my own feet, the whisper of the gown against my waist, the mesmerizing rose-gold blush that held the room captive.

In the enchanting way Malakai watched me still, that faint tilt to his mouth. Like nothing in this room existed but us. As if we could be anywhere, not just in an assassin's manse...and wherever we were, that's where he was content to be.

My gaze wandered, wanting to find the faces around us; Malakai released my hip, spun me out from him to a loft in the strings, then drew me back—holding my chin fast for a moment, fixing my eyes on his before he gripped my waist and started us twirling again.

"Remember...they do not matter," he reminded me.

I drew in a long, quivering breath through my nostrils. "How are we doing, really?" I let an edge overtake my voice—warning him against a lie.

His gaze glimmered behind the seat of his mask. "Poetry in motion."

He spun and dipped me, his nose gliding along the arch of my throat; my breath snagged as his face loomed above mine.

Nearly against my lips, he breathed, "They will never see us coming."

In one smooth pirouette, he spun me back upright, twirled me on the balls of my feet—and slipped away.

Reality crashed back over me with the parting of our fingers—with our arms still upraised, outstretched, reaching for each other even while he turned away, vanishing into the crowd.

He'd made his mark.

It was time to steal the serum.

I let my arm fall, guarding my fluttering middle with the spread of my fingers, breathing in deeply through my nostrils and pushing the swell of air out through my mouth.

And it was time for a distraction.

CHAPTER 62
ONE LAST DANCE

FROM ONE OF THE card tables, three hands deep and several coins lighter, I
watched Malakai chat casually with Solomyn and Katia Degrace at the edge
of the dance floor, wine flutes and finger sandwiches in hand.

Our gracious hosts struck me as the last people in the world one might think
were assassins.

If anything, they reminded me of my maternal grandparents, who I'd only
met a handful of times before my mother's funeral—and then the grief had taken
them shortly after. But the Degraces sported the same coiffed gray hair, the same
kind smiles, the same gentle, invested gazes that had dipped in and out of the first
near-decade of my life, there for birthdays and the occasional *Spirited Sunrise*.

They laughed with Malakai like old friends; they paused to shake hands and
greet gushing commoners and friends utterly refined. And the longer I watched
them, the more I began to see how all of this was possible—the leaders of a
Guild being the elderly, well-trained assassins who had earned their notoriety and
trained those beneath their rank. Who'd learned to play the part *exceptionally*
well...and who'd gathered enough coin through enough affluent killings to host
a Jubilee of this magnitude.

There was also no mistaking their love for each other—a devotion shown in
the smallest ways. Hands on backs, hands on arms, swift glances, secret smiles.
Occasionally, Solomyn pressed a kiss to his wife's temple, or nuzzled her hair; in
the middle of conversation, she propped an arm on his shoulder and wound her
wandering fingertips through his silver curls.

It shouldn't have made my throat ache, seeing the way assassins could hold
death and love with the same confidence in two well-trained hands.

It shouldn't have unleashed a strange, uncanny flutter of hope in my stomach.

I drowned that uninvited sensation with splashes of wine and too many
chocolate truffles to count.

For most of the night, I circled around the Degraces—and around Malakai while he spoke with them in the kind of animation I'd rarely seen from him before. It was no wonder, really, that the Poet Poisoner had evaded capture so long; if I hadn't lived with Malakai myself these last several months, I might not have been able to tell the mask of the suave savior in Amalgard from the one who flirted with Valessa, or this one who talked the ear off a pair of assassins about who-knew-what.

Or the one who'd smiled at me beneath the fireworks. Who'd shown me his vault. Who'd leaned against me at his most broken, and let me hold him. Who'd danced with me in this dreamlike place, his mouth an inch from mine.

I ground my teeth into my lower lip until it pulsed, nearly bleeding. *Not tonight.*

I dropped my gaze back to the cards and resumed playing once I caught a glimpse of Malakai charming Madame Katia—pressing a kiss to her knuckles, murmuring a question, then escorting her to the next dance.

My heart raced with anticipation. It was almost time.

I gathered my winnings from the latest hand, then moved toward the next card table the way someone truly playing for keeps would—but a hand snared my elbow along the way, halting me on the edge of the dance floor.

"Madame Beris, isn't it?" Solomyn Degrace offered me a smile far too appealing for a man so much older than me—a smile meant to charm a common woman in grand halls, not a healer in disguise. "Seeing as my wife and your husband are sharing a dance, I thought perhaps we could do the same?"

I flashed a glance at Malakai; he watched me over Katia's head, but gave no indication if he thought this was a wise or foolish choice.

Think like a commoner.

Stitching on a sweet smile, I drizzled my coins into my dress's pocket and melted into the man's gentle grip. "I'd be so delighted at the honor, sir!"

We took to the dance floor, his hands so formal in how they floated above my waist and lightly cradled my fingers that it made me sharply aware, for the first few steps, how intimately Kai had held me before.

Shaking off the thought, I focused on my current partner. "Your home is just...unbelievable. Absolutely stunning, breathtaking, almost like a storybook..." I swallowed and looked away. "Listen to me, rambling like that. Of course, you know how magnificent it is. It's *your* home."

"It is magnificent, isn't it?" Solomyn chuckled. "And it's a joy to share it with people like you."

He might've thought I missed the slight; I struggled not to roll my eyes.

"Your charming husband was just singing the praises of your bistro work," Solomyn remarked after I kept my silence through several turns. "I can't say I have ever had the pleasure of visiting *Beris's Bistro by the Canal,* but when my work next takes me into Rastra proper, I'll be sure to visit."

"We'd love to have you," I replied sweetly—and with our next turn, I shot Kai a withering glance across the room.

We'd come here to steal from these people tonight, not to torture them unduly.

"And what work is it that takes you into the city?" I asked demurely as we made our next turn around the dance floor. "Something more exciting than owning a bistro, I'm sure!"

Like slitting throats. Or assigning others to do it.

"Land redistribution," Solomyn replied with the casual grace of a man who had been telling the same lie for countless years.

"That sounds..." I searched for a word, wishing I had Addie and Reiko's talent for them. Or even Malakai's.

Which made me think of the poem he'd recited earlier—his own work, about—

Stop, I ordered myself. *Not here, not tonight.*

"It's incredibly mind-numbing work," Solomyn chuckled, rescuing me from my unspoken chaos. "But it allows me to afford the lifestyle my sweet Katia deserves, so I'm hardly one to complain."

"Humble, mind-numbing, entertaining..." I shrugged. "All work is worth the effort if it supports the life and people you love. Even if it never lets you sleep."

"Is your bistro so busy?" he joked.

"Not the bistro, but I have other work that takes up my time."

The strings strained to an end, and we halted; Solomyn pressed a chaste kiss to my knuckles. "Well, if we should find one another on the dance floor again, I'd love to hear of your other pursuits."

I effected the same mocking curtsy I'd used to annoy Malakai the last several months. "If the souls love us enough, sir."

We turned our separate ways—him to find Katia, and me to nearly collide with Malakai, waiting among the crowd. His hand was extended, his gaze fathomless behind his mask. "May I have this last dance?"

So, it was done.

Pulse thundering, head and chest a bit fuzzy from it all, I clasped his fingers and let him draw me in for a slower dance, the strings sweeter this time, far more melancholy. I rested my head against his chest, fragrant fennel and pine erasing the spicy aroma of Solomyn's clothing from the folds of my dress.

"Everything is going to plan," Kai murmured against my hair. "Are you prepared?"

"As I'll ever be," I whispered into the lapels of his coat. "Word at the card and dice tables has it that the western wing is the most heavily occupied...people are being allowed into the powder rooms in the east wing, but the door to the west is double-latched, with some guards patroling in the windows."

"Excellent work." Malakai's knuckles trailed up and down my bare spine, eliciting an endless parade of shivers that danced across my skin. "I knew you could do it, troublemaker."

"Be careful, Malakai," I warned. "Not everyone is going to fall for this ruse. You'll still have to fight your way through."

"I've done it before...I'll gladly do it again." His lips brushed the crown of my head; there was no mistaking it this time like I had the night I'd last seen Phin.

And there was nothing to drown that feeling squirming through my middle, making me feel weightless, fearless, and fully capable of *anything*.

"Happy hunting," I whispered against the hollow of his throat.

His arm snugged me just a bit tighter against him, for just a moment longer. "The happiness comes after."

Glass burst with a piercing *crack*, shattering on the floor behind us; boots skidded on the slick ballroom floor. An awful, gagging, retching sound put the resonance of the strings to death.

And then the screaming started.

CHAPTER 63
PAINFUL PURSUITS

MALAKAI AND I WRENCHED apart; his arms slipped away from me, and as I turned to the mayhem behind me, he fell in with the first flock of people doing precisely what commonfolk did when trouble manifested itself: fleeing from screams and havoc, looking for a safe place to muster.

And there was plenty of both those things as Katia swayed and bent double, clutching her middle, crying out so loudly and with so much agony it likely burst all the blood vessels in her eyes.

"*Katia!*" Solomyn roared, shoving aside the nearest guests to reach her; he lunged to her side just in time to catch her when her strength gave out and she tumbled toward the floor.

"Madame Degrace!" I yelped—then staggered backward when someone elbowed me out of the way, hurtling me into the crush of bodies fleeing for escape at the top of the steps.

Solomyn's head whipped up, his furious gaze latching onto the sound of retreating bootsteps. "*No one leaves this room!*"

Spinning on my heels, my eyes flashed to the top of the steps, where Malakai and several others froze...where the butler who'd taken my coat swept forward from the doors, arms extended, ushering them back.

There was no time to hesitate; I dashed up the steps after them, catching the butler's wrist, whirling him to face me. "My cloak—you took my cloak, didn't you?"

Confusion crinkled his brow as his eyes shot past me, to the bedlam below. "Madame?"

"I'm a healer!" I shouted. "Get me my cloak, I have a cure-all that may help whatever's wrong with her!"

Indecision held the butler fast for another heartbeat; but when Katia's next anguished scream rattled the mosaic glass above, desperation made the decision for him.

He turned and slipped out the door, barking orders at someone beyond not to let anyone through; but several guests shoved through anyway, and with a curt nod in my direction, Malakai vanished among them, swift and silent as ever.

I darted back down the steps, so Malakai's absence at the top wouldn't seem so stark; then I shouldered through the crowd, tugging the vial of cure-all from the chain around my neck and holding it tight in my fist.

"Let me through—let me through, I'm a healer!" I snarled, throwing elbows and kicking at legs in front of me until finally, *finally*, the people parted enough that I reached Solomyn and Katia.

They were already surrounded by several sturdy bodies making space for them—most likely friends. Most likely assassins who knew cures as well, who were already trying to decide how to fix what we'd broken.

But they wouldn't be able to fix this...Malakai and I had seen to that.

"I'm a healer," I repeated, tumbling down at Katia's side, gripping her floundering, fisting hand and meeting Solomyn's frantic gaze.

"Healer?" he snapped. "You're a bistro owner!"

"I'm that, too, yes...you said you wanted to know about my other pursuits!" I turned my fingers to his wife's wrist, checking her pulse. "Is she sensitive to any foods? Allergic to them?"

"No, of course not—I wouldn't serve anything like it if she were!"

"I'm just trying to understand what's happening," I soothed, brushing loose hair from his wife's wrinkled brow and cupping a hand over her nose and mouth to monitor her breaths. "I don't like the sound of her lungs...has she been ill recently?"

"Not even a touch of a cold all season."

"Here, sit her up, that will help her breathe more evenly." I steadied her wrist, and he took her shoulders, propping her back against his chest; the position reminded me so achingly of Kai and Sofi that for a moment, the tension in my throat turned genuine.

Even if this was necessary—even if these were assassins, and even if I held the cure concealed in my hand—this was still a man's beloved wife we were harming. Threatening to take away from him.

The notion sent me into a flurry of the usual examination I would do if I hadn't already been aware what was abrading her from the inside—checking the eyes, monitoring her pulse, testing the flow of blood to her extremities. The crowd bolstered around us, some weeping silently, others weeping loudly...some so chillingly quiet, it left no doubt they had faced death of this nature before.

I strung the ruse of examination out for as long as I could—for Kai's sake. And as long as I knew Katia could bear.

Then it was time to land the blow.

"This...this seems like poison." Effecting a raspy tone, I glanced up from pressing gently on Katia's abdomen—already warm from the inflaming poison twisting through her veins. "Sir...does your wife have any enemies?"

Solomyn's gaze held mine, his ashen complexion paling even further.

"This may have been deliberate," I murmured. "I've seen it before, in the infirmaries in Hyraith where I trained. And if that is the case, sir, there may be only one way to save her."

The butler's thundering footfalls clapped through the crowd just then as if I'd summoned him for my act.

"Your cloak!" He flung it into my lap; I plunged my fist into the pocket, making a show of extracting the vial I already held from the inner folds; then I held it out to Solomyn.

"This is a cure-all," I said. "It's been handed down through my family for generations as a protection against the unknown. It may help your wife...it *may*. I can't promise anything, since we can't be certain what caused this."

"An heirloom cure, and you'd give it up for a stranger?" one of the assassins scoffed behind me.

I twisted to pin a glare on him. "Did you miss me saying I'm a healer? That's my duty—healing! Now I can help, or you can bicker and call for someone else, but with a pulse this thready and her breathing so labored, and with the distended feeling of her abdomen...I doubt she'll survive the wait."

Solomyn supported his wife against him, eyes half-mad with desperation.

Luck, I knew that desperation so well. I had seen it so many times, it still ached and twisted in like a knife—even if he was an assassin.

And it struck me sideblind how *recently* I had seen it.

Hadn't Malakai looked at me with a tinge of that fervor when I'd returned from confronting Phin?

"Let me help her," I urged. "If I even can."

Another long moment spiraling out heartbeat by heartbeat, while he searched my gaze and clung to his wife, whose pained breaths corroded the air between us.

Then, cursing, he tipped her head back against his shoulder and parted her jaw with the pinch of his thumb and forefinger—like this was far from the first time they'd done this.

I tried not to imagine a life fraught with that much peril as I uncorked the vial and tipped the antidote into her mouth...watching weeks of work disappear in a syrupy, opalescent stream. Gone in moments down the gullet of an assassin.

But if this worked—and I was confident it would—then we could escape tonight without any blood on our hands, including our own. And that was worth all the effort in the world.

Seconds thudded past, while I gripped Katia's wrist and monitored her heartbeat; while, to my relief, her breathing eased as my antidote danced with Kai's poison, nullifying its agonizing effects, just like we'd practiced and planned. Soothing the raw, inflamed flesh of her innards before it rotted to the point of leaking; bringing drowsy comfort as well as healing to what had been so rapidly and ruthlessly ravaged.

"Did it work?" another guest asked anxiously, bending over my shoulder.

"I don't know for certain," I lied. "It may take time, depending on what she was poisoned with. But she shouldn't be alone until she's awake and lucid."

Solomyn straightened, bearing his wife up in the span of his shockingly-strong arms. "I'll take her to rest, and keep watch over her. No one steps from this room until I have questioned every soul who danced with her, drank with her, spoke with her. Is that understood?"

Wide eyes met across the ballroom—far too many pairs to belong just to the commoners here.

This stroke of ours had rocked the Guild Garrote; all at once, even dancing and drinking and showing off among each other wasn't safe.

After all, who was more likely to have poisoned Katia Degrace—an assassin, or a commoner?

Cold sweat broke down my spine.

It was time to disappear.

CHAPTER 64
THE RUINED RUSE

LEAVING, IT TURNED OUT, was far easier said than done; not only because everyone was kept to the ballroom for questioning, but because, after Solomyn and Katia slipped out through the upper doors, their guests descended on me like maggots on necrotic flesh.

They all wanted a bit of the cure-all for themselves. They wanted to know where I'd learned healing and poisons. They wanted to know my family name and how they'd brewed such an antidote, and what precisely we'd feared enough to pass it down.

The pressure on every side was like an encroaching headache; a half-hour after Solomyn and Katia left, there was absolutely nowhere in the ballroom left to retreat to. These assassins and terrified commoners had chased me out of every corner I'd slunk into for a moment to breathe and think, and I'd repeated the lie I'd first told Mistress Merrietti when I'd stolen the Lightbane—of my humble origins in a town not far from Rastra— so many times that I was beginning to wonder if I had a touch of Storycrafter in me, after all.

And that was when the butler found me, thank Luck; when I hurried toward the shadows below the broad steps for the second time, trying to escape the barrage of questions, he swooped in and took me by the arm, leading me up them instead...and out into the foyer, where the guests who had escaped during his absence were clustered in groups of dozens, trembling and muttering and glancing at the doors.

Many watched me pass with wide, frantic eyes as the butler ushered me into the eastern wing—into a pearlescent hallway accented in whorls of powder-blue and soft violet paint. The teal carpet matched the drapes drawn closed over the floor-to-ceiling windows, and both whispered at the passage of our steps as we started down it, his hand still around my back.

"You looked as if you needed to catch your breath," he said as we went. "And I assume if you were responsible for any of tonight's excitement, well...it would make little sense to poison Madame Katia, only to save her."

"Thank you for the rescue." I didn't even have to feign gratitude for that. "And I swear to you, I wouldn't do anything to hurt these people...this night was supposed to be *enchanting*, not..."

"Nearly fatal?"

"Yes. That."

"Well, we have you to thank that it wasn't. And I do thank you for that...Madame Katia is resting comfortable and starting to come around. She doesn't seem to be in pain anymore." The warmth of his smile suggested a personal sort of relief—the kind that came from a friend's safety after a brush with death.

Luck, I knew that feeling too well.

"I'm just glad I decided to bring the vial with me. My papa says you can never be too careful, and what do you know—he was right." I rubbed a hand over my eyes, then cursed when it smeared my cosmetics in sparkling streaks of charcoal along my fingers. "Oh, fl—rotting—"

Chuckling, the butler dropped his arm. "The powder room is the first door around the bend in the hall. I'll wait for you here, if you'd like to freshen up."

"*Thank you.*" I squeezed his wrist as it swung back to his side, then hurried up the hall and hesitated just shy of the corner.

The way around the bend was...darker, without a lining of windows. It reminded me in a flash of Dashian's playhouse, of the mirrored wall where I'd caught the real Beris looking back at me.

It reminded me that success in this country was never more than one deft maneuver away from being thieved right out of your hands. That the moment you thought you were alone, or safe—in a city street, in a playhouse washroom, with a guaranteed kill at the tip of your throwing knife—that was when something came slithering from the shadows.

I couldn't bring myself to turn that corner. Something about all of this...

Now you're thinking like an assassin.

My hands curled into a fists at my side. I whirled back to the butler. "Actually, I just realized I left my—"

The door at the mouth of the corridor whispered shut behind him.

I hadn't even heard him *move*.

The peppery odor of citrus and cinnamon struck my face like a slap from my right, bursting from around the corner—and I spun, one heartbeat before the bolting force of a much taller, much more muscular figure than mine rammed full-speed into my chest.

My feet swept out from under me; I lost all my air before it even became a scream. I would've been flattened on the teal rug if not for the hand that seized me back the throat, sweeping me up and flinging me back against the wall.

Every last one of my ribs vibrated in a single, resonate note of keening agony. I gasped, then broke into staggered, violent coughs that tore off without a prayer to Luck when iron fingers banded around my windpipe—and bore down.

My panicked, sparkling vision filled with Solomyn Degrace's snarling face.

"I—I d—"

I don't understand! The lie roared in my mind, begging to be pleaded, but I couldn't catch enough air to voice it.

Solomyn's fist clenched around my throat, his weight flattening me against the wall with so much smothering force, it felt like my spine would crack in half—if my windpipe didn't cave first. Or the wall itself.

"Whatever you and your husband are scheming, it won't come to pass," he snarled. "You think you commoners know poison? You think *we* don't know *cures*?" Nothing of the gentle, genial old man remained in the assassin who raised his free hand to pinch the nerves at my shoulder, shooting a piercing, numbing stroke of agony down my arm to the tip of every finger. "A family heirloom, *really*—and a healer in our spare time? Healers don't come to Rastra, they're run out by the likes of Merrietti if they keep their lives at all…but I suppose whoever hired you to infiltrate this Jubilee didn't bother to share that with you. They must have offered you far more coin than you won at my tables, to slip my wife a poison and a cure." Malice nearly blackened the soft brown of his eyes. "We are going to visit the private wing, you and I…and you will be telling me all of your secrets, who hired you, which assassin gave you that poison and its cure, and why my Katia was the target…if I have to remove every fingernail from your hands and both your eyes before you scream them to me."

Luck, no, no, no—

I tried to thrash, tried to lift a hand and claw at his arm, or free the vial of contact poison from its chain around my neck…but it was still a struggle just to breathe.

He pressed in even nearer, hot spittle flecking my face. "It's pitiful they thought a bistro owner could outwit the Guild Garrote with some measly poison and a jar of cure."

I would never know if the way my heart skipped was because he was so close to suffocating me, or because of the fury that banged off the insides of my skull. Only one clear-headed thought slipped through the haze my mind was becoming:

They know.

No more pretense.

The ruse was up.

This was life or death—just like my first day in this country. And Malakai couldn't save me this time.

My half-numb hand fumbled at my thigh, rucking up my skirts, grasping desperately for my dagger and seizing its handle—

I had one second to realize that was *not* my dagger's grip—not the polished wood I'd clutched so tightly so many times since that night when I'd been prepared to wield it in defense of my life against a murderer in the streets. Or whenever holding it had simply made me feel safe.

The grip in my palm was...woven like ivy. Like thorn branches. Slick gemstone angles kissed my palms and stilled my darting fingers.

That was all I noticed. As much as I could let myself think.

Then I whipped the Navarian blade from my sheath and slashed it across Solomyn's forearm.

He didn't block the blow—maybe because he was inebriated, or still shaken by his wife's near-death, or because he hadn't expected a bistro owner to carry a blade. But he seized and stumbled backward instead, his vicious howl ripping through the dull roar my ears like a blaring foghorn as his iron grip unlocked from around my throat.

My knees cracked against the floor, and I flung myself sideways, swimming in my skirts, staggering back to my feet; I backed away up the hall, holding the blade out toward Solomyn, who clapped a hand in the bloody mess the unhealing dagger had made of his arm and stalked after me.

He didn't even seem to *feel* it.

"I'll gut you, you boneless, rotting little *maggot!*" he roared. "I'll feed you your own entrails until you tell me everything—*everything* you did to her, everything you had planned tonight—!"

He tried to swipe for me with his dominant hand, but the cut of movement unleashed a bellow of pain that chased me back quicker than the stroke of his arm itself. Blood sprayed and spattered against the wall as if I'd severed an artery, not just flesh and muscle and sinew.

The horrifying work of the Navarian blade.

"What—" Solomyn gasped with disbelief—and maybe the first strokes of pain—then staggered after me when I retreated. "What in every sullied soul did you—?"

A second, far more brutal shout belted from around the corner, slicing across his demand: "Get your filthy, *rotting* hands away from her!"

And then a shadow descended on us, gloved palms slamming into the assassin's wounded forearm, ripping a piercing shriek from him that sounded more like a wounded animal than a man as he stumbled back against the wall. That pointed blow crumbled him too quickly to block when those same deft fingers flashed up to the head a heartbeat later, took it at an angle, and *wrenched*.

For the first time since my earliest lessons in Harrow Hall, the crack of shearing bone turned my stomach. I retched, stumbling back another step, fingers strangling the grip of the Navarian blade.

And just like that—it was over.

We had killed Solomyn Degrace. Leader of the Guild Garrote. Host of the Jubilee.

And for a muddled, empty-headed moment, the only thing I could think—the thing that filled my eyes with tears—was envisioning Katia's heartbroken, hate-filled face when she learned we'd taken her husband away from her.

Well, your choice cost a good family their wife and mother. So, I hope you can live with that.

My back struck the corridor's opposite wall, and Malakai spun on me, his eyes widening at the blood that stained my dress—that dripped from my hands. "*Naomi.*"

"Oh, Luck, we killed him," I choked. "They're never going to let this go, an entire guild of *assassins*—and *Katia*—"

"I have gambled with far worse odds."

"Don't tell me that!" Hysteria cracked my voice. "This was supposed to be clean, it was supposed to be *neat*, I can't believe I let him corner me—I can't believe I—"

I'd used a poisoned blade against someone.

I'd killed with *poison*.

I did it again. Again. Again.

Now we would have to run. Now we could never stop running.

Again. Again.

Malakai approached me with hands outstretched, his wide eyes framed in a constellation of blood spewed from Solomyn's arm. "You...are *marvelous*," he breathed. "You were absolutely perfect, you did precisely what you needed to do to defend yourself. And you did it without hesitating, and that...that is remarkable." A hint of a smile grazed his lips. "That's done now, troublemaker...give me the dagger."

His dagger.

I was still angling it outward, as if the threat lingered in the hall. As if I could swipe at the horrific shadows of the assassins who would soon be pursuing us.

"Why did you...why did you give this to me?" I choked, fighting to find the shape of his face through tearstained eyes.

He straightened all at once, stepping forward, so near the Navarian blade's black-opal edge pressed against his chest. A button unthreaded from the top of his night-dark shirt.

"Because I knew that I was putting you in a place of danger tonight, regardless of how well we'd prepared," he rasped. "And I would far rather lose that blade than ever lose you."

My fingers unlocked. The knife dropped from my hand, and he stooped to catch it deftly by the handle before it struck the carpet—and he caught *me*, too, when my knees buckled, completely without warning. So fast I couldn't even brace myself.

I gripped the shoulders of his coat, and he supported me with one arm around my waist until he sheathed the dagger somewhere I couldn't see; then he gripped my hips in both hands and settled me back against the wall, grinding his forehead gently against mine until the motion forced my eyes open.

"Look at me," he said, low and husky. "Did he harm you?"

I shook my head, but the truth nudged its way out in a cracked whisper. "My throat is on fire."

No change in his earnest expression. "Can you walk?"

I wanted so desperately to nod. To sashay out of this place with all the grace that we'd strolled in.

But my knees were still threatening to buckle, and my hands were stained in blood, and all I could think of were death throes and bloodshot eyes and my fingers locked around Raynes's shoulder—threats on every side.

My eyes squeezed shut. Another shake of my head, my brow shifting against his.

In one deft movement, the world shifted height—the Poet Poisoner scooping me up behind the knees and around my bare back, adjusting me in his grip until my face was cradled in the crook of his neck. And I clung to him, not caring in the least how weak that might make me seem.

I'd had to drag myself away from the last bloodbath I'd caused. To stumble on alone. To bury it so deeply it had been gnawing holes in my heart ever since.

This time, there was someone to hold onto. A strong, sturdy chest to lean against. A neck throbbing with an uneven pulse that held me in myself like roots in the soil.

So I held on tightly. And I let Malakai carry me out from a house of assassins.

CHAPTER 65
THE HEALER'S HISTORY

I REMEMBERED VERY LITTLE about escaping the Degraces' manse.

Some bloodstained blur of muttered threats. Stepping over a corpse that looked suspiciously like the butler just outside the hallway door. Shattering glass and the smell of trodden-down grass. The long, dark, silent carriage ride back to the heart of Rastra.

The first thing that struck with any sort of clarity was the feeling of blood leaving my hands.

I blinked for what felt like the first time in hours, peeking down at my fingers; Malakai ran a dark, thick cloth between each one, and pinkish water dripped into a bucket between us. We sat on the edge of my bed in the house, him with his shirtsleeves rucked to the elbows and arms balanced on his knees while he washed the blood away.

"Ah, there you are." His voice was low, soothing...like how I'd speak to my patients. His gaze was trained on my hands. "I wondered when you would find your way back to me."

I swallowed, which did shockingly little for the swelling in my hot, throbbing throat. My voice was still a croaky rasp when I said, "You don't have to do this."

"But I want to."

And I wanted him to; so I fell silent, watching him clean away the blood, squeeze out the rag, and set back to work again. And again. And again.

How we'd escaped the Jubilee without anyone noticing the blood was beyond me. I expected I owed Malakai's quick thinking and familiar escape from tight scrapes for that. But I couldn't even find my voice to thank him for it...or for what he was doing now.

The blood on my hands felt like a hundred people's. It could have been mine, if the night had gone differently. Solomyn's threats still rattled in my head and itched under the fingernails he'd threatened to rip off.

Fingernails caked with his blood.

"Do you have the truth-telling serum?" I blurted at last.

"Safely accounted for." Malakai tugged an iron-dark chain from the collar of his shirt with one hand, then let it fall again. "You played your part perfectly."

"You're *sure* it's the right serum?"

"It will need to be tested." He let that hang on the air for a moment, then added, "But given the number of men I had to kill on my way to it, one would easily ascertain it is."

"I suppose that's the end of our partnership, then," I teased weakly.

His eyes flashed to my face; a last, sharp squeeze of the rag poured out a hefty deluge of blood-tinged water. Then he sat back, scouring his hands down his thighs. "Get changed."

He gave me the room, and I slipped from the dress that pinched more and more like deathbed restraints the longer I was aware of my body again; I felt more like myself once I'd changed into soft, silk pajamas, their gentle embrace erasing the feeling of Solomyn's shove to my body—though every inch of my chest felt as bruised as my throat.

It wasn't the first time I'd been cornered by a person who wanted to do me harm—it likely wouldn't be the last, given the cities I liked to visit and call home—but I'd never felt so helpless in one's hold before.

Such a strange flip of Luck, that he was also the first one I'd helped kill for laying hands on me; I supposed killing a known killer was easier than stabbing a simple drunk in the neck.

Blinking away the memory, I wrapped my cardigan around myself and slipped back out into the hall.

Malakai's study door was ajar, the light of the hearth a silent invitation my sluggish feet took without hesitation. He sat on the cot, glancing up when I joined him; the shift of his jaw erased a stormcloud from his eyes...a burning tempest that made me think I wasn't the only one reliving our time at the Jubilee and its disastrous end.

Slowly, I sank down beside him; he swiveled slightly to face me, offering something in his hand—another cloth, this one dripping icy water.

I banded it around my throat, moaning as my eyes tumbled shut; relief made me all at once so exhausted, I could've put my head in his lap and slept right then.

"It takes a very particular sort of person to best an assassin," Malakai remarked. "Even one intoxicated and rattled by his wife's near-death."

"Maybe you think too highly of your kind," I scoffed quietly.

"Or perhaps I think more highly of *you* than you do yourself." He didn't give me a moment to digest those words, or remark on them; instead, he added, "You were not afraid to kill him."

"You know what he would have done to me if I hadn't."

The face of a leering redheaded soldier flashed through my mind; my stomach twisted itself in a knot to rival the scuff of straining fabric. I opened my eyes just in time to witness the curl of Malakai's hand over his knee into a trembling, white-knuckled fist. "I'm well aware."

We were quiet for several moments.

"You possess an extraordinary amount of poise," Malakai said at last, "and an extraordinary lack of hand-wringing over the necessities. The way you've aided me these last few months has been...nothing short of admirable. Especially for a woman not raised in the Hadrassi life."

It was a compliment, coming from him; from anyone else, it might've been an accusation.

"If you would be willing," he added, "I would like to know why."

A harsh swallow ripped at my throat. "Why—?"

"Why you are here, Naomi." He grimaced at the rough edge of his own voice, and gentled it when he added, "Why you are *still* here, not shaken, not vomiting into the sink, not dissolved into weeping after the blood I washed from your hands tonight."

I leaned back from him a bit—escaping the lure of those words, spoken without a trace of malice. "You *know* why."

"I know why you came to me—why you agreed to this mutual partnership." A slow shake of his head. "But I am asking for the truth of *you*, Naomi Weathers...freely given. Where your strength comes from. And how I can help you where it's needed."

He wanted my side of the story.

Something Calten had never bothered asking for before she'd wielded my actions to her own ends. Something I'd been terrified to tell Arias, or Addie, or anyone else over the years...fearing the judgement. The arguments against the choice I'd made. The advocation for any path other than the one I'd taken. All looking at me the same way everyone did whenever I mentioned my fascination with poisons.

With Malakai, there was no terror. In fact, staring into his blameless gaze, it struck me that I'd been waiting to tell him this story from the first time our paths had crossed in Rastra.

I'd just been waiting for *him* to ask *me*.

Now he offered his hands upturned on his knees, and watched me. And waited.

Slowly, I laid my palms over his. His long fingers closed over, caging mine, his thumbs brushing my knuckles.

"Now." His tone lacked any venom, any vitriol, any judgement I had expected for years when the inevitable question came: "Tell me what these hands have done."

I stared at them—my fingers safe in his grip.

No one had ever protected me from this. No one had been able to—this secret had made *me* the defender. The liar. A woman set apart.

It had kept every friendship and relationship I'd forged since fleeing Vallanmyre as shallow as the dregs of a perfume bottle. Friends in Dalfi had never been closer than warm acquaintances. A dalliance here or there had still kept suitors at arm's length, terrified they would come close enough to see my secrets.

With Malakai...

One glance into his eyes, and I could see the truth.

He already knew. He'd likely even suspected what I was capable of, what Calten was holding above me, since our first meeting. It had just been a matter of waiting until *I* was ready to tell him, and...

And I was. After tonight. After what we'd just endured together.

"It was...there was an important man in the Mithran army." The words emerged as a quiet croak, my gaze dropping back to his hands holding mine. "General Arlo Gryffen. One of the Sha's chief advisors since they were young men. He was everything you would expect of a man in charge of the ranks...stubborn, skilled, fiercely loyal to Mithra-Sha." I swallowed, the next words scraping like scalpels: "He even helped reassign a soldier who was harassing me, somewhere so far away it wasn't likely I would ever see him again."

"And yet," Malakai said—nothing more.

"He had some prejudice against Hadrass-Drui...I'm sure you could invent any reason and it would be near enough to the truth to matter." I appreciated the faint flex of his fingers around mine—a nod to just how complicated this country was, with its neighbors and within itself. "He hid it well enough, I think...at least so much that the Sha never knew, which I suppose was the point. Everyone knows

Tobyrus Lothar is hopelessly enamored with his wife. He would never hear a foul word against her."

Not unlike Solymon and Katia. Perhaps, if Tobyrus had ever known what his general was like, things would have gone differently for me. For all of us.

Sniffing, I dashed my nose against my shoulder...keeping my grip on Malakai's hands.

"But then General Gryffen was injured in a skirmish near the Vensair Mountains against some Hadrassi detractors," I went on softly, "and it...it changed something in him."

"Unleashed his prejudice to the uttermost?" Malakai ventured.

"You could say that." I swiped my tongue over my lips. "They brought him to me for triage, because of my reputation by that time with the Sha's family. I did my usual routine of herbs to calm him for assessment, but with all of that in his blood, he started ranting about his hatred for Hadrass-Drui...how he wished the Storycrafters would make themselves useful and wipe this part of the map clean."

I chanced a glance up at Malakai, my stomach roiling more at the notion now than it had even back then, in the infirmary—knowing that such an action would've meant Malakai was gone. And Lu. And Phin. And Caspian.

People I had come to respect and admire—at the very least.

"I tried to ignore it," I added softly, "to be sympathetic, considering it was a Hadrassi blade that had dealt him so much hurt. But then he wouldn't stop *talking*...going on and on about how much he despised the Shadre, how she was the biggest mistake Mithra-Sha had ever made, how she'd clearly seduced Tobyrus and made a fool of him. He called her all manner of filthy names. And then he said that her half-breed children would never sit in power, not as long as he drew breath."

His foul slurs stuck like a sideways bone in my throat. That was *Arias* he had been talking about. And Mahalia. Two of my closest friends, and he'd spoken of them like homeless dogs he would've kicked aside in the street—at best.

"The nonsensical ramblings of a man influenced by strong drug." Malakai's words held no inflection—an argument just for argument's sake, not a conviction. Knowing I'd tried to convince myself of the same, before I couldn't anymore.

"No. He meant every word," I whispered. "But I still tried to reason with him. I reminded him of all the good the Shadre and her children have done for Mithra-Sha, for its people. And when he wouldn't listen, I told him he didn't really have any say in the matter, that Arias would inherit regardless of anyone's personal opinion. And he said, *We'll see about that.*"

The echo of those smug, certain words on the verge of unconsciousness wracked a shudder through me. I'd heard less cruel confidence in the voices of men holding knives to throats, a second away from spilling blood.

"For two days after that, I just sat vigil at his bedside," I added. "I couldn't sleep. I couldn't stop hearing that threat, over and over in my head. And I realized that this Hadrassi attack...it had changed General Gryffen. In his mind, it somehow confirmed his prejudice...and it gave him permission to act on it."

I tightened my fingers around Malakai's, preempting the chill that always came when I remembered this part.

"He started writing coded letters addressed to his contacts in the army—many of them close to the Sha. He asked me to deliver them—"

"Of course, you never did."

"Of course I didn't," I scoffed. "But my friend Jaik had taught me that code years ago. When I deciphered it, I realized he was asking for the guards to be pulled away from the Shadre and her children. For them to be left exposed. I think he was hoping for an accident to happen...and if one didn't, he would create one eventually."

At least, that was what I'd consoled myself with all this time. It made the next part easier to tell...easier to bear.

"He wasn't going to stop," I murmured. "So he had to *be* stopped."

I startled at the brush of Malakai's fingertips, grazing a strand of hair from my brow and tucking it behind my ear. "Tell me what you did, you magnificent, clever troublemaker."

Those words shouldn't have warmed me as much as they did. They shouldn't have made telling the next truth so simple. So freeing.

"I wrote to some contacts of my own," I confessed. "I acquired some Hadrassi poison. And instead of his curative drugs..."

"You poisoned him." Malakai sat back a bit, his gaze touched with awe—and an unexpected glint of the muted respect that always made me feel a bit steadier on my feet.

"With Mummer's Dance." My mouth jerked at the widening of his eyes. "I fed him just enough that when his organs burst, it seemed like a complication of his wounds. But I gave him nothing for the pain...I did *nothing* to try and save him. Or to ease his passing."

That strange braiding of guilt and satisfaction wedged in my throat just remembering how the General had perished...how I'd held Raynes back when she'd tried to intervene, and then threatened her the moment I'd seen the horrified recognition dawning in her eyes.

"He died too kindly compared to the deaths he wanted for the Shadre and her children." The words emerged steelier than I'd expected—a fair attempt at convincing myself.

"You," Malakai murmured, shifting nearer to me again, "are downright dangerous."

"Aren't most murderers?"

The last word hitched and stumbled on my tongue.

I had murdered General Gryffen.

By no means an innocent man, but...he had been under my charge. Entrusted to me by the Sha, who'd grieved his death never knowing the way the man had plotted against his family. And I had kept that secret because Tobyrus Lothar's paranoia had grown wings by then, and claws, and it had already started choking the life out of Addie. I'd known that revealing the cruelty of his close friends would've only made things worse for her...for all of us. And that, for letting him suffer, for killing him myself...I would have hung. At best.

Because I *was* a murderer.

Malakai's quiet snort wrenched me from those thoughts. "This was not as simple as *murder*, and I believe you know that. It's why you walk with your head high, despite the blood no one else can see on your hands."

His thumbs grazed my knuckles again—a stomach-fluttering reminder of the scarlet stains he'd just cleaned from them a half-hour ago.

"People prefer to believe that countries are sustained by the noble choices of good leaders," Malakai went on quietly, his gaze fixed on my hands. "But you and I know better, don't we? Because good leaders accumulate the greatest enemies. And in order to keep their image unsullied, it falls to others to filthy their hands for the sake of righteousness."

"You believe it was *righteous*, what I did to General Gryffen?"

"It saved your new Sha and his sister, did it not?"

I had no argument for that.

"Doing what must be done is rarely easy," Malakai added. "Doing *right* makes you unpopular, unlikeable, and earns you a long list of unfavorable names." The corner of his mouth twitched. "But that's how countries survive: by the righteous actions of people who are willing to fall on blades and bloody their hands to stop wickedness from spreading. Even if it costs them everything."

"For an assassin," I murmured, "you know an awful lot about nobility."

"You forget, I read poetry."

A half-hysterical laugh sprang from my lips, and I tumbled forward, burying my face in the crook of his neck; after all of this time, the story was told. My actions had been laid bare—by my *own* choice, not like a blade dangling on a string above me, waiting to drop and cleave into my skull.

Someone knew—someone I trusted. Someone who understood every reason I'd done what I did, even if it was cruel. Even if it had been an impossible choice.

Someone who was so much like me.

After a long, hesitant moment, Malakai freed one of my hands to curl his fingers in my hair, holding me against him. "Knowing you as I do...I know you didn't make that choice lightly." The faintest brush of his nose against my temple. "Mithra-Sha is fortunate to have you at its leader's side."

"Not after what I did."

"You will never make me believe you regret that man's death. Not you."

I bit back my protest, forcing myself to sit with his words—to feel out the error in them.

Or...the truth.

"You don't regret saving their lives by ending his," Malakai murmured. "Tell me what you *do* regret, Naomi."

Heat stung my eyes, and the prickle of pain forced the words free. "That I ran away."

I'd abandoned my friends and all of the difficult choices I'd seen on the horizon...because, knowing I'd been capable of killing General Gryffen, I'd felt capable of *anything*, easy or difficult. Good or wicked.

So I hadn't been there when they needed me; when my skills and my sensibilities—even as rough-edged as they'd become—could have done the most good.

I'd run away. And other people had been forced to make impossible choices...like Tobyrus Lothar, choosing murder to preserve his strong arm. And Audra, rewriting the world itself because of Jaik's death. And all of the weight Reiko and Arias and Mahalia had shouldered alone for years in our absence, knowing I could have helped.

That was where my guilt truly lived. Not in the death of murderous, prejudiced Arlo Gryffen...but in the cowardice afterward that had driven me away.

I had put my own safety over their wellbeing. But now...

Hadrass-Drui had made my safety a gamble at best. And still the work here *had* to be done—whether it endangered my future or not.

That was how it should've been in Mithra-Sha.

I never should have left.

But I couldn't remake that choice now—I didn't have Addie's power. All I had was my next breath—drawing in the scent of pine and fennel from just above the pulse in the side of Malakai's neck—and my next step.

I gripped a fistful of his collar and pushed myself back, just far enough that I could meet his eyes.

"Because I killed him with poison," I rasped, "that was why I was sent here, to the Moravens."

Understanding overshadowed Malakai's gaze. "To face retribution from both sides...for his death, and for those who might've taken the blame for it."

I nodded—let him live with that conclusion. Because even now, I couldn't bring myself to give him *that* entire truth.

But I'd still given him more than I'd ever willingly given to anyone else. And that made me feel braver than I'd ever thought possible.

"Now that you know my secret," I murmured, "I think it's time to make sure what you stole was really the truth serum."

CHAPTER 66
TRUTH AND LIES

TWO PIPING-HOT MUGS OF cocoa in star-glazed mugs shouldn't have seemed so intimidating. They really shouldn't have.

But my hands trembled a bit as I sat on one side of the low table before the study hearth and watched Malakai extract the tapered vial of the truth serum from the front of his silky indigo nightshirt, holding it up to the light.

It seemed only fair we *both* sample the contents—in fact, that had been my idea. Different bodies metabolized substances at different paces, after all; both of us sampling it would allow for a broader understanding of its effects.

Still, I found myself second-guessing the choice as Malakai swirled the golden, nacreous liquid in its thick glass vessel.

"Are you ready?" His eyes flicked to me, weighing—testing.

The only person who would say no would be someone with truths to hide. But I'd already given him the one that most terrified me.

I bit my tongue between my teeth, then grasped my mug and held it out to him. "Born ready."

"Just one drop should be enough," Malakai said—possibly to reassure me.

"Well, in Harrow Hall, they like to say *one drop can destroy everything,*" I joked.

A drip of thick, syrupy gold spooled into my cocoa, blending in like caramel swirled into the milk and melted drinking chocolate. Malakai tapped out a drop for himself as well, then hastily corked the vial and returned it to the inner folds of his shirt; he lifted his mug out to me. "To vengeance."

"To honesty," I countered; we toasted and sipped.

The full-body flavors of the cocoa—arguably one of my best batches yet—wasn't dimmed at all by the truth serum. In fact, it added a layer of sweet richness that almost made me wish we'd added more than a drop.

Flipping Hadrassi poisons.

Malakai and I sat and sipped in silence, gazes averted from one another; the anxious pounding of my heart slowed over time, a deep, mellow, almost buttery warmth soothing through me. I relaxed into the shabby wingbacked armchair, tossing him a smile. "This isn't so bad."

"Comparatively speaking." But his smile was also more relaxed than I usually saw it; it reminded me a little of when we'd snuck into the playhouse to watch *Four Brothers, Four Brides* perform. Or when he'd left the scraps for Valessa and put on a fireworks show for her grandchildren.

It was a glimpse of the Malakai he could've been, if his family and future hadn't been stolen from him.

Swallowing a rapidly-cooling mouthful of cocoa, I murmured, "I'm really, truly sorry about the hand life's dealt you, Kai."

His gaze jumped to me, brows tweaking upward; it was a long moment before he answered, "I appreciate the sympathy. And the feeling is mutual."

A laugh cracked out of me, and I waved my hand. "Oh, what? At least I have...*most* of my family." My throat snagged as my mother's face flashed through my mind; snugging both hands tight around my mug now, I added, "Or...did you mean the circumstances that brought me to Hadrass-Drui?"

"Yes, about that. I've been meaning to ask you..." Though he didn't clear his throat, my heart kicked up its rhythm a bit; the trailing off, the significant pause, hinted at what was coming.

A difficult question. A test of truth.

"Why did you ask for a partnership, rather than fleeing Rastra once you escaped the Moravens?"

I dashed my tongue over my lips, tasting the sweet sting of inevitable *truth* glossed across them.

Then I said, "Because the Moravens wanted me to handle you for them. They still do."

Malakai searched my face for a long, long moment; then he leaned forward, cupping my chin in one hand, his eyes holding mine.

"Are you plotting to betray me, then, Miss Weathers?"

The hair on my nape prickled.

"Never," I whispered.

And that was also the truth.

I didn't know exactly *when* it had become the truth...when I had crossed that line I would never step back from. All I knew was that, somewhere between the routines of mornings and evenings, somewhere in the midst of learning pieces of why he did what he did—what drove the Poet Poisoner to kill—I had begun to see him differently. And the more I'd chiseled away the mask to find the man beneath...

That man had become precious to me. Someone I really did want to help, somehow...for the sake of his family's legacy. For his *own* sake, so he could finally find peace.

It was why I'd done what I had in the Guild Garrote. Why I'd stopped meeting with Phin.

Why I could look him in the eyes now, unflinching, and tell him the truth:

"I will never betray you, Malakai."

Relief shattered through the familiar darkness of his gaze; he freed my chin and bowed his head over his outstretched arms, and he spoke down toward the table between us.

"Understand something...I have been the villain of every story I've been a part of since my family's passing. Every one...a nightmare in every mind, a curse in every mouth, a shadow in the corner of every eye." His head tipped up and tilted at an angle—puzzled. And almost predatory. "Except yours." Those enchanting eyes fixed on mine. "When you look at me, it's...perplexing. As if you believe there's still some mystery to solve here."

"There is. You saved me the night we met."

"I didn't do that for your sake. I had a score to settle...saving your life was happenstance."

"And staying, after? Bothering to ask if I was hurt, talking me down from my panic?"

"Perhaps I'd heard about the Drui's Mithran visitor. Perhaps I was curious if it had anything to do with me...if you'd come to ruin me."

Tension rolled down the dip of my spine. He had no idea how right he was...or else I wouldn't still be drawing breath.

Breath that tasted of fennel and pine. He was so close now, every shallow pull of my lungs drew in the taste of him.

"Malakai," I whispered, "tell me why you *really* saved me that first night."

Slowly, he leaned back in his seat. "I saved you because I had business with the man who attacked you." Before I could muster a groan at that same tired truth, he added, "But I stayed because yours was the first life I'd *saved*, not taken, with my own hands since all of this started. And ever since the moment I spilled blood on your behalf, I've felt..."

His hand wandered across the table between us; when he took my fingers, played idly with them, I didn't stop him.

I had never had less of a desire to.

"*Responsible*." His brow furrowed, and he shook his head. "No, that's not the right word. It isn't an obligation. I just can't seem to stop saving your life...watching over you wherever I find you."

I had words for it. Words for the way he'd looked at me, even back in that night-drowned street when he'd first kissed my hand. For the way he'd held my wrist while he slept with his head in my lap.

For how he was looking at me *now*, peering up through his lashes, setting my core alight.

"At first, I agreed to a partnership because I had some hope of using you as a shield." The blunt words struck like the butt of a blade, springing my mouth open. "From the night we met, your escort betrayed your importance to the Moravens. I thought that perhaps if they ever cornered me, you could be some sort of bargaining piece."

He waited—giving me time to search myself for anger. For a sense of betrayal, but...I found none. Because no one had ever danced this dance quite like Malakai and I were doing it; so, of course he'd seen me at first as a means to an end. Hadn't he been the same for me?

I didn't know...*exactly* when it had changed. For either of us.

All I knew was that, staring into his eyes across the table that had become such a staple in my nightly routine—*our* routine—I saw no trace of the indifference that would make a man turn a stranger into a shield. Nor had I seen that man in the one who'd come rushing to my aid like a storm in the Guild Garrote's Jubilee.

The villain he claimed to be.

"And now?" I whispered.

"Now..." He searched my face without a hint of guile. "No, not just now. From the moment you stepped into my life, you have been the only trustworthy truth in a world built of lies. I deal in deception daily, with my enemies...with my past. And you are the first person I have known in *years* to be so unabashedly herself. All the best. All the worst." The smallest shrug as he turned his mug around in his hands. "When I'm near you, I don't feel as if I'm waiting to join my family in their graves. I feel...alive. As if I could begin to think of a future on the other side of all of this."

"I think of that, too," I blurted. "When I look at you."

His gaze wrenched up to me, and for the first time I saw something in it I'd never witnessed before.

It almost looked like *hope*.

"I've been hiding such a large part of me for so long," I admitted, "because I was afraid anyone who saw it would turn against me. But you saw that side of me, the part that was capable of that, long before I even told you the truth tonight...and you still wanted to be closer to me. To *know* me." I pressed my lips together, biting back a wave of emotion that threatened to free tears from my eyes. "I've felt safer with you...closer with you than I've let myself be with anyone in such a long time."

The firelight caught the flickering curve of that same smile he'd shot me in the street, months ago.

Swallowing, I whistled lowly and glanced down at my cocoa. "This is strong stuff, isn't it?"

A beat of quiet; then he spoke in a voice that was hardly much louder: "As a matter of fact, the effects of the truth serum are notoriously short-lived."

My gaze whipped back to him; he watched me, hand outstretched on the table, knocking a soundless tune on the knotted wood.

"Oh," was all I could manage.

A moment longer of silence; then Malakai said, gruffly, "I don't like to sleep with pants on...my legs feel trapped."

A giggle burst out before I could suck it back. His eyes narrowed at me, and I retorted hastily, "Well...I actually have a notorious black thumb. Most of the plants I try to grow live painfully short lives, and then I just buy new ones. None of my friends know that, though...they all think as a healer who works with herbs, I'm some adept horticulturist. But I find poisons are easier to grow."

His smirk erased that warning glance. "The first poem I ever penned was to a girl I was infatuated with. She tore it to pieces and fed them to me."

"Good Luck that one wasn't penned with poison!" I wagged my brows. "I've broken at least two dozen of my father's favorite peddling finds and blamed them all on my brothers."

"I made *my* brother my scapegoat as well. I doubt if he tasted a single dessert for a whole year thanks to my sneaking out."

"I think merfolk might actually be real."

"I have long been fascinated with dragons."

"I always wished I had a sister—I used to make Behn dress up in my mother's old clothes and act out stories with me until I met Addie."

"I often wish I had died and my sister had lived."

We stared at one another for a long moment; I had nothing to say to that. Nothing to offer when death hugged us close like the shadows, its fingerprints imprinted permanently across the faces of our lives.

"I'm not afraid to die," I whispered at last. "I've faced death too much, I just...I'm afraid to lose the people I love. To be left behind."

Malakai tapped his fingers gently against his mug. "I only fear one death: suffocation. Drowning, strangling, smothering...I couldn't train that fear out of me."

"I made everyone in my family their own signature scent so that, if something were to happen to them...I could still smell them sometimes and remember them as clear as day." I sipped my cocoa before I added, "But they don't know that's why. They didn't really notice I came up with that right after we lost my mother."

Malakai settled back in his seat, pinching and rubbing the bridge of his nose, then settling a hand over his eyes. "I am *tired*," he rasped. "I am so rotting tired of being the only one upholding this crusade to bring justice for my family. Some days, I wish I could forget them and pursue a different life...even knowing I could never enjoy one."

Compassion knotted in my throat; I reached across the table to curl one hand over his around his mug.

"You aren't alone," I reminded him. "You have me now, and we're fighting on the same side."

He peeked at me from beneath the shadow of his tilted hand. "That terrifies me."

"It terrifies me, too." I brushed one finger over the back of his knuckles. "But I'm not leaving until this is over."

"Not even for the chance to disappear and avoid absolution for Gryffen's death?"

"Not even then."

Malakai's hand fell, fingertips tapping the armrest of his own tattered chair as he studied my face—that searching, peeling-apart look that made me feel so vulnerable. And so *known*. "Is that the truth?"

"Yes," I said. "I won't leave you, Malakai Kane."

His breath blew out quietly through rounded lips. "Nor I you, Naomi Weathers."

We sat with that for a long time—until our cocoa was cool and the hearth had dimmed.

Then Malakai said, softly, "Caring is a death sentence."

"No," I replied, "caring is what keeps us alive."

Another beat of silence.

And then we began to trade truths again—wishes and wanted things and loves and hates that drove us to laughter and rage and tears. We gave them up to a safety neither of us had ever known before...a truce that had long ago started feeling more like an alliance. Like a friendship.

Like, maybe...

Some other truth neither of us was willing to broach tonight.

It must have been late, the night long gone outside the walls of his study, by the time waiting for the next volley of courage for one of us to say something turned to a drowsy darkness.

I woke briefly, when a braided blanket fell around my shoulders and tucked under my chin; when knuckles swept backward along the line of my jaw, up to my ear. When serum-stained lips touched my hair. "Troublemaker."

I was asleep again before I could muster a reply.

CHAPTER 67
TO HOLD A VILLAIN'S HEART

E VERYTHING WAS DIFFERENT AFTER the truth-telling serum.

I couldn't quite put a frame to it, like an obvious diagnosis hovering just at the tip of my tongue; all I knew was that my hands still smelled like the soap Malakai had used to clean blood from them, and my skin was patterned with a whole galaxy of glitter-stains from the Jubilee even days later, and my head rattled with a feeling like *unfinished business* whenever Malakai and I brushed up against each other, moving around the manse.

We didn't leave—waiting for the Guild Garrote to launch a search for us in the street. To surveil Beris's bistro and realize I was not her. To begin unspooling truths and falsehoods, to try and figure out which assassins exactly could've hired us both.

I doubted if they would ever guess that the Poet Poisoner himself had been there; but just in case, we kept to ourselves in the one place no other assassin had ever found him. A manse all our own.

As the days wore on with us trapped together, I wasn't certain if Malakai could feel the change, too; but I caught him watching me from the corners of his eyes now and again while we cleaned the manse or sat in the upper vault at the long table, reading together, or when we shared coffee and meals every morning and night. Always with a slight smile across his lips playing havoc with my heartbeat.

And occasionally he'd make a remark about little truths I'd told—how I preferred my cocoa made with cream, not milk, so was I going to milk a cow myself today, or not? And did I wish to practice my assassin's skills with this little plant he'd purchased at the market a few weeks ago? And should we go hunting for merpeople in the river?

I stole his pants and hid them after he went to bed for that jab. He didn't remark on it—ever—but his quiet cursing while he banged around the lair looking for them had me muffling my laughter in the covers until it was safe to come out and greet my no-longer-pantsless partner.

But it was more than a partnership now...we both knew it.

Partners came and went. They were for a set number of days, or until a contract ended, or only so long as the aims were mutual. A partnership would've been over and done after the Jubilee, regardless if we had to lay low for safety's sake.

This...this was different. And it was thickening the air between us like a sweet, syrupy serum full of truths neither of us wanted to tell.

Finally, I'd had enough. I was the one with more civilized skills, after all—if anyone was going to broach the shift between us, it had to be me. And maybe that would do something about the strange dreams I couldn't shake—dreams of truth-telling that ended an entirely different way.

It started with a cup of coffee, enriched with the perfect amount of milk—not cream—and a drizzle of molasses sugar. Made with care and carried just as delicately through the manse to Malakai's desk, where he hunched before the map, scribbling notes in his latest ledger.

I tapped him on the shoulder, and he glanced up; a rakish tuft of black hair fell wayward into his eye, and it stole all my composure not to brush it away.

"What's this?" he asked. "It's the middle of the afternoon."

"It's a thank you." I set the coffee in front of him, over his shoulder. "For coming for me at the Jubilee."

He twisted a bit, draping one arm over the seatback and holding his fountain pen loosely between his long fingers. "You think an afternoon coffee makes us even?"

"Well, it's a *delicious* cup of coffee."

"You sampled it?"

"I had to make sure no one poisoned it." Shrugging, I rounded the desk to lean against the workbench across from it, folding my arms—a little more space than my usual chair gave us. "But, to your point, no. Coffee doesn't make us even. I just thought you deserved the show of gratitude."

He stared into the coffee mug for a long moment. Then, quietly, "Well. You're welcome, then."

A swift sip, then he was back to poring over his ledger.

I couldn't help studying him, peeling back the layers of him with my eyes the way he always did with me; the cool, unattached assassin. The man who gave herb scraps to ailing old widows and set off fireworks for their grandchildren. The brutal avenger of his family's premature deaths. The poet who almost shed a tear at an aerial performance. The shadow of vengeance who'd descended twice now on men threatening me—who'd assured both were dead, even when the fate of one had ben assured by the venom-blade he'd slipped secretly to me.

A killer. A protector. An orphan. A lone survivor still struggling to survive. A man who was relearning what surviving *meant*—the same way I'd been struggling to define living ever since I'd taken a life.

The scratching of the fountain pen didn't change, but Malakai's low voice jolted me from my thoughts: "Perhaps you should stop looking at me, Miss Weathers."

"Maybe I wouldn't have a reason to keep looking twice if you would stop surprising me."

Now the scratching stopped; his head lifted slowly. "And what have I done to surprise you this time?"

Edging out a small smile, I shrugged. "You're just an interesting mess of contradictions."

"Says the healer who poisons."

"Says the poisoner who's saved my life...more than once."

A quiet snort. "Don't you have something else to do?"

"Not really. Not unless you want to whisk me off to the sunroom I just finished cleaning this morning and show me your talents with the piano."

"You should leave." His brusque tone struck like a slap to the face; the sting might've lingered if not for the bob of his throat, or the next words that dropped from his mouth. "Or I may do something that would surprise us both in the worst ways."

It was hard to know whether it was the curiosity, or the courage of seeing beneath every mask he wore, or maybe just a drop of truth serum still swirling somewhere in my veins.

Because I didn't take the escape he offered.

We were done dancing around this—the tension in the air. I was done letting him be the shiver that crawled up my spine every time our hands brushed. Every time I remembered his knuckles trailing along my bare back when I'd dressed before the Jubilee. When we'd danced. When he'd dipped me, his mouth an inch from mine.

It was now, or never.

So I pushed up from the worktable and leaned both hands on the desk, bending toward him. "I dare you, Poet Poisoner."

Slowly, he raised his head; we were so near the wisps of coffee and sugar on his breath tickled my nose.

He stared at me. I stared at him.

Disappoint clattered through me when his expression didn't shift—another mask fixed firmly in place. The unsocial recluse, warning people not to take a step nearer.

I knew the look of running. And there it was, stamped across the darkness of his gaze.

A wry smile wrung across my lips, though I couldn't infuse it with any humor. "I thought not." I pushed back, straightening. "If you need me, I'll be in the vault."

I pivoted away, and then...

He did surprise me.

He surged to his feet, caught my chin in the cradle of his hand, and pulled my face smoothly back toward him.

The next thing I knew, I was tasting those lips for the first time.

Burnt coffee. Dark, sticky sugar. A hint of the spicy leaves he sometimes chewed to help him work long hours into the night.

Intoxication.

My hands fastened to his shoulders, and with one arm he swept his ledgers off the desk; the other hooked around my waist, and he slid me effortlessly across the empty surface until I was sitting on the edge before him, legs wrapped around his waist, never breaking the kiss.

His hands tangled in my hair, pushing it off of my cheeks; mine slid up from his shoulders to lace around the back of his neck. I kissed him until I forgot every reason why I shouldn't—why this was a terrible idea that could only end one way. I kissed him the way I'd never dared to kiss anyone since I'd left Vallanmyre, for fear of all the places it would lead.

With Malakai...there was no fear. Only a feeling that I'd been waiting to do this since the first moment I'd met him. And that, now that I *had*...

There was no turning back.

With a shared, wild gasp, we finally broke apart; my brow fell against the unsteady cadence of his racing heart, and he buried his face in my hair.

"You," he rasped, "are the only good thing in my life. The only good I've held since my family was ripped away from me."

His shirt soaked up my tears before they could fall. "And you make me feel *safe*. Like I can finally stop running and come home."

We leaned against each other for more minutes than I could count, doing what we did best: grappling silently with how the world had just shifted for us both. *Again.*

"It's a dangerous thing." Malakai's molasses-dark words stirred my curls at last. "To hold a villain's heart in your hands."

Leaning back, I met his gaze—touched with dampness and desire.

"I've held fouler poisons," I murmured. "And things far less precious."

He cradled my face in the spread of his hands...killing hands.

The gentlest hands that had ever held me.

"That makes a pair of us, troublemaker." The corner of his mouth crinkled up. "A perfect, powerful pair."

He kissed me again—one. Two. Three.

And by the third, I knew my life would never be the same again.

CHAPTER 68
KISSING THINGS

I KISSED THE *POET Poisoner.*

My first thought when I woke the next morning, wrapped in silk sheets and a soft duvet, my lips still bruised from the sheer amount of kissing we'd enjoyed the day before.

Not a dream. Not a fantasy. I had actually kissed the man I'd been sent to capture.

I had kissed him passionately. And repeatedly.

And I...I wanted to do it again.

Groaning, I ripped the pillow out from under my head and hugged it over my body, pressing it flush to my face.

If I smothered myself, that would solve this entirely new, completely unexpected, and not entirely unwelcome dilemma.

But the longer I lay there, wrestling the problem in bouts of alternating panic and intrigue, it occurred to me that kissing Malakai might've been the least of my concerns; it was the *reasons* I'd kissed him that changed everything.

Because he was not just the Poet Poisoner to me. He wasn't an immoral assassin or some other country's trouble to deal with.

He was the man who'd saved my life when I'd first come to Hadrass-Drui. He was the one who'd fled with me in Rastra, who'd let me lie my way into sanctuary in his lair. The one whose wounds I'd bound, whose daily life I'd shared, whose secrets I'd held and with whom I'd shared mine.

The one who'd come for me in the Guild Garrote. The one who'd tested truth with me...and we'd both found we liked the taste of it on our lips, even when it wasn't forced against our will.

I couldn't precisely find the place where that wound began...where we'd become so inextricably stitched into one another's lives. All I knew was that kissing Malakai Kane hadn't been impulse or lust or morbid curiosity or one of a dozen things that had fueled countless kisses with other men I'd dallied with in Dalfi...kisses that had led to nothing.

It had been a next step. A consecutive heartbeat. A natural breath in the rhythm of living that consumed my time in Hadrass-Drui.

I'd kissed Malakai because it was what people *did* when they felt this kind of bubbly warmth in their middle. When they couldn't wait to see the other person. When something deeper than survival and necessity bound them.

Shoving myself up straight, I bent forward, buried my face in the pillow wedged against my cocked knees—and screamed into it until I lost all my breath.

Oh, flipping *Luck*. I was in such deep trouble.

Because, even realizing what all of that *meant*...

I *still* wanted to kiss him again.

Malakai was in a foul mood.

That much was evident from the moment I wandered into his study, yawning to force air back into my deprived brain and hugging my cardigan close in the crooks of my arms. He looked as if he'd already been up—and deep in the coffee—for hours. Harried motions jerked him from one side of the lair to the next, shoving pins into the map, flipping through ledgers, jotting notes and mumbling curses to himself like we hadn't left *that* habit behind weeks ago.

Purpose arrested every motion, but there was a certain manic quality to his movements, too. A feeling like every step could break into a run...like he was just on the verge of losing his composure.

Not a good time to discuss kisses or the implications of them, then.

"Good morning," I greeted dryly, stepping back as he breezed by me to rifle through a perpetually-locked chest of poisons. "What's biting *your* well-shaped backside today?"

He didn't even react to the quip, nor did he look my way. "I'm a bit busy, and unfortunately my plans for last evening were consumed with...other things."

Kissing things? I almost teased him—but judging by the set of his shoulders and the deliberate way he was inventorying his poisoner's stock, this was not the right moment for teasing.

"Surely one night couldn't throw *everything* off balance," I wheedled.

"It's not the one night. It's been a litany of them."

So, he'd noticed, too; how both of us fell so easily into those quiet evenings of eating dinner or chatting over mugs of cocoa at the fire. How often we'd lapsed doing the work he'd first brought me on to assist with.

That flipping binding of our lives together. How had neither of us noticed what was happening until it had culminated in a *kiss*?

I'd had friends swooning on my sofas for years now, telling me how a kiss could change everything. I just hadn't fully grasped how *true* that was.

"Time is short," Malakai added when I didn't say anything—possibly mistaking my silence for disbelief, "and despite your not-altogether-*conventional* assistance, things are not progressing at a clip with which I am comfortable."

"And what *clip* is that? Breakneck, with a dash of reckless and careless?"

"What have I told you about cracking jokes in my presence, Miss Weathers?"

"That it's the light of your life, and you'd be lost without it?"

Luck love me. I just couldn't help myself.

He paused, disbelieving dark eyes whipping my way. I mustered a smile at that look. "See? You're proving it right now."

He slammed his chest of poisons shut with a strike from the heels of his palms, but the sound didn't jolt me the way it maybe once had; I held my ground at his approach, knowing by the angles of his face precisely what was coming.

His long, graceful fingers gripped my elbows; then his palms swept up my bare arms, to my shoulders, and back again. A soothing, rhythmic motion for us both; we let out our breath in the same instant, and the knot between his brows eased a bit. He bent his head, his nose skimming my hair.

"You don't deserve my temper," he said through a kiss to my curls. "The morning has been trying my patience."

"Is that what this is? I thought you had a bout of spring fever."

"Would you please try to be a *tad* serious, troublemaker?"

"It just seems to me like you're plenty serious enough for the both of us." Settling back on my heels, I found the uneven cadence of his heart with the center of my palm, letting that crooked, reassuring rhythm wash through me. "Why the urgency? We've been plotting for the Jubilee for months, and now it's behind us. I thought you would be able to relax at least a *little* bit after that."

"Unfortunately, time is still working against us. Particularly all the time we've spent keeping our heads low in the manse."

"Time? Time for *what*?" I cocked my head. "What is it you're so worried about?"

He was quiet for a long, long while—so long I wondered if he was waiting for me to give up and change the subject.

But I couldn't. Not with the dart of unease through his eyes or the way his brow crinkled; and not when it felt like, after everything—the heist, sampling the truth serum, the way he'd *kissed* me the day before—he was finally choosing honesty. And that the things he'd chosen were bringing him to a crossroads, unleashing whatever this *franticness* was inside of him.

This was a moment for him...a pivot. A choice he couldn't come back from. And I wasn't certain he would trust me with it...if he even should.

But I wanted him to. As badly as I'd wanted him to kiss me last night.

Maybe that kiss had changed more for him, too. More than the desperation it lit in his gaze or the way it drove his movements. And whatever that change was...I wanted the whole truth about it.

So I held my silence, tracing my thumb against his sternum. Waiting.

And waiting.

And *waiting*.

"I am...*concerned*," a soft, seething note perforated Malakai's cool tone when he finally spoke, "because rumor among the underworld holds that Athicus Moraven will abdicate by the start of spring. Which is now, thanks to our waiting here in the manse, only a few weeks away."

CHAPTER 69
ONE DROP

SHOCK STRUCK *ME* SILENT now, my tongue cleaving to the roof of my mouth. A wisp of candied peaches and sharp herbs stroked the tip of my nose, teasing it into a crinkle that almost made me squint—looking backward at a memory of Phin's windowless chamber in the heart of Fortress Ferregrand. Peering back on a conversation I'd almost forgotten until now...one that made sudden, shocking sense.

A Moraven family secret. The reason Phin had come home from Thrasmund exactly when he had. This was what he hadn't been able to tell me back then...a changing of the watch that kept this fragile country in some semblance of stability. A swift trade of power from one hand to the other.

I'd seen what chaos that had wreaked in the transition from Tobyrus Lothar's hands to his son's—in a country that trusted its leaders, that was held together by more than necessity dabbed in treachery and paranoia. How much worse would Hadrass-Drui suffer?

This had to be why Phin had finally left Thrasmund after spending half his life training and living there. If his grandfather rescinded power, it would pass to Serai and Varros...and Phin would assume the active role in the rulership that his mother had held for his entire life.

His desperation to end Malakai's schemes, to protect his own—the burden that seemed to bear down heavier and heavier on him whenever we'd made contact here in Rastra—crystallized all at once.

He wasn't only protecting himself. This was about the ruling power in Hadrass-Drui.

And Malakai...

"What does this mean for you...for your revenge?" I demanded. "For *us*?"

Malakai blinked down at me. "Us?"

"Clearly, this rumor had a hand in shaping your plans." Folding my arms tight over my middle, I forced a shrug. "And those plans involve me now. That's why you even brought me on to help you in the first place, isn't it? Because, like you said that first night in Rastra, you're short on time. So I want to know what all of this *means*."

His jaw tightened. "It means that all the power in Hadrass-Drui is about to be like bones cast into the air. No one knows where they will fall...how things will crack...except for me."

Disbelief wrenched my head back. "*You* alone, out of *all* of Hadrass-Drui, know what's going to happen next?"

"Do you think I would be doing all of this if I didn't?"

My volley of arguments choked silent. We stared at one another.

And all at once, I realized just how much I *trusted* Malakai.

Not the way I'd trusted my family or my friends for all of my life. Not the way I trusted my own healing talents or the convictions that splinted most of the choices I made—even the most badly fractured ones. I didn't trust him like I trusted sunshine days to be good ones or the smell of rain on the wind that I was always, always right about.

But I trusted his ruthless focus. I trusted his unbroken word. I trusted that what he said, he would do. And more than anything, I trusted that he hadn't overlooked anything in this violent obsession of his.

"What's going to happen, Malakai?" I whispered.

His gaze waged a war I'd only seen a handful of times since we'd first met: when he was battling his own convictions. When he was deciding something that would change everything.

The same way he'd looked at me when he'd agreed to a partnership. When he'd told me of his family's deaths. When he'd kissed me last night.

That conflicted gaze crawled slowly down from my eyes, past my lips, to my shoulder and down my arm; and then his fingers followed, binding between mine. His grip strangled like a man on death's doorstep, clinging to life; I wasn't certain anyone had ever clutched my fingers so tightly, even in the throes of a surgery without ether.

"This," he said huskily, "is a truth I have never shared with anyone."

There was a strange lilt of pleading to his tone...as if he hoped I would tell him not to share it. To keep his secrets. To shut me out.

Oh, Kai. He knew me better than that.

"So, it will be a truth *we* don't share with anyone," I offered.

His eyes flicked from our hands back to my face. "It will be a danger to you. It has been a danger to me for half my life. This secret is why no one has ever come to this place...why I have never called anyone a friend, or a partner, or a true ally."

Until I met you.

A chill winked down my spine; I shuddered it off. "I'd like to take my chances on knowing precisely what it is we're dealing with." I mustered a smile that felt as if it pulsed at the corners with every pound of my racing heart. "Kai, help me understand this. What does your family's deaths have to do with Athicus Moraven abdicating?"

His tense jaw flickered, his gaze dipping to my lips for a distracting second; then he tugged me toward his desk, and I followed...my stomach knotting in on itself and my hand absurdly glad of his grip around it. It was a grounding point, like a healer's mantra, keeping me steady as we reached his worktable.

With one rough sweep of his arm, he dumped books and papers and stacks of ledgers to the floor. His powerful fingers caught my waist, and he lifted me like I weighed nothing, plopping me on the edge of the desk, my knees wedged around his hips.

For a moment, I wondered if this was about to go an *entirely* different way—the same way it had gone last night.

Then he reached past me, dragging a stack of loose-leaf parchment even with my thigh and flicking a fountain pen from his pocket. He uncorked it with his teeth—*unfair*—and bent over my knee to ink a sable stripe down the top sheaf of parchment. "This is your rulership in Mithra-Sha." A tap of the fountain pen at the top of the line. "One Lothar inheriting from another, and another, so on and so on, for as long as memory holds."

I let my legs swing slightly, heels striking numbly against the face of the table, knees brushing his sides with every stroke. "To my understanding, yes."

A faint crook to one half of his mouth. "Hadrass-Drui is not like that."

He brushed aside the ink-slashed page with the side of his fist, then twisted off the head of the pen. As he tilted its sculpted edge delicately above the next parchment sheet, a thought blew through my mind—a whisper of shadow.

A single drop of poison is all it takes.

Ink gathered, swelled...and dropped from the pen's painted neck.

One drop can destroy everything.

With the softest splash, the droplet landed—and spread like venom from an adder bite, branching rapidly across the page.

"Hadrass-Drui holds only an illusion of rulership," Malakai murmured, his gaze darting to trace every tendril that spidered out from that single drop of ink. "Some answer to the Drui and his family…but they are only one power. Leagues like the Guild Garrote, the Nightforge, Silent Shroud, Children of Bones, all of these sects are powers that have clustered together to evoke some sort of change. To knock this country out of joint. But most remember their places and keep to the code."

A wicked twist seized his mouth, feathering tension all along his high, sharp cheekbones.

"There is one that isn't like that."

He slammed his thumb against a branch of ink, smudging it like puddled blood against his skin.

"Grave Dominion." The name fell from his lips like a curse and crawled in chills up my bare knees and exposed thighs. "What they lack in common sense, they more than make up for in ambition. This guild has been a blight in this country for nearly a century."

The thunder of my heart nearly drowned out the words—and even then, they mattered *far* less than the glaze crossing his eyes.

That vulnerability, that anguish…I'd seen it in him just once before.

I palmed his bearded cheeks, dragging his head around. "Look at me."

A slide of his teeth bared in a snarl staying grief; but he *did* look at me, so long and so hard that I caught the only tear I'd ever seen him shed, its warmth soaking into my thumb…an invisible match to the ink that stained his.

"Flipping Luck," I choked. "*Grave Dominion* took your family. Is that what all of this has been? Every person you've poisoned—"

"All members." He brushed an arm between us, pinching the bridge of his nose and squeezing his eyes shut. "Every last one."

My heart wouldn't stop its wild, out-of-control gallop; it took me a moment to piece together *why*, what the tension was lurking under the surface, squeezing my chest like an iron band.

"Malakai, the people you poisoned were *all* high-ranking elites in the Hadrassi ruling class."

"Infiltrators." He practically spat the word, dropping his hand and fixing that ebony stare on me again. "Assassins who have taken power at every level. Grave Dominion has been worming its way into the heart of Hadrass-Drui for decades. My family was no exception."

My mouth popped open on its hinge. "You—what?"

"My family was established, wealthy, influential in Hyraith—as renowned as Raversen and his wife, once." Malakai bent his hands on either side of my thighs, his shoulders arching beneath the slip of his silken burgundy shirt. "My great-grandfather was the one who consigned us to that guild. My brother and sister and I, we were born into Grave Dominion...trained from childhood, all of us, as assassins."

His focus cast over my shoulder, but his gaze was even more distant than that. Witnessing horrors I was most likely Luck's favorite friend not to know.

"Grave Dominion is the only guild that rarely recruits from the outside. It trains its children, and their children, and *their* children in the art of assassination." Bitterness dripped from every word like infection pulsing in a wound. "Blades. Poisons. Elements of the world...in the hands of *children*." His posture shifted, his hands balling into fists, knuckles shoving down against the desk. "We were one of dozens of families that make up the guild. And my father would've never had a qualm about any of it, if Grave Dominion hadn't set its ambitions too high."

"Higher than high-ranking *assassins*?" I choked.

"They want Fortress Ferregrand." Malakai's hoarse snarl stopped my heart altogether for a moment. "They want the Drui title for their own."

Before my mind could even *begin* to feel that out and shape it into a way that didn't make it crushing, devastating, *horrifying*, Malakai was speaking again—still in that rasping growl.

"That was when my father realized how dangerous all of this was. That it could only end one of two ways: with the slaughter of the Moraven family, or with all of us hung for treason." A sharp shake of his head. "He and his closest friend, Louka Nassar, thought they could remove their families from Grave Dominion before the plot unfolded. But word of their plan to flee Hadrass-Drui came to light, and when the stroke fell..."

His complexion paled corpse-white so rapidly, I thought he might drop to his knees. I seized his face again in my hands, steadying him, brushing my fingertips gently through the hair beside his temples—then anchoring them to his cheeks.

"Malakai," I murmured. "Come back to me."

His eyes flickered. He blinked. Slowly, he drew his gaze back to mine, that terrible sheen blooming across the surface again. His calluses chafed the wooden desk as he forced his fists to relax; then, slowly, his fingers curled around my hips. He drew me nearer, and pulled himself against me in the same smooth motion; I wrapped my legs around his waist and settled my face against the staggered beat of his heart.

"Only two of us survived," he rasped. "Myself and my friend, Gydeon Nassar. In the weeks that followed, we compiled as much of a list as we could of everyone we knew to be a part of Grave Dominion, from the Nassars' contacts and my father's and mother's, and then...Gydeon fled the country. He begged me to escape with him, but I couldn't leave my family unavenged."

So he had stayed—alone. An only survivor, a single assassin against a guild.

He'd been just a *boy*. And he'd taken on a country of killers alone—with an incomplete list of their names.

I spared a peek over his shoulder—toward the map on the wall. Toward the names he must've been writing for *years* now...names that had once meant alliance, maybe even safety. And now they were a list of betrayers and supplanters to destroy.

Flipping Luck, no wonder he needed the truth serum. No wonder it had been worth risking the wrath of the Guild Garrote—and both our lives—for.

His work would never be complete until he could wrestle the names of every member of Grave Dominion from some high-ranking official of theirs...someone like Solomyn Degrace had been for the Guild.

"How do you know there are people who can complete your list?" I wound one hand tight around his collar. "How can you be *sure* when you've gotten them all?"

"For the same reason my family finally chose to flee: because the Grave is coming close to completing their schemes. That means those of high rank and status are being given greater knowledge of those beneath them. Among those, *someone* has the entire list. I simply haven't been able to find who...but I know it's near." The lightest brush of his fingertips up and down the ridges of my spine. "It has to be, because Grave Dominion finally found a way into Fortress Ferregrand, through the Moraven family itself," he murmured against my hair. "And that was how they learned what *my* family and the Nassars planned. Their newest recruit, desperate to prove himself, when he learned of the plot...he told the guild. And by the end of that night, I was the only Kane still breathing."

Shock yanked me back from him, to the tips of his fingers, with mine splayed on his chest. A numb fuzziness crawled across my mouth, deadening my whisper: "*What?*"

But even when his lips framed the name of his family's murderer—I already knew.

Of course I did.

Because Malakai had spent all these years bringing members of Grave Dominion to justice, piece by piece. He did not break his patterns. He did not change his code. And now I knew all of his victims had held one single thread in common.

Not their notoriety. But their loyalties to an assassin guild jockeying for power in this unstable country.

Malakai had only slipped once. One act so uncommonly bloody, so unusually vicious, so sloppily *unlike* him, that everyone else had thought it was the work of a partner, or a break in the pattern...not the wildly-aimed blow of a man against his family's true killer.

A killer who had vanished for over a decade.

A killer who had just now emerged from the shadows.

Phineaus Moraven.

CHAPTER 70
GRAVE DOMINION

I WAS GOING TO be *sick*.

I lurched back from Malakai, pressing my hand over my stumbling, struggling heart, sucking down heaves of air to quiet the nausea that churned in my stomach as the realization settled. As it smothered me like a burial shroud.

Phin couldn't—he *couldn't*—

But...yes, he could.

Yes, he *had*.

It was all falling into place—symptoms stacking up to a single diagnosis.

A diagnosis I had *missed*.

Phineaus, the sweet, smiling, guileless victim, his feet set on the road to power.

Phineaus, helpful to a fault, eager and earnest to catch the Poet Poisoner. To protect himself and his family.

Phineaus, who'd *followed* me to Rastra...who'd shamed me for my choices, bruised me for my defiance, made me doubt myself over and over again on this road *his* family had shoved me down.

This had never been about defending me, about helping me. He'd wanted to make sure Malakai was dead, so that no one would stand between him and his intentions. The schemes of *Grave Dominion*.

I crushed the heels of my hands over my eyes, but it didn't stop the torrent of thoughts cracking and colliding in my head, ricocheting off the walls of my skull.

I should have known. Luck, I should've suspected him first!

He'd burned the note Malakai had left with his name on it. Why would he burn a note like that...unless it hadn't only contained his name? Unless it had been incriminating somehow. We'd only ever had his word about what it said, no proof whatsoever.

The note. Malakai had left it as soon as Phin returned to Fortress Ferregrand. His first chance since his family's deaths to reach their betrayer, because Phin...

Phin had been gone.

"Thrasmund." I dropped my hands and spun back on my heels. "It's not what they say it is."

"It is, and it isn't." Malakai reclined against the desk, arms folded, watching me. "To those unawares...the Moraven family, for instance...it is only known to host the most prestigious schools for the elite. The same schools, as I understand, that your Sha was invited to attend." Horror lanced through my veins; whatever emotion it stitched across my face had Malakai's brows slanting inward when he added, "Unbeknownst to them, Thrasmund also serves as the the beating heart from which Grave Dominion pushes all its intentions along. Cerene, Geovany, and I all spent years there honing our skills while we underwent our schooling."

I shoved my palm against my mouth, holding a shriek of disbelief and *fury* at bay.

That sweet-faced *lucker* had *lied* to me. And I...

Oh. Oh, no.

I'd been working all this time, not only for the Moravens, not for Calten, but...

All of those people I'd helped Phin save, with a gentler poison and a swift escape...assassins. Murderers in positions of power. And him, the worst of them all.

I'd been doing the dirty work for Grave Dominion. Reporting to them. Slowly chiseling away at the plans of the only man who knew who they were...who had the power to stop them.

"What is Phineaus going to *do*?" I hissed.

"From what I gather, once Athicus rescinds power, the plot is to have him pass away quietly in his sleep. Then a brutal death for Serai, Caspian, and Varros, which will throw the country into unplumbed depths of chaos and terror." Malakai swept an arm in a broad, graceful, mocking bow. "Enter Phineaus, now with unhindered power. He'll sweep in and calm their fears, seize control...and by effect, share it with Grave Dominion."

A murderer ruling a whole country. The same unconscionable outcome that had completely altered the course of Mithra-Sha's future.

"What about Lu?" I demanded. "Coraline?"

Folding his arms again, Malakai shrugged. "They're beneath him in succession. I doubt if he has any reason to see them dead." His jaw tightened. "But if that were to change, he wouldn't hesitate. He didn't hesitate for an instant when he betrayed us."

And I was *helping* this man.

Had been helping him.

We were not safe. Not here. Not anymore—if we ever had been.

I whirled on Malakai. "We need to leave Rastra. *Now.*"

His dark brows sketched upward. "Any particular reason?"

None of the urgency seething under my skin lived in his tone; somehow the question felt like a door swung open. An invitation for honesty.

Does he know?

He couldn't. If he suspected I'd been in league with the man who'd murdered his family, he never would've agreed to our partnership...in fact, I'd likely have gotten a poisoned poem line of my own. And if he learned *now*, at best, he would be gone in a heartbeat, and I...

I didn't want him to go.

I didn't want him caught.

I hadn't, for *far* longer than I dared admit to myself.

"Valessa's rumors were right...Phineaus is here," I said, and the sudden, sharp slam of those dark brows back over his eyes was all the proof I needed that Phineaus and I had hid our movements well.

Too well.

"How do you know?" Malakai shoved himself up from the table with a backward thrust of his palms.

"I've seen him," I hedged, and Malakai's mouth jerked back at the corners.

"Has he approached you? Harmed you?" When I shook my head, he added hoarsely, "Why didn't you tell me?"

"Because I wasn't certain at first that it was him, I just spotted him from a distance...and then when it happened again, I...I assumed he was here searching for *me*, and that was after you'd been hurt, so I didn't want you involved. I was careful—"

"Careful is not enough where he is concerned!" Malakai swept around me, cobbling books and notes into a pile and snatching a weatherworn pack from drawer of the desk.

"Do you think I don't *realize* that now?" More than I could've ever possibly fathomed before. "You're telling me he's the worst of *all* of them, and he's out there—looking for us!"

And after our last encounter at the canalside, I didn't have a prayer to Luck that there was enough good will left between us that I could barter, cheat, or beg my way into mercy for Kai or me.

Not knowing what Phineaus was really capable of.

Malakai hesitated, one handful of ledgers shoved into the pack; then he crossed the room to the hearth and gathered our plates and mugs. Wrapping them in his blanket from the cot, he settled them into his pack, then surrounded them with more ledgers. He kept his gaze fixed on the contents when he finally said, "I was careless when I struck Phineaus in the Fortress. I used a different poison, a crueler one, because out of all of them he deserves to suffer the most for what he's done." A muscle ticked in his cheek. "That was a mistake. I let his death slip through my fingers, and now it's endangered you as well as me." His jaw squared, and with a sharp yank, he shut the pack. "That will never happen again."

He slid his mask into place, shrugged into his pack, and offered me his hand. My chest crumbled, shriveled up like a withered plant stalk.

I don't deserve this.

To flee with him. To remain in his confidences. Not when I'd been an unwitting accomplice to a true murderer...a man who planned to keep on killing indiscriminately, anyone who crossed his path on his way to power.

But staying with Malakai was the only way I knew of to stop Phineaus.

So I took his hand.

CHAPTER 71
POSSESSION AND POWER

W E TORE THROUGH RASTRA'S glistering streets like a pair of shadows sprouting wings, bound for its outer fringes and the salvation of the open roads and wildlands beyond. Grief and shame made it hard to breathe; at my insistence, we'd left my pack behind, my notes, the gifts from my friends...everything. I wasn't willing to risk another minute in this city, even for my valuables.

Even to let myself grieve for the things we were leaving behind...the manse we'd made so beautiful together. Those rooms that had begun to feel more like home even than my empty dwelling in Dalfi.

With every thudding footstep, with every crash of my heart in tune, I reminded myself we had everything that truly mattered; we just had to get *out* of this city unspotted. By Phineaus and his contacts, by the Guild Garrote.

After that, I would tell Malakai. I would apologize with every scrap of strength I had. And then, somehow, we would find a way to fix all the things I'd broken trying to help one assassin stop another.

My breaths scraped my lungs raw. Malakai's hand never faltered from mine, tugging me down side streets and along curving paths at the canalside. Places we'd walked confidently before, certain of our anonymity, now lurked like the rest of this city—seething with secrets. Every shadow a threat.

I didn't even trust myself to know what was a real threat and what wasn't; but I trusted *him*.

The darkness shifted above the city like a cloth shaken out as we flew; the patterns of the night rippled and changed, a faint lightening gathering in the east just as homesteads thinned out to smaller novelty shops near the outskirts, with small plazas clustered between.

"Almost there," Malakai muttered.

And then, swearing, he drew up short. His hand around mine jerked my arm in a painful twist, and I stifled a shriek, wrenching back to his side.

A furrow of dark clothing and gleaming swords blocked our way—just this side of the road to the outskirts, where we'd ducked from the city to visit Nera and Sofi that first time.

Sentinels. A posting. A *patrol*.

Waiting. Watching. Weapons agleam.

There, at the outer edge of the very last plaza in the chain stretching to Rastra's edge, lounged a figure in fine Hadrassi core darks, feet kicked up on a bistro table, lean, muscular body stretched in the accompanying chair.

Waiting for us like a dinner meeting.

"And there it is." Phineaus's tone was as jovial as ever; for the first time, it sliced like a blade against my belly. "I figured this was how we'd find you...running away together, thick like thieves. Or, you know...like assassins."

His eyes cut to me, and right then, I knew I'd lost.

All these weeks I'd spent avoiding him, he hadn't been waiting for me. He'd been plotting against me.

"See, that's the thing about assassins." His cool tone, the casual way he delivered those words, was proof of my worst fears; he was no longer hiding his truths from me. Which meant I no longer had any guise of safety with him...not when he'd already seen me like this. "Trouble is, we all know the same ways in and out of things. Same places the Guild Garrote's been watching the last couple weeks, the same places Merrietti knows like the back of her hand. So when you two finally poked your heads out tonight..."

A whisper of moving cloth at our backs; I jerked my head to the side, my heart plummeting at the glimpse of leather armor sliding from the pockets of shadow behind us.

More sentinels, closing in.

"Yeah, didn't take long to figure out which way you'd go." Phineaus lurched up from his chair, his nightshade attire rippling in gasps of purple and black like blood touched by the air. "Bet you can figure out where it's going now, right?"

The sentinels all lunged at once, streaking in from behind us and around Phineaus's flanks; Malakai thrust me aside with a shove of his arm, and by the time I'd stumbled two steps, he was armed and whirling to meet our attackers.

The battle was brief, and brutal—a sickening mess of spilled innards and slit throats, blood spraying the cobblestone road. For a dizzying moment, I thought Malakai would win—that, even more than a dozen against one, with all those knives and garrote wires he pulled, he could bring them down before they landed a blow.

But he'd only dropped five when a sixth darted past his guard; and this one didn't attack with a blade. He rammed something into the back of Malakai's shoulder, deadening his dominant arm before he could manage more than a feeble stroke that severed the sentinel's hand at the wrist.

A blink later, two had his arms; a blow to the stomach cost him his air, and then they were wrestling him down on his knees, restrained—all before I could do anything more than catch my own breath and bite back a shriek of his name.

"Well, that went *perfectly*, didn't it?" Phineaus chuckled, watching Malakai writhe and wrestle in the sentinels' hands. "Just the way you said it would, Miss Weathers. You really have a knack for betrayal, don't you?"

Malakai's head whipped my way; horror cracked down every one of my ribs, my focus lunging to Phineaus. "*Excuse* me?"

"Now's not really the time to be coy, is it?" His tone held all the same teasing I'd come to know over the last handful of months, but for once, the lightness of it didn't touch his eyes. They blistered with malicious triumph, no trace of warmth touching those tawny depths. "You said if we gave you enough time, you'd be able to lure the Poet Poisoner out...and here we are. *Right* out in the open."

Malakai cursed profanely—cursed *me*—and my stomach tied itself in a stabbing knot. "Don't you *dare*—"

"Don't I dare...what? Applaud you for the greatest act I've ever seen?" Pocketing his hands, Phin whistled lowly. "I've been going to playhouses my whole life, but I've never seen a part like you just pulled off. Getting the *most* prolific poisoner in Hadrass-Drui to let down his guard? Walking him like a dog on a chain right into the hands of Hadrassi justice?" He cocked his head. "It was beautiful. Worthy of a standing ovation, really."

"That's not—!"

"You can drop the act, Weathers." Phineaus's tone edged into foreign territory—forbidden territory. A warning laced every syllable. "We've got him. You don't need to pretend anymore."

And all at once, I saw *exactly* how Phineaus Moraven had become the man he was.

The easy lies. The earnest charm. And the way he kept twisting and twisting and *twisting* this moment, deflecting my protests at every spin. Tightening a torniquet until all blood stopped. Until everything bruised and blackened. Rotted and died.

Until there was nothing left that could be saved.

I whipped toward Malakai, restrained by six sentinels now, his masked face angled my way; and though he didn't say a word—he didn't *dare*—the hatred seething from every bend of his body was enough to choke me. To hold *me* silent while I stared at him.

He believed Phineaus. And why shouldn't he? I'd led us into this. Not just tonight, in my own ignorant desperation...but ever since I'd first crossed the threshold into Phineaus's room in Fortress Ferregrand.

That I hadn't known what I was walking into until tonight made absolutely no difference whatsoever. Because I was supposed to be better than this. I'd outthought and outsmarted the Poet Poisoner.

But I hadn't outsmarted Phineaus.

Not yet.

Slowly, ever-so-slowly, I curled my hands into fists.

One. There was still time. There was one poison in my pouch I could still use against him...and against myself.

And against Malakai. Because the moment I did it, he would lose any scrap of faith he still held in me.

Two. This might be the only thing that would save him. And *that* might be the only hope we still held of stopping Grave Dominion in its tracks.

Three.

Easing out a breath, I turned to Phineaus. "Thank you."

He blinked. "I'm sorry...what?"

"*Thank you.*" I set free just a seam of the agony ravaging my chest, letting it crack my tone. "For finally listening. For finally *doing something*. I've been trying to show you for *weeks* how scared I was, how I was out of my depth, how I couldn't keep up with his cruelty anymore...and you *finally* came for me."

A brief, sharp shift of bootheels on stone behind me; I refused to look back as I crossed the open span of cobblestones—and wrapped my arms around Phin's neck, pressing myself against him.

"I'm so tired of playing the part," I whispered into the side of his neck. "I've been afraid for my life every single day. But you kept your promise, that you wouldn't let anything happen to me. Thank you, Phin...*thank you.*"

He caught my shoulders and pushed me back, eyes narrowing. "What do you think you're doing?"

"Something I should have done a long, *long* time ago."

I seized his hands, dragged them up to the sides of my neck—and lunged forward to kiss him.

With Phineaus Moraven, *trust* was not the thing that shattered his defenses. *Mutual understanding* and *respect* were not words that meant anything to him...at least, not beyond the realm of death and chaos where he and Grave Dominion reigned.

But possession? Power? Having everything he craved, even the things he'd kept himself from claiming so far?

Just for a moment, he buckled.

And a moment was all I needed.

I pressed in, covered his mouth with mine, crushed my body to his until he gave way. Until his hand seized the back of my head and *he* took power, capturing me against him, his tongue forcing my lips to part until it danced with mine.

I kissed him with everything in me—kissed him with the memory of a Luck-flipped redheaded soldier who'd wanted exactly this from me. Kissed him with fury and hatred masquerading as passion, with the vengeance I'd soaked up from Malakai seeping back out of me. I dug my fingernails into his shoulders and marked him with all my might—let my anger out the only way I could.

This wasn't about him. Phineaus was taking, but he would never give. And he would never fully succumb.

He didn't need to.

The moment he let me breathe, I freed the smallest moan from the back of my throat, as if I couldn't bear to be parted from his kiss.

One of the sentinels coughed. Shifted.

There it is.

Bone fractured with a guttural *crunch*; before the man had even finished screaming, flesh sliced wetly and a body dropped to the cobblestones. Phineaus jerked backward, and I seized his collar in both hands, winding fabric around my fists, dragging him back down and sinking my teeth into his lower lip.

His bark of pain was lost in the chaos erupting behind me—slashing blades, snapping bones, grunts, cries, *screams*.

Phineaus's open palm struck against the side of my face in a skull-rattling *smash*, and sparks erupted across my left eye; my fingers jolted free of his collar, and I staggered sideways, slamming shoulder-first into the nearest shopfront and almost buckling to my knees. Heat flared across the side of my face in a pulsing wave, and when I staggered around to face the havoc behind me, it took several blinks before I could even see it.

See *him*—Malakai, the incarnation of death and bloodshed, the blade strapped to his wrist unleashed...the same weapon that had saved my life my first night in Amalgard. Even with one arm slack, the Poet Poisoner fought with a rage that should've sent every last one running; he carved his way through the lesser-trained sentinels like a bonesaw through a femur. It wasn't an easy glide, it was a brutal hacking and riving that left a trail of gore spattered in his wake.

It was vengeance...for himself. For what they'd done to him at Vespertine's manse. For what they'd done to him *tonight*.

And at the corner of my foggy vision, Phineaus drew wicked, serpentine dagger from behind his waist, his gaze fixed on Malakai.

"*Kilgrave!*" I shouted.

Another sentinel dropped with a severed femoral artery, and Malakai's focus lunged to Phineaus—the only assassin among this contingent.

For a half-second, that mask angled my way again.

And then Malakai was gone from my life just like he'd come into it—a shadow among the shadows, slipping back into the darkness between the buildings. A vapor of smoke brushed away by the hand of the wind.

"*Get after him!*" Phineaus barked at the handful of sentinels who still stood.

I couldn't blame them for hesitating...not when their lives been spared tonight by nothing except Malakai's disappearance. And I almost admired that they went, even reluctantly, at Phineaus's command; though my muddled head wondered dully just how threatened by him they must feel, to risk the certainty of death at Malakai's hand over whatever awaited if they disobeyed.

That was the last thought I had to spare for anyone but myself; because then Phineaus was approaching *me*, with that dagger in his fist and a ferocious glint in his eyes.

"You," he said in that cheerful tone that convinced me of *nothing* anymore, "just made a *very* bad choice! Didn't you?"

"I made the *only* right choice," I hissed.

"Mmhmm." Phineaus halted before me; his thumb brushed my inflamed cheek, and even that slight pressure streaked fresh tears from my eye. "Well, let's see where doing the *right thing* gets you, huh?"

The pommel of the dagger slammed into my injured head. Shadows smothered the world.

CHAPTER 72
THE MUMMER'S DANCE

T HE SECOND TIME I woke in Fortress Ferregrand from deep unconsciousness was nothing like the first.

There was no soft duvet, no stained-glass mosaic, no warmth and welcome. When I cracked my heavy eyelids apart for just a moment, there was only firelight interrupted by slats of black, and pain everywhere. In my head especially, but also in barbed tingles everywhere my body made contact with frigid stone.

The dungeons. How marvelous.

It couldn't be anywhere else; not after what Phineaus had done. Because, if he'd wanted me dead, I would be.

Imprisoned meant something else. Likely something far worse.

It took me a long moment, orienting myself with my eyes pressed shut again, to realize what had woken me: the distant echo of whistling, floating down the corridor like a mockery from Luck itself. A shrill, scornful melody that warned me of imminent discomfort worse than what was pounding through my addled head already.

Behind my aching eyes, I remembered now that I'd been dreaming. Of hair that slid through my fingers like black silk. Of strong, gentle lips roaming over mine. Of mingled breaths that tasted like coffee and sugar and a wild wondering that made my heart feel like it was going to claw out of my chest...and I was happy to allow it.

But that wasn't what lingered with me in the echo of that whistle approaching like a funeral dirge.

It was the essence of betrayal, angled my way like a scalpel in a frenzied patient's hand. It was the last impression of Malakai Kane that I would most likely ever have...and it was the way he'd cursed my name.

I almost preferred the whistling over that. *Almost.*

Groggy, my head pulsing, I rolled to my opposite shoulder and pressed my face into the cold stone floor. Sweet, sweet relief as the chill seeped into my bruised jaw and up my battered cheekbone, soaking into my throbbing temple.

I could've laid like that for hours. Days, even. If I didn't have company.

So I did what I'd been doing, for better or worse, every single day since my mother's death, every day since I'd left Vallanmyre that first time: regardless of how I felt, regardless of the weight towing me back, regardless of how close I felt to drowning, I dragged myself upright instead. I shoved my hands into the stone and levered myself away from that cool respite, so that from the waist up, at least, I faced him when he arrived.

Phineaus, sauntering down the torchlit corridor, whistling merrily as he ran his fingers over the bars of empty cage after empty cage...all the way to mine.

"You know, I always imagined you'd look more put-together first thing in the morning," he jeered, strolling to a halt outside the bars. "I've got to say, I'm regretting how things ended between us a whole lot less, seeing you like this."

"Nothing has *ended*," I seethed, shoving my mangled curls off my brow.

"Now, see, *that's* where you're wrong. I knew it was over the second we talked beside the canal...I knew you'd somehow picked him over me. So, here we are, with my grandfather deciding what to do with you now." He leaned his arm against the bars above his head, chafing the tip of his thumb and forefinger together. "There's an argument going on about whether you were coerced into the Poet's services, or if you're a spy, or if Mithra-Sha sent you *specifically* to try and finish what that assassin started with me." A humorless smile tugged at his mouth. "I'm fond of that one, personally, since it was my contribution to the confusion."

"And that's what you want, isn't it?" I spat. "Everyone confused, everyone afraid, so that no one looks twice at you."

A crooked shrug. "It's going to make things that much easier when my grandparents, and my parents, and my cotton-headed uncle start to drop like bones." He snapped his fingers, two, four, five times—one for each family member he intended to assassinate. "If they take my advice and consider that the Lothars sent you here to destabilize us...hey, even better. I think a few of them could easily disappear in the conflict that comes from *that*."

Disgust bubbled like acid in my throat. "Do you even *hear* yourself? That's your family you're discussing!"

"Oh, cry me a canal and sink a corpse in it, *Weathers*," he scoffed, tucking one toe behind his heel and slouching deeper into the bars. "Rulers don't have time to care about *family*, they have a country to be concerned about. And thanks to my grandfather's raving paranoia and my mother's absolute ineptitude, there isn't much of a *country* left for me to inherit once they're buried where they belong."

"And a *murderer* is going to mend that?"

"He's going to start." Phineaus shrugged. "Start with knocking out all of these guilds, uniting the assassins into *one* group." He cocked a finger. "Anyone who doesn't want to rally up—like everyone's favorite Poisoner—will be hunted down and, ah, what's the *official* word for it? Right!" Shadows billowed across his eyes when they narrowed on me. "*Executed.*"

"Beginning your imaginary rulership with *more* death," I hissed. "How poetic."

"Yeah, well, we all know how *you* love a good poem." Rocking back on his heels, he swept me with a cursory look. "Funnily enough, all of this was possible because of you. And to think I almost wasted that chance with a little bit of bloodshed."

It was the first thing he'd said that made no sense at all. But I didn't give him the satisfaction of that—I just watched him.

"That first night you came to Amalgard was meant to be the end of it," Phineaus went on, his fingers dancing along the dungeon bars—a slow, taunting cadence. "That was one of ours you encountered in the street...our newest initiate with one simple task from me: make you disappear."

My breath clunked hollowly into the bottom of my lungs and didn't crawl back out again. Not for several long moments while his words chased themselves around my head, annealing into an awful, cruel sense.

My attacker in the street that first night in the city—

Grave Dominion.

"It was the perfect plan," Phineaus added. "My aunt's meddling little pet poison study, throat slit, tossed into the gutter. Just another casualty of a country lacking for real leadership. At worst, we'd have to send a sympathy note to Mithra-Sha." A caustic snort. "At best, maybe my spineless cousin would've gotten his hackles up and done something for the first time in his short and thus far incredibly *disappointing* tenure as Sha."

His fingers stilled, his gaze flashing up to seize mine.

"But then he *saved* you." The word slid through gritted teeth, a flexed tongue that curled around it like a sour aftertaste. "I didn't know why at the time, but the Poet saved you. And that had me thinking there must be some sort of weakness in that armor of his…something that couldn't look away where an assassin worth his mettle should. So I decided to keep you around…to slide you in under that armor and see where I could pry it back."

My knuckles strained against my skin, fists aching so horribly they nearly erased the pain in my joints from the dungeon's perforating chill.

The sheepish, guileless *victim* I'd first met lying in that bed, surrounded by his concerned uncle and doting sister…the caring older brother who'd escorted Luminae on a nighttime jaunt for cocoa, and talked of legacy beneath the stars…

Such a lie.

I'd met a strategist that first day. My own almost-killer by another's hand. And he'd drummed up that ridiculous plot to ingratiate me to Malakai…pulling my strings all along, stitching my life into Malakai's just to bring the Poet to his knees.

There was only a small sliver of satisfaction in knowing this: my mere presence in this dungeon was proof I'd won.

"And now don't *you* feel like a fool?" I shot back. "He wasn't *saving my life* that night, he was removing another member of Grave Dominion from the gameboard."

Phineaus's cruel smile didn't falter. "Unless that was just a bit of what you Mithrans call *fickle Luck*."

"You *are* a fool, Phineaus." I shook my head. "He abandoned me, didn't he? He left me here with *you*."

Phineaus tilted his head, measuring me with snakish eyes. Unlike when Malakai gave me that look—*had* given me that look—it didn't loosen my tongue. It didn't make me feel like spilling my secrets.

It made me want to coil into myself and retreat from him.

"Maybe," he murmured. "Or maybe the Poet is pacing in his lair right now, tearing out his hair, regretting that choice he made in the heat of the moment. Maybe he's already scheming up ways to get you back."

I hated the way hope raised its head and stirred, beating against the cage of my ribs. I hated that hope was more fickle than Luck itself.

Most of all, I hated that I *knew* Phineaus could see it—that he scented my desires. That they stirred that malevolent gleam in his gaze.

"The trouble with regret," he added softly, "is it puts you one step behind."

Swift as a snakebite, he launched an arm through the prison bars; in the narrow space, there wasn't enough room to dodge. Even when I jerked back, his iron-strong fist encircled my wrist. He yanked me against the iron slats, my sternum impacting first, then my belly, forcing all the air from my lungs in a violent heave. I doubled over, retching, chest straining and shuddering—so dizzied with the loss of wind that it was a moment before the pain lunged to the forefront.

Before I realized that a dart tip had pierced the skin at the inside of my elbow.

Swearing, I dug my fingernails into Phineaus's wrist and ripped skin from the hinge to the middle of his forearm. He barked a sound somewhere between a curse and a startled laugh, tearing his arm from the cage and shaking it out, scrubbing the side of his fist against the wheals. "Rancid, reeking *bones*, he must've had a lot of fun with you!"

I tumbled back a step, clapping a hand over my elbow; the thick, heavy tension that preceded true pain thudded beneath my sweat-slick palm, spidering out, climbing up toward my biccp and down toward my wrist.

"What was that?" I snarled.

"A bit of incentive." A wicked smile hooked his full lips up at one side. "By the time the Poet gets his little wits together, stops arguing with himself, and finds his way to the Fortress, he is going to find you in a *very* compromised position." Winding one hand around the bars, he tilted conspiratorially toward me. "And that is going to make the rest of this much, *much* easier to get over with."

Bashing his palm against the bars and chuckling when I jumped in my skin, Phineaus snapped around on heel and strolled down the dungeon hall, whistling to himself. I held still, trembling, fear and hate souring on the back of my tongue.

I didn't dare glance down until he was too far gone to enjoy the reaction.

Beneath my palm, the veins inside my elbow were already blackening, spreading outward in varicose branches.

Poison.

Not just any poison.

I'd seen these veins before. On a patient turncd to an enemy. On...

Gryffen.

My back struck the wall. Slowly, I slid to my seat, digging my head against the stone, biting down on a sob as pain pulsed and radiated from the hinge of my arm.

I'd told Malakai that I wasn't afraid of death...that I'd seen it in so many faces and so many ways over the years that it as just another *thing* that happened to people. That would someday happen to me.

But I was a liar. This moment was making a liar out of me.

I didn't want to die *here*. Alone, frozen to the stone, ravaged by Mummer's Dance. Here, without a proper goodbye to my Papa and brothers, to Audra and Arias and the others.

I didn't want to die hated, forgotten, thought of as a traitor.

I didn't want to die without a hand holding mine, the way I'd done for so many people I couldn't save. I'd walked more patients than I could count into death's arms, released them to it with our fingers slipping apart.

I didn't want to die without someone to walk me to it, either. To hold my hand. To tell me goodbye.

"Malakai, please." A whisper. A prayer. A sob.

As if he could hear me. As if he really was watching over me wherever I was.

As if he would still come, after what Phineaus had done to us.

As if I really wanted him to, knowing it would mean his death.

His death, or mine.

Clinging to my arm, I crumbled sideways to the floor.

And I began the long wait for my own demise.

CHAPTER 73
A WEAK AND WANTING HEART
(MALAKAI)

THE MANSE WAS DESOLATE.

Not merely because I had ransacked it upon my return...though I had. Nor because it was an absolute boneyard of desecrated ledgers, tomes cracked at the spines, and overturned tables and chairs...though it was.

No. Sitting astride an overturned chair, cradling a chilled cloth to a not-in-consequential knot of bruising at the back of my shoulder, I *felt* the cold and quiet crawling along my bones.

Desolation, as it happened, did not only come in the wake of a fit of temper like the one that had seen me overturning my desk and hurling bookcases to the floor.

Desolation was...emptiness. A void where something had once been.

I had rarely returned to a place of life after death fell like a funeral shroud. My childhood home, I could only assume, had been snapped up by some member of Grave Dominion who'd coveted it while my family still lived. An unexpected mercy, in the end...I had never been forced to walk haunted halls.

Until now.

Whispers lurked in the shadows of the lair, like flares of light guiding travelers home. Laughter. Endless conversation mortaring the cracks of silence that had once brimmed in this place. The smell of freshly-brewed coffee, the clatter of two plates and two mugs together—

"*Enough,*" I snarled to myself.

Days she'd been gone. Days since her betrayal had come to light. I should've been able to walk through my own manse without overturning the places where she'd sat—where *we'd* sat together.

I shouldn't have to destroy my own semblance of a home just to erase the impressions she'd left behind on it, like fingertips pressed into dust.

But here I was, straddling an overturned chair while I studied the map with its countless intersections, its endless bloodlines intertwined.

Grave Dominion, everywhere. Spreading like an infectious disease, like a poison all their own.

She had served them. Aided them.

"Stop," I ground out, lifting the cloth and pressing it over my eye instead. "*Enough*, Malakai."

But it was not enough. For days I had been here, evading the eyes of the city, of the Guild Garrote, sentinels and their master...and it *still* was not enough to erase those moments in the streets, the last time I had seen her.

Focus was preeminent. What had happened here in Rastra—what I had allowed to happen with the machinations of a weak and wanting heart—could not be allowed to transpire again. Grave Dominion had struck too close; Phineaus, the self-named Kingslayer like some figure from Mithran fiction, had come *far* too close to laying his hands on me.

Because of whatever rapport he and Naomi had shared.

A flicker of her face traced my mind. I curled my lip, squeezing the rag to my brow until water dripped down my cheek and plopped from my chin.

Rapport. Wasn't that a pleasant way of saying she had all but turned me over to him? And why—to save her own skin? Or because—

Ah, sullied souls. There it was.

The flicker fanned to a full memory...the infuriating sight of her stretching up on her toes, her mouth crashing over his.

All at once, the simmer of temper rolled to a boil that would not be contained.

Flinging the rag from my hand, I kicked up from the overturned chair and tore the map down from the wall. I swept the table of all the trinkets, papers, pots, and pans that cluttered its surface. I spun for the upended contents of my satchel scattered across the overturned cot, hurling them one by one aside. Lists that meant nothing. Ledgers that counted for less. The things I had intended to scaffold my plans with when we fled the city, when we started anew—because somehow, foolishly, I had believed in that moment that so long as I had my partner with me, I had *everything*.

My fingers encountered softness and sturdiness, smooth as silk. Rage and vengeance scorched my tongue—a comfortable taste of ash, familiar as a friend after all of these years.

The first glazed stoneware plate shattered into three shards at impact with the wall, the *crack* of it ricocheting through my head like the slam of a hand on a cheekbone. I raised the second, readied to throw—

And waited.

And waited.

And rotting *waited*.

My reflection glowered back at me from the midnight glaze, a warped rictus of undefinable emotion. I could almost mistake the pale streaks across it for the star trails in the glaze.

"*What are you doing*?" I bellowed, seizing the plate with both hands—screaming at the only pair of ears left to listen. The only ones that had been listening for too many years. "Just let go!"

I couldn't hurl the plate.

I couldn't silence the echo in my ears—the shattering of the last one.

The impact of his hand against her cheek.

The dagger-sharp thrust of certainty that the kiss had not been what it seemed.

"Don't do this," I warned myself—but my tone was feeble, as seamed as the dish lying broken across the room. "Do *not* go down that road, Malakai."

It was too late.

The resonate *thud* of dagger pommel to tender flesh rang through me like a blow—the blow that had struck her unconscious.

From the rooftops, veiled in shadow, I had watched him drag her away...dragged, like a satchel full of priceless things. Dragged until her tender flesh had peeled on the stone, leaving streaks of blood behind.

Streaks I had followed to the edge of Rastra, until they had vanished. As *he* had vanished, towing her behind him. And I had lost the trail...after hours of searching, until his sentinels had drawn too close for comfort, forcing my steps back into the city proper, back to this empty tomb of a manse.

Why in the grave had I even looked? Why had my scant few hours of sleep since seen me dreaming of finding the bloodied trail—finding *her* at the end of it?

I had no excuse, save one.

Conspirators did not drag their accomplices behind them on the stone.

The plate tumbled from my fingers, dropping unharmed into the churned folds of my puddled bedspread, and I faltered backward until my shoulders struck the wall. Slamming my eyes shut, I pinched my nostrils and smothered my mouth, pulling in thinner, longer heaves.

There were two ways to stoke fire, they had taught us in Thrasmund. Great bellows and small breaths.

Kingslayer. That was how Phineaus Moraven had introduced himself the day my father had decided our time in Grave Dominion was over. He'd chosen his assassin's alias before he'd even made his first kill...but not *long* before.

He'd charmed my sister with a smile...and followed it with a blade through her heart.

A serpentine dagger. A pommel to the temple.

Some victims, the Kingslayer destroyed outright. And others he toyed with, a jaded predator with confined prey.

He teased and taunted their precious hearts. He dragged them back to his lair to play...bodies scraping over stone.

I lost the trail.

I lost her.

"Let her go," I hissed. "Let her *deserve* it."

A slap to the face. A scream.

Kilgrave!

She hadn't betrayed my name. She had warned me of the Kingslayer's coming, as if she'd known my moment of weakness—too desperate and disoriented to keep watch of every person in that deserted span of a plaza.

Disoriented by *her*. What she had done. *Everything* she had done.

She kissed that rotting bastard.

An image branded behind every blink of my straining eyes. A betrayal different from all the rest. A moment I relived over and over, saturated with a sickness and *wrongness* that remained unshakeable.

I knew precisely how she kissed. I was fully and inescapably aware of what *passion* tasted like on that woman's lips—as well as fury, and hatred, and a host of other things.

She hadn't given him an ounce of her passion. Only her rage.

Hatred and betrayal could exist in the same space—if there was coercion.

If he had coerced her...*why wouldn't she tell me?*

Did it truly matter that she hadn't?

There was a reason I couldn't focus. That I had been alone here for days, undiscovered, and failed to find my way back to my purpose yet. My cause.

Small breaths burned like wisps of smoke crowding my lungs. I dropped my hand and slammed my skull back against the wall, unleashing pain and fury and ruin with a snarl aimed for the lonely rafters.

He has her.

He has everything.

The thought caught me like a hand around the throat, squeezing until my eyes flared wide.

Not my schemes. Not the plans Naomi was aware of.

He. Has. Everything.

I had sworn I would never leave her...never let him take her back to that place.

Rage had made a liar of me.

And, with his hand tangled in her hair, her body scuffing behind him in the streets...

It had made a prisoner of her.

And I knew what would come next.

Small breaths. Great bellows.

If a man strikes you on the cheek, you strike him through the heart.

I knew *precisely* what would come next—because his sentinels had found me tracking the bloodpaths paved on the cobblestones. Because I let my composure slip to the tips of my fingers when she had kissed him.

Because of how she had screamed my name.

I knew what the Kingslayer would do...it was what I would have done. What Grave Dominion had taught us to do.

And whether she had once been his willing coconspirator or not...it would happen because of *me.*

Because he knew where my heart lay. And the Kingslayer would strike true.

Slowly, I bent—my elbows to my thighs. My back sliding down the rough stone until I fell to a crouch on my heels, palms pressed together, fingers braced to my lips. My eyes fixed on the three pieces of a shattered dish lying halfway across the room.

The first and final signs that there had ever been something *more* in this place.

It was desolate now.

But the walls were singing.

A resonance, a rumble rising up from the lowest parts. A shaking which tolled on into war drums in the confines of my thundering head.

I was shaking—shudders of fury and hate wringing out the strength from my bones. Pouring something greater than that into the space my strength left behind.

Something endless and almighty. Something that did not bend to sinister schemes and Grave fabrications.

My eyes tumbled closed, and in the darkness behind them, I met her at last.

At the end of bloodstained streets. At the end of trail lost in the wilds beyond Rastra.

A bruised arm. Panicked eyes. *I've been trying to tell you for weeks how scared I was.*

All those nights she'd returned from the city streets shaken, distant, distracted—cajoled and threatened by him. The way she'd crumbled into my arms after visiting with a *patient* who'd refused to see her any other time.

Whatever else had been a lie, it had never been that...her fear. Her reluctance. Her shifting moods.

A betrayer...but an unwitting one.

The glide of her mouth against mine. The heat. The desire. The *vulnerability*.

I grimaced at memory's retort of her lips crushed over his; a shake of my head dislodged the notion, but another slid sharply into its place.

My sister's smitten smile. The bedazzlement morphing into shock, then agony, then mortal terror when the Kingslayer's dagger found a home precisely in her sternum—and shoved in up to the crossguard.

Hadn't I vowed, half a lifetime ago, that I would never believe Phineaus Moraven's lies again?

She had deceived him with a kiss because he didn't know her.

She had deceived me because I *did*.

Naomi Weathers wept for the necessity of death. She cried for cruel men with their wicked intentions silenced forever. She straddled the line of healing and harm with a vicious, violent grace that set everything within me alight.

She was not like the Kingslayer. She was not like *me*.

But I could stand to be a bit more like her.

I could stand to reason that even if she had betrayed me...she did not deserve the Kingslayer's rage.

Slowly, I raised my head. Slowly, I let my hands drop, palms still aligned, hanging from my knees as I stared at the desolation before me.

She had enleagued herself with him. But that was not the entirety of it.

The only truth I knew for certain was that he had her. And that he would never let her walk away, accomplice or not...back to Mithra-Sha. Back to the home she loved.

Not when I had escaped his grasp *because* of her.

Not when he had dragged her away.

"What is it all worth?" I murmured. "What is vengeance worth to you?"

Everything, I would've answered once. *Anything*.

That was before I had met a healer in darkened street, knife in hand. Before she had taken an interest in me, in the ways of this manse, in the brew of my coffee and the shape of my mind. Before we had entered the Guild Garrote together, turned to thieves together; before she had mended my wounds and, utterly against my will, pierced her needle into my innermost parts and mended things beyond what sight could see.

Naomi Weathers had infiltrated me. The first single drop of her presence that fated night in Amalgard's streets had fanned out ripples that moved me still.

One drop can destroy everything, she'd told me.

Well. Damn.

It was time for destruction.

CHAPTER 74
BRING HIM TO HIS KNEES

THE WORLD WAS BURNING.

Stars winked and withered in the darkness. Fire scorched one side of my face hotter than the other.

There was no relief. Pressing my cheek to the floor turned the world topsy-turvy. My mind muddled through stanching cotton. Decadent agony followed the black maplines down my arm, across my chest, along my torso.

It crawled out of my fingertips. The soles of my feet. My eyes.

The shadows visited me.

Papa, drowning in peddled wares, suffocating under the fine cloth that wrapped his face. I clawed at the smothering silk, but then when I ripped it away—

A burial shroud. My mother lying beneath it, her eyes wide and white and opaque, her skull rotted to bone, her mouth agape in a wail of agony.

I screamed, I hurled the shroud back over her with all my might, but it drifted high. It erased her as it passed, and in her place...

All four of my brothers lined up in a row, their throats cut in neat flaps.

The screaming wouldn't stop. The sobbing *wouldn't stop.*

And the shadows wouldn't stop coming, melting through the cage bars, taking on the shape of new torments with the deft precision of a ticking clock.

Addie, wearing the color of arterial blood, more of it gushing from her shoulder and side while she begged me to save her...and I couldn't force my heavy, hurting limbs to drag me near enough that I could even try. Jaik, already dead with a dagger through his heart. Reiko devoured by the manifestations of Misspoken stories. Mahalia, gored with a sketching lead jammed through her eye. Wyat bleeding out slowly from a belly wound, weeping for help I couldn't give. Arias dragged away by those shadows, slipping from my fingertips when I tried to crawl after him.

The shadows parted. Malakai stepped through them, masked and magnificent and devastatingly beautiful. Like a storm at night or a well-made blade.

I knew I was thinking nonsense. That the poison was ruining me, one pulse at a time. But that didn't stop me from dragging myself by my fingernails and wobbly legs to his boot tips, gasping, panting, "Be here. Be with me. *Please* be with me."

Slowly, Malakai crouched. Slowly, he threaded his fingers through my hair, down my cheek, raising my head by the gentlest grip on my chin.

And for one absurd moment, my terrified, anguished weeping turned to tears of joy.

Take me home.

"You *disgust* me." The words dripped from his mouth like skeins of shadow—like poison all their own. "Little *betrayer.* They're welcome to have you. And I truly hope they make you suffer until your very last breath."

He shoved my head aside, setting a lance of fire rampaging down my swollen cheek when I toppled shoulder-and-face-first to the floor.

Curled into myself, I sobbed until I vomited, opening the door for the pain to crawl inside. To have its way with me from the outside in.

I had no concept of passing time. Hours—days—did it really matter? Death always came at its own pace, and it had its way with me like a cat with a mouse.

It peeled me open, claw by claw. It dug its talons in at my hips and scoured its way down my legs. No matter how I lay, where I slumped, whatever corner I dragged myself into...it just kept raking and ravaging and burning. Until there wasn't an inch of me that didn't pulse with agony.

Faces came and went in flares like fireworks—the faces of patients I'd failed to save. The faces of their families, split open in screams that pierced my ears until I ripped at them for relief. Until they bled.

General Gryffen's corpse lay beside me, ravaged with burst vessels, eyes blackened with the spread of old blood. He rolled to an elbow, fingers around my throat, wrapping the pain around me until it hovered somewhere between real and imaginary, throbbing in my waking and delirium.

I screamed for Malakai until I lost my voice. But he wasn't watching over me anymore.

And then, somewhere in between the tears, the pleading, the bleeding and anguish—

Whistling.

A thrum of footsteps that jolted through every inch of my shivering body. A resonance against the stone beneath me that *hurt* like rat teeth nibbling at my flesh.

"Don't *you* look like you're having fun?"

I pried my swollen eyes apart, squinting in the torchlight—finding Phineaus's familiar, detestable face rimmed in firelight like an eclipse.

"What, not happy to see me?" A smirk lanced across his lips. "Come on! Where's the witty quip? Where's the *banter*?"

Choking, panting, I couldn't even pry myself up to face him this time.

"Almost wish I could join you." He freed the words like a confession, head dipped toward the cage bars. "I've tried a taste of it, you know that? Mummer's Dance. Before that note the Poet sent, I mean...in Thrasmund, they train you on a taste to help build up your immunity. If you take just a *little*, you'll imagine some things like you wouldn't *believe*." He leaned on his heels and cast his head back, hands still gripping the bars. "*Hoo!*"

Chuckling, he rocked on the balls of his feet again, spreading his palms wide on the cage slats. One finger stirred in the air between them, pointing casually my way.

"In *your* case, I'm guessing the wild part—the hallucinations—must be over. Good news for me! That means the poison's fully infiltrated your brain." His head tilted. "Bad news for you, it's going to get *really* painful from here."

A shudder rocked through my limbs, and even *that* ached, like someone was holding a torch a few inches from my skin.

"Other good news: I know exactly what I'm doing. Because the fun part's just starting, and...you'll never guess who just called a meeting."

It took a moment for the fire to abate enough that I could swallow those words, digest them past my cotton-dry mouth, force them into my thudding head and mash them into sense.

No. No, no, no...

Phineaus peeled the cage door open and stepped over the threshold; I dug my frail fingertips into the stone until they scraped raw, struggling to push myself back from him, but there was nowhere to escape.

There had never been.

Pain exploded from the pinch of his grip around my upper arm like he'd stabbed a blade straight through the muscle, scraping bone. He smiled when I screamed, heaving me up to dangle from his hand. "That's it, good *girl*! That's *exactly* what I want him to hear."

All the force tumbled from my voice in a wretched sob—like my lungs had given up, too. Screaming didn't make the agony end, so why bother with the effort?

"Just...rotting *perfect.*" Reverently, Phineaus palmed the matted hair from my brow. "Now, try to make yourself look presentable, all right?" Glee rattled his tone. "Not every day you get to help bring an assassin to his knees."

CHAPTER 75
THE POET AND THE KINGSLAYER
(MALAKAI)

*T*HE DUNGEON ATRIUM. MIDNIGHT.

The only words my trembling hand had managed to articulate on the note I'd wedged into the Kingslayer's windowframe. I had considered jotting it in poisoned ink, but it was too great a risk with Naomi in his clutches; if he perished at my hand, doubtless he had others in Grave Dominion poised to ensure she suffered the same fate.

The only way to spare her life was to confront him, one assassin to another.

I could not recall the last time I'd been afraid before a mark. The tremble in my hands had died long, long ago. Vengeance had promised a long, straight road to mutually-assured destruction; it was not a matter of *when* I would perish, only a question of whether it would be before Grave Dominion's utter demise, or in landing the final blow.

Yet when I slipped through the same seam in the lower stones by which I'd gained entrance to first strike the Kingslayer, and made my way drenched from the moat and dripping along the old, bricked-over escape tunnel up toward the dungeons...my hands would not be still.

I curled them into fists, chasing the shaking into a thick sort of heaviness that encircled my forearms like shackles.

Fear would make a fool of me. I had only the need for focus and fury.

One I owed to Naomi. The other to the Kingslayer.

The dungeon was unguarded—doubtless a sign that my arrival was anticipated. But when I turned the handle of the thick, sturdy outer door and pushed my way inside the atrium—finding it lit with a blazing chandelier in the upper reaches of the rotunda—I was still not prepared for the sight that greeted me.

The Kingslayer, waiting, casually whistling and flaking his thumb along the fingertips of one hand. And in the other—

My steps ground to a halt. My jaw tightened far beyond the point of pain—and still it was *nothing* matched to the anguish that rived through my chest.

Naomi hung in this murderer's grip by a fistful of hair, crumbled and weakened, hardly holding her weight on her own feet. Ravaged, panting, doubled over...she didn't even raise her eyes at my arrival.

Shame wrenched the dagger piercing my heart.

I had left her to this. I had given her up to this fate.

"*Naomi.*" Her name seethed from me, and both of them jerked—the faintest twitch of her limbs. The sharp upsweep of his head, the blinding smile tearing across his face.

The same smile that had beguiled my sister to her own early grave.

"Ah, there he is!" That voice I had despised with all of me since he'd cackled down at my sister's corpse...it raked against my ears. "Right on time, Poet."

I gave no answer. It was Naomi I couldn't keep my eyes off of.

This was not the woman I had broken my promise to in that plaza. It was a shadow of her—a gaunt, gutted thing, spoiled in her own soiling and sickness, bloodied and battered from outside and within.

And along the lines of that precious body I had craved to the point of madness...

Varicose tendrils spidered up and down every path of her veins. They coiled like fetters around her wrists and ankles and necklaced her throat like a noose.

I had known he would do this...had predicted it from the moment I'd heard him strike her in the street and watched him drag her away by a fistful of hair. And still I was not braced for the blow it dealt me, for the panic and fury that tore my heart from my chest and upended my insides.

Mummer's Dance. A favorite among Grave Dominion. A poison even I had never dared inflict on any victim...save one.

The poison with which I had nearly ended the Kingslayer's life was his weapon held against me. Just as I had suspected he would.

"*Poetic,* isn't it?" he grinned. "Thought you'd like the gift. I've got to say, I think *my* packaging was better."

"Release her." The snarl that ripped from me was hardly my voice—hardly human. "*Now.*"

"Is...is that supposed to intimidate me?" The Kingslayer pressed a hand over his heart. "Gah! Just shaking in my boots, really." His arm swung back to his side, and all at once he was serious, not a hint of showmanship in his tone: "Take off the mask. Let's see who we're dealing with."

"Don't." Naomi's tearful plea was paper-thin. Nothing like the unyielding edges my pride and plotting had cut themselves against all the months we'd lived in the manse together. "Don't give him this."

I was already reaching back, already unbinding the mask that had kept me safe and secret from everyone, all this time.

Everyone but her.

Tugging it away burned like skin rendered from bone; but I let the porcelain clatter to the floor between us, and raised my eyes to meet the Kingslayer's—finding the shock, first. The disbelief. And then the first seams of perverse joy cleaving through the depths of his amber gaze.

"No way," he breathed—then whooped, "no way in the *grave*! *What?* *Malakai Kane*—the Poet Poisoner is *Malakai Kane*!" He swiped a hand down his face, settling it over his mouth. "Oh, you've got to be joking...this is too perfect. You're supposed to be *dead*!"

"Likewise," I growled.

"I don't know how you slipped away all those years ago, my friend," the Kingslayer laughed, shoving Naomi a step nearer and striding after her. "But that's not happening again. You've got a *lot* to pay for. Starting right now."

"Malakai, you can't give up," Naomi pleaded. "You can't do this for—"

The Kingslayer shook her viciously by a fistful of hair, and her mouth cracked in a silent wail, her head arching back to seek some semblance of relief. With the Mummer's Dance spooling through her veins, even the lightest tug would deal the same pain as being scalped.

My fists throbbed at my sides, begging for the Kingslayer's throat. Or to hold her against me, far from his reach.

"Shh. Healer. The men are talking," he hissed against the shell of her ear. Eyes pinned on me—ensuring I captured every movement—he added, "Show me what you've got, Malakai. You remember the old drill."

I did.

Before every meeting with Grave Dominion, there had been a ceremonious stripping down. A show of every nook and crevice where a weapon of any sort could be hidden. I'd expected that. Come prepared for it. And though the lack of armament chafed at every angle of my body, it was a pain *nothing* like watching Naomi dangle from his grip without the strength to hold herself upright.

She was a weapon—the one that had burrowed under my flesh without my notice.

Arms outflung, I turned a full circle for the Kingslayer's assessment. He watched with predatory enthusiasm until I faced him again.

"Excellent! Now, don't mind if we get intimate."

He cast Naomi against the wall, the strike of her body on stone echoing through every inch of mine. My feet jerked in her direction as she slumped to her knees, head tipped forward, erratic breaths echoing off the atrium walls; but the Kingslayer stepped into my path, one hand outstretched.

"Ah-ah-ah," he scolded. "Keep to the *code*, Poet."

For her sake—her *survival*—I did. Submitting myself to the Kingslayer's hands scouring my person...the hands that had rammed a blade into my sister's heart. That had thrown a knife into my brother's back. That had dealt unspeakable agony to my parents, all as a stepping stone to where he'd ascended now.

"What do you know? You actually did it!" Chuckling, the Kingslayer clapped a hand on my shoulder, setting it twitching with the press of his lethal fingernails into the fabric of my shirt. "Just one more thing..."

The bash of his knuckles to my cheek erupted my vision like a spatter of blood, whipping my head aside; I kept from staggering only because I had known the blow would come from somewhere, at some time.

It was Naomi whose head bobbed up sharply; Naomi whose gaze cleared in a few stuttered blinks. Her fingers dug into the atrium's uneven stones, and her feet churned beneath her, forcing her up, shoving her a staggering step in our direction.

The Kingslayer met her with a deft pirouette, snatching her by the back of her neck and scruffing her like an unruly canine. "Where do you think *you're* going, spitfire?"

Her knees buckled and pain danced across the contortion of her features; one hand struggled back to swipe at his knuckles, but he batted them effortlessly aside, stilling her with a rough shake that dragged another sob from her chest.

I had killed until my hands ran red. But I had never *gloried* in any death the way I would bask in this man's. I had never craved it to the brink of salivating, dreamed of it while awake.

This moment changed *everything*.

"So, here's what I want," the Kingslayer drawled. "I want *all of it*, Malakai. That means your plans, whatever list you've been working from, and, ah, let's see...how about your lair?" A crooked smirk tilted his lips. "And then I want *you* behind bars until I'm ready to finish what I started with the rest of your spineless, runaway family. You give me all of that..." another sharp shake setting Naomi's whole frame swaying, "and I'll give you what's left of this one. Might still be enough left to have some fun with before she's gone."

Naomi panted and trembled, utterly slumped in the Kingslayer's grip; but she still found it in her to be my stubborn troublemaker, to raise a protest with the last of herself.

"Malakai, *no.*"

As if those words, choked out with such a desperate, brittle crack in the very center, would do anything but *convince* me of this choice.

For my family, I had tarnished my hands beyond cleansing. In their names, I had killed and killed and *killed* until I no longer recognized the face in the mirror.

But for her, I would do far more.

I would break the man in the mirror, if it meant sparing her this agony.

"Don't take your eyes off of me, Naomi," I warned. "I'm about to surprise you again."

Her eyelids fluttered, struggled, lifted in one last slow, painful sweep—then tumbled shut. My body wrenched forward another step as if some tether bound me to those eyes; when I lost them, I lost my footing. And my composure threatened to follow when she sagged in his grip and did not lift her head again.

Rotting contrarian!

I tore my gaze to the Kingslayer's grinning face, pulse tuning itself to the wild, staggered ticking away of borrowed time. "You will find all of my plans and all of my poisons in the old Nassar manse on the outskirts of Rastra. And I will tell you how to enter it when you give her to me."

His brows arched, his fingers flexing against the nape of Naomi's neck. "You really expect me to believe you're just...handing all of that over?"

Fury lashed from me in a shout: "*Why are we doing* any of this *if you didn't expect me to come back for her*?"

Naomi's head bobbed faintly. The Kingslayer's lips pushed out to one side. "Fair point."

He debated a moment...an eternity held in the hands of the man who'd taken everything from me.

"Nassar, eh? After all this time?" he finally echoed.

"Isn't that what I said?"

"Hm." The slightest nod. "It tracks, doesn't it?"

Without warning, he released Naomi—an unceremonious drop from an unmoved hand.

Uncoiling, I lunged across the atrium, knees scraping stone as I slid to catch her, sweeping an arm around the back of her neck, steadying her head. Our chests collided, our knees pressed together on the cold and cruel stone, her head lolling limp in the crook of my elbow; old tears had carved paths through the grime that coated her face and throat.

She did not move. Did not even raise her head.

Panic clamored in my fingertips, a vicious hum of warning that refused to abate this near to the Kingslayer. But for once, I gave no attention to the instinct that had sustained me all these years; I chased it out with a palm braced over Naomi's chest, finding the wild leap of her heart greeting my hand as if it rejoiced at seeing me.

How could a heartbeat almost be a man's undoing?

"Troublemaker?" I hissed, searching her shadow-scorched face for a hint of awareness.

Not a movement. Not a flicker.

"Oh-ho, sullied *souls*," the Kingslayer gloated. "She actually got you to fall in *love* with her, didn't she?"

I tore my gaze to his wicked, grinning face; he pressed the side of his fist to his mouth, but it did nothing to hide his vicious delight.

"Almost makes me wish I could've dragged this out a *little* bit longer." He thrust his hands into his pockets. "But, ah...my grandfather's not getting any younger, and that seat of power's looking better every day. Now, here's what you're going to do."

He stepped to the iron door across the atrium, opening it with a backhand twist of his wrist and sweeping it wide.

"Walk yourself and your pet poisoner down into the last cell and do me a favor—shut the door behind you. You can do whatever it is you do together until I come back from Rastra." Vicious delight lit his gaze like a pyre flame, intent to devour flesh and bone. "And once I've got the truth out of you—whether that's it or not—I'm going to finish what I started with you and your pieceless brother and your pretty little sister. And if she's still sucking down air by that point...I'd love for her to be the audience."

For a moment, I considered what it would require of me to end his life, here and now.

Every last scrap of my strength. Every element of surprise. And not an inconsiderable amount of what Naomi called *fickle luck*.

But none of that was the risk that kept me on my knees when the shadows whispered for vengeance from the edges of the atrium. For a score to be settled at long last.

If I struck...if I even tried...Naomi was the cost to be paid.

She did not have the time for an unwinnable battle. Not when hers was breaths from being lost.

Of its own accord, my thumb brushed a spidering vein that stretched upward from her clavicle to her jawline; a shiver pulsed through her flesh beneath my hand, and a weightless sort of rage lifted through me, congealing in a hard knot at the top of my throat.

The Kingslayer was a deadman walking. Every breath he borrowed now was stolen against the ones he'd taken from her.

I had learned mortal patience in the pit of my family's empty graves. It could pinch a bit longer if it meant I did not have to dig hers.

Slowly, tenuously—mindful of the Mummer's affects with every shift of muscle that jostled her—I swiveled Naomi in my grip, slid an arm beneath her knees, and brought her to my chest.

When she lay there, for the first time since that blackened plaza in Rastra, I released the entirety of my breath. But it hitched again when I rose, as smoothly as possible...and still she whimpered, curling into herself, wounded even in her delirium by the smallest motions.

This suffering the Kingslayer had inflicted on her.

He grinned as I crossed the atrium to him; wrist propped against the edge of the prison door, he watched with venomous, predatory glee while we passed.

"I have to say," he purred, "I just loving seeing the pair of you like this."

I would not give him the satisfaction—though every nerve screamed that I was near enough to snap his neck, if I only dropped Naomi and got my hands around his head.

I would not give him the pleasure of her death as my doing.

So I strode down the torchlit corridor, to the narrow cell at the very end; I nudged it open with a boot tip and stepped inside. And I kicked it shut—my eyes clanging closed of their own volition with the rattling impact of the lock clattering into place.

This was my choosing. Grave Dominion had not subdued me. And as long as I was not subdued by their hand, I could still escape.

We would escape this place.

"Got to admit, I didn't think you'd actually go all the way," the Kingslayer called down the hall. "Finally, the Poet Poisoner in a cage."

He waited. I gave him nothing, measuring my breathing, forcing my arms not to tighten their grip around Naomi.

I would not allow myself to be made the cause of her pain.

"All right, all right," he sighed, "a deal's a deal. You're locked in there with her, now give me the details."

And that was precisely what I did.

While I bore Naomi to the brutal stone shelf that mocked itself as a bed, I gave him the way through Rastra's twisting outskirts to a manse long thought abandoned—now abandoned in truth. Cradling her in my lap with one arm tucked behind her neck and ripping my cloak free with my unburdened hand, I explained the keying on the doors. Wrapping her in the loose fabric and settling her gently on the shelf, I murmured the means to disable the defenses. Told him where to find the vault key, the keys to my workroom.

I gave him everything. And precisely nothing more important than the woman crumbled on the shelf before me, clinging to her fate by the tips of those life-giving, death-dealing fingers.

The Kingslayer listened with rapturous intent while I shifted loose curls from Naomi's brow, watching the sinister play of pain acting itself across the stage of her face: from her twitching eyelids to her trembling mouth and tight jaw, to the pinch between her eyes that refused to ease no matter how many times I stroked my thumb against it.

"Fantastic!" the Kingslayer belted out when I'd been silent for a full minute. "So, you enjoy watching her choke to death on her own blood once her organs start popping like little soap bubbles. And as for *you*," a click of tongue against teeth, and likely a finger angled in my direction like a blade, though I refused to pay him the satisfaction of a glance, "I'll be back to let my family know you snuck in, silenced your partner down here in the dungeons, and I caught you trying to slip back out."

Retreating bootsteps were nearly our salvation; but of course, he couldn't leave it at that.

He had to gloat.

"Just in case it hurts anything," he added, "I worked her over for *months* in that city, putting pressure in all the best places, and she never gave me anything useful about you."

My traitorous heart stumbled over its rhythm even more than usual; though I still didn't spare him a glance, something in my posture must have shifted beyond my control. The Kingslayer twisted into that seam like a blade.

"That's right...she protected you, and what'd you do? Turned around and abandoned her for nothing." A low, gravelly chuckle. "I mean, when it came down to it, my word or hers...you believed *me* over her. Have fun explaining that one to her before she goes under. I'll see what's left of you both really soon."

The door at the end of the hall clanged shut—not soon enough to mask his triumphant whistling.

Let him leave, I warned myself. *Do not give him a place in your mind to lurk while he's gone.*

I'd given him Rastra—a few days' journey even by the Moravens' flighty carriage rides. Once there, it would be a few days more to raid the manse when he realized I hadn't deceived him after all. Then a few more days back.

It would be enough. It had to be enough for our escape.

But for now, none of it mattered.

All that *did* matter was saving Naomi Weathers.

CHAPTER 76
SLOW DECAY

*T*AP. *TAP. TAP.*

A relentless drumbeat on the side of my head.

Tap. Tap. Tap.

Like the tick of the old clock halfway between mine and Conor's bedrooms in our childhood home.

Tap. Tap. Tap.

A familiar beat—

One. Two. Three.

Pain flared at the edges of my body, tucking itself behind my knees and into the hinges of my elbows, bracing to awaken as soon as the rest of me did. But something chased it at bay—something quiet and unrelenting and so agonizingly trapped between real and just another hallucination.

"Open your eyes, Miss Weathers. It's time we made some trouble, you and I."

Oh, I knew that voice. That challenging, satin-soft, midnight tone.

It just *figured* he wouldn't leave me to the sweet escape of sleep.

But I'd never been one to back away from a challenge. And even with the Mummer's Dance coursing through my blood...I wasn't about to start now.

Prying my tacky eyelids apart, I blinked, setting a film of dampness rippling across my vision...enough to reveal I was back in my cage. That I was flat on my back, wrapped in warmth that threatened to burn, but hadn't quite started to just yet.

And hovering above me, congealing into focus—

A hollow face with sharp-cut cheekbones. Eyes the color of a shadowed sky, sprinkled with stars. Lips slightly parted, damp and glistening as if they'd been scoured by weeping. Dark hair tousled forward instead of back, for once, half-masking the ridges of worry that lined his scarred brow.

Malakai's face, inches from mine.

Please, be real. Please, please, please, *be real this time.*

I wanted to reach up, wanted to touch him, wanted to frame that bearded jaw with my hands and push his hair back to its place on top of his head. Tell him how sorry I was for what Phineaus had put between us. And assure myself this wasn't just another twisted attack of the Mummer's Dance infiltrating my brain.

But my arms wouldn't lift, even when I willed them to; they were dead-weight at my sides. I couldn't twitch a muscle, couldn't push my legs out across his. Even the thought of movement ignited small, screaming pinpoints of agony in my joints and the hinges of my bones.

All I could do was blink—setting free tears from the corners of my eyes. They dripped and drizzled into my ears.

The grooves deepened across Malakai's forehead; his thumb swept the burning trail from beside my left eye. "I know," he rasped. "I know how badly this hurts. And it's all my doing…I broke my vow. I should never have left you."

Clearing my throat burned like shoving my arm through a tangled mess of thorns, but I couldn't choke back my voice anymore. I wouldn't. It was the only part this Luck-flipped poison hadn't taken control of.

"Why," I croaked, "why did you—?"

Ferocity flashed through his eyes; his fingers flew, gently unbinding something warm and scratchy from around me…something that smelled of fennel and pine. *His cloak.* "Spare me the questions until I'm through saving your life."

"Kai, you can't—"

"Just you rotting *watch me.*" His fingertips brushed lightly along my arms, down my sides; every press of fingertips burned like a torch. I gasped and sobbed, and his hands jerked away. "Rotting bones, it's *everywhere.*"

"It's Mummer—Mummer's—"

"I know the poison." His gaze darted over me as if he was reading one of his ledgers out of my skin. "And I brought the antidote for it."

"Phineaus searched you. You don't have anything that can help…this."

This slow decay. This dying from the inside out.

"Ah, Miss Weathers. We both know you're keener than that." A smile slashed across Malakai's mouth that didn't hold a flicker of mirth. "I didn't bring the cure on my person. Well…not precisely."

I blinked again, catching the sheen on his lips I'd thought were tears.

And all of a sudden, for the first time in *days,* I wanted to laugh.

"You…" I panted. "You brilliant, *ridiculous…*"

He planted his hands on either side of my head, leaned his full, shielding height over my poison-wracked body—and pressed his life-giving kiss to my lips.

The taste of chilled water and bitter herbs and sweet nectar exploded in my cottoned mouth, saturating every parched inch. A gasp of craving wrenched through my shriveled lungs, and when I arched with need, Malakai met it without asking; one hand seized my wrist gently, and he slipped my arm effortlessly around his neck, weaving my frail fingers into his hair.

With all the might his presence provided, I willed my fingers to curl—and finally, they behaved. Sifting silky strands of hair through the raw, stone-scuffed tips. Curling and releasing, bringing him closer. So close the shadows that cradled him and the shadows of my death mingled.

I drank down that promise of healing—of salvation—until I'd licked every drop of it from his lips. And when that small flare of vigor abandoned me like the vim before someone's last days, I crashed back down without any strength to brace myself.

Malakai swooped an arm beneath my shoulders, bearing me up before my body could make painful contact with the stone. So swift and lithe I barely felt it, he shifted me into the *much* more forgiving shelter of his lap, leaning me against his shoulder.

"There she is." His gloved fingertips carded aside the few curls that had managed to escape the mat clinging to my scalp. "It will ease soon...just breathe, you violent, terrifying troublemaker."

One fingertip at a time, I curled my fist around his collar, and held on.

Through the waves of agony. Through the fading ecstasy of the antidote's taste on my tongue. Through the relief, and the shock, and the despair that he was here—and what he must've given Phineaus after I'd faded from consciousness.

I was too weary and wasted from the poison to ask. I was too tired to keep my eyes open a second longer, sinking into the first semblance of peace I'd found since I'd woken in the dungeons that first day.

I floated. Drifted. Almost dreamed.

A groan blistered in my throat when Malakai shook me gently awake. Had it been minutes? Hours? Days? I couldn't be sure...I just knew the smell of fennel and pine and the rumble of his voice from just under my ear.

"I know you'd rather sleep," he murmured, "but the antidote should be taking effect now. And the sooner it counters the poison, the sooner we can put our brilliant minds together and find a way out of this place. Now, make fists for me, will you?"

I tried. I tried with all my might, pushing intention and command through every muscle, all the paths my blood traveled, but...

"Malakai?" I whimpered.

Nothing moved. Not even a twitch of a fingertip this time.

He was quiet for a long moment. Then a shallow, shuddering breath that spelled destruction for anyone responsible for this. "*Why isn't it working.*"

His fingers tightened around me, tugging me closer to his chest—

And everything *shattered*.

Something deep inside of me *snapped*, sheared, sundered, wrenching me doubled up in Malakai's grip. Blood spurted up my throat and spewed from my lips, a scarlet shower spraying against the stone bench.

The world tipped and whirled—Malakai, bolting his feet, spinning me with one arm so I wouldn't choke, the other hand wrenching my hair back—

Every movement, every brush of his fingers an agony. Everything fracturing, splitting when I gasped, retched, vomited again.

For a moment, a muffled, cloaking silence descended over my head. The world faded to a distant blur.

Some awful, guttural sound prodded through the tatters of my mind. Deep and croaking at first—then louder, louder, *piercing*. So sharp and anguished, I couldn't ignore it.

So deafening I couldn't understand at first that *I* was making that sound.

That it was coming from me, an endless, agonized wail tearing my throat to tatters.

I was screaming. I was screaming even though it was making me bleed, even though I could *feel* my throat erupting in a gush of thick, hot-metal blood...

I couldn't stop *screaming*.

Let me die, let me die, just make this stop*!*

Brutal light slashed through my mind, a thousand thoughts unraveling and spinning out of control all at once—

General Gryffen. He felt this when I killed him.

Jaik. Bleeding to death, alone and afraid...I wasn't in the Shastah to find him. To save him.

Malakai's family.

All of those people in Grave Dominion.

The Moravens.

My mother...

Her countenance flickered in and out of focus. Out of reach...but coming nearer.

Pain erupted through my face, tuning my screams to an ear-splitting fever pitch.

"Naomi—*Naomi*!" Malakai's voice, somehow louder than mine— "I can't fix this...I don't know how to *fix this*! Tell me how!"

He couldn't.

Neither of us could.

"I—I'm—" The hacking syllables emerged with a burble of blood.

I'm sorry.

I never meant to betray you.

I think I love you.

Hold my hand.

Did I think it? Plead it? Scream it?

All I knew was that his fingers wrapped around mine, a cage of anguish dimmer than the rest of it coursing through my body. That his lips brushed my knuckles and a slow burn spread out from them, consuming everything.

This time, when the shadows came, I didn't resist them. I fled into the darkness with open arms.

They felt like his shadows.

And I was more afraid of living for one second longer than of dying with his hand holding mine.

CHAPTER 77
ASSASSIN IN THE SHADOWS
(MALAKAI)

NAOMI WEATHERS WAS DEAD.

The thought possessed me, consumed me, *destroyed* me the moment she slumped onto the shelf, slipping out of my grip. I reclaimed my hold on her arms at once, jostling her, though I knew the pain it would inflict—because pain could bring her back to me.

But it didn't. She was utterly slack, mouth agape, eyes fallen shut.

"*No!*" The word *roared* from me, as if it had any staying might against the power of death. Slamming my hand against the bench beside her head, once, twice, three times, I dropped, burying my face in her hair, losing my next shout—and a surge of tears, the rage, the hopelessness, the guilt of my futility—in the press of a kiss to her temple. "*No, Naomi!*"

The faintest flutter of breath brushed my wrist between sleeve and glove.

An exhale. A silent vow.

The moment I wrenched back, took in her face, the blood weeping from the corners of her lips—hinges creaked. Far down the hall.

You enjoy watching her choke to death on her own blood.

He'd been waiting. Watching. Ready to gloat.

The world dipped red—the same sickly crimson as the constellation sprayed against the wall. Soaking my clothes. Dripping from her chin.

Palming the bench on either side of her head, I shoved to my feet and clapped hold of the cage bars, shaking them until their percussive rattle set my head aching.

"*What are you waiting for, Kingslayer?*" I belted the challenge down the torchlit hall. "*Get in here and finish it!*"

Stillness. Silence.

And then, all at once—absolute darkness.

All those torches snuffed out at once, with a single puff of some acrid dust that stung my nostrils, burning away the stench of blood and sweat and terror that clung to our cell.

Footsteps drummed on stone, and a man's leonine shape barreled into our cage bars, gloves snaring iron, his frame rocking against the bolted cage. "*Is she alive?*"

"Barely," I snarled. "Who—?"

"Someone who knows why the antidote didn't work." Brass rattled on brass—the report of clanking keys—which sent my pulse into an utter frenzy when the man added, "The Mummer's Dance was refashioned. Not what you would have known as a boy."

"What—?" I slipped back a step as he wrenched the cage door open, spreading my arms to shield his view of the bed.

Heedless—foolish—he barged into the cell, brushing back his hood.

Unfathomable hate and unfathomable disbelief pealed through me like death knells as Caspian Moraven shifted, peering past me at the stone shelf. At Naomi.

"Sullied souls," he rasped, "tell me I'm not too late."

He stepped nearer, and I backstepped again, keeping myself between them...as if this man who knew of Grave Dominion secrets could possibly do her more harm than his rotting nephew had already wreaked. "Keep your distance, Druavas."

His gaze snapped from her, to me, sharpening in the all-to-familiar press of a blade to my neck. "Listen to me, Malakai, she is already almost gone. If you want the cure—if you want to *save her*—you'll pick her up and follow me."

I should have hesitated.

But ask me if I did.

Tucking Naomi's arm behind my neck, I swung her up from the stone, keeping my jaw set against the trembling breath that fought its way down my throat at the limp roll of her head. At the ashen pallor of her skin. "*Where?*"

"My lair." Caspian backed from the cell, keeping his eyes on me. "Every assassin has one."

Every one of us.

Oh, a reckoning would come for this man. Swift. At the point of a venom-tipped dagger.

But for now, I had little choice but to trust, and follow.

Because Naomi had no hope at all unless I did.

CHAPTER 78
INTERLUDE

BREATHE, NAOMI.

A whisper in the shadows.
Don't be afraid.
Softness. Sinking. Safety.
Salvation.
I'm right here, troublemaker.
A prayer smelling of fennel and pine.
Just keep breathing.

One...

Two...

Three.

CHAPTER 79
COUNTING TEARS

T HE FIRST THING I knew when I woke—before pain, before softness, before anything else, even that I was alive at all—was that someone was holding my hand.

A soft, textured warmth. A permanent, bracing squeeze. There was no flex, no lessening—as if, with even the slightest change in pressure, I could just seize that gap and leap through it. To whatever came next.

Screaming, blood spraying, something inside of me rupturing—

I sucked in a swift breath, which sliced down every muscle from beneath my ribs to above my pelvis on the way down; and for the first time in longer than I knew, I left the shadows, stumbling through slow blinks and swift breaths back to the light.

Chandelier light; the old, cobweb-laced thing drifted just a bit in the recesses of an unfamiliar ceiling arched overhead. The smells of old, dusty books, peppery ink, and poultices tickled my nose into a scrunch. When I blinked—when my vision cleared more—I found the definition of bookcases beyond whatever bed I was lying on, piled with ancient tomes and loose-leaf pages.

The hand around mine dared to tighten just a bit; rolling my head against the pillows, I finally found him...with a rush of relief that dragged out all my breath at once.

Malakai perched on the bedside, gloved fingers closed around mine. His usual shadows were all gathered up around his eyes now, so deep he looked like he'd been punched—though I supposed on the left side, that *was* the case. A stark, ugly purple-black stain spread along his defined cheekbone from the bite of Phineaus's knuckles.

That hadn't been just another hallucination.

The atrium—the cage—the blood, the breaking—

I tried to shift, but a dull, throbbing pain in my lower midsection warned against it. I settled for wrapping my hand just a bit more firmly around his.

"Well, hello, you." I winced at the abraded tone of my own voice—like I'd been gargling glass.

His eyes tightened, deepening the grooves on either side; gingerly, he brought my knuckles to his mouth, pressing a featherlight kiss to them. "Hello, Naomi."

The most wearied relief wrung out his reply; it was the kind of sleepless tone I'd known too well from too many infirmaries, the exhausted gratitude that came after days and days, sometimes *weeks* of bedside vigils, when hope had been clung to so tightly that upon release, it gasped and flopped in a shriveled heap.

No one had ever said *my* name with *that* tone before.

I swallowed, and that hurt, too; Malakai watched my face for a moment, then bent past me to lift something from a bedside shelf. Water swished on porcelain, and ravenous thirst bubbled in my gut; I could barely wait for him to release my hand and support my neck, to help me sit up so I could drink.

Sweet, cool water flooded me to my innermost parts, and I moaned, flopping my head back in Malakai's hold. His grip around my nape spasmed slightly. "Must you do that?"

"Shh. I'm enjoying myself."

"That makes one of us."

I popped an eye open, taking him in more clearly with the water soaking through my desert-dry insides. More than just shadows around his eyes...he was utterly bedraggled, his hair oily and unkempt, his skin sallow. The sharpness of his cheekbones was more than just inherent now, it looked as if he hadn't been eating. And he moved...stiffly, setting the cup back on its board, settling me against the pillow and leaning one hand on the mattress beside my temple.

"How are you?" he murmured, hooking a bit of hair off my brow with his smallest finger.

I winced at the gesture; by the way the strands pulled against one another, I could feel how matted my hair was. "Like I've been asleep for a long time."

The tension tugged again around his eyes. "Nearly a week."

"*Nearly a*—?" Flipping Luck, how could it have been *that* long? "Kai, what *happened*?"

His jaw tightened, the faintest feathering at the hinge.

"The Mummer's Dance," now it was *his* turn to sound like he was chewing glass, "ruptured one of your organs. We had to bring you to a surgeon and threaten him into seeing you. He barely halted the bleeding in time."

Oh. So the blood, the agony that had sent me fleeing into the shadows—

Not a hallucination. Not some dark dream brought on by the poison…not precisely.

"At least tell me it was one of the ones I can live without." Though those were precious few, I'd performed enough surgeries to know that there were organs that *could* rupture and those that *never should*.

Flint-dark eyes flicked up to mine. "You're still here, aren't you?"

I set my breath free, settling back more deeply into the pillows. "I take it you kept me sedated?"

"To expedite the healing. As well as…"

He broke off, rocking back upright, his hand sliding down to brace beside my opposite hip; the bend of his arm across my body was almost protective, but the amalgamation of emotions playing in his face was impossible to define.

"To spare me the pain?" I ventured.

The corner of his mouth jerked, a tremble passing over his lips. "I have never heard…*anyone* scream for death the way you did."

And he was an assassin.

I toyed with the edge of the bedspread—genuine silk, likely imported. The real stuff. "I'm sorry if that frightened you."

He pinched the crease of his nose, eyes squeezing shut. "Please tell me that you are not *apologizing* for anything that happened in the throes of your near-demise."

"I can accept I couldn't control myself *and* be sorry you had to see it," I argued. "I…I know what it's like to watch someone die of that poison when you *despise* them. I can't imagine what it's like when you…"

I trailed off. Swallowed.

Malakai's eyes flashed back to mine; this time, he didn't look away. And the longer we stared at one another, the heavier the weight became…the less I could mask it behind the cavalier of a healer's training.

I had nearly died. *Things* had ruptured inside of me. I'd been vomiting blood, screaming in pain, begging for death. That poison had undone me to the last inch, until I'd fled toward my demise rather than fighting against it.

Phineaus had almost killed me—and Malakai had almost been forced to watch, helpless to mend it. A double-edged blade of vengeance rammed through both our chests.

He'd twisted us so *perfectly* against each other. He'd played us off one another like well-used gamepieces. And we'd both fallen into it so completely, I didn't quite understand how we weren't rotting in the dungeons still.

I just knew we hadn't gotten out because of *me.*

A trickle of heat scoured my cheek. Then another. Malakai frowned, shifting nearer to me. "Are you in pain?"

"No, I'm flipping *furious* with Phineaus. And with myself." I sniffed and scoffed, scrubbing viciously at the itching tip of my nose. "Why are you looking at me like that?"

"Counting these." He brushed a stray tear away with two fingers. "So that I know how many cuts to kill him by."

"No...Kai, these aren't for him. These are for *me.*"

Oh, there it goes. Now that those first words had tumbled out—now that he blinked, and regarded me with that careful look in his eyes—I wasn't about to stop.

"I lied to you for months," I rambled. "I learned how to dilute your poisons, to put the members of Grave Dominion to sleep instead of killing them. And then Phineaus was dragging them off somewhere, I don't know...maybe Thrasmund, maybe to some lair of his own. They're not even *dead*, Malakai, not most of them. And it's because of *me*, because I became this twisted servant of Grave Domin- ion...and I am so sorry. For all of it." Bracing a hand to my aching midsection, I added softly, "I didn't know how to trust you, at the beginning. And by the time I did...it was too late."

Malakai listened without moving, without so much as blinking. When I was silent again, his eyes slid away from me, fixing across the room—then tumbling shut. The prominent arch of his throat rolled with a few swallows; he stretched and rolled his head, loosening a kink from his stooped neck.

Then he said, "That doesn't matter."

I blinked. Rubbed the heel of my hand over my ear. "I'm sorry...are you answering me, or talking to yourself again?"

"The rotting plan doesn't *matter.*" Ferocity fletched every word...a convic- tion he was maybe cladding around himself, syllable by syllable. But when his gaze snapped back to me, sincerity gleamed in those adamant eyes. "It was a bare sketch in desperate need of refinement. Otherwise, how could a Mithran healer have put so many cracks in it?"

"Kai. Don't try to make me feel less awful than I should. I *betrayed* you." The words tasted like ash...worse than the slick slide of my own blood on my tongue. "I *was* sent here, to the Moravens, to find you. To turn you over to them."

I'd gone to the verge of unraveling myself out of loyalty to my friends, time and time again. Knowing I'd betrayed one—that I'd betrayed *him*—made me feel like a stranger to myself.

"The woman fleeing from her fate, from her shame, yes. Yes, she betrayed me," Malakai said with that bluntness I adored—and that drove me absolutely mad. "And I don't need her help anymore. But the poisoner who killed for her future Sha, whose only regret was that she abandoned him after…will *she* still help me?"

Help him—to bring down Grave Dominion. To put right the mistakes I'd made. To put a stop to Phineaus's schemes.

Whatever he meant by it, my answer was just the same: "Without one single flipping *second* of hesitation."

Something dark and decadent swirled in Malakai's gaze, and he tipped his head, inclining toward me, his focus fixed on my lips—

Iron chuffed on stone, and we both leaned away at the same moment—Malakai with a low curse, me with a small flare of relief that the first time I'd taste his lips after my near-death wasn't with my hair itching like it was full of spiders and my body reeking in ways I was just now becoming fully conscious of.

But I forgot all of it—betrayal, and vows, and reeking, and kissing him—when the last person I'd ever expected to share breathing space with us strode around a bend in the bookcases and halted in the chandelier's dim glow.

"Oh, sullied souls—thank the *grave* she's awake."

"*Caspian?*" I sputtered—then wrenched my gaze to Malakai. Maskless. Watching the Druavas with predatory intent as he shucked off his own gloves and approached the bedside.

"Well, she recognizes me…mark in favor of no persistent addling." Caspian flashed both palms my way like I might try to bite them off at the wrists. "The question is, does she remember the pair of you are married?"

"*What?*" I whipped my focus to Malakai.

"The Druavas thinks he has *jokes*," Malakai remarked stiffly, his focus never deviating as Caspian halted at the bedside and drew a stool from around the base of it.

"I'll have you know, I'm absolutely filthy with humor." Caspian's smile lacked any real mirth, but there was no wanting for warmth in his eyes when he offered his hand, palm still upraised. "May I?"

Completely mystified—and just now realizing how much I'd missed his careless humor and gentle gaze—I surrendered my hand to his; he brushed up my sleeve, and for the first time I noticed I wasn't wearing the tattered, soiled sleepshirt and billowy pants that had barely kept me warm in the dungeon; the overlarge, pine-green shirt that tumbled beneath my collarbones, so well-made it was almost achingly soft...

I pressed my nose briefly to my shoulder; beneath my own stench lingered a hint of fennel and pine.

Cozying back against the pillows, I watched Caspian inspect my arm, as high as my shoulder; then he tugged a bit of the front collar down, ignoring the bass clearing of Malakai's throat while he examined my sternum and clavicles.

"What are you doing here?" I asked quietly—a weak effort to soothe the tension climbing the cracks of this room.

"You're in *my* lair," he said, a hint of teasing fletching the words as he moved his assessment to my neck and throat.

"The Druavas freed us from the dungeon after Phineaus departed Fortress Ferregrand," Malakai added stiffly.

There was the faintest tremble to Caspian's fingers when he peeled down my eyelids, one after the other. Then a soft breath rushed from him, fanning the bitter scent of coffee brew across my nose, and he fell back on his seat. "It worked."

"What worked?" I demanded.

"The antidote to the Mummer's Dance." Caspian smiled again, this one shaken with relief—but far more genuine. "You'll be weak and woozy for a while yet, but you should make a full recovery in time."

"And the risk of infection?" Malakai demanded—before I could even fully catch up to the fact that *Caspian Moraven* knew the cure for a strain of Mummer's Dance that had fooled Malakai and me—and that he was hiding us *here*, in a lair to which he had access—

"I'd say nominal, given how the last week has gone." Caspian eased the blanket down and rolled up the hem of the shirt that fell along my thighs; his fingertips traced over the dull center of pain just along my hipbones. "She's had the strongest course of herbs known to poisoners, not to mention how well I packed the wound. If she were going to show signs of illness, we would've seen them by now."

"Good." Malakai's tone brittled. "Then we've run out of use for you."

The words had just pierced my mind—horror filling in their wake—when Malakai surged across the bed. Both hands wrapped around Caspian's fancy lapels, and with a full-bodied *shove*, Malakai hurled him into the workbench near the bed.

A scream popped through my lips at the smash of breaking beakers and the *crunch* of bone on wood. Caspian barked with agony, but Malakai was heedless, throwing him flat on his back and plucking a knife from across Caspian's hip.

The moment the brutal edge caught the chandelier's glow, a bit of strength poured back into my veins. I shoved myself up in the pillows. "Malakai, what are you *doing*?"

"What I've always done: removing an assassin in a seat of power." Malakai didn't budge an inch, knife in fist, flattening Caspian down on the worktable. "The Druavas is a member of Grave Dominion."

CHAPTER 80
THE TWO-FACED COIN

MY BREATH RETREATED TO the bottoms of my lungs in one sharp, ripping intake. I held it captive there, frozen, silent—waiting for Caspian to call Malakai mad, to beg for his life, to try to squirm free of that murderous grip.

He didn't do...any of that.

He slumped back on his elbows against the worktable, tossing his gray-streaked hair from his eyes. "I wondered if you put that piece together. It didn't seem like it, when you didn't mention it this past week."

"The only reason you are experiencing the privilege of drawing breath in my presence is because I had use for you." Malakai's stiff lips barely cringed around the words. "And that use is ended."

The blade reared back, then dropped, a silver slice severing the cords that held *me* rigid with horrified disbelief.

"Malakai, *stop*!"

He froze, the tip of his blade kissing Caspian's neck. It was several seconds before he ground out a retort: "*What*, troublemaker?"

"Phineaus wanted me dead, and you captured. Caspian set us free and cured me." I shuffled the blanket off, pushing myself by increments to the edge of the bed—bracing my abdomen with one hand, just to be safe. "Two men! Two members of Grave Dominion, doing opposite things! Don't you think there must be something more to this than we're seeing? Something we can *use*?"

"You might want to listen to her," Caspian hedged, his eyes nearly crossed as he stared down the blade balanced at this throat. "Isn't that why you wanted to keep her around?"

"My reasons for keeping Naomi alive are *none of your concern*!"

"But *his* reasons are *mine*," I countered. "Leave him *alone*, Malakai. I want to hear this."

For some of the longest heartbeats of my life, none of us moved. None of us really breathed. Because none of us knew what would happen next.

And then it happened...something I had never thought possible before the moment in the atrium when his mask had fallen to the floor. But now it had happened *twice*.

For the second time, Malakai Kane surrendered a kill for my sake.

The knife eased back. He spat the word, honed like a shard of broken mosaic glass: "*Talk.*"

The breath rushed out of my lungs, and I sagged a bit—then shook my head when Malakai darted a glance my way.

It wasn't likely I possessed the strength to interfere if he'd chosen vengeance over common sense this time. Thank *Luck* for whatever it was that made him listen to me.

"You heard him," I added to Caspian, keeping my voice low and brittle. Best if he knew he didn't really have an ally in this room yet...just a curious benefactor at best.

"Malakai is right. I *am* a member of Grave Dominion." Caspian pressed a fingertip to the point of the blade, shifting it away from the dip of his throat. "And, much like the Poet Poisoner, I've been a catalyst for its downfall."

"Not from where I'm standing," Malakai scoffed.

"Then *move.*"

The two men glared at one another, heating the air like water boiled for bandages—full of all the same bitter curatives and stripping agents. It was comically—and corrosively—too much like my brothers arguing over broken wooden swords.

As in, *what is the point of this pissing match*?

"Malakai, give him space to breathe, for Luck's sake," I groaned, and after a hesitant moment he pulled back, pitching himself against the edge of the bookcase adjacent to the worktable. "Caspian? You're getting on *my* nerves, too."

"Souls forbid." He arched up on both hands splayed out behind him, keeping a wary eye on Malakai as he scooted himself back to sit on the edge of the worktable. "What more can I say? I've been working for years to unravel Grave Dominion from inside its ranks."

And all at once, with those earnest words, several things made sense.

The antidote he'd given me. This lair he'd brought us to. Even the way he had taken me under his arm—quite literally—when I'd arrived, nudging me by gentle thrusts down the path to meet the Poet Poisoner.

Not only to save his family, but...

"You're playing both sides of Luck's two-faced coin," I breathed. "You're trading secrets from the inside. Working against Grave Dominion when they think you're one of them."

"That isn't possible," Malakai seethed, knuckles creaking over the knife.

"My father may just be the most paranoid man who's ever lived," Caspian scoffed. "Worse than my sister's husband, and given what sort of trouble Tobyrus has kicked up for his country, that's saying *quite a bit.*" Disappointment flared across his eyes when they cut to Malakai. "Do you really think he never caught a whiff of an assassin's guild with its eye on his title? Why do you think he's never abdicated, when he's so old and feeble a strong breeze could blow him over?"

"He knew it would lead to all of this, didn't he?" I demanded. "Exactly what's happening...a grab for power."

Caspian nodded. "He was well aware that unless Grave Dominion was dealt with in his lifetime, a war would break out when power traded hands. It's always been his greatest fear. So he's been preparing for it...for decades now."

I smoothed both hands down my warm cheeks. It was almost too much to fathom—having learned the intricacies of Grave Dominion for myself less than a fortnight ago, and now to realize how deep and *tangled* this web of assassins and power-mongering ran—

"Keep speaking," Malakai growled, setting the knife twirling over his fingers, "or I'll start slicing."

"All right, all right." A deep breath, and then Caspian murmured, "All three of us—Serai, Callie, and I—we were trained for particular purposes, to face specific challenges. Serai, to rule, of course...and to ferret out supplanters from the old clans who hide away in the mountains. Callie, he shipped away to mitigate the possibility of a threat from Mithra-Sha and their Storycrafters. And I...I was turned loose with Grave Dominion."

My heart clenched like a fist, and twisted so painfully I sucked back a whimper.

I couldn't even *imagine* that life. Children, born and raised like soldiers, set apart for specific—and deadly—purposes. We'd always known in Mithra-Sha that Calten had been shuffled off to us by her father...and maybe we were just Luck-loved that she'd fallen into blissful marriage with Tobyrus instead of remaining a spy for her family. That certainly explained why they disliked her so much.

Another thought seeded and took root so quickly, I didn't have a chance to snip it at the bud.

Were the Moravens really so different from Grave Dominion—also raising and training children like Malakai and his siblings to dole out their own retributions?

Malakai seemed to be knitting the same thoughts together; the look he pinned Caspian with now was bled dry of resentment. There was something else nudging its way into his guarded expression, tracing familiar lines beside his eyes.

Comprehension. Maybe even kinship.

"You infiltrated them," he said, slowly.

"When I was little more than a boy." A grim smile cut across Caspian's face. "It was easy enough to convince them of my intentions...people craving a power they're deprived of tend to look for others with the same complaints, to build a new power of their own. And what was I? The third child, a tool for my family at best, a bit of extra padding between them and their detractors at worst. I begged Grave Dominion to make me something more."

"You've been doing this for *decades*?" I murmured.

"That I have." Grimacing, he rubbed the side of his neck. "What I didn't expect was for the Grave to realize they couldn't fulfill all of their desires through me. So they decided to keep me as an informant against my family...and they moved on to another ruler."

"Phineaus." Malakai's gaze sharpened. "How long have you known?"

"Not long," Caspian admitted. "My list of contacts, like the rest of Grave's, is incomplete...it never included Phineaus's name, and his schooling in Thrasmund left nothing to be doubted. That truly is where many of the elite receive their lessons, whether the Grave snatches them up or not...best academies in the country, and all that." A deprecating smile flashed across his lips, harkening to some storied history that was better left to tale-turned minds like Addie's. "But I had some concerns...suspicions, I suppose, when I saw how well you kept to your pattern with Corylus's death, Malakai. It made me realize you *hadn't* changed, not really. Corylus was one of us, after all. But I didn't let myself grasp that notion...not until Phin disappeared to Rastra. Then I couldn't stop thinking of how fiercely he'd tried to convince us that the attack against him countered the Poet Poisoner's code. I sat with that long enough that I realized he must know something more about what that code truly *was*...which is something only Grave Dominion should have been aware of."

"The true connection between the victims." I glanced sidelong at Malakai; his face paled slightly.

"Precisely." Caspian swallowed. "Once I allowed the idea that *Phineaus* knew what linked the deaths, so many pieces fell into place. The patterns of his absence, the timing of his return with my father's forthcoming abdication, the attack against him...and I realized the precise moment he became their favorite gamepiece." His gaze fixed on Malakai, shaded with weariness. "It was when your family and the Nassars fled. I never thought the informant who turned against them could be my own flesh and blood, or I would have put a stop to it long ago."

Malakai's grip shivered around the knife. "You knew what they did to us."

"I more than knew." Caspian shook his head slowly. "I tried to stop it."

I blinked. Malakai straightened, lips peeling back from his gritted teeth around a single bladed word. "*What?*"

"I sent a ciphered missive, warning them that the Grave was aware of their plans to desert. I thought I'd given them enough time to get out, but someone—Phineaus, I assume—must've intercepted it. And then he decided it was time to set things in motion, beginning with Cerene."

"Yes," Malakai said softly. "He did."

This silence hung heavy with something we all knew—witnesses and secret-keepers alike. The fate that had fallen on Malakai's family, on the Nassars. The absolute bloodbath that had begun all of this pain and tragedy, leading us to this room, to be together now.

Victims of Phineaus. Victims of the Grave.

"I thought it might be you," Caspian added quietly. "Ever since the first killings. I remembered you differently from the others, I suppose...they saw a born assassin shedding criminal blood in Thrasmund, but I remembered a kid with a love for poetry." Malakai shifted his weight; I swallowed a sharp, needling pain in my throat. "I've been diverting suspicion as much as I can, keeping the sentinels turning circles and distracting Grave Dominion with false trails and theories. It's why I volunteered to handle things when Corylus turned up dead...I was concerned that after the attempt you made with Phin, you'd gotten sloppy enough that someone would be able to trace it to you."

Malakai's jaw shifted. "Until then, I was *exceptionally* careful."

"That you were." A hint of a smile touched the corner of Caspian's smile—then vanished again. "But I'm afraid all of that is behind us now...when Phineaus returns and realizes you're both gone, he's likely to suspect me. I have a sense, given some of our conversations over the years, that he's been aware all this time of my status with the Grave...even when I wasn't told of his."

"Then you're on the run from them," I murmured. "Just like we are."

"So it would appear."

Malakai and I traded a glance; he gave the subtlest shake of his head, but I didn't return it. I stared him down, waiting.

Because the Poet Poisoner wasn't a fool. With his true face known, he wouldn't be able to stay quite as many steps ahead of Grave Dominion. And when Caspian's loyalties became known, he wouldn't be safe, either.

I had come here to stop a poisoner from destroying the Moraven rulership—and that was precisely what I was going to do.

"Phineaus isn't going to stop until every Moraven above him in rank is dead." I grimaced at Caspian's subtle flinch. "He made that abundantly clear to me...he wasn't even the least bit regretful about it. So we can't afford to be, either."

"A handful of days to reach Rastra," Malakai said, his eyes fixed on mine, "several more to go through my things there. And another handful to return."

"Where does that leave us?" Caspian wondered aloud.

"With a week left at most to come up with a way to trap Phineaus," I said, "and put an end to his scheme once and for all."

CHAPTER 81
HANDS THAT BREAK, HANDS THAT HEAL

I T WAS A DISCUSSION we had to have—and one, it turned out, that none of us were ready for just yet.

Caspian refused to pursue the matter without a good night's sleep and a hearty brew of coffee in him; to my surprise, Malakai allowed him that, allowed him to shuffle off into he recesses of the lair while he sheathed his knife and approached me at the bedside. "I am available for whatever you need."

The words were already on my lips before he'd even finished speaking: "A *bath*, please, thank Luck."

"There's a washroom." Malakai nodded to a corridor mouth yawning between a pair of bookcases—then watched quietly as I bent, cradling my twinging middle with one hand, measuring the distance I would have to walk—and dreading every possible step.

"Would you help me?" I whispered.

Something flared in the depths of his eyes—then shuttered behind a blink, a deft dip of his head.

There was something different in the way he took hold of me, wrapping an arm around my waist and pulling the other around his shoulders. But possibly the tilt of his hold only felt strange because I had expected him to carry me, like he had after the Jubilee.

Still, he took the brunt of my weight, and we made our way down the hall to the not-entirely-unimpressive washroom; though there were no windows letting in light on the way to it—or within—but Malakai helped me settle against the wall and lit a cluster of candles in the corner, their rich currents of molten wax cascading in pink swaths over the floor.

Perhaps Caspian had lit those candles for the souls he'd killed as a necessity to keep his cover with Grave Dominion all these years.

My head still reeled with that revelation while I took in the rest of the room: stone lined with brassy pipes, a sink stand set against one wall and a clawfoot tub beneath a pattern of mosaic tiles that decorated the opposite side. The tiles depicted a vague imitation of a forest in pinks and blues and greens, marbled with black webbing.

I loved it instantly.

"Where *is* this place?" I trudged to the corner soapstand, peering at the various bricks and bottles there while Malakai crouched beside the tub, fiddling with its pumps and levers.

"Still in Amalgard, but belowground." Malakai's reply suffered slightly under the ear-aching *squeak* of the neglected faucet handles. The resulting shudder, burp, and gargle of water chugging through disused pipes had us both wincing, flashing one another sheepish half-smiles.

But when the water guttered out into the tub, I forgot the pain in my ears and every other part of me. The only thing that mattered was tossing myself into that steaming water as expediently as possible.

"Eyes closed," I warned; with a sigh and a groan, Malakai lowered his face into the crook of his elbow, braced on the tub's glazed edge. I hastily shucked off the shirt—his shirt—and the underclothes—his bedshorts; then I paused to take stock of what I could see.

The varicosity was gone from my veins, thank Luck...the poison had receded, just as Caspian had claimed. But there were bruises everywhere, splotched across my arms and legs, my abdomen; I looked like I'd been beaten, like a soldier at the city infirmary or like one of the men and women I'd helped escape from violent abuses at home after they'd come to me with injuries they couldn't quite explain. Or were too frightened to.

Phineaus had marked me without hardly lifting a hand. He'd given me scars to remember him by.

And to think I'd once been so worried about this mission, the same sort of marks on *him*.

Trembling with disgust, I snatched a foaming soap from Caspian's bath rack and poured a generous dollop into the water; then, bracing my middle, I slid a leg over the tub's edge—pausing with a caught breath when pain wracked through my nerves, flaring like a sunburst across the span of my midsection.

Without so much as a blink in my direction, Malakai offered a hand; throat tight with gratitude, I welcomed the aid, clambering over the edge and slipping into the tub where I sank beneath the foam.

I had to bite my palm to muffle the moan of pleasure that surged in my throat as the bubbles closed around my chest. *Luck*, I had missed bathing...I had never let myself go more than two days without *some* form of washing, three at the most in the most desperate times, ever since I was a girl. Now there were weeks of grime caked on my body, turning the bathwater murky almost as soon as I slid beneath the surface.

"Ugh," I muttered, and Malakai's head popped up from his arm. "Excuse me! Did I say you could look?"

"You can hardly make sounds of disgust and expect me to..."

He trailed off, his gaze taking in my bruised arms spread against the edges of bath, bracing myself so I wouldn't plunge up to my chin beneath the water. Fury shattered across the surface of his eyes, and his fingers curled around the faucet tap until the fastening creaked.

Grimacing, I stretched forward inch by inch and pried his grip off the handle. "Breaking Caspian's things—not advised."

"I am going to *kill him*."

"I know." Phineaus, not Caspian. Still, the words needled around my skin. "Malakai, would you do something for me?"

His gaze still traced my wounds above the water. "I thought I'd made it obvious I will do almost *anything* for you."

My stomach lunged at that, then fluttered back down to its resting place; I wished those words only brought giddiness, instead of ushering in the reminder of what he'd given up for me.

Rastra. All his plans. That beautiful manse I'd come to love, that vault he treasured so much. Everything that put him a step ahead of Grave Dominion and everything he held onto that helped him still be *Malakai*.

I shook my head, rattling that thought away. "Could you please look at me and see *me*—not another vengeance to pay Phineaus back for?"

Malakai blinked, leaning back on his knees; the play of emotion in his tightening mouth and the widening of his eyes was like nothing I'd seen from him before. I couldn't possibly begin to define it.

"I *do* see you, troublemaker," he murmured; then he caught my hand off the knob, pressing a swift kiss to my knuckles. "Forgive me."

I wasn't certain whether he meant for this, or...for all of it.

I slid forward and touched my lips to his, just to address every possibility; Malakai startled a squeak from me with his fingers tangled in a fistful of hair, drawing me nearer, his lips pressing more firmly against mine.

It reminded me for a furious, flagrant instant of when he'd tried to kiss me back to life in that dungeon—the *only* pleasant memory from the whole sordid affair.

With a teasing nip to his lower lip, I pulled free; Malakai hung against the edge of the tub, fixing me with a look that absolutely *burned*.

"That, you can't do," he growled. "You can't kiss me while you're in the bath, in this state."

"This state?" I pointed to my bruise-freckled arm. "Or *this* state?" Biting back a wicked grin, I gestured a hand to the length of me, hidden beneath the ashy water and foam.

"As usual, with you, it's both." He rocked back from the tub, rising to his feet. "What sort of shampoo do you prefer?"

Hiding a smug smile behind the bubbles, I offered a small consolation prize: "Surprise me."

And he really did: of the variety of soaps the posh Druavas kept on hand, Malakai chose one infused with cucumber water and flecks of mint. The full-bodied, faintly peppery scent smelled like cleanliness itself. When I lathered it between my fingers, my senses sparkled with the relief of escaping my own stench.

Heart thudding with the water's heat, I tangled my woozy, soap-slathered fingers in my hair; but my weakened body rebelled against the particular angles required to address the hopeless matting, a position that leached the strength from my arms in seconds. It felt as if I was running with a full healer's pack held over my head; heaviness wound down my shoulders, curled around the backs of my biceps, and almost deadened my fingertips.

"Um." I chewed my lower lip. "Malakai, if—would you mind—?"

He stayed me with gentle fingers around my wrists, lowering my arms gently back to the water and tucking them around me as he pressed a kiss behind my ear. "Must you ask?"

A snide retort died on my lips with the first stroke of his fingers against my scalp; I ducked my head, the tip of my nose brushing bath foam, and shut my eyes as he worked the layer of grime from my skin. As he reached the places I couldn't, and chiseled away the marks of hurt hidden there.

It was quiet work, so oddly intimate I didn't dare break it with jokes or conversation. Every now and again, Malakai cupped handfuls of water over my shoulder and upper back, then returned to his work—untangling, scraping, cleansing. Removing so much evidence of where poor choices and secrets—ours and others'—had brought us.

It took more than an hour—so long I tugged the drain pipe stopper up with my toes, let out a bit of the cool water, and refilled it with fresh and warm while Malakai worked carefully over my hair. Then, finally, just when I'd started to drift—when the steam from the tub dulled my senses—Malakai's hand slid beneath my chin from behind. He tilted my head back against the dip of his shoulder, his fingertips grazing down the arch of my throat, his palm resting over my heat-thrummed heart.

"Finished," he murmured, searching my eyes. Water ran in soapy rivulets from his fingertips, beading down my chest, into the water.

"Thank you." I let my eyes fall shut, stretched up to find his mouth—and winced, breath catching a bit as the lines of my abdomen pulled taut. A reminder not to move certain ways too swiftly.

Boots snickered on stone; Malakai lurched up, away from me, my eyes snapping back open to find him retreating. He scoured his arm against his nose and mouth, then shook his head fiercely. "Finish your bath."

He all but stumbled to the standing sink in the corner, cranking it on and shoving his sleeves up to his elbows. But he didn't wash; he braced his forearms on the edges and bent over the stream of water, head hanging. A violent shudder rollicked down the lines of his back.

Alarm bolted through me, and I pushed myself up carefully against the curve of the tub. "Malakai?"

"Finish your *bath*." The words cracked, staggering from a command to a plea.

Oh, not a chance in flipping Luck.

Tugging myself from the bath—hating how woozy the heat had rendered me on top of the weakness I already felt—I lashed a towel around myself, tucked it beneath my arm, and padded to the sink. "There, I'm finished. What's wrong?"

His head swayed up just enough to catch my eyes for a brief moment in the reflection of the rose-glass mirror; then it bobbed low again. "You're in pain."

"You're saying that like it's new." I forced a chuckle, circling to his side with one hand on his back. "I've been in pain, but I'm healing. I—"

"Your suffering is my doing."

"What—just now? No, I moved the wrong way, it had nothing to do with you."

"*Don't.*" He shrugged off my hand. "You shouldn't...it was me."

My rebellious fingers curled into a fist in the folds at the back of his shirt. "Malakai, you're not making sense. *What* was you?"

"It. Was. *Me.*" Every word carved out of him like the point of his own knife, his shoulders scaling down and inward. "You broke when *I* held you. When I tried to move you. You made a sound just like that, before you started screaming."

Oh.

Oh.

I swallowed a prickle of my own discomfort at the memory, leaning low, pressing my cheek to his stooped shoulder. "You didn't know. You couldn't have known how near I was to breaking." A shaky laugh crawled from my throat. "*I* didn't know, and it was my own body...I've lived a good portion of my life in it, you know?"

The heel of his hand reared back and then crunched the edge of the washbasin with a sickening snap. "This is *not* something to make light of."

No. He was right. Not because of what he'd done...but because of what it was doing to him.

He was in no state for jokes.

I reached around him, gently tapping the faucets off. Then I took his forearms and pulled him around to face me, stroking my thumbs over his wrists. "Malakai. I'm not afraid of you."

"Perhaps that's a mistake." The words weren't envenomed—in fact, they were dangerously near to fracturing. He didn't lift his gaze from my grip on his wrists. "These are the hands that broke you."

"These," I kissed every one of his fingers at the first knuckle, "are the hands that carried me out of the dungeons that was supposed to be my tomb. These," I slid my nails gently up his wrists, his forearms, to his shoulders, "are the arms that held me together when I was falling apart. And *this*," I laid my palm over his shuddering chest, "is the heart that brought you back to find me."

His face dropped into my hair. "I should never have left. I am...sorry beyond what words can say, troublemaker. I don't even know how to ask for your forgiveness."

"Kai, it's already forgiven. I wanted you to go," I reminded him. "I never wanted Phineaus to have *either* of us, but...especially you."

His breath shuddered against my damp curls. "I broke my vow. I let him take you back to that place."

"Then make a new one." I rested my chin against my knuckles, my hand still braced over his heart. "Never again?"

"*Never* again," he echoed with a toe-curling adamancy. "Never, Naomi."

We were quiet with that for a time—my face resting over his chest, his in my hair, the steam soaking into our skin. Malakai was the first to draw away this time, grazing a kiss to my temple as he slipped past me.

"Get dressed."

I was more than happy to oblige, sliding back into his shirt and undershorts and toweling the ends of my hair; but when I was cozy and dressed, turning to find him again, he was slumped on the stool in the corner with his head in his hands.

Slowly, I strung the towel over a hook beside the wall, then joined him. Stroking my fingers through the hair at his temples, I eased his head back until his weary eyes found mine; in the dimming candlelight, the depth of the shadows below them struck me like a wild blow from a patient emerging out of a drugged stupor.

"When did you last sleep?" I demanded.

A quiet scoff. "Sleep—and leave you alone in the care of Grave Dominion? I think not."

"You must have slept *sometime* this past week. You're still lucid."

A faint lift and slump of his shoulders. "I dozed here and there, when he was gone. When it couldn't be avoided." His gaze strayed to the mosaic tiles. "It...has not come easily. I'm not often given to nightmares, my line of work simply won't allow for me to carry terrors from waking to sleeping. But ever since that rotting dungeon..."

I had never wanted to murder someone so badly as I wanted to kill Phineaus Moraven with my bare hands right then—not even the one man I'd actually *killed*.

Every moment seemed to reveal new depths of his brilliant treachery. What he'd subjected us both to beneath Fortress Ferregrand had broken us so precisely, whole armies could've learned strategies from it.

Thank Luck, my life was built around fixing what was broken—inside and out. And with us, I knew where to start.

So I laced my fingers between Malakai's, leading him up to his feet and toward the door. "Come here."

We slipped back out into the heart of the lair—which I could see now was a rotunda of sorts with a recess for the bed, the bookcases pulled away from the walls just enough that a body could slip between the curve of the stone and the back of the shelf. To peruse for more books and papers, maybe...or to duck for cover if the wrong person entered.

Caspian could've been lurking anywhere, but the lair was silent apart from the cheery flicker of flames in the chandelier as I led Malakai to the bed and shoved him down onto it; he fell in a sprawl of propped elbows and bent knees, frowning up at me. "What is this?"

"It's you, sleeping." I crawled in next to him, tugging the blanket over my hips. "And it's me sleeping, too."

He held very still as I snuggled my back against his side; only once I'd settled did he mutter, "This is not precisely proprietary."

"So tell Caspian to report us to the sentinel watch," I yawned; the embrace of the pillow and the softness of the blanket were already finishing the work of the warm bath. I'd never craved sleep so much in my life.

After several long moments full of silent debate, Malakai eased on his side, his chest to my back. One arm slid carefully around my waist, as if he was waiting for me to break—for the screaming to start again.

Gnawing the corner of my lip, I rested a hand over his where it dangled before my stomach, tracing the ridges of his taut knuckles with my fingertips. "Do you want to tell me about it?" I ventured. "I don't really remember much. It's all a bit of a bloodstained blur."

He snorted at my very weak attempt at humor, then fell quiet for several long moments.

"You said...many things just before you fell unconscious." His throat bobbed audibly. "You pleaded for death. Apologized. You begged me to hold your hand."

His fingers wound through mine, pressing our hands together over the lateral scar that bisected my lower abdomen.

"I'm sorry you had to hear all of that," I whispered.

"There are plenty of things I'd much rather hear." He tucked his face against the back of my shoulder, his warm breath whispering along the side of my neck, crawling down to my clavicles, fanning across my chest.

It was a strange, *delicious* relief to have my hands behave this time when I tucked one backward, sinking into the soft strands of his unkempt hair. I shifted in increments, glancing back at him with his head still cradled against the arch of my shoulder. "Whatever you want to hear me say, I'll say it."

"You've said enough for today." His lips grazed my eyelids, then the tip of my nose. "Sleep, Naomi. Tomorrow we make enough trouble to send this country to its knees."

And we would just have to hope it had the strength to straighten up again.

It was a handful of heartbeats before I drifted on the cusp of sleep, my endurance tested by the heat of the bath and the comfort of Malakai's body curled around mine. He'd relaxed, too, his head heavy in the crook of my neck and shoulder, his arm loose around my waist as he tucked me back against him.

And just as I took that blissful step from awake to asleep, surrendering to the fantastical precipice where thoughts turned to dreams, a quiet, night-dark whisper took my hand and guided me over the edge:

"*I love you, too.*"

CHAPTER 82
AMBUSH

WE WERE DIFFERENT PEOPLE in the morning.

No more time for sweet-smelling baths and bodies snuggled together in a too-small bed; I knew it the moment I woke from dreamless sleep, a sharpened awareness pricking at the edges of my mind.

I'd slept long enough. I'd let Phineaus make a liability of me for *too long*.

It was time to work.

I crept out before Malakai started to stir, changing behind the shelves into a shirt and skirt Caspian had left folded on the worktable for me...retrieved, it looked like, from the closet of my old room in Fortress Ferregrand. A subtle hint that he was still playing the part of the gregarious Druavas even as his family crumbled around him.

Finally dressed in ways that felt so much more like *me*, I followed the rich, nutty scent of brewed beans and poured two steaming mugs of coffee from a steel pot set on the mantel of the lair's only hearth. My heart wrenched with regret when I filled the plain stoneware cups...no glaze, no decoration to them whatsoever.

Fitting for this place. But I missed the manse, its kitchens, its rooms. I missed our routine there.

"Feeling better?" Caspian's voice drifted in before the rest of him, emerging through one of the lair's two arched doorways; one led the washroom. The one he stepped through, dusting a fine sprinkling of snow off his shoulders and ruffling it from his hair, clearly led outside.

"Much." I handed him one mug of coffee, then poured another. "And you?"

A sigh heaved through him as he shed his cloak. "Let's not make this a matter of feelings for me, because I *feel* as if I'm walking to my own execution. Or willfully laying my heart on a table and asking someone to stick a knife into it."

I leaned back against the hearth for a moment, clinking my nails against my coffee mug. "You love Phineaus, he's your nephew. That kind of lifelong love doesn't go away overnight."

"No, it certainly does not." A painful smile plunged into the rim of his mug. "And it also doesn't change what must be done."

The necessity of which prodded me across the room, to the bed; I kicked the foot of it gently, jolting Malakai upright with a slice of drowsy eyes, and met his glower with upraised mugs. "I brought coffee."

"Your saving merit," he muttered, accepting one from me—and leaning forward to steal a brush of lips before he swung his long legs off the bed, alert as if he'd never slept.

But at least, cranky as he was, it was a sign of his strength returning. He hadn't stirred once all night long; and he was the picture of shadowed grace as he reclined against the corner of the nearest bookcase while Caspian and I slid in at the worktable.

"So," Caspian began, "the problem of Phineaus and Grave Dominion. How to solve it."

"Killing them all comes to mind," Malakai offered mildly, sipping his coffee.

"Yes, but *how*?" Caspian shot back. "Lines of poetry penned with poisoned ink won't do the deed anymore...yes, I know about your little trick," he added when Malakai and I both stiffened. "One of the many things I've been guiding the Grave away from considering over the years."

Malakai's jaw worked for a moment, chewing over the revelation that he hadn't be quite as hidden as he'd thought, even before I'd winnowed into his life; I sidestepped his shock, addressing Caspian instead: "Three of us against a whole guild of assassins won't work, either."

"Very true." He curved one arm around himself and smoothed his bearded mouth with his other hand.

"It will work if we can keep one step ahead of them," Malakai said.

"They have the lair in Rastra now," I reminded him. "They have all of your plans."

"Let them have it." He met my disbelieving snort with a shrug. "Those schemes no longer matter."

"He's right," Caspian agreed. "The focus is off of Grave Dominion as a whole now. It's Phineaus that needs dealing with." Even when pain stretched through his tone like gauze unraveled, thin and tense, the conviction didn't flicker out of the set of his mouth.

"It's a new strategy entirely," Malakai added. "And if Grave Dominion is kept busy with the old one, with their focus on names pinned to a map, so much the better for us. What Phineaus finds there will buy us time to deal with *him*."

I ticked my nails along the mug, soothing my mind into motion with the steady cadence. "What about the truth serum? Your own poisons? What can Phineaus do with those?"

A wicked smile tugged across Malakai's mouth. "Please give me *some* credit, Miss Weathers. Everything of *lasting* significance, I removed from manse. What was left behind is still significant enough to keep the Kingslayer entertained, particularly what pertains to my schemes against Grave Dominion and what lies in the vault." A ripple of regret twisted one corner of his mouth when he mentioned that sacred space—but his tone held firm when he went on, "Rest assured, regardless, I didn't completely cripple us."

Relief snipped the tension from my body, letting me slouch in the chair. I loved grand gestures of heroism and absolutely senseless affection as much as any girl from one of Addie and Reiko's stories; but I'd be flipped on the dark side of Luck's coin if I didn't admit, at least to myself, how glad I was that Malakai hadn't thrown *everything* away when he came to rescue me.

There was still a *real* villain who needed defeating, after all.

"So, what do we have left?" Caspian asked.

"Several poisons against which the Grave has no antidote," Malakai offered. "A battery of my best weapons. The truth-telling serum stolen from the Guild Garrote—"

Caspian choked on his next sip of coffee and rocked upright in his chair, pounding himself on the chest. "You—the pair of you infiltrated and *stole* from the *Guild Garrote*?"

"What, like it's difficult?" I plastered false innocence all over my tone, though my fingers strayed up to rub the places where Solomyn Degrace had bruised.

"Oh, sullied souls...is *that* what they've been on the hunt for, ever since that rotting Jubilee?" Still coughing—and now laughing in between—Caspian shook his head. "You *have* been busy."

"Unfortunately," Malakai cut in without a hint of his own humor, "this doesn't quite solve our trouble."

"That Phineaus will be looking out for someone to poison him," I sighed, resting my nose against the edge of my mug and inhaling the bitter steam. "Moreso now than even after the last attempt on his life. So, Caspian is right...the Poet Poisoner's usual methods will be useless."

"And I'm afraid I can't get close now." Caspian scratched sharply above his brow. "I won't even be able to show my face in Fortress Ferregrand once he returns."

"Unless you play your part well." Malakai tipped the rim of his mug toward Caspian. "Make him believe you had nothing to do with our escape."

"I'm not willing to risk that," I cut in, and both men shot me raised brows and wide eyes. "What? Caspian, you're our friend, aren't you? Why would you expect me to be happy with you trying to lie your way around that absolute madman?"

"I wouldn't call him a *friend*," Malakai grunted.

"I wouldn't expect it in the least," Caspian spoke over him, a glint of affection in his eyes.

I spread my hands, one still wrapped around my mug. "We've all seen now what Phineaus is *truly* like. And he wants you dead besides...every Moraven older than him is a threat to the power he's trying to claim for himself."

"My soul is forfeit regardless." Caspian streaked a hand back through his silver-threaded hair. "Rotting bones. I've heard this sort of talk most of my life, but to know my own *nephew* is plotting it this time..."

"It's tragic, and truly heinous." Malakai swept his mug before himself in a herding gesture. "Let's keep our focus on outwitting him."

"I can't think of many ways to do that," I admitted, "except..."

My ears tingled with the memory of rifleshot echoing through Shastah halls—a sound that had sent me running like my own life was in the balance, out of my room in the guest wing and flying toward the Convening Chamber, the day Addie and Jaik had been brought back to those golden halls by Galan Fiordona.

My eyes drifted up to find Malakai's; though we didn't share the memory, the intention in my tapered-off words found a home in the depths of his eyes.

"In true assassin fashion," he finished quietly. "Weapon against weapon."

Caspian frowned, glancing between us. "Would you be a match for him?"

"Once, perhaps," Malakai said. "We've had the same training, to a point."

"But yours ended half a lifetime ago," I pointed out. "Phineaus just left Thrasmund within the last few months."

"Hence the concern." Malakai shoved up from the bookcase and came to the table, hooking out another chair with his foot and dragging it out to settle into. "Caspian?"

"We might be a better match, but that's in part because we've had sparring matches in formal fencing." Caspian shook his head. "So of course, he knows my tactics and tendencies...both as Druavas and as a fellow assassin."

Malakai's eyes flashed to me. "Do not even suggest it."

Laughter spurted from me, and I set my coffee aside so it wouldn't spill with the giggles that shook my hands. "Malakai, have you *met* me? What makes you think I'd suggest I'm any sort of match for an assassin? Flipping *Luck*."

"You have surprised me countless times...for better or worse," he scoffed. "Not to mention you pulled a dagger on a member of Grave Dominion your first night in this country."

"Pulling a dagger to defend myself is nothing like staging a battle with an assassin!"

"Then we're agreed: you'll take no part in this."

"Well, I didn't say *that*—"

"The part *itself* is what's in question," Caspian spoke over both our protests, "because there is absolutely no sense whatsoever in picking a fight none of us will win."

"That *is* true," Malakai grumbled, sinking back with folded arms. "But if not a fight, and not a poisoning, then what do you suggest?"

We all looked around at one another, unspeaking.

Then I murmured, "Could it be an ambush?"

Caspian and Malakai both stiffened, studying me with new, shrewd interest.

"When I was a girl, and I wanted the advantage over my brothers, I had to accept they were always going to be bigger and brawnier than me," I went on. "So I would creep out of closets and attack them that way...sometimes I could even win a wrestling match if I started it with the element of surprise."

"And were your brothers also assassins?" Caspian asked. "Unless so, I'm not certain—"

"The Navarian venom-blade." Malakai's gaze was fixed on me, brimming with respect, even a sprinkle of reverence.

I couldn't help but smile—then jerked around in my seat as Caspian lurched forward in his. "Stop. *No*. You actually *have* one?"

"Yes. Kept aside for a purpose precisely like this." Malakai's focus flashed to Caspian. "Even a small wounding with it would incapacitate the Kingslayer long enough for us to escape without engaging in a full-fledged fight."

"And an ambush would put us near enough to do it," I added.

Caspian blew out a long, staggered breath, knocking on the tabletop. "Infiltrating Fortress Ferregrand to deal with Phineaus will not be easy. My father has the place locked down...I'm afraid Phineaus's suggestion of your spywork rattled him deeply, Naomi. He believes Callie herself may have turned against him...he's terrified for his family's wellbeing. I'm the only one he's allowed in or out, to continue my work with Grave Dominion."

"What about Phineaus?" I demanded. "He's in Rastra!"

"He departed just before my father gave the order, claiming he'd left some important legal documents in the city." Caspian snorted. "My sister's attempts to call him back have fallen on deaf ears...naturally. But no doubt he's spun some lie about how he's taking a few extra days there, lying low, waiting for things to blow over."

"And your grandfather is willing to accept that, because it keeps Phineaus out of harm's way."

Caspian shrugged. "Clearly we've all gotten quite used to turning a blind eye where my nephew is concerned."

Malakai scoffed under his breath. "Then that leaves us thoroughly banned from the Fortress."

Caspian nodded. "*I* can walk through the front doors unscathed, which is how I've been coming to see the pair of you. But Naomi is now considered a spy, possibly an enemy...and as far as my family knows, she's meant to be interred in the dungeons." He waved a hand at Malakai. "*You*, we won't even discuss."

"Your sentinels don't know my face."

"No, but Phineaus does. And any informants he has within the halls will no doubt report to him even if I smuggle you inside well before he returns home."

"What about the ways you crept in before?" I demanded of Malakai.

"The Kingslayer will likely have seen to those as well." Malakai rubbed a hand along his bearded jaw, then the nape of his neck. "We barely slipped from the dungeon ahead of the sentinels dispatched to barricade the way I'd taken in."

"An ambush on the road, then?" I offered.

"Not the best variables," Caspian hedged. "Particularly on the road to Rastra. You've traveled it...you know how it's been laid for safety, to prevent that very thing, given the state of the country."

I slid my fingers into my hair and bent forward, scratching my scalp, trying to dislodge a good thought, a brilliant solution—

Nothing.

And that was how it was for the rest of the day; pouring countless cups of coffee, taking turns pacing circles around the table, discussing and arguing and suggesting and declining until we were weary of it all. And Caspian and Malakai, I worried, were one dismissed notion away from drawing knives on each other.

"Clearly, none of this is helping," I cut in before the latest quarrel could squirm from between Malakai's gritted teeth. "We're exhausted, we're hungry, we've all worked our minds to the bone. Let's try again in the morning, shall we?"

"Possibly for the best," Caspian agreed grudgingly, rubbing his temples. "We're talking ourselves in circles and still have no means of getting the pair of you safely inside the Fortress."

"If we ever will," Malakai grumbled, shoving back from the table and thrusting a hand out to me. I took it, rising stiffly, cradling my midsection while we circled the table and returned to the bed; after a squeeze to my elbow as I passed him, Caspian let himself out the way I'd spotted him coming in that morning. I hoped to Luck he would be safe, not reckless, after the absolute nightmare of a day we'd had.

Malakai watched through narrowed eyes as I lowered myself gingerly onto the edge of the bed. "Are you in pain?"

"Not really pain. Just discomfort." Logically, I'd known how even sitting up after so much time inert could strain a patient's strength; but it was one thing to learn it from textbooks and teach it to others. *Experiencing* it was another matter entirely.

How was I going to be of *any* use when it came to confronting Phineaus?

Scratching behind my ear, I bent my elbows onto my knees and covered my face with my hands. Outthinking the masterful deceptions of a secret assassin was so much more difficult with a brain that felt like it was made of pus strained through a sieve.

"I just need to sleep on this," I mumbled—to myself and to Malakai. Then I lowered myself to an elbow and stretched out, lying upside-down in the bed, propping my feet on the pillow.

Perched beside my head, Malakai traced his fingertips lightly through my hair. "Some solution will present itself."

"How can you be so sure, without Giddy Gus here to advise you?"

He scoffed low in his throat. "I can be certain because all of that excellent advice he gave me was, in fact, *me* advising *myself*."

I mimed a gasp, laying a hand over my heart. "*No.*"

"I'm afraid it's true."

"Shock! Horror!"

"You will recover, in time."

"I may swoon first."

"I would rather have you swooning for other reasons entirely." Malakai bent, his nose brushing mine, the skim of his breath stealing all the air from my lungs for itself—

And then he drew back, stroking his thumb over my lips.

"But, first," he said, "sleep."

Grumbling a litany of abuses against sensuous assassins who knew *precisely* what they were doing, I curled onto my side with my head tucked on my arm; through half-lidded eyes, I studied the drab stone walls of the alcove, the dim rotunda washed in chandelier candlelight. I stared at the pillow, at the mortared stones, at the headboard of the bed—

And went on staring, an idea blooming like the flowers bursting in perfectly-rendered buds along the bed's iron framework.

"Malakai!" I shoved myself up one elbow, twisting over to face him. "When you left the lair in Rastra, did you bring any of *my* things?"

He grimaced. "Rotting sentimental—"

"Did you, or didn't you?"

"Against my better judgement at the time, believing you'd betrayed me...yes."

"All of my clothes, too? My necklace that I took off when we went to the Jubilee?"

"*Yes*, all of it, you thieving raven. Why?"

"That necklace, it was a gift from Arias...it's a Moraven family heirloom his mother handed down to him!" I gripped his hands, squeezing with all my might. "It's a bone key, Malakai. It can open any door in Fortress Ferregrand."

Comprehension broke like daylight in his dark eyes, and his fingers tightened around mine in turn. "A way into every room."

"Even Phineaus's." I nodded. "It can get us in. And then we can end him and his schemes, once and for all."

CHAPTER 83
ALL THE LUCK

IT WAS A MARK of how much Malakai had grown to trust Caspian—or of how desperate we all were to have this over with and be free of Phineaus's stranglehold threat—that when I woke from a night of fitful dreams, there were clear signs Malakai had gone from the lair and come back.

A scent of the city streets hanging above the bedcovers. A pair of familiar satchels strung over the seatback at the worktable. And on the bedside table...a starlight-glazed mug full of steaming hot cocoa.

A smile crawled across my sleep-heavy face, and I stretched—my toes digging into the solid warmth of a familiar thigh. Rolling over, I found Malakai seated at the foot of the bed, threading my key pendant between his knuckles.

Something about those long, lethal fingers cradling the key's delicate, vine-wrapped shaft and rose-plated bow felt...right. In a sort of darkly romantic way.

"You kept the dishes?" I mumbled.

"Most of them." He didn't elaborate on that—or on the fact that, when he'd been tossing together the *important* things to keep from the manse like the Navarian venom-blade and the cure for Mummer's Dance, he'd also deemed these necessary enough to bring along.

Our gazes met over that precious key to all our ends, and his mouth tugged down at the corners, hollowing deep dimples on either side.

"I would prefer if you didn't come along for this."

I pushed myself upright, stifling a groan that just might be a blade in his arsenal. "Surprise, surprise."

"There's no need for it." Malakai's tone was clipped, factual; but the sharp groove of his brow and the clench of his fist around the key betrayed his concern. "We are more than capable of inserting a key into a lock and twisting."

"Fair enough." I scooted back against the pillows, hooking my hair behind my ears. "And what are you going to do if either one of you is wounded? Hm?"

"I would assume we would treat our wounds, as we both have been doing for *several* years before we met you."

"Malakai. I'm a healer *and* a poisoner. And you're going to ambush an *assassin*," I reminded him, taking the mug in both hands and wrapping them tight around the silk-smooth glaze. It was absurd that the brush of that silky-stern texture made me want to cry; I'd have rather blamed the heat in my eyes on the topic we discussed. "If he deals either of you a wound you can't manage on your own, you could be dead before you make it back to the lair."

"It seems a worthwhile risk to me."

I stretched across the bed, cuffing one hand over his wrist. "Not to *me*."

We were quiet again after that, me settling back to sip my cocoa, Malakai resuming his study of the key. Likely looking for some indication if there was any door in Fortress Ferregrand that wouldn't open for it.

I shivered despite the warmth seeping from the mug into my palms.

We only needed one thing to go right for this—but there were so many possible ways it could go horribly wrong.

I didn't *want* to be there for any of it. I had no desire to look Phineaus Moraven in the face ever again after what he'd done to me. But with a bevy of antidotes and far more training in healing than either Caspian or Malakai possessed...

I was their best chance of surviving any one of those possible horrors.

Malakai seemed to be thinking along the same patterns as me—as usual—because after several minutes, he said, "If the choice were mine, you would stay here in the lair, safe. Where you can't be harmed or used against me."

"I know." I blew out a breath, stirring the hair off my brow.

"I also recognize that you are trouble incarnate," Malakai added, "and that regardless of what I say, you'll make the choice you deem best." His dark eyes lifted to mine. "I trust that choice, even if it will never be the outcome I prefer."

Warmth radiated through my chest, touching every place the cocoa's fading heat couldn't quite reach. "I appreciate that."

"Would you go armed?"

"Luck, *yes*." A breathless laugh scraped from my throat. "And I would listen, and follow your lead *exactly*. I don't have any interest in being some sort of hero, I just want to make certain the three of us all walk out of that Fortress together."

"And if I told you to leave," Malakai asked lowly, "to leave *me*, if it meant your own salvation...would you do it?"

My lips popped away from the rim of the mug. For a long moment, we just watched one another—the echo of a story he'd told me ringing in my ears.

The brother who'd begged to be put down. The body he'd had to leave behind.

"You know the answer to that," I murmured at last.

He scrubbed a hand along the side of his neck and up his nape, then slowly let it drag back down and tumble into his lap.

"So," he said, "what will it be, troublemaker?"

"You know the answer to that, too."

"Sadly, yes." He stretched forward, planting his fists on either side of my hips and brushing a fleeting kiss to my brow. "Caspian has invited me to spar with him, to hone both our skills. Wish me some of that Mithran Luck, would you?"

"You don't need Luck when you're the Poet Poisoner," I teased, tilting my head back to catch that kiss against my lips.

"Alas, that might have been true before I met you. But with your precise breed of trouble wreaking havoc in my life..." His lips turned upward against mine, and he withdrew, delving into my pack to retrieve something else—something that sang like music when he slipped it over his wrist.

Good-luck charms on a silver chain, disappearing beneath the cuff of his tugged-down sleeve; they glinted as brilliant as the arrogant smile he shot me when he backed away from the bed.

"I still need all of the luck I can get."

CHAPTER 84
ANTICIPATION AND ANTIDOTES

OUR INFILTRATION OF FORTRESS Ferregrand required a surgeon's precision.

Caspian hadn't made it any secret how much the timing of it all disturbed him; he'd warned us over and over again how tight it would be. That we would have to sneak in after Phineaus returned from Rastra, to avoid being in the Fortress long enough to arouse suspicion...but if we gave him too much time to himself, he would realize we were gone from the dungeon and put up his guard.

That left us relying on Caspian's reports from the Fortress—waiting for Phineaus to inform his family he was making his way home.

We didn't go idle those days; we reviewed maps and building sketches of the Fortress, plotting our way through its halls until we could recite our way to Phineaus's chambers with our eyes closed. Malakai and Caspian sparred every day, honing their skills just in case. I delved into my pouch of antidotes and cures, laying them out one by one, refreshing myself on their uses and applications. And I added a handful of tinctures to my repertoire thanks to Caspian—bottled and powdered remedies created by Grave Dominion itself.

Perhaps I should've felt a tweak of conscience about using the assassin guild's cures...but I much preferred wielding their tools against them over being robbed of something I might need to save our lives.

We passed nearly a week that way...days spent preparing, nights where Malakai and I lay in the bed together, his arm always around me, talking quietly about the manse and about Rastra and whatever else came to mind...but never what waited ahead. My dreams were riddled with different outcomes of the ambush and a relief of having it over with that faded quickly whenever I opened my eyes to the lair's familiar depths again.

And then, finally—just when the claustrophobia of the rotunda and wash-room started to itch under my skin—Caspian greeted us one morning with a grim set to his mouth and red-rimmed, sleepless eyes.

Malakai and I both jolted upright at the worktable where we'd been passing the time playing Suits; my stomach turned in a vicious, slippery knot. "Phineaus?"

"On his way back to us." Caspian leaned his shoulder against the same doorway through which he always entered, then knocked his temple to the stone. "He'll arrive by week's end."

Malakai stood, any hint of leisure from our game shedding from him like a cloak. "Then at week's end, we'll be rid of him...and my family's blood avenged."

CHAPTER 85
INTO THE FORTRESS

ASPIAN'S LAIR, IT TURNED out, wasn't far from Fortress Ferregrand at all—which fit fairly well with how I knew him. I'd never met a man who was *such* a mingled mix of cleverness and contempt, likc he was daring the entire world with a one-fingered salute to guess his machinations and next moves.

So he'd built his lair inside abandoned ruins along the northern rim of stone that ran along the sea, a crumbled memory of a castle cordoned off with warnings posted everywhere against trespassing—by order of the Moraven family, punishable by fining and imprisonment.

I supposed no one looked twice at it long enough to notice that the old pipes were still drawing water from the city reservoirs.

I'd never been happier to smell fresh air than when we climbed out of the bottom of the turret plunged deep into the earth like roots and picked our way through the rubble, three in a row, disguised under the cover of a gathering sunset. Wrapped in my cardigan, my pouch belted at my waist, I moved between Malakai and Caspian, accepting the hand Malakai occasionally offered to help me over clots of ruined stone. The rush of the sea and the tumble of waterfalls muted our movements as we rounded the stone rim, the Fortress looming on its solitary spit of an island to our left.

I shuddered, remembering the last time I'd been inside its halls—a memory that was thankfully dimming with every passing day. But, like most horrors dealt to human flesh, my body kept the score: in visceral twinges and a crawling sense of dread while we made our well-plotted approach.

We would infiltrate Fortress Ferregrand from below—not the secret way into the dungeons that Malakai had used twice, but by an old tunnel we'd discovered during our perusal of the maps. Caspian had never visited it, so it stood to reason it was an escape corridor hewn out by his paranoid ancestors...a perfect way in. And Luck's smiling face landed on our side, insomuch as we had him to guide us. His intrinsic sense of the sentinel patrols inside and outside the Fortress would be our saving grace tonight.

We reached the sea by way of a set of chiseled steps leading down the face of stone the cliffs; it was slow going, the rock made slippery by seaspray, and more often than not we were catching ourselves from falling, moving like crabs down the stairwell.

Full night found us at the bottom of the slope and clambering into a small vessel Caspian had lashed there days ago; as the Druavas thrust us out from the shore and clambered aboard, and Malakai took up rowing, I gauged the height of the moon in the cloudless sky.

According to reports the Moravens had received along the road, Phineaus would be riding down the drawbridge within the hour. And one hour invading the Fortress was the precise amount of time we'd agreed on for the ambush.

I slowed my pulse with several deep breaths and a count of three.

This was no dream. It was finally almost over.

Malakai ran us aground in a furrow of toothlike stone shards at the base of the Fortress; we picked our way up the steep, rocky slope among them, searching swiftly and silently for the door.

The slow going dragged over my skin like a cat rubbed backward. I wanted to scream with every glance I shot at the moon, knowing time was already short—and growing shorter.

Phineaus was inside Amalgard by now. How much longer until he crossed the bridge?

Before I could round the stone base and check to see if the halves of it had already been lowered, Caspian's fluting whistle gathered us back to him; he'd found a door pressed into the steep slope at the base of the Fortress, padlocked shut. Its weatherworn iron was the same exact shade as the stone around it; I would've walked straight past it.

"Time to see if that key of yours is everything Arias said." Caspian sidestepped, gesturing me forward.

I held my breath as I took his place, inserting the key into the lock; with a silent prayer to Luck, I gave it a twist.

All that breath tumbled out in a sigh of relief when the padlock gave way.

The tunnel beyond was dark, dank with disuse, smelling strongly of minerals and dampness. I wrinkled my nose as we slipped inside, and Caspian took the lead again—running us up the winding corridor without a light to see by, our only guide the twist of the tunnel walls. I kept my palm flat to the stone on the left, Malakai to the right, feeling for any sideways or divergences—but there were none. The corridor funneled straight up for what felt like nearly a mile, until Caspian called quietly, "There are steps here."

His footfalls ascended; then, a shallow *thump* up above.

Another door. This one had no padlock, but a two-sided knob that refugees from the Fortress could lock behind them. I opened it with the bone key, and we hefted ourselves out of darkness, into dim light.

Not from the room we'd entered, but from the hall beyond it; a warm glow seeped under the door, carried on the smell of buttered dough and sugar.

"I think we're near the kitchens," I whispered, my chest tightening at the memory of the last time I'd been here...with the Moravens, sharing cocoa and concepts of legacy.

"That we are," Caspian murmured. "Best to set your fortress for escape in such a way that you can steal food on the way out." He crept to the door, then peered back at us; only the edges of his eyes caught the gleam from below the door. It made him look more frightened than his breathy tone betrayed. "I'll draw the cooks out, then create a distraction for the sentinels...move them to the eastern side of the Fortress, then double back and sweep the halls to ensure they're clear. If possible, from there, I'll join you."

"Don't rush yourself," I warned at the same moment Malakai growled, "Don't be sloppy."

"Neither of you give me enough credit," the Druavas snorted, flinging up his hood to mask his familiar features. "I've been doing this longer than you've been alive."

I wasn't certain that was *precisely* true, but I didn't question it; I bumped shoulders with him as I unlocked the door and let him out, then dropped the key's chain around my neck and tucked it into my cleavage.

Malakai and I leaned against opposite sides of the door, listening for the fluster of retreating footfalls as Caspian spoke with, then herded out, the cooks and kitchen maids. I'd never bothered to ask him what lies he would tell to the people he *did* encounter about what was happening tonight...and I supposed it hardly mattered.

All we needed was a bit of chaos and confusion to mask our steps.

"Are you ready?" Malakai murmured as the bustle retreated further and further from beyond the door.

"Of course I am. It's just another infiltration," I joked weakly. "Just like the Guild Garrote."

He didn't remark on the faint quaver of my tone, only asked, "You're certain you know the way to the Kingslayer's rooms?"

I nodded. "I have those plans memorized by now, and…" I swallowed, shame pricking the base of my throat. "Phineaus showed me the way himself."

Malakai cradled my cheek for an instant, the brush of his thumb against my jaw erasing the guilt of how I'd unwittingly aided the Kingslayer's crimes. "Then let's use that against him, shall we?"

Spurred by that notion, I led us out—first into the deserted kitchens. And then into the heart of Fortress Ferregrand.

Caspian was right—we shouldn't have doubted him. All the clamor in the Fortress stayed somewhere ahead of us, like a distant, throbbing heartbeat shoving blood down different paths as we ran through the deserted halls. Arias's gift unlocked door after door for us—ways that had been shuttered by order of the Drui. Paths to reach his family that should've been sentinel-guarded and sealed shut gave way before us thanks to Caspian's con and Calten's key, and we ascended level after level only dodging the occasional sentinel.

All of them were moving the same way—toward whatever commotion Caspian had raised. I *had* bothered asking about that, and he'd informed me lightly that every sentinel in the Fortress would believe they'd chased the Poet Poisoner tonight.

Possibly not the *best* ruse, but it was certainly doing the trick. We reached the upper floors and the Moraven family's wing of suites with minimal delay, though I counted every lost second against the beat of my heart as we sprinted for Phineaus's door.

It all felt a bit like one of my dreams…especially remembering when I'd stood here last. How I'd been so thoroughly on Phineaus's side, how deeply I'd despised Malakai then. Now I soaked in the strength of his back pressed to mine, leaned into the comfort of his eyes watching down the corridor while I swiftly undid the locks—three of them—and swung open the door.

Now it was just a matter of hiding—on his balcony, we'd decided, so we couldn't be cornered in any part of the room—and waiting for his return.

But *wrongness* struck me like the Kingslayer's own slap to my face the moment we slipped into his parlor, shutting and locking the door behind us.

I froze, sinking at once into my own senses, gaze darting through the entry parlor's shadowed corners; like a patient presenting with uncertain symptoms, I felt out every inch, searching for what lurked under the surface as Malakai stole toward the door to Phineaus's bedchamber—and the balcony beyond.

"Malakai, wait," I hissed.

"There isn't any time," he retorted.

"No, something isn't right." My voice sharpened. "This room...it doesn't smell musty at all."

"Perhaps they've cleaned it in their Druavas's absence." Malakai's tone was tight, tense.

"No...it's not that, it's lived-in," I hissed. "I can smell lathered soap, turned bedsheets, cologne, the *hearth*—"

It was dead now. But the taint of ash tickled my nose.

Someone was here. Someone had *been* here, by the smell of it, for quite some time.

Malakai reached the door to Phineaus's bedchamber the same moment the thought settled in my head; I lunged across the parlor, catching his wrist, yanking us both aside—

And the door pounded outward, a throwing knife sailing through the gap the moment it widened, the tip *crunching* into the doorframe we'd just entered through.

A second after, and it would've been embedded in Malakai's heart.

And from the bedchamber beyond, the Kingslayer strolled out, drawing a second knife, his eyes fixed on us.

"Hey," he purred, turning the blade over his knuckles, then angling the lethal point at us. "Aren't you two supposed to be in the *dungeon*?"

CHAPTER 86
VENGEANCE INCARNATE

FLIPPING LUCK, THIS IS not good.

"You really do have a nose on you, don't you, Weathers?" Phineaus's grin was the smile I'd come to know in Fortress halls and seedy taverns, markets and cathedral steps and canalsides—bright, brilliant, fully lighting his eyes this time.

That his joy came from catching *us* sneaking in churned my stomach with horror.

"You look good," he added smoothly, "for someone who was choking on her own blood the last time I saw her."

Malakai spread his arms like the bristling wings of a sleek, shadowy raven, backing us both toward the high windows paneled with those drapes Phineaus had once claimed to love—possibly our only hope of escape. "Behind me—get behind me, Naomi!"

"Like *that's* going to deter me," Phineaus snorted as I ducked behind Malakai's back, a hand to my dagger. "When I'm ready for her, there's not going to be enough pieces left of you to even break her fall, Poet."

Malakai's head sank beneath the line of his shoulders—a bracing stance I knew all too well. "I see they've added showboating to the training regimen in Thrasmund."

Phineaus chortled. "They've added a *lot* of things you—"

Malakai tore forward without warning, dropped the venom-blade from inside his sleeve and slashed in an opalescent streak—a dangerous maneuver that was the closest to an ambush we had left.

It was almost enough.

Almost.

Phineaus doubled back with a chuckling "*Whoa*!", unleashing a cuffed blade from the inside of his wrist and catching Malakai's in a deft swivel. He thrust them apart from one another, Malakai guarding me again as I slipped with my back to the door, Phineaus sniffing as he swiped his wrist beneath his nose.

"Honestly, surprised it took you this long to come back," he said. "Soon as I got the word you broke out, I turned right around and came back to wait. I'll tell you, it's been *mind-numbing*, sitting around in my rooms, letting my family think I was in Rastra while I waited for you to get the guts to take a swing. I actually had to resort to *reading*...how pathetic is that?" He scooped up one of the books from the table in front of the hearth, flashed the cover at us—one of Kilgrave's volumes, a special sort of taunt that sent a shiver dancing down my spine—then tossed it idly into the flue. "Anyway, when you didn't show, I started to think, '*Now, what could make them take their sweet time?*' And then I realized...ah. Right. Ambush. So I got the word spreading that I was on my way back, and..." He gestured to the room with a broad sweep of his arm. "Rotting bones, you people are *predictable*."

"You were *never* in Rastra," I hissed, desperate to keep him talking as my hand fumbled backward with the door.

"Uh...yeah. Just said that." Phineaus jerked a thumb at me. "That Mummer's Dance really did a work on her, huh?"

I snagged Malakai's shoulder before he could leap for the Kingslayer again. "You weren't the least bit curious about the Poet's lair?"

"Oh, don't get me wrong. I have friends tearing that old manse apart." Phineaus shrugged. "Thing is, I figure this one's smart. He probably kept a few important pieces for himself. So, why not divide and conquer? Let the others sort out the lair...figure out where the Poet's stashing the rest of his goods."

"As *if*," Malakai seethed.

"Mmm...right. You can play tough all you want, Malakai, but I know exactly where that chink in your armor is." Phineaus wagged the tip of his blade between us. "All I've got to do is start carving. She starts screaming. *You* start talking."

And he might've started carving right there—if the sinister dip in his tone and the tightening of his grip around his dagger were any indication. But before he could advance another step, the door slammed open against my back, crashing me forward into Malakai, both of us stumbling off to the side; a dark shape barreled through the doorway, hurtling full-bodied into Phineaus, catching him in a headlock and dragging him away from us.

My shout of relief at Caspian's appearance turned to a bark of warning as Phineaus pivoted smoothly in his hold, shoving him backward with both hands. His shoulder struck the door, slamming it shut again—sending both of us leaping aside.

Caspian cursed, blocked Phineaus's downward slash with an upraised arm—then buckled when Phineaus swept his ankles and hurled him against the sofa.

My cry choked off when Malakai shoved me back into the curtains, out of harm's way; Phineaus seized Caspian by the throat, hefting him back to his feet.

"Oh, you are *beyond dead*, Uncle!" Phineaus's glee didn't quite mask the rage bubbling beneath every word. "The Grave is going to swallow you *whole* after tonight, and I can't begin to explain how much I'm going to *love* that."

"After tonight, it won't matter," Caspian snarled, "because they will be far too busy fleeing from your cooling corpse with all their schemes in *shambles*."

"You really think you have it in you, big man?" Phineaus taunted.

Caspian faltered, sagging in Phineaus's hold; then he shrugged. "No. I don't. I've never had it in me to hurt you kids." A slight tilt of his head. "But *he* does."

Phineaus hurled Caspian away—hard enough to crack his head against the sculpted trim of the wall and drop him in a heap on the floor—as he whipped to follow his uncle's gesture.

He stumbled when Malakai sprang on him from the opposite side, the venom-blade ripping a shred of Phineaus's sleeve just before he thrust free.

They dissolved into a duel of fast hacks and brutal slashes, blows held so close to their bodies it was like a secret...like a dance. Steel blurred with the quick complexity of their movements, and the air bottomed out from my lungs as I watched, clinging to the panel of rich red fabric wrapped around me, waiting for my moment—to leap to Caspian's aid, or Malakai's. To end Phineaus, if I saw half a chance...even if it put me in harm's way.

But there was no breaking into their dueling waltz even if I'd had any desire to; the air clouded like blood in the water with years of warring ambition and vengeance, with the memories of Malakai's dead family—his sister, his brother, his parents—with the fates of another family that Phineaus was all too ambivalent about cutting down on his way to power.

Except, this time...it was his *own* family hanging in the balance.

And even though it was the Kane legacy Malakai fought for...he was fighting for Hadrass-Drui's survival, too.

Shadows and burning red backdrops painted Malakai as a tarnished hero this time—a man at war for the salvation of the ruling family, without a drop of love for them in his veins. But what he *did* possess was enough wrath and ruination and enough hunger for absolution to keep him dancing with the Kingslayer even past the point where trained soldiers would have faltered. Beyond what I'd ever imagined when I'd faced this moment in my nightmares, back in Caspian's lair.

He was vengeance incarnate, as darkly beautiful as the blade he wielded; and he didn't stop, even as the minutes tore on—even when he couldn't land a single blow on the Kingslayer.

And...maybe Malakai was more of a match for Phineaus than any of us had thought; maybe Phineaus could feel it in the stroke of his arm, in the surety of his steps...that Malakai was fighting for more than just vengeance now. In this room, in this moment, he was fighting for something that made him equal—even greater—than a selfish, pampered heir craving power.

Maybe that was why Phineaus took the coward's way out.

Maybe that was why he blasted Malakai away with a kick—and lunged for me instead.

My fingers were on my dagger's hilt, drawing it before my mind even fully caught up to the Kingslayer's change in course; I plunged a hand into the folds of the curtain and whipped them across my body, distracting him with the flash of crimson fabric. When he caught it in his free hand and tore it back, I was ready to block his downward thrust—just like Caspian had done. Just like Jaik and Wyat had taught me.

The tip of his blade *almost* pierced my collarbone; but I shoved up and back with all my might, unbalancing him just enough that I could wrap the curtain fabric around his wrist and jerk his knife arm aside.

Which left just enough of an opening for Malakai to sweep in from the side, lashing out at Phineaus's ribs.

Three heartbeats was all it took.

One for me to realize what was coming by the dart of a menacing grin along Phineaus's mouth.

One for the shout of warning to form on my lips—too late.

Because, by the third, Phineaus had pivoted, his wrist and blade still shackled in the curtain fabric—and whipped the taut drape twice in a noose around Malakai's throat.

With one deft rip, he tore the fabric from my hands, skinning them raw—and kicked Malakai backward through the mosaic window.

CHAPTER 87
OVER THE EDGE

S HATTERING GLASS. COLD NIGHT air tearing against my face. Pain sprinkling in whizzing shards along my body.

The scream that ripped from me was so loud, I couldn't hear if Malakai's neck snapped when he hit the end of the noose.

I threw myself against Phineaus with all my might, ramming him out of the way, shoving him stumbling over the low table before the hearth, his knife clattering from his hand; then I sprang on the drape, fighting to drag Malakai back inside.

Sharp fingers dug into my nape; Phineaus hurled me down against the floor, shoving all the breath from my chest. I rolled just before he landed his weight on me, my dagger slicing against his cheek—then ripped it back and slashed again, and again, scouring his shoulder and collarbone but missing the side of his neck in my fury, my desperation.

His fist slammed into my lower belly, and blinding pain erupted through my abdomen. I seized up, screaming, and toppled sideways; Phineaus crawled over me, fists pounding in the exact places I'd slashed him.

Shrieks and sobs shattered my throat as more hurts joined the first, though they dimmed under the agony rolling in my middle; then Phineaus had me up by the throat, thrusting me against the bricking beside the window so hard all the breath choked from me at once.

"You know, I think I'm *always* going to miss the fun we could've had together," Phineaus panted out a laugh, retrieving his dagger with a slope of the arm and brushing the hair from my brow with its edge—slitting a small seam against my forehead that freed a trickle of blood into my eye. "I'm honestly a little glad he *did* get you out of the dungeon...I like this ending better, because I get to do it myself. Have a last little *hurrah* before you're gone."

"*Kingslayer!*" Malakai's voice was a glottal, brutal rasp from below the window edge that broke off with a choke—a feeble echo that ripped through my chest.

"Sounds like his neck's still intact! Hopefully he's got enough air left in him to *really* feel it while he watches me cut out those pretty insides and hang you next to him." Phineaus stroked his thumb over my trembling lips. "What do you say, Naomi? First you, while he's strangling out there...then I'll take my time with Uncle Caspian." A jerk of his head toward the dazed form of his uncle, still slumped at the hearthside. "And then, since the three of you were kind enough to draw the guards away from their watch...I think it's about time Mama and Papa shuffled off the gameboard. Sullied souls, I could clear the whole thing with one sweep! And it's all thanks to you."

A cough. A curse. Malakai thrashed, but the drape swung less with every buck of his body—his struggles becoming more feeble as he strangled.

Don't give up! I wanted to sob—wanted to scream at him. If he could just stay conscious—

A slim slash of movement darted in the corner of my vision—a silver flicker like a needle dipping in and out of flesh. I couldn't help it...my focus pulled away from the assassin in front of me, just for a moment.

To the fingers lifting the fallen venom-blade from the floor.

Phineaus's attention averted, too; he followed the slant of my gaze—then released me and spun, lashing out wildly with a stroke of his hand.

But for the first time since I'd known him...the Kingslayer was too slow.

Too slow by just a breath, just a heartbeat. Maybe he was too stunned to strike with all his might; if he was half as shocked as me, that was our salvation.

Because he wasn't keen enough to block—or to retaliate—when Luminae ducked beneath his skewed slash and plunged the Navarian dagger straight into his gut.

For a moment, the whole room went silent as an infirmary after a patient's last breath.

Phineaus's arm flopped boneless at his side; his chin tucked to his chest, his gaze turning down on the dagger that stuck out from his middle.

One hand wobbled up—and Luminae screamed, a cracked sound of heartbreak and fear. She twisted the blade, leaning all of her weight against it—shoving in until her brother buckled with a soft, shocked hiccup.

"I won't stand by while you hurt this family," she gasped. "I won't let you *murder them* for your own gain!"

With an anguished sob, she ripped the blade out and flung it clattering aside, skidding and sparking across the stones; Phineaus lunged, a drunken, stumbling misstep, grabbing for his sister's throat. But she pirouetted gracefully out of reach, backing away as he pursued...every step weaker and more wavering than the last.

When he broke down to his knees, so did she—still out of reach. She spun and fell, skirts pooling around her, and pressed her hands over her ears as Phineaus collapsed into heaving death throes.

I finally willed myself to move—to peel myself up off my knees and lunge for the window. Shards of broken glass macerated my palms as I leaned out over the side of Fortress Ferregrand, gasping against the wind tearing across my face.

Malakai swung just out of arm's reach below...not fighting to draw himself up, not clawing at the noose.

Utterly still.

"Kai—*Malakai*!" Flattened on my stomach, I clawed at the drape, struggling to reach for him.

But he dangled just beyond my fingertips.

Twisting back into the room, I screamed, "Caspian, help—*help me*! I need you!"

He had already started to rouse, half-lidded eyes straying between his nephew—thrashing on the floor—and his niece—sobbing with her hands pressed over her ears.

At my shout, he blinked, rolled slowly to one side...then crawled through blood to my side, leaning out the window...cursing at the sight of Malakai swinging limp below.

"Tell me you can reach him!" I clawed my hair from the wound on my brow. "Caspian..."

"I'm *trying*," he grunted. "Hold on to me!"

I braced him with my weight, my blood dripping and staining the back of his shirt, while he plunged to the hips over the window's edge. And all I could think of was every lesson from Harrow Hall about how long it took a person to strangle, the noosed pressure on the carotid arteries turning the mind murky, the thoughts to a panicked shroud...

How Malakai had told me once that suffocation was the only death he feared. Drowning, smothering—

Strangling.

Choking on that thought, I nearly missed Caspian's muffled whoop of grim triumph. But his command bit through: "Help me lift him!"

Hauling Caspian back by his belt and a fistful of shirt, I stabilized him on the window's edge; then I sprawled next to him and reached down, hunting desperately until my fingers struck purchase on a sagging shoulder. A bearded cheek brushing my knuckles.

Panting prayers, I slipped both hands beneath Malakai's arm and pulled with Caspian—until, after too many agonizing minutes to dare count, my abdomen a mess of wailing agony, we all spilled backward onto the bloodsoaked floor.

Malakai crashed into the bend of my arm, half-sprawled in my lap, his face mashed against my aching middle. His eyes draped shut.

He didn't move.

"Malakai." Jostling him with the arm that braced him, I fumbled with the noose—then flinched as it gave way all at once.

Caspian dropped the venom-blade, the limp halves of the severed drape pooling at his feet. Working the noose from around Malakai's neck, I eased him down onto the floor.

My arms were numb. Chilled. Utterly empty without him.

A furious red wheal circled beneath his jaw; a horrific bruise was already spreading down his windpipe.

He was—

He wasn't *breathing*.

"Luck, *no*!" The shout burst from me, and I laid my head over his chest.

No uneven cadence greeted me. No rush of air into his lungs.

I jerked back from him, jaw tumbling open, fighting to draw breath for myself.

A shadowy flicker of movement; Caspian crouched beside me. "I'm here, what do you need?" When I stuttered, stammered, tongue tangling, he barked with a cracked voice, "What do you *need*, Naomi?"

The shout jolted me with clarity like a strike of lightning. "You pump his heart, and I'll breathe for him!" Lacing my fingers together, I bent over Malakai's chest, showing Caspian what to do. "Like this! We have to keep up the flow of blood—"

My head clamored with Luminae's gasping sobs and Caspian rucking up his sleeves and shoving me aside to take my place, while Phineaus bled out his last breaths beside us—and none of us helped him.

Swinging my leg over, I crouched with my knees pressed to the tops of Malakai's shoulders, angling his head back. The sweat-and-blood-tacky drape of my hair fell over us, obscuring the room...blotting out the Moravens.

There was only him, and me. His slack face. The lingering furrow between his brows.

He was afraid. He was so flipping afraid to suffocate.

Biting back a sob, I pressed my mouth over his.

It was such a familiar rhythm I had fallen into uncountable times. But everything else was wrong—the room, the setting, the *silence* as Caspian and I worked.

The silence from *Malakai.* From his chest, his mouth, each time I checked.

"Come on, kid, don't do this!" Caspian snarled, thrusting his interlocked hands so forcefully over Malakai's unmoving sternum that it shifted his whole body across the bloodstained floor. "Breathe for us, Malakai—*come on!*"

No answer. He didn't stir at all.

Not at Caspian's shouts. Not at my sobs.

This can't be happening.

I couldn't lose him *now*—after Phineaus was gone. After *everything.*

When Caspian crashed back on his heels, staring vacantly down at Malakai, I didn't know how long we had been working over him. But something in my own chest snagged—threatening to rip, to tear me wide open. "What are you doing? Why are you stopping?"

"Naomi, I think—"

"This isn't the time for thinking! Just *do what I said!*"

But he didn't. He stared at me, a trail of dampness snaking through his stubble. "Naomi."

"No!" I shoved him aside with my shoulder—and, seized with violent desperation, I slammed my fist over Malakai's unbeating heart. "It's not over! *He's not done!*"

"Naomi, enough—if he could have come back by now, he would have!" Caspian seized my fist. "Stop—help me with Lu—"

"*Let go of me!*" I ripped my hand from his grip. "I am not giving up on him—I will *never* stop fighting for him!"

Caspian cursed as I spun back, jamming my fist with all my strength down Malakai's chest. Again. And again. And again.

"Please!" I choked. "Please, Malakai, you have to breathe for me...don't you dare break your promise!"

Don't leave me again.

449

CHAPTER 88
THREATS AND VOWS

M*ALAKAI, PLEASE.*

Death was...softer than I had envisioned. Quiet. Unfeeling. Peaceful.

Oddly poetic.

I know you're still with me...open your eyes!

Drifting away seemed utterly simple. Terror and hate faded to distant notions, shrinking by the moment. A soothing balm after what had come before.

So what was this flickering thread that clung to life?

Don't you dare break your promise.

Cotton and freesia. Blood and salt.

A threat. A vow.

I won't leave you, Malakai Kane.

Nor I you, Naomi Weathers.

Deep within the darkness, something pulsed.

Naomi—

The thread. The oath I had sworn.

I'm afraid to lose the people I love. To be left behind.

She was screaming for me.

Screaming. The Kingslayer taunting her, hurting her—

Malakai, I love you. I love you...please!

I took hold of death, on every side of me. And I bent it to my last and greatest will, on the threshold of oblivion.

I will not leave her behind.

CHAPTER 89
THE SLAYING HAND

*O*NE. *TWO. THREE.*

At first, I thought I imagined it.

The cruel stammering of hope. A crooked rhythm brushing the center of my hand.

One—two—three—

Thrusting the heels of my palms against Malakai's heart again, I drew back...and stilled.

Had...had his chest just lifted?

"Kai?" I whispered.

One, two, three.

Cursing fickle Luck, I dropped my hands on either side of his cheeks and crushed my mouth over his, fisting my hand in his hair—pulling his head up off the floor.

The wild, whooping gasp of his inhale sucked all the breath from my lungs; and then his hand shot up, gripping the nape of my neck, and he yanked my mouth tighter against his.

Sobbing, I crumbled against him, framing his cheeks with both hands and mingling our breaths.

"Found you," he grated out, his voice little more than a desperate wheeze broken by the strangling cord. "Kingslayer?"

Tears blistered in the corners of my eyes. "Dead," I rasped, and his fingers tightened around my neck. "He's gone, Malakai...it's finished."

"You're all right?"

"I am now." An absurd, hysterical giggle burst from my lips. "Don't you ever, *ever* scare me like that again, you idiot."

His only answer was a panting breath and a hard kiss to my hair.

Squeezing my shoulder and clapping Malakai on the arm, Caspian got shakily to his feet and turned to the gruesome scene behind us. With my forehead pressed over Malakai's stumbling heart, I didn't need to look with him—I could *feel* the absolute void of silence where Phineaus lay.

Dead. The Kingslayer was finally dead...and not even by any of *our* hands.

My fingers trembled at the notion of other hurts in this room that needed mending...ones I couldn't touch yet. Ones I had to leave for Caspian while I dealt with the agony in front of me...and the fear still soaking away from my parched throat.

Still, I couldn't help chancing a peek as I curled against Malakai's chest, my curiosity drawn by the murmur of Caspian's voice.

"Lu." His tone was the gentlest thing I'd ever heard; he approached his niece with palms raised, blood streaking from his brow down his cheek. "Lu, sweetheart, it's all right. He's gone. You don't have to look, but he isn't suffering anymore."

She jerked away from him as if he raised a blade against her; there was a horrific, glazed quality to her eyes...not tears, but utter hysteria. It unhinged her jaw and a rambling mess of words spilled forth, tumbling all over each other: "I was coming down the hall because I heard a commotion, and—and I know I wasn't supposed to be out of bed, but Phin said he was coming back tonight and I just wanted to see him, to make certain he made it home safe...and I heard him from all the way down the hall, he was shouting something, and I thought he was in trouble. I should've called the sentinels, I don't know why I didn't, I just...then I heard what he was saying, and I—I couldn't let him do it," she retched, shrinking in on herself. "To Mother and Father, to *you*—"

"Honey. I know," Caspian soothed.

"He wasn't—that wasn't my brother."

"I *know*." Caspian crouched before her. "No, it wasn't. Phin has been gone for a long time...since before he went to Thrasmund."

Luminae crumbled into sobs, flinching out of Caspian's reach; dragging myself up to sitting again, I looked back to Malakai, measuring my own breaths to the familiar rhythm of his. It was the only thing that kept me from crying, too.

I hated Phineaus. I always would. But I hated even more that Luminae—sweet, sincere, earnest *Luminae,* my first real friend in this country—had been forced to finish this mess for us.

My fingers quavered a bit when I offered them to Malakai, helping him sit upright; he pressed a fleeting kiss to my knuckles, his red-rimmed eyes fixed on mine until a fresh, rolling sob from Luminae had us both jerking around to face her.

"What am I going to do?" The Druella folded over herself, arms strung around her willowy body. "What will Mother and Father say?"

"They'll say nothing," Malakai croaked, "because they will never know."

All of us turned to him at once, Luminae's eyes blowing wide; Caspian seized the moment to slip an arm around her, bringing her to rest against his unhurt shoulder.

"This country needs two things." Malakai's gravelly tone made the words all the grimmer. "Steadiness to step forward from this moment, and a villain to rally against. To suggest otherwise will lead to collapse."

Like a bone snapped, or a tendon severed, or a critical organ removed—

He was right. The reasons for Luminae's choice would mean nothing to a country teetering on the brink of ruin.

Gritting his teeth, Malakai went on, "Knowing assassins infiltrated the Hadrassi ruling family—that a sister killed her own brother, and a son nearly murdered his parents—will destroy whatever semblance of control the Moravens still hold."

"Hadrass-Drui will never survive it," Caspian said bleakly. "The guilds and factions will all rise up at once. It would be a massacre."

"Precisely. So we will give them what they need." Slowly, Malakai rocked to his feet; I rose with him, steadying him with a hand to his chest. "As far as anyone beyond the four of us will ever know, Phineaus Moraven was as innocent as every lie ever painted him...his death was the Poet Poisoner's work." His brows mashed low over his eyes. "And that work isn't finished."

Caspian nodded slowly. "Grave Dominion will be on the run after this, without Phineaus at the head of the ranks. They're still a problem that needs dealing with."

"Consider it dealt."

I couldn't tear my eyes from his face—I couldn't stop my heart from ripping in half at the faintest tremble in the corner of his mouth that only I could see.

He had told me once that he was the villain in every story of every person whose path he'd crossed for too many years. Now he would be the villain of an entire country...the most wanted and hated man among them.

His legacy, right now, was being written in this room. Written as a murderer, a thief of Hadrass-Drui's shining future.

He can't survive that, the healer in me screamed.

But the poisoner knew...lesser men had survived far worse.

"Malakai Kane," I whispered, "is that a streak of *heroism* I see?"

His flinty gaze warned away any ounce of sentiment. "You can't make me care about this broken world." Bloodied fingertips caressed the arch of my cheek and traveled down my bruised face and collarbone. "But as long as I know you're living in it, I'll do what I can to keep it from burning to ashes."

"Then we haven't a moment to waste." With a deft curl of his arm and a slow bend of his knees, Caspian lifted both himself and Luminae from the floor. "The sentinels will be on this place like grave dirt on bones soon. Malakai?"

"Give me a five-minute headstart, if you would."

"I'll give you six."

Malakai's grip tightened over my shoulders; he tugged me toward the bedroom doorway, and Luminae broke her uncle's hold, stepping after us. "Wait! How...how can I repay you for this?"

Malakai cast her a long, assessing look over his shoulder; and it painted an entirely different picture of Luminae than I'd ever seen, that she didn't quell under his cool consideration. Even with tearstained cheeks and her brother's blood on her hands, she held her head high.

"You can become something better than he was." Malakai jerked his chin at Phineaus's cooling corpse. "Better than a mess I have to mop up in the next half a lifetime."

Luminae sucked in an audible breath and answered with a wobbly nod.

Then we were gone—stumbling across the parlor, through the bedroom, out onto the balcony on a course for the thing I'd felt us hurtling toward from the first moment he'd saved my life in the streets of Amalgard.

Our goodbye.

CHAPTER 90
THE HEARTS THAT HAUNT US

MALAKAI AND I BURST out into the chilly night, catching ourselves against the railing, spinning to face one another.

It wouldn't be difficult for him to climb down, even from this height—to disappear into the slimmest sliver of space between the scene of Phineaus's death and the places where the sentinels were rallying by now, realizing they'd been deceived…if not by whom.

There would be no other time and no better place for a farewell.

I stepped forward, tying my arms around Malakai's neck, pulling him flush against me. "I'm not ready to say goodbye to you."

"You've made that abundantly clear." His hand splayed in the small of my back. "I can't imagine a fate worse than this…but it's the only choice. To keep you safe, and free…and to have the chance to put an end to the rest of Grave Dominion and spare this country, once and for all."

A choked laugh cracked from his chest. His hold on me tightened like a death grip.

"Sullied souls…listen to me." A sharp huff of breath against my ear as he nuzzled his face into my hair, his chest rising and falling in stilted gasps. "You are the only reason I have ever wanted to be a good man."

"You *are* a good man, and even if no one else ever knows it…*I* will. You're the man who does the right thing, even if it's not the easy one." Tears burned in the corners of my eyes. "And I know this won't be easy, either, but…when you get your things from Caspian's lair, and run…promise me you won't look back."

"I'm afraid I could never keep that vow." His voice trembled slightly. "But what I *will* swear to you is that, when I look over my shoulder, I'll know precisely where you're standing."

Somehow, that was the greatest comfort he could give me in this moment that felt like ripping pieces of myself away, bit by bit. Tiny petals tugged off a dying flower, each one plucked with a prayer that this was not the end of us.

Drawing back, I spread my hand against his bruise-blackened neck, hating every heartbeat that was taking him away from me—that wouldn't allow me to look after him, to make certain he was safe, to ensure he wouldn't succumb to the strangulation, somehow, days or weeks from now. "Take care of this."

"I will."

"And take care of *this*," I pressed my other palm against his unsteady heart, "until I see you again."

A bright sheen danced across his eyes. "You have my word of that. And that I'll be watching, troublemaker." His voice cracked over that ridiculous name, his thumb pressing fiercely against my chin—like a mark I could carry with me. Something to remember him by when he was gone. "Always."

"You had better be." I shoved his arm down and surged forward, seizing his face in both hands, towing his head down for the last kiss I was ever promised to have with him.

With this villain who'd carved a way into my heart. With this shadowy hero Hadrass-Drui would never know it had.

With the only person I'd ever trusted with every last part of me.

His hand seized my side, slid under my arm, gripped a handful of fabric and flesh and held on, wrenching me against him; his other, bloodsoaked and hotter than flame, tangled in my hair and angled my head to one side, crushing my mouth tighter against his.

It was the smallest in a long list of foolish, insane things I had done and desired since I'd first met him. But Luck if I didn't want to kiss Malakai Kane until the world burned. Until the sentinels caught up to us. Until it destroyed everything.

But that was the thought—*destruction*—that gave me the power to hold on tighter. Then to force him back, when all I wanted was to lose myself in him, like dusk blending into night.

We parted with a stumble and a shared curse, and his teeth dragged at my lower lip, his chest rumbling with the first groan I'd heard since I'd dragged him back to life. As if, out of *everything* we'd faced tonight, letting go of me was the thing that caused him the most pain.

When I drew in enough breath that my senses roared back to clarity, it brought the distant churn of thundering footfalls...shouts from below, as the sentinels mobilized. As they began to comb the Fortress in search of intruders. Hunting for the Poet Poisoner.

"Go," I hissed, fisting my hand over Malakai's thundering heart. "You have to *go*, Malakai."

"I wish I could take you with me."

"I know." But, as usual, the Poet Poisoner was his own downfall; he'd helped shape me into the woman I was now—the one who had to stay. Who couldn't run away with him. Who had duties calling from somewhere else...across the mountains. Far from wherever he was going now.

"Promise you'll haunt me," I blurted out as he backed away—a silly stroke of desperation, a last reach of the hand from the part of me that wasn't ready to let him go. That would never really be ready to say goodbye.

A wicked smile cocked up one side of his mouth, and he twisted his wrist—jangling a whisper of luck from beneath his sleeve. "Would you expect any less?"

A last graze of his lips to my knuckles; then he was gone, scaling over the balcony railing, disappearing into the void of the dark, endless night that wrapped around Fortress Ferregrand.

Bracing my hands to the lip of stone, I leaned all my weight into it and let the tears scour my hot, aching cheeks; I let them fall as I searched and searched for Malakai's shadows among all the rest of them soaking the city.

But there was no trace. He was gone.

And with blood caked between my fingers and his kiss branded on my lips, my hand, my heart...

I wasn't really sure if I would ever see him again. Or if hauntings were all we had left anymore.

CHAPTER 91
RUNAWAY LOVE

M Y JOURNEY TO LUMINAE'S rooms was nothing short of an ambling, tearstained mess. I barely had the clarity to remember the way, or the presence of being thankful Caspian's ruse had worked so well; the commotion from the sentinels still rumbled several floors below by the time I reached her door.

If I were found staggering, soaked in blood, through Fortress Ferregrand, I wasn't certain they'd wait to question me before running me through this time.

But after three tries to turn the knob with shaking hands that kept slipping from the brass, I forgot the sentinels. I closed my eyes and leaned my head and shoulder against the sleek wood. And I let everything wash over me.

The infiltration. The confrontation with Phineaus. Luminae's intervention. Malakai...

Malakai is gone.

Tears burned down my cheeks and tucked into the creases beside my nose, like tiny secrets that belonged just to me. And to him.

I was the only person alive to cry for the Poet Poisoner...for Malakai Kane. So I let myself weep, just for a moment, like the tears shed before moving to a dying man's bedside. Before I had to clad myself in steel and be the strongest one in the room, for however long it mattered.

Then, sucking in several deep breaths, I steadied the knob, twisted, and slipped into the parlor.

A fire roared in the hearth, fighting against a chill that had absolutely nothing to do with the temperature of the room. Humidity steeped into the cracks of the stone, wafting from the partially-ajar washroom doorway. Caspian leaned against the wall outside, sacked back against it, face buried in one hand and his other arm curled tight to his ribs. He'd done nothing for the wound weeping blood down the side of his face.

His head whipped up when the door clicked shut behind me; for an instant, a lethal trace of tension rode down the lines of his body...a keen reminder of what he was, what he had *become* to protect this family.

A family that had turned on him from one side. A guild that had struck from the other.

"He's gone," was all I could muster as I trudged across the room to join him. "Luminae?"

"She's..." He tilted his head at the doorway, his red-rimmed eyes fixed on my face. "Insisted on taking care of things herself."

A kernel of respect—and fresh grief—ignited in my chest. "She's stronger than she lets on."

"I know, but would you...would you look in on her? She won't speak to me, she won't bathe, and I need her to wash the blood away before..." Caspian sucked in a strangled breath, sweeping a hand down his face, leaving it settled over his mouth. "Before I send for the sentinels and tell them I found—"

His nephew. His personal betrayer. His sister's beloved son.

I seized his free hand, squeezed it with all my might and pressed a kiss to his cheek. "Take care of your head first, all right?"

His eyes slammed shut. "If my healer insists."

One more squeeze; then I slipped past him into the washroom.

It was the most nondescript of all the ones I'd seen in Hadrassi homes so far...no mosaics, just simple tiled marble and a few engravings strung along the curved walls. Luminae perched on the edge of her clawfooted tub, knees plunged into the steaming water; her bloodstained hands rested upturned in her lap, and she stared at them, unmoving.

Quiet, steady dripping echoed from her fingertips, splashes turning the water pink. From her cheeks as the tears fell.

For the first time that night—for the first time since I'd let go of Malakai and watched him blend with the shadows that kept him safe—calm stole through me. And I remembered everything I was.

The person who saw hurt...and healed it.

Heal this.

I padded across the room, hovering a careful hand beside her shoulder. "Lu?"

She jumped, twisting to face me; her wide, glossy eyes pinned to my face with the desperation of a woman who'd taken a rifleshot through the middle, begging me to save her.

"I killed him," she whimpered. "My own—"

"The Kingslayer," I cut her off gently, sweeping a damp tendril of silvery hair from her brow. "You ended the Kingslayer's schemes against your family."

Her chin trembled. "He was still Phin, before he was that." Her face turned back to the blood-tinged water. "I'm still a murderer."

I steadied myself with the count of three—bracing for what I had to say next. What I'd known was coming from the moment I'd watched Luminae drive the knife into her older brother's gut and save us all...save her entire country.

"May I tell you a story?" I murmured.

Her head shot back around, a glimmer of something fiercer and more earnest shattering the shock at those words. "I...I would like that, yes."

So while I crouched beside the tub and gently bathed her brother's blood from her hands, I told Luminae the story of a Mithran General named Arlo Gryffen. Of a Shadran and Shadress who were good and noble, but how the good things hadn't mattered enough to outweigh the crimes invented in a cruel man's mind.

I told her the story of Naomi Weathers, who'd become a poisoner to save what was precious to her. How she had made the most horrific choice possible, sullying her own soul and dirtying her hands to protect people who did not deserve retribution for harms they'd never committed. I told her of a woman who'd fled, who'd hidden away...who'd stepped back into the light to protect her life. And found the truth of herself along the way.

The water was murky and Luminae's hands and arms pristine by the time I fell silent; we both stared at the water for a long time.

Then her voice, small and soft as a thread of moonlight: "I never knew that about you."

"Only three people do." I nudged her ribs gently with my elbow. "And you're the third, by the way."

A strangled snort pushed through her nose, and she wiped the tip of it hastily on her damp wrist. "Can I find myself again after this, do you think?"

"Yes." I brushed my fingertips up and down her back. "*Yes*, Lu, I think you will. And you won't be alone. Caspian knows, and *I* know. You'll always have us, no matter what."

The last word had barely left my mouth when she twisted on the tub's edge, wrapping her slender arms around me. She clung to me, and I held on to her, and we both wept for what felt like an eternity.

For a dead brother, lost long ago. For love that was running away, one mile at a time. For everything in our lives that had been broken or stolen in this wrestle for Hadrassi power...things we could never have again. And things we hoped we could someday hold tight to, and never let go.

At long last, Luminae pulled back, blotting her eyes with her sleeve. "Oh, I'm a mess. Would you help me dispose of this night dress?"

"Of course." I took her hand and helped her rise, shaky as a surgery patient, from the tub. "And then I'll have to go."

"To help Uncle Caspian with the ruse." Her lips thinned as we stepped back into her rooms; mercifully, Caspian had made himself scarce. "I've been thinking of that. You should tell the sentinels that the Poet broke you out of the dungeons so that he could force you to help him get close to Phin. That Phin found you sneaking in and rescued you from him, and that Uncle Caspian came across you in the rooms, begging for your life and Phin's. That will explain your capture and coercion...it will convince them you were never a spy."

I halted, struck by the shift in her tone—from sorrowful to scheming when the moment demanded it.

Paranoia wasn't the only thing that ran thick in the Hadrassi blood. There was cunning, too, and quick-wittedness. And as much as Phineaus had worn those traits like a badge across his chest, Luminae wore hers like a bandage under a bloodstained dress...far less visible, but still the stuff that stanched the bleeding. That kept her back straight and her feet moving, one after the other, as she crossed the room away from me.

I owed this woman my life. But I knew that wasn't what she needed to hear...just like I hadn't needed it when I'd killed Gryffen.

So I gave her what I *had* needed...what would've given me so much more strength.

"Your love of stories really serves you well, Lu," I murmured. "You're excellent at coming up with them on the spot."

She tossed me the smallest, nastiest little smile over her shoulder—a hair-raising, deprecating smirk that reminded me a bit too much of her brother.

"I'll have to be, won't I?" Bearing down a deep breath, she slid the straps of her nightdress off, stepping out of it to the thin chemise beneath. Wadding up the ruined fabric, she hurled it into the fire. "Because I'll be telling one story and living another for the rest of my rotting life."

CHAPTER 92
LIVING STORIES

After that night, we were all living stories, it turned out.

My time in Hadrass-Drui came to a swift end after the discovery of Phineaus's body. Caspian and Luminae's corroboration sealed my place as the unwilling and unwitting victim of the Poet Poisoner's schemes, at least in the grief-addled minds of Athicus, Estrella, Serai, and Varros.

It was my second and last conversation with the rulers of Hadrass-Drui, bled of all interest once they were certain I wasn't involved in Phineaus's death. No one, it seemed, was convinced enough of my work as a spy to risk pursuing conflict with Mithra-Sha; and there was no thanks for what I'd risked, or regret for what I'd endured, when they dismissed me from the cold, dim chamber where I'd met them the first time.

Not that I blamed them. Hadrass-Drui had its own troubles to manage…and its own villain to hunt.

The day I packed my satchel full of my old clothes and books, and a few things new—a plate and two mugs glazed with starlight, a necklace with a teardrop bottle, a dress I couldn't bear to part with, and a cloak that smelled of fennel and pine in the creases—the bulletins were being surfaced on every shopfront and side-alley wall in Amalgard.

We had *Wanted* notes just like them in Mithra-Sha. But the familiarity of the practice didn't make the familiarity of the masked countenance sketched across them any easier to bear when I caught glimpses of it nailed to columns and corners even throughout the Fortress halls, on my way out of its doors for the last time. As if the servants might forget who was wanted for Phineaus's death between one hall and the next.

My steps ground heavily on the stone floor, and grief wedged itself in a thick ball at the base of my throat.

Flipping Luck. I just wanted to be away from the baleful gaze of the Poet Poisoner's mask lurking down every hall, with a vow of a lifetime's sum of gold for the capture of Phineaus Moraven's murderer plastered above his head.

I just wanted to go *home*.

Shadows found me on my way out of the Fortress, though not the one I'd been missing and watching for out of the corners of my eyes for days now: one was willowy and seek, ash-blonde hair twisted into an ornate topknot, deep, flowing burgundy dress hiding unseen bloodstains that might never wash clean. The other donned a suit of deep slate, his hair combed back, looking more trimmed and put together than I'd ever seen him.

I didn't have to glance twice at Luminae and Caspian, one on my right and one on my left, to realize why they were dressed so nicely. Or to understand why the Drui and Druaeva had firmly requested I vacate their city before midday today.

"It's the funeral today, isn't it?" I tucked my satchel more firmly across my front, welcoming the pressure of its strap against my prickling skin.

Caspian pocketed his hands, nodding vaguely. "We were on our way out to the Grand Mausoleum when we heard you coming down the stairs."

"We'll ride with his body in the soul-sender's carriage." Luminae's tone was remote, her words almost dreamlike as she stared ahead at the broad, soaring doors leading out to the Fortress's front steps, her long fingers fiddling with an ivy-and-rose-twine cuff fitted around the shell of her ear. "It only seems right."

That she walk her brother to his final resting place, after she'd sent him there with her own hand.

The implication sent chills scampering down my spine and made the dagger in my sheath—washed clean, but wearing the memory of Phineaus's blood—feel heavier than ever. I slipped my arm around Luminae's back and squeezed; she tipped her head against mine, but that was the only acknowledgement she gave.

If her family had let me, I might've stayed a little longer just to make sure she was healing. But our time together was a book shutting when the sentinels drew open the front doors; and though Luminae traced her fingers down my arm and squeezed my hand in passing, she didn't even say goodbye on her way to the long, dark carriage posted on the curving footpath between the garden hedges.

She climbed inside with her brother's dark pinewood coffin, leaving Caspian and I alone on the stoop.

"It's going to take time." Caspian dropped an arm around my shoulders and rubbed my bicep briskly. "For all of us. But she'll be all right, in time...I'll be watching over her."

I didn't doubt that at *all*. If I had learned anything about Caspian Moraven in my whirlwind of a visit to this country, it was that he loved his family more than he loved anything else—anyone in the country, his title, his honor, even his own life and soul.

"What happens to *you*?" I asked.

Caspian pocketed his free hand, offering an unperturbed shrug and a glance over both shoulders to ensure we were alone once the sentinels shuttered the doors at our backs; then he tipped his head to murmur in my ear, "I haven't heard so much as a whisper from the Grave since Phineaus's death. I have to suspect they're a bit blade-shy after losing him...they're afraid to draw attention my way."

"Are you worried that will change? That they'll reach out again, or..."

Or try to do to you what they did to the Kanes and Nassars?

"I suppose my only hope is that somewhere out there, there's a villain doing his work well enough that I won't have to be bothered with them anymore." Caspian winked.

Tension curdled in my gut; not for the first time in the last fortnight, fretting strangled my throat.

There'd been no word—not a mark, not a letter, not a flirt of aberrant shadow—to suggest Malakai was still out there, doing everything he'd promised. I'd spent more nights awake lately than I cared to count, wondering if I'd made the right choice after all, letting him go off alone.

What if his windpipe had collapsed afterward? What if there had been more damage to his mind, his heart, his lungs from the near-strangulation than I'd been able to assess in the whirlwind moments after? What if he'd turned delirious, stumbling into some gutter and collapsing before he'd ever made it out of the city, too weak to help himself? What if the bleeding had broken out beneath the surface, or he'd been hemorrhaging internally, profusely, and I'd missed it?

What if he was well and truly gone, and I would simply never know?

I dispelled those worries with a sharp shake of my head; like I always told my most fretful patients, it was no use worrying about things that hadn't happened yet. At best, it simply meant you suffered twice—and no amount of agonizing could stop the terrible from coming. It could only make the good things dimmer while you had them.

I ducked from beneath Caspian's arm and faced him, cinching my satchel strap tight across my front.

"Take care of him, Caspian." It was not a request.

"As much as he'll let me." With a soft smile edged in grief, he gripped my shoulder and bent me toward him, his lips grazing my brow. "And you look after *yourself*, you little troublemaker."

Tears scalded against the backs of my eyes; I blinked them hastily away, wrapped my arms around his broad shoulders and kissed his cheek fiercely, and then did what I'd been yearning to do for so long.

I walked away from Hadrass-Drui.

Through the twisted streets of Amalgard, darkness lurking down every vein like Mummer's Dance waiting for a new victim to claim. Past the markets made to slumber today in honor of a Druavas who'd lacked any semblance of honor at all. I passed cathedral after cathedral swimming with firelight that slid itself under my skin, fever-hot...a reminder of all the death in my wake. And how I'd nearly joined them.

And how some death was necessary...even if it left the deepest scars.

My heart hung so heavy in my chest, I was shocked it didn't slow my feet by the time I reached the port; relief stung my eyes at the sight of the familiar Mithran airship tethered at the portside where the letter I'd sent to Arias last week had summoned it. I made my way hastily up its familiar rungs, pausing just below the very top to look back down over the city.

A city of sorrow and shadows, ringed in golden flames, at the heart of a land full of spice and secrets.

Soon, Caspian and Luminae would arrive at the Grand Mausoleum. There would be reverent words spoken over Phineaus's coffin—not a bit of them true. My friends would shed tears for a brother and nephew lost long ago, and for the way they'd sullied their own hands to put to death what sprang out of that boy's cruel ambitions when he'd succumbed.

There would be new candles on every cathedral step, burning in the Mausoleum tonight, lit in the Fortress windows. Candles for the soul of a fallen Druavas who did not deserve the people's love...but he kept it anyway, carrying it off with him like one more stolen thing, even into death.

Villains would be remembered as heroes. And the heroic actions of the eternally tarnished would be forgotten...all for the sake of saving a country that had no clue how close it had come to dying. How close it still was, one foot on the edge of its own grave.

Disgust and grief wrapped around my throat like Phineaus's own fingers. I hauled myself over the last rung onto the deck, and met the Captain's raised brows and offered hand with the only words I could muster.

"Take me home."

CHAPTER 93
SECRETS KEPT AND CARRIED

T HE AIRSHIP TRIP BACK to Mithra-Sha was uneventful—which was, oddly, everything I needed and nothing I wanted. There were still hurts I needed to heal, inside and out; I was exhausted and heartsick in ways I couldn't even tell anyone, my wounds stinging, my abdomen tense and sore from Phineaus's blow and from dragging Malakai back through the window.

And still I found my eyes drifting to the port in my familiar room, longing for excitement...the kind I would never wish on anyone I loved. But the kind that had made me come alive in ways I hadn't thought possible during my stay in Hadrass-Drui.

Thank Luck I would be making my own excitement from now on.

I barely waited for the airship to fully dock before I was on the deck, ready to disembark. Shoving open the belowdecks hatch, I breathed in the familiar smells of my childhood—and almost lifelong—home.

Rich foods, decadent drinks, burning airship fuels, roaring water, hot sweat and warm stone...it all greeted me at once, wrapping around my senses like a hug. And underneath it all, that deep, zesty undercurrent I'd come to recognize like my own signature scent over the last few months.

The unique spice of Hadrass-Drui, like a secret tickling the tip of my nose.

I held in a breath full of it as I shook hands with the soldiers and thanked them for the escort. Then I let myself down the ladder and jogged as fast as my healing middle would allow, over the Storycrafted glass bridges, bound for the Shastah.

The people I'd been avoiding ever since I'd fed that poison to General Gryffen...they were the only ones I wanted to see now.

Startled *helloes* and a few pats to the shoulder greeted me as I breezed through the familiar halls. I'd known them all this time, so well I could've walked them with my eyes shut...but I'd been walking them like a stranger ever since I'd come back to appeal for Audra and Jaik's safety from the Sha's bounty, years ago.

Not anymore; I held my head high as I crossed the gilded halls, relishing the certainty in my stride echoing off the walls. I had a place here—I *belonged* here. And the impossible choices I had made to protect my country—and its leaders—made me no less deserving.

In fact, it made me *moreso*.

Carried on the current of that confidence, I entered the Convening Chamber, knowing full well it would be occupied at this time of day.

And sure enough, there was Arias Lothar, lounging in the seat at the far end of the soaring chamber, temple resting on his fist, looking as if he was trying to steal a short nap before he saw his visitors for the day.

And at the sight of him, all the breath spilled from my lungs; I almost choked on his name.

Luck, I'd *missed* him. I'd missed all of my friends, for longer than I'd even been in Hadrass-Drui.

Arias's head bolted up at my entrance; he blinked several times, then shoved himself sharply to his feet. "*Naomi.*"

"Surprise! I'm back." I spread my hands a bit. "I...I should've said more in my letter, but there just wasn't—"

"No, there was no need...we received more correspondence from Hadrass-Drui while you were en route." Arias descended from the dais with dazed, slow footfalls. "I...we were informed Phineaus—"

I swallowed the surge of hot, tangy hate that bubbled in my throat like blood at that name. "I did everything I could."

Grief traced the lines of Arias's downturned mouth and the stiff angle of his jaw when he halted, nodding slowly, his gaze tracing over me. His brows mashed lower, and the tension splintered out from his jaw, winding into the corners of his eyes. He took it all in silently, at first—me, my bruises and cuts and still-healing wounds, the way I carried myself.

Then he said, quietly and lethally, "Who did this to you?"

Oh, Luck. "No one. It doesn't matter."

His fingers creaked into fists. "It. Flipping. *Matters*. Who *did* this, Naomi?"

"I'm not going to do this with you. There's no one for you to take a swing at, even if that would do any good—and it wouldn't." I took a step nearer to him. "You're the Sha now, not the Shadran who chased off Galan Fiordona because he harassed me. You have responsibilities, duties...an image to uphold. I'm not going to let you squander all of that because of a few cuts on my face."

"A *few*—" He broke off, rubbing a hand over his mouth, then letting his arm swing limp at his side; his gaze crawled over me again, up and down and back up again, slowly digesting what I'd said like a slow-acting tonic. "I've never heard you talk about my position that way before."

"I never understood it like I do now," I admitted. "What it demands of you...and what's demanded to keep the peace. I'm so sorry I've taken it so lightly, that I haven't been here the way you've needed from someone who's a member of your inner council. But I swear on both sides of Luck's coin, from now on, I'll be here. I will be *everything* this rulership needs."

Even the things you'll never know you needed me to be.

His shoulders loosened slightly, his eyes softening at the corners—and for just a flicker, his likeness to his uncle struck me like a slap to the face. It made my breath catch.

Then, in two long strides, his embrace engulfed me, a storm of leather and ink and patchouli—the familiar smell of every hug he'd given me since the first, when I'd spared his life from a plague as an initiate at fifteen.

I wrapped my arms around his waist in turn, leaning into him as he slowly swayed us both.

"I broke my promise," I confessed into the safety of his strong shoulder. "I didn't...the poisoner got away."

It ached worse than I'd imagined, lying to him while he crushed me in his embrace.

"I don't care," Arias retorted fiercely, the sharpness of that sincerity cutting across the path of my shame and spurting surprise in its wake. "After all this time...that was never the comfort I needed. That justice is a Hadrassi matter, and I'm sorry you were ever tangled up in it. That you ever felt it was your duty to solve it, and that you were harmed fighting for it all the same." His hands found my upper arms, and he set me back gently from him, meeting my gaze with a wide smile, eyes damp. "The only comfort I've missed all this time is knowing that my chosen family is safe. Including you. *Especially* you."

Heat stung the tip of my nose. "I've really missed you."

He squeezed my shoulders. "Mutual, Noni."

I buried my face in his chest, and for several moments he just held me; and I was just Naomi Weathers again, a talented Mithran healer with eyes for her own country's borders.

But I couldn't stay that way. Not for long. Not anymore.

Arias freed me when I squirmed back, and I squeezed his hand once before I stepped away. "After I've gotten settled back in my old rooms here in the Shastah," I grinned at the way his eyes brightened, "we'll need to talk about everything that happened. And how I think it might affect Mithran interests going forward."

"You know I always am, and always have been, open to your council."

"I know. And I think I finally trust myself enough to give it." Pulling my pack more securely onto my shoulder, I shrugged. "So, what are a few bruises, if they win me that?"

We parted with a promise—that I would be ready to speak with him over breakfast in the morning. Just like we'd done before I'd slipped poison to General Gryffen and set myself on the inevitable path to Hadrass-Drui. To losing and finding myself down that long, winding road.

I'd just reached the Convening Chamber door, my hand on the ornate handle, when Arias's voice wound quietly after me: "Naomi. If something more had happened with my family, in Hadrass-Drui...am I right to believe you would tell me?"

Bracing my fingers swiftly around the cool metal of the handle, I pivoted on my heel to meet his gaze; it searched mine with the familiarity of half our youth and our entire adulthood as friends, and the realization struck me that I'd known Arias for as long as Phineaus had been a murderer...and as long as Malakai had been on the hunt for revenge.

Despair wriggled deep in my core. Was there any hope of keeping the truth secret from someone who'd known me so well for so long?

"What makes you think anything more would've happened?" I hedged.

"Because that country drove out my mother's love and broke her heart," he said quietly, "and she was one of their own. I know how Hadrass-Drui treats its people...and I am fully aware that it's a far more ruthless and complicated country even than ours, with all of...this." He gestured to the length of himself, and my heart pinched at what that indicated: things with his father, with his mother, within himself.

Wounds I couldn't heal *or* protect him from.

But I would carry what I could—what I had to—so that while he bent under the weight of his family, he didn't break under the rest of it.

"It wouldn't surprise me," Arias added softly, "if you were to tell me that the whole affair was complex, and that more was involved than what the letters say."

For one moment, I considered telling him all of it. Phineaus, Grave Dominion, his grandfather's impending abdication...the assassin who held my heart.

But the Sha had duties and responsibilities that required him to use knowledge a certain way...knowledge that would affect our relationship with our neighbors to the east.

I knew what secrets I had to keep...what *I* had to carry now.

So I stitched my lips up in a reassuring smile. "If there was anything more, of course I'd tell you, Raz."

He inched his breath out in increments, mouth tilting up slowly in turn. "I appreciate you more than words can say."

That might've made me feel guilty, before; but now, slipping out of the Convening Chamber, it only strengthened my resolve.

Arias couldn't afford to know the truth of his cousin's treachery...not with the state he was in, and had been ever since we'd all learned what his father had done to our friends and this country.

Maybe, someday, he would be able to hear it. But for now, this was my burden to bear.

And I bore it gladly.

CHAPTER 94
WOMEN OF SMOKE AND MIRRORS

I BARELY HAD TO think on my way to my old rooms; my feet knew the path there from the Convening Chamber like I'd just walked it yesterday, not years ago. Even the lanternlight streaking the walls felt like a glow winding through the past to light the present as I slowed in front of my old door.

Budding florals and tendril vines were hewn deep into the wood—a thing made of Storycraft. Audra had spoken it into being the day we'd moved into the Shastah.

Luck, I couldn't wait to see her...and Jaik, and Reiko, and Mahalia, and Wyat. And my Papa and brothers, too. The thought of their smiling faces filled me with new purpose; I twisted the familiar knob and let myself inside.

Nothing had changed in my absence; the sitting chamber was all just the same, from the neutral and green tones of the furnishings and rugs to the items I'd deemed unnecessary and left behind when I'd fled. Trinkets, macrame planters, gardening stands all divested of their growing things...

Relief pricked my eyes, slowing me to a halt on the threshold; I had to blink before I fully took in the other thing that was *precisely* the same.

The hearth was lit, shedding cheery warmth over the table-and-chairs arrangement where I'd sat with Audra and Arias countless times when we'd all served the Sha together.

And seated on the plush lounging sofa was Calten Lothar.

A strange feeling of relived life muddled my thoughts for a moment; this was such an echo of our meeting in Harrow Hall's receiving room, but I didn't feel like the same woman who'd dragged herself there in fear, the tip of a threat held to my throat.

In fact, no fear beat in my veins at *all* when I approached the seating arrangement, drawing the Shadre's eyes to me.

"I hope you don't mind the intrusion, Miss Weathers." She raised a brow—a blunt greeting I'd grown used to in the company of her equally-blunt family.

"Not at all, Shadre." I unshouldered my satchel, slinging it onto the spacious floor of the sitting room. "My first priority was visiting Arias. But I take it you're eager for a full report."

Though even the long flight from Hadrass-Drui back to Mithra-Sha hadn't helped crystallize exactly *what* I was going to say to her—to this woman who'd been raised as an infiltrator and then turned her back on her paranoid family out of a sense of love and duty to Mithra-Sha.

Maybe we weren't so different, after all. Maybe it took all the same determination and cleverness and steely stuff to make the choices I'd made as the ones she had.

That notion had me holding my head high as I approached her, sinking into the almost-forgotten softness of the plush emerald armchairs by the hearth. And I fought not to think of another hearth, another pair of chairs...another Hadrassi I wished with all my heart was here in this room.

"So?" Calten prompted as we faced each other. "Report."

"Why don't you tell me what *you* know," I pressed, "and I'll fill in the gaps."

She assessed me for a long moment. Then: "If you've spoken to Arias, then you're likely aware my brother's correspondence reached us before your airship did."

"And?" I prodded. "How did he put it?"

"He said that Phineaus's fate was sealed before you ever stepped foot over the Hadrassi border." Grief glistened in her adamant eyes. "But that you did all you could for him. And that your insight and the risks you took were invaluable in ensuring that this assassin is no further threat, and that my family is safe."

It was an effort not to let all my breath out at once. To nod and play along as if I'd heard that truth a thousand times.

Not everyone can play that part, Phineaus had said to me once.

As usual, Luck was mocking him. He'd died in his role, the curtain fallen on his stage...and I would be playing mine for a good long while yet.

"I was able to find and identify the Poet Poisoner," I said, "and with what I learned, the whole country will be hunting him. I may not have brought him to justice myself, but the things I did made Hadrass-Drui a far safer place...despite the casualties."

Or rather, because of them.

"Yes. Caspian said as much in his letter." Calten smoothed a hand over her knee.

"So," I ventured after a moment, "Where does that leave *us*, Shadre?"

"You mean, the matter of General Gryffen?" She let the name clatter between us, her eyes riveted on my face—assessing how I reacted. Whether I flinched or winced or withdrew. Whether I cowered from the act I'd committed.

I did none of it. I simply held her gaze and said, "Yes. That one."

She let the silence swell. I let her have it—another test.

I'd faced worse.

"You now hold Hadrass-Drui's respect," she said at length, "and that is not lightly earned. It would be a shame to stir up conflict over a death that, by all accounts, was a tragic accident." She rose, brushing invisible dust—or the last frecklings of the choice that had nearly cost me my life—from her dress. "No, I don't suppose we need to pursue recourse over one mistake that cost a patient his life, in an otherwise unreproachable reputation."

A different healer—one who had not stepped foot into the Hadrassi underbelly, who had not deceived and thefted the Guild Garrote, who had not faced the truth of her own mortality and her reflection in the mirror, and was not irrevocably entwined with the Poet Poisoner—would have accepted that. She'd have bowed and scraped and then fled and hoped—*prayed*—that the nightmare would never catch up with her again.

I wasn't that healer anymore.

I was done running.

"I never said it was a mistake."

Chilly silence swept the room, stirring Calten's eyes back to me.

"Arlo Gryffen was a swayed dogmatist who held more hatred for you and your children than he held love for the Sha and this country." I couldn't help enjoying the faint flicker of shock in Calten's eyes. "And we are never going to speak of this, or of him, ever again."

"Oh?" She arched a sculpted brow. "Aren't we?"

"We aren't, and I can tell you precisely why." I wound my arms around each other, outstretched on my legs, and laced my fingers together. "Because you know Arias is in danger again...that the coin flipped against him when he took his position. You know better than *anyone* how power plots from the shadows, what it does to untested rulers." I cocked my head, measuring her the same way Malakai had so often measured *me*—looking for the truth behind the smoke and mirrors, all the secretive sharp edges that made up the woman before me. "Between a new

Della in the south and all the dangers you grew up facing in Hadrass-Drui, and what just happened to Phineaus, you're afraid for Arias. Afraid of what's coming for him."

Calten's gaze strayed to the lofty windows. "Amere-Del has always been tumultuous and treacherous. And now you've met my father and mother...you know the sort of land that lies to the east."

Luck, did I. From its gutters to its grandest cathedrals, I knew...and I knew the shadowed sentinel who watched over its paths and byways now. Who had for so many years.

Whose charge was the same as mine.

"Well, I can assure you...you have nothing to fear anymore." Bracing my hands on the table, I inclined toward the former Shadre. "Because the woman who killed for your family's name then is the same woman serving at your son's side now. And I promise, I would do it again in a heartbeat if it kept him safe...if it kept this country safe." Every word bore fresh strength and conviction down into my bones. "Arias is my friend, and Mithra-Sha is my home. I would do no less than what's necessary to save both...so you can trust that, even if it filthies my hands, I am going to *ensure* Arias Lothar serves this country well, for a very, very long time."

Calten regarded me with immutable focus, for endless moments that unraveled like thorny vines—barbs plucking at the skin, peeling away a shred at a time.

Then, at long last, her lips tilted up at the corners. "I knew I chose rightly when I came to you for this task."

I trapped my breath behind a cold smile. "Then we have an understanding?"

Smoothing down the crushed velvet of her skirt once more—turning the rich emerald to core black—Calten nodded. "We will never speak of Arlo Gryffen again. And I must say, Healer Weathers...you've impressed me."

Impressed the woman bred and trained to infiltrate Mithra-Sha, to seduce its young Sha, to hold sway over the land of stories and their power. I might never know if that was a compliment or a blow, and I decided in that moment I didn't care.

I knew what I was, who I was...what I was capable of.

And that allowed me to be everything I was meant to be.

"Likewise, Shadre," I replied with saccharine sweetness. "I'm sure we'll find other things to speak of in due time."

"I have little doubt of that." Calten swept for the door, then paused, one long-fingered hand braced on the knob. I'd always thought them pianist's hands, or penman hands…perfect for filling the Shastah halls with haunting music, flawless for legislating and bringing aid to the Mithran people.

Now I knew they were capable of so much more. And what she held in abeyance with those hands watered my respect for her until it flourished upward, choking my throat.

"Speaking of what might or might not come for Arias," she murmured down toward the knob strangled in her white-knuckled grasp, "while you were away, we received correspondence from an unexpected place."

I pushed up from the chair, unease bolting down my spine. Arias hadn't breathed a word of this to me in the Convening Chamber—and that spelled trouble all its own. "And that would be—?"

"Torr-Kal." A faint flex of her fingers around the knob that matched the twist in my gut at the latest mention of that country. "The most distant country from our own. It just so happens they've fallen on difficult times, in several regards, and they're eager to make an alliance."

The way her shoulders stooped, the bend of her back as she said it—

"A marriage alliance," I croaked.

"That was the gist of it, yes." Calten's tone steeled slightly. "Though Torr-Kal suffers much, they do have unlikely talents in many regards…which makes them both a threat as well as a shard of hope, considering how tenuous things tend to be when new rulers ascend to power. So Arias is considering it heavily…that's what Mahalia tells me."

The slightest twist of heel angled her shoulder and one hawkish eye back toward me.

"I would keep your gaze keen and your potions at the ready, Healer Weathers," she warned. "We may someday find ourselves hosting Torrian guests. And if we allow the kin of the infamous Kal Marwan through our doors, I fear Arias will face dangers we cannot predict."

The thought almost had a moment to poison me with dread. But just before it truly burrowed in, it was Malakai's face I saw in my mind; Malakai's voice I heard in my head.

Now you're thinking like an assassin.

Not just a compliment—a warning, and a charge for my future.

I could never go back to the healer I'd been after what I'd seen. What I'd done, years ago, and in Hadrass-Drui. All the things I knew now about myself and others.

And that was good. Because that was not the healer I needed, or that this country needed.

It needed someone who could think like a poisoner, like an assassin. And meet them challenge for challenge, threat for threat.

Teeth set, shoulders peeled back, I said, "You're going to find that I can predict quite a bit more than you might think, Shadre. And I'll be ready for all the rest."

A flicker of a smile tilted her mouth. "Then I should think my son is in very good hands, indeed."

Hinges creaked in a cold punctuation, somewhere between a challenge and a threat, as she glided from the room.

EPILOGUE

FOR THE FIRST TIME since I'd left Fortress Ferregrand, I was alone.

Alone as I emptied my satchel, dumping the contents on the wing-backed sofa. I set the mugs and plate above the hearth, watching firelight turn the shimmering glaze to an absolute starshower; then I stacked the books on the dusty shelves and hung the pendant key from a hook beside the mantel.

I slipped into the bedchamber I used to call mine...that hadn't belonged to anyone since I'd fled the Shastah in fear and shame all those years ago. I expected to find those feelings of terror, my own inadequacies, gathered in the corners with the dustballs and cobwebs...but they were nowhere to be found.

It was just a room, ready to be occupied again. And it started with hanging my new Hadrassi dress and my spare clothes in the familiar, cavernous walk-in closet...pieces of the old and new Naomi, hung up and waiting to be drawn like soldiers drew weapons.

A smile dug a dimple into my cheek when I stepped from the closet—

And my eyes found what I'd missed until now.

Propped against the pillow, the heavy cardstock languished like a lover in the sheets, waiting to be stumbled upon.

My breath hitched, then hurtled out as I lunged for the bed; diving across it, ignoring the tug in my scarred middle, I snatched up the note and traced my thumb over the shivering ink scrawled across the front.

A single word:

Troublemaker.

Tears slashed across my vision, setting that precious name swimming; I hugged the note to my chest, squeezing my eyes shut until the dampness seeped through.

"Oh, *Luck*," I breathed. "You're alive. *Thank Luck*."

Urgency chewed at my nerves, and all at once I couldn't stand a *second* longer not knowing the contents of the note; I ripped it hastily with my teeth, dumping out the folded cardstock from within, laying it open on my lap.

Miss Weathers,

It seems you will soon return to your establishment at the Shastah. I hope you find the accommodations to your liking…a bit drab for my taste, and woefully undersecured.

But if it allows me to steal moments with you, I suppose I can let the rest lie.

My work will take me away for some time, so this is the only correspondence I can presently send. However, you can expect to receive reports from our mutual friend. I leave this note for you as a token—and a vow. That I will still find you, wherever you are, and that I will come back to you whenever time allows. Until then, leave a candle lit…you know who it burns for.

Know, too, that I will come back. As I always have, I always will.

Forever, affectionally, and against my better judgement and will, begrudgingly and irrevocably yours,

Kilgrave

An elegant postscript lay beneath, every curve of every letter teasing and full of private jest:

I assure you, this letter is not penned in poison. When I devastate you, Naomi Weathers, it will only ever be face to face.

Until that time, you can always find me in the shadows at the corners of your eyes.

For a moment, I let my eyes tumble shut—I let myself believe the glint of darkness as my lashes clung together was him. Reclining against the wall, arms folded, watching me in that completely unfair, devastatingly handsome way of his.

When I blinked my eyes open again, there was nothing. Just me and my imagination.

I would have to keep him with me in all the small ways, then. In shadows and shared secrets and notes tucked safely in my journal like pressed flowers, eternally shedding the smell of fennel and pine.

That was where I stashed the letter, then tucked the whole thing away in a seam of the Shastah stones where I'd chiseled out the mortar years ago.

Then I dressed in my favorite tunic and serrated skirt, bound my hair beneath a handkerchief, and lashed on a cloak that pinned against my left shoulder.

It was time for the *Bean and Brew*. I could already feel the embraces from my friends winding around my shoulders, hear their delighted shouts at my arrival, and practically taste the rich, caramel blend of coffee and alcohol on the back of my tongue.

Oh, it was *more* than time.

Still, I made sure to add one last piece to my attire before I slipped out of my room again: the teardrop vial necklace Malakai had given me, resting beneath the line of my bodice like a dagger in a hidden sheath, waiting to be pulled.

I felt safer with it. Surer of what I could face and overcome. Wearing it brought Malakai close, along with everything he'd helped awaken in me...like the Poet Poisoner himself was striding with me through the Shastah halls, always watching over me. Keeping his brutal, beautiful vows.

I tweaked the delicate glass bottle, a smile curling across my lips.

You never knew, after all, when you'd need a little poison in your life.

Just one drop to change everything.

A POSTSCRIPT PENNED LIKE POETRY

For anyone else, that might have been the end of it. The perfect final stitch, as Malakai would have said—a word that, for us both, could be the forever close of something. As it had been for my mother and father...a bond so beautiful, timeless, priceless—severed. Something sacred left tattered and frayed. A wound not sealed properly, healing at awkward angles, twinging during cold nights

But that was not us. Not our story.

It's strange how the best and worst things in your life can start to bleed together, like poisons and cures. And, given enough time, they can all become part of the same hazy, half-forgotten dream.

That was what my time in Hadrass-Drui became, as the months wore on. As my feet bonded back to the familiar brick walkways of Vallanmyre. As my hands reintroduced themselves to the bone-aching, heart-filling labor in the city infirmaries. As my days filled up with council sessions surrounded by friends, and nights with my brothers' teasing and laughter and talks of the future, my father's smile fuller and happier than I had seen it since we were children.

Mithra-Sha was true, and real, and enduring. And day by day, Hadrass-Drui faded to a mirage in memory, something one wakes from and can't recall if it was wonderful or wicked.

All I had for months was twinges in my side when I tugged against healed places just right. A vial tucked beneath my shirt, thumping like a small heartbeat separate from mine whenever I ran to a patient's room, to another crisis that demanded my hands...frequently bloodstained, frequently trembling by the time the crisis was over. A headful of dreams that sometimes seemed far more real than what I had witnessed and done and endured in the Land of Spice and Secrets.

And then...all of a sudden, I had more.

First, I had one of the longest days in memory—a full morning of meetings, a full afternoon in the infirmary, a full evening helping plan Behn's whirlwind wedding to a fellow traveling musician he'd met on the road exactly halfway between Allorae and Dalfi...the fingerprints of fickle Luck all over their chance encounter.

But I also had an empty belly and an emptier smile after I had to endure my brothers teasing me about how it could be possible they'd all be married before me. How I could be the last of the five Weathers Wonders to find love—what unexpected flip of the coin was *that*?

And then, once I managed to pry myself away to my rooms, I had quiet for the first time that day. Quiet as I toed off my flats and dipped my head, kneading stiffness from my spine on the way to my bedchamber. Quiet melancholy that wrapped around me like the favorite cardigan I snagged off the back of the sofa on my way through the door.

I had my bedchamber...dim, cozy, bathed in cool core darks. I had my bed, perfectly made, and my windows cracked a bit to let in the warm summer breeze. I had my books of healing and a few Mithran poetry volumes Addie had given me after my return, and I had my table set before the hearth—

And that table.

That table was not the same as I'd left it.

I gripped the bedpost at the first stumbling lurch of my heart. Disbelief snagged my feet to a halt on the rug that encircled the bed.

Two starry glazed mugs sat on the tabletop. Two shiny, night-dark plates complemented them—one sporting twin gashes that met as one, gold poured into the seams where they'd once shattered.

Fingers slipping from the bedpost, I floated to the table, no longer feeling the floor beneath my feet. Soft glaze drew like satin against the calluses on my fingertips, and my hand darted past them, reaching for the lantern between the place settings. Irrational fear jabbed at the edges of my heart—that when I coaxed up the light to see better by, all of this would evaporate. Another part of the Hadrassi daydream—

"Leave it."

My breath hitched. I whipped around toward the narrow washroom door—

And there he was. Propped in the open frame, one boot tip resting casually behind the other, eyes fixed on the task of cleaning between his fingers with one of my washcloths. The smell of freesia soap and line-dried cotton rose from its fibers, but something spicier tickled my nose, too.

Something piney. Something *wonderful*.

He sloped his head, fixated on his task...sparing me a moment to assess him. The fall of his damp, messy hair over one eye; the long column of his neck, bared gracefully to the wash of moonlight through the windows, marred with rashes and scrapes that looked weeks old, at most. A bruise around one eye, a split in the corner of his lip. And an old, burn mark that wrapped beneath his chin—a noose scar healed over.

The steady rise and fall of his chest. The tilt of his chin this way and that as he cleaned grime and what was likely old, dried blood from the creases of his hands. The painless way he held himself despite his visible wounds, and how at *ease* he seemed—a vision of splendid shadow, just another of many splashed against the walls and frames of my room.

But...he was *here.*

He was *alive,* and he was *here,* in my rooms in the flipping *Shastah.* Where I'd dreamed him and envisioned him and prayed him back to me.

Are you real? I almost choked.

Did you use my bath while I was gone? I wanted to ask.

Or, *How precisely did you get into my rooms without one of Jaik's goons noticing you?*

But all that escaped, with none of the pert confidence I fought for, was just his name.

"Kai?"

His gaze snapped up, finding me from beneath the thick fringe of his lashes...and the dampness of that stare betrayed the casual focus with which he'd tended his hands.

He had let me see him. But now he saw *me,* and in that one look, we were both undone.

Balling the rag, he cast it aside into the washroom behind him and shrugged up from the doorframe. "Hello, beautiful."

The chair banged into the table legs as I thrust it aside and lunged across the distance to him; he met me in two strides at the foot of the bed, catching me up in his arms. And I was crying into the side of his neck while he spun me around and clenched me against him, pressing kisses to my temple, my jaw, my throat. Then he buried his face in my hair and gripped the back of my neck with trembling fingers, fastening me so tightly against him that the smell of warm water and fennel and pine became mine, not just his.

I'd never smelled anything so wonderful.

Malakai fell back to sit on the edge of the bed, tugging me into his lap, and I swung my legs over sideways and pulled myself into the breadth of his chest and that funny cadence of his heart. He settled his face in the crook of my neck, and I folded my arms around his shoulders, nuzzling against his temple.

"I missed you," he said, hoarsely—almost unsteadily, with a deep, dragged-in breath. "Sullied souls, I missed you *so much*."

"I think I may have missed you more." My tears were already adding to the dampness of his hair.

"Debatable. And thoroughly unlikely." His lips brushed my collarbone, twisting my insides into delectable knots—then he drew back a bit, shifting me in his lap. He freed one hand to tease out the chain that rested along my clavicle, tugging until the weight of the bottle rested in his palm. "You still wear it."

"I carry you with me everywhere I go. Every day." Hands on his shoulders, I shifted to wrap my legs around his waist and tied my arms around his neck. In the moonlight, I searched his face...every scrape and bruise, every hurt I hadn't been present to heal; my thumb strayed to the laceration at the corner of his mouth, and a throbbing tangle of grief and fury rocked through me. "Flipping Luck, I wish I could be there."

He caught my hand, bringing it to rest over my abdomen—over the scar that still itched now and again just to remind me of its presence. "I can only do what I do there knowing you are as far from my work as possible."

And maybe that was always how it would be with us. But here, tonight, his presence in my rooms—it proved something else, too.

"You came back."

A last squeeze of my hand; then his returned to fit against my hip. "I will *always* come back for you, troublemaker."

Catching my lip between my teeth, I dropped a kiss on his hair. "Well, I want to know what's happened while you were gone. Tell me everything."

His throat bobbed as he gazed up at me, a shine of wonder stealing through his stare like I'd never seen before—maybe just a glint of it in that Hadrassi alleyway beneath the fireworks. It carved away the man I'd known all this time, the poisoner assassin, the graceful poet; it left a vulnerable, wide-eyed, half-stranger before me.

But...still the man I was in love with. Still my Malakai.

"You *are* everything," he breathed, sliding both hands around my back.

Laughter bubbled from me at that absurd truth—and another truth my brothers and father and friends would never really know.

That I *had* fallen in love. With the most unexpected and secretly wonderful person, hidden behind so many masks.

"Then tell me all the rest," I murmured, laying my brow against his.

He sank back on one elbow on the bed; the other hand fisted in my hair, guiding me down to lie against him until our mouths met. Until I had the truth I'd needed most since our parting on that balcony in the Fortress.

That this was not the end of anything. We were just beginning.

Kiss-bruised and delirious, we drew apart after several moments; and with a mischievous smile, Malakai Kane said, "Let me tell you of all the trouble I've gotten myself into."

CHARACTER GUIDE

NAOMI WEATHERS (**NAY-OH-ME**): AMONG the most talented and infamous healers and poison studies in Mithra-Sha

Patrik Weathers: Naomi's oldest brother; a welder.

Felyx Weathers: Naomi's second-oldest brother; a canal-worker

Conor Weathers: Naomi's third-oldest brother; an architect

Behn Weathers: Naomi's fourth oldest brother; a traveling musician

Sha Arias Lothar (sha-uh-RYE-us low-thar): Ruler of Mithra-Sha, son of Tobyrus and Calten.

Shadress Mahalia Lothar (ma-HAY-lee-uh): Daughter of Tobyrus and Calten, first in line to rule Mithra-Sha.

Reiko Nayori (ray-co nay-OR-ee): Close advisor to the Master Storycrafter and one of Naomi's closest friends

Audra Grissom (AW-druh GrISS-um): Former Master Storycrafter and one of Naomi's closest friends. Jaik's wife.

Jaik Grissom (Jake GrISS-um): Arias's bodyguard, Audra's husband. One of Naomi's closest friends.

Tobyrus Lothar (toe-BYE-russ): Former ruler of Mithra-Sha. Husband of Calten, father of Arias and Mahalia.

Shadre Calten Lothar (sha-dray kal-tehn): Wife of Tobyrus, mother of Arias and Mahalia. Hadrassi by birth.

Drui Athicus Moraven: Ruler of Hadrass-Drui. Father of Serai, Calten, and Caspian. Grandfather of Phineaus, Luminae, and Coraline.

Druaeva Estrella Moraven: Co-ruler of Hadrass-Drui. Wife of Athicus. Mother of Serai, Calten, and Caspian. Grandmother of Phineaus, Luminae, and Coraline.

Druella Serai Moraven: First in line to rule Hadrass-Drui. Mother of Phineaus, Luminae, and Coraline.

Druavas Varros Moraven: First in line to co-rule Hadrass-Drui. Father of Phineaus, Luminae, and Coraline.

Druavas Caspian Moraven: Second in line to rule Hadrass-Drui.

Druavas Phineaus Moraven: Third in line to rule Hadrass-Drui.

Druella Luminae Moraven: Fourth in line to rule Hadrass-Drui

Druella Coraline Moraven: Sixth in line to rule Hadrass-Drui.

Malakai Kane/The Poet Poisoner: One of the most prolific assassins in Hadrass-Drui

Mistress Merrietti: A Hadrassi shop owner with assassin ties

Solomyn and Katia Degrace: Prolific assassins among the Guild Garrote

Assassin Guilds:

The Guild Garrote

Grave Dominion

LOCATION GUIDE

AMALGARD (AH-**MAL**-GUARD): THE CAPITAL city of Hadrass-Drui

Amere-Del (AH-meer dehl): Country to the south of Mithra-Sha. Ruled by the Del and Della.

Dalfi (dal-fee): Airship port and trade city

Fortress Ferregrand: The Hadrassi palace where its ruling family resides

Hadrass-Drui (ha-drahs droo-ee): Country to the east of Mithra-Sha. Birthplace of Mithra-Sha's Shadre.

Hyraith: The spice capital of Hadrass-Drui

Mithra-Sha: Naomi's birthplace and home country

Rastra: One of the most prolific trade cities in Hadrass-Drui

Thrasmund: The city where Hadrassi nobility receive their training

Vallanmyre (val-en-mire): The capital of Mithra-Sha; home of the Shastah and Fablehaven Academy

Valorkeep: The Hadrassi academy of scholarship

The Vensair Mountains (venn-sare): The mountain rage spanning the eastern border of Mithra-Sha; separates Mithra-Sha from Hadrass-Drui

ACKNOWLEDGEMENTS

2024 – THE YEAR I drafted this book – was one of the toughest of my life. Yet in the midst of the darkest time, God gave me light...a plot I'd been searching for during six months of wilderness wandering. *This* plot – a darker, more difficult story to pour all of my rage and hurt and frustration into. And to heal. And to find beauty on the other side of the breakdown.

So, to God, first forever...thank You for this unlikely gift. Thank You for showing me that this series was not done by any means...that *You* aren't done with *me.*

To Cassidy, without whose enthusiasm I might not have kept the courage to finish this one. Thank you for loving (and tough-loving!) me from the starting gate to the finish line. For your beautifully unhinged adoration of Naomi and Kai and your insight that has made this story come more alive for me than it ever did in my own head. You were such a key part of God's plan for this book, in countless ways...this is 500 pages of me giving you the story I always wanted to, the story you deserve. Thank you for being my person. <3

To my family who held me up, supported me, put their own lives on hold and made me a priority when I faced my mortality, and then disappeared into my writing cave for a solid month to work it through on the page with Naomi and Kai. You were all a piece of Naomi in my life – healers, helpers, seeing the good in the darkness – that helped make this book a rich writing experience. I am so thankful for you all.

To the friends and fans and readers who have invested in the TALES OF WONDER & WOE...who have read, reviewed, shared, supported, messaged me, screamed, cried, all of the things. You also played such a tremendous role in my ability to come back to this series and declare I'm not done yet. THANK YOU. You will never probably know how *much* your support truly means...in good times, but especially in hard times. I hope this book pours back into you the way you poured into me.

ABOUT THE AUTHOR

Renee Dugan is an Indiana-based author who grew up reading fantasy books, chasing stray cats, and writing stories full of dashing heroes and evil masterminds. Now with over a decade of professional editing, administrative work, and writing every spare second under her belt, she has authored dozens of books. Living with her husband, son, and not-so-stray cats in the magical Midwest, she continues to explore new worlds and spends her time in this one encouraging and helping other writers on their journey to fulfilling their dreams.

ALSO BY R. DUGAN

You can find other R. Dugan books, including...

The Chaos Circus (Young Adult Portal Fantasy)
The Curse of the Blessed (Adult Fantasy Trilogy)
The Starchaser Saga (New Adult Epic Fantasy Series)
Tales Of Wonder And Woe (New Adult Epic Fantasy Series)

at online retailers Amazon, Barnes & Noble, and more,
and at reneeduganwriting.com/shop

Find Renee Dugan online at: Reneeduganwriting.com
And on social media: @reneeduganwriting

www.ingramcontent.com/pod-product-compliance
Lightning Source LLC
Chambersburg PA
CBHW061036310726
48969CB00004B/970